IDENTICAL

SCOTT TUROW

IDENTICAL

MANTLE

First published 2013 by Grand Central Publishing,
a division of Hachette Book Group, Inc.

First published in Great Britain 2013 by Mantle
an imprint of Pan Macmillan, a division of Macmillan Publishers Limited
Pan Macmillan, 20 New Wharf Road, London N1 9RR
Basingstoke and Oxford
Associated companies throughout the world
www.panmacmillan.com

ISBN 978-1-4472-4478-3

1 3 5 7 9 8 6 4 2

A CIP catalogue record for this book is available from the British Library.

Printed and bound by CPI Group (UK) Ltd, Croydon, CR0 4YY

For Dan and Deb

IDENTICAL

I to the world am like a drop of water
That in the ocean seeks another drop,
Who, falling there to find his fellow forth,
Unseen, inquisitive, confounds himself.

William Shakespeare,
The Comedy of Errors

I.

1.

Paul—September 5, 1982

*M*any years from now, whenever he thinks back to Dita Kronon's murder, Paul Gianis's memories will always return to the start of the day. It is September 5, 1982, the Sunday of Labor Day weekend, a lush afternoon with high clouds lustrous as pearls. Zeus Kronon, Dita's father, has opened the sloping grounds of his suburban mansion to hundreds of his fellow parishioners from St. Demetrios Greek Orthodox Church in the city for their annual celebration of the ecclesiastical New Year. Down the hill, in the grassy riverside meadow that serves as a parking lot, Paul arrives with his mother and his identical twin brother, Cass. The next few hours with both of them, Paul knows, will be an ordeal.

On the driver's side, Cass is out of the old Datsun coupe instantly.

"I need to find Dita," he says, referring to his girlfriend, Zeus's daughter.

Their mother climbs from the passenger seat with Paul's assistance, watching her other son sling his suit coat over his shoulder and bound up the hill.

"Theae mou," she mutters in Greek and quickly makes the sign of the cross after invoking God in dismay.

"Mom," Paul says, now that his brother is gone, "what are we doing here really?"

Lidia, their mother, condenses her thick eyebrows, as if she doesn't understand.

"You refuse to come to this picnic every year," he says, "because of how much Dad hates Zeus."

"No more than I," quietly answers Lidia, who rarely concedes priority in anything. Together, with Lidia hanging on to her son's arm for support, Paul and she start up the gravel path toward Zeus's vast white house with its low-pitched gables and Corinthian columns. "This picnic is for the church, not Zeus. I've missed many of our former neighbors, and I have not been face-to-face with Nouna Teri in months."

"You talk to Teri every day."

"Paulie mou,"—literally 'My Paul,'—"I didn't make you come here."

"I had to, Mom. You're up to something. Cass and I both know it."

"Am I?" asks Lidia. "I didn't realize that when you received your law degree, you also became a mind reader."

"You're going to make some kind of trouble about Dita."

"Trouble?" Lidia snorts. At sixty-three, their mother has grown somewhat stout, but she retains a regal manner, a tall woman with fierce dark eyes and a wide spray of graying hair pushed back from her brow. "Dita makes enough trouble by herself. Even Teri admits that, and the girl is her niece. If Cass marries Dita, your father will never speak to him again."

"Mom, that's just old-country nonsense like believing in the evil eye. Cass and I aren't going to carry on your crazy feud with Zeus. And we're twenty-five years old. You have to let Cass make his own decisions."

"Who says?" answers Lidia, adding a sudden chuckle and a squeeze of Paul's bicep to lighten the mood. That is their mother's idea of wit, laughing when she says something she means.

At the top of the hill, the picnic is a sensory barrage. The gums and spices, still smoking in the censers after a brief religious service, mingle with the aromas of four whole lambs roasting over oak, while the frenetic, high-pitched music of a bouzouki band lances the air to welcome the hundreds of guests crowding onto the lawn.

Teri, Zeus's sister, their mother's best friend since Lidia and Teri were both seven years old, awaits them with her scarecrow mop of dyed yellow hair. She embraces Paul and his mother. Zeus's son, Hal, is beside Teri, greeting the guests. At forty, Hal is fat and awkward and overeager, the kind of person who always approaches you in the pathetic hapless manner of a slobbering dog. Even so, Paul retains a soft spot for Hal, whom Cass and he used to follow around like puppies twenty years ago, in the days before a quarrel about the lease on Paul's father's grocery divided their families. Like Paul, Hal seems willing to ignore all that. He hugs Paul's mother, whom he still calls "Auntie Lidia," and chats idly with Paul before Teri leads Lidia away. A covey of their friends awaits them in the deep shade of one of the many blue-and-white-striped tents pitched across the lawn. Reluctantly, Paul heads into this jumble of people from his childhood whose old-world ways and ponderous expectations he's always longed to escape.

A few paces in, his girlfriend, Georgia Lazopoulos, catches sight of him and starts forward with her adoring grin. In her blue gingham sundress, Georgia is short and curvy and cutely dimpled—people always mention Sally Field. Although they have dated since their senior year in high school, their lips barely brush when they reach each other. Georgia is the daughter of Father Nik, St. D's priest, and realizes she is under constant observation on occasions like this.

She has already prepared Paul a paper plate of lamb and pasti-tsio, both favorites, which he accepts with thanks, but he steps away from her for a second to look for Cass. Paul finally spies his twin amid a clutch of people from high school. Even at a hundred feet, Paul knows he can catch Cass's eye, and when he does, he hitches his chin slightly so Cass is aware of their mother's location. They have resolved to keep watch and intervene if Lidia comes near Dita. She is unlikely to approach Dita's parents, to whom she has not spoken in years.

Privately, Paul shares most of his mother's opinions about Dita, but he feels Cass's fierce need for autonomy and has always treated his brother's desires as synonymous with his own. Despite their parents' furious opposition, Dita, with her caustic tongue and daring manner, seems to delight Cass far more than any prior woman.

Other people—normal people—don't really understand what it is to grow up not fully knowing where you start and your brother ends. For Paul, humans fall into two classes: Cass, and everybody else. Even their mother, a titanic force who has always loomed over them with the strength and unbending will of a marble column, does not stand in the same realm of emotional proximity.

Therefore, it has been one of the most surprising challenges of Paul Gianis's life that his brother and he began to become so different in college. Cass partied too much and openly resisted their parents. After graduation, Paul went on to law school, while Cass drifted until successfully applying to the Kindle County Police Academy, where he will start next week.

As Paul turns back to where he left Georgia, his legs tangle with someone behind him, and he is suddenly on the way down, arms helicoptering as he yelps, sending his plate flying. He ends up flat on his back, while the young woman he tripped on bends toward him, pinning his arms against the grass.

"Don't move," she says. "Give yourself a second to be sure you're all right."

It's Sofia Michalis.

"Where have you been?" are the first words out of his mouth. He does not know if he means simply that he has not seen her in several years, or that the time has transformed her. Both are true. Sofia was always self-possessed, a smarty-pants, but not the kind of girl you would have thought would end up so attractive. In high school, she was one of many young women the boys, with typical cruelty, referred to as 'a Greek tragedy,' meaning her nose is far too large for her face. But she always had that air. And a killer body. Now she knows she's something special.

Laughing, he sits up to examine himself. There is a grass stain on the sleeve of his tan Brooks Brothers suit, but no pain anywhere. He accepts her hand to return to his feet, while several people who came close to help now turn away.

In answer to his question, Sofia tells Paul that for the last seven years, she has been in a combined college and med school program in Boston. She got her MD in June and began a residency here at U Hospital.

"In?" Paul asks.

"Surgery," she answers.

"Jesus," he says. He never would have imagined. "Does that mean I could have gotten free stitches, if I needed them?"

"My mother keeps telling me I should have let her teach me to sew."

Sofia asks about him. He will be sworn in to the bar in two months and become a deputy prosecuting attorney in Kindle County in Raymond Horgan's office.

"And what about the rest of it?" Sofia asks. "Still going with Georgia?"

"Still going with Georgia," he answers. Her two small front teeth

appear over her skinny lower lip and that fine set of honkers seems to perk up somehow. He recognizes what she's thinking: *When are you going to figure it out?* "She's here somewhere," he says and gestures widely, as if he did not know that Georgia is bound to have stayed close, almost as if he otherwise might get away.

"I'll have to find her," Sofia says. "And say hello."

"You should," he says, feeling that Georgia has somehow thwarted the momentum of their conversation. Sofia parts with a quick wave and he resists the temptation to let his eye follow her. But the impact of her presence lingers. Sofia, he senses, has become one of those people he has longed to be, able to make herself felt in the world. It is a jarring sight when he finally glances back a second later to see Sofia with Georgia, who holds no similar ambitions. At Father Nik's urging, Georgia skipped college, and is already a senior teller at a local bank. Paul loves Georgia. He will always love Georgia. But he is not sure he wants to marry her, which is what she and her family have long expected. That is his problem. Life with Georgia would be good, but not necessarily interesting.

Caught up with these thoughts, Paul realizes that he has lost track of their mother, and when he finally spots her, he is alarmed to see her engaged with the host. But Lidia is considering Zeus with an unyielding expression. Dark and still improbably handsome at the age of sixty-six, Zeus with his rushing silver hair is turned out in a white suit, doing his best to appear jolly in the face of Lidia's coolness. Paul would have thought that Zeus is too obviously stuck on himself to succeed in politics, but he became the Republican candidate for governor, and is neck and neck in the general election race with barely two months to go. If Zeus wins, he will presumably leave his vast business, which owns shopping centers across the nation, in the hands of Hal, who is virtually certain to run it into the ground.

In the meantime, Paul notices Zeus's beautiful daughter headed toward him. Dita glides up and plants full on Paul's mouth a humid kiss, in which the ether of alcohol lingers. Whenever he sees Dita, she seems to be smashed. It takes Paul an instant to understand that she is pretending she can't tell the twins apart—most people still cannot—and he eases her away.

"Is that you, Paul? Lucky for me you didn't play along. Would Cass be jealous or do you two share everything?" Raven-haired and statuesque, with full, well-shaped features and striking dark eyes, Dita laughs and draws her breasts against his arm, forcing him to take another step back.

Because of antics like this, Paul tries hard to avoid Dita, even though he knows intuitively that is exactly what she wants, to separate him from Cass.

"Dita, I know you think you're funny, but I wouldn't be hanging by the phone waiting for your guest shot on Carson."

"Oh, Paul," she says, "you're totally uptight. If somebody shoved a lump of coal up your ass, it would turn into a diamond." Having plainly triumphed in this impromptu round of the Dozens, Dita pauses for a measuring look. "Why is everybody in your house against me?"

"We're not against you, Dita. We're for Cass."

"That's right. Cass needs a girl like Georgia. Bor-ring."

The pain of hearing someone speak so callously about Georgia is surprisingly sharp, and he has to suppress the impulse Dita frequently inspires to slap his hand over her mouth. Dita is smart. That is another thing that makes her so dangerous. He turns away, but Dita cannot resist a final shot.

"Really," she says, "I think I would have dumped Cass a long time ago, if I didn't know it would give the rest of you such a thrill."

Over the years, when Paul revisits this day that will change his family's life forever, Dita's thrashing unhappiness with herself will grow plain to him across the distance of time. But in the moment, he can feel only the peril to his twin that Dita poses, and his painful inability to save Cass from it. Paul walks off, while the thought comes to him with the force and clarity of a trumpet blast: He despises that woman.

2.

Pardon and Parole—January 8, 2008

Evon Miller, fifty, senior vice-president for security at ZP Real Estate Investment Trust, ran with the uncommon speed of a former athlete through the basement of the State Building Annex, not knowing where she was going or why she was here. Short and strongly built, Evon unexpectedly made out the number of the conference room she was seeking, and jerked to a halt. Within a plastic holder beside the door, a misprinted placard read PARDN AND PAROLE BOARD HEARING. Inside the conference room, she found her boss, Hal Kronon, CEO of ZP, whose urgent e-mail had summoned her. He was speaking with his personal lawyer, Mel Tooley, and another man in a suit she didn't know.

Evon had spent twenty years as an FBI special agent before taking this job, and she had learned that the power of the state, frequently spoken about as if it were a dread disease, was often most notable for the utter lack of majesty with which it was exercised. The Pardon and Parole Commission's monthly deliberations about the liberty of several dozen humans were going to be conducted in this low-ceilinged windowless room from metal folding chairs placed at two card tables. Behind the seats, the great seal of the state, thirty inches across and all plastic, hung slightly askew on the streaked wall. A lectern with a microphone was centered between the commissioners and two more card tables reserved for the participants, the state and whoever would speak for the prisoner. The hearing, which the card at the door said would commence at 2:00, had apparently been delayed.

Evon's boss, dark and burly, with his shirt gathered over the waist of his bespoke suit and his necktie askew, finally saw her and drew her toward a corner of the room. On the way, she asked why he was here. His message had offered no explanation.

"I'm trying to keep Cass Gianis in prison," he said. Evon knew next to nothing about the murder of Hal's sister, Dita, in September 1982. The case was long past being news by the time she'd moved to Kindle County fifteen years ago, and Hal preferred not to discuss it. Her knowledge was limited to what had been in the papers recently, that Cass Gianis, the identical twin of Paul Gianis, a state senator now running for mayor, had pled guilty to killing Dita, his girlfriend at the time. "That's not what I need first."

"What is?"

"It's YourHouse," he whispered. Hal had been in negotiations for months to buy YourHouse, one of the nation's largest builders of planned communities, for several hundred million dollars. With the downtick in prices for single-family homes, he believed he could bargain hard and diversify ZP, as he'd been advised to do for years. "We missed something in our due diligence. In Indianapolis. Sounds like there may be a brownfield on part of the site. We need environmental investigators. ASAP."

Evon was not even sure there was such a thing. Worse, knowing Hal, she was wary of chasing phantoms.

"Where did this come from?" she asked, meaning the information.

Hal kept his voice low, his lips barely moving.

"Tim shadowed Dykstra and the rest of the YourHouse crew, after they flew in yesterday."

"Jesus, Hal." ZP had kept Tim Brodie, an elderly former homicide detective, on an annual retainer for decades to do occasional work as a private investigator for Hal. Evon had little use for private investigators, most of whom were wannabes and used-to-bes who didn't know where the lines were and could get the company in trouble. Having Brodie spy on his business adversaries was typical of Hal's impulsive and risky stunts.

"Get somebody on this," he directed Evon, "but don't go far. I may need your help here."

As a boss, Hal Kronon, who had run ZP on his own since the death of his father, Zeus, twenty years ago, seemed to exist in a state of constant agitation. He could be by turns imperial, outraged or pleading, and always loud and opinionated. In every mood Hal required instant gratification from his employees. Evon was often baffled, therefore, by how fond she had become of him in the three years she'd been at ZP. For one thing, he had been astoundingly generous, making her far richer than a girl from Kaskia, Colorado, ever would have imagined possible. But mostly she liked Hal because he was so abject when he needed her help and so thoroughly appreciative afterward. Hal was one of those men who required plenty of women to take care of him, especially now that his mother, Hermione, was gone. There was Hal's wife, Mina, funny and bossy, and pudgy like her husband, and ancient Aunt Teri, his father's sister, who scared everyone a little bit. At work, Evon had become one of Hal's principal confidants, frequently nodding for hours, and gently attempting to save him from himself.

She went out to the hall to call her assistant VP who covered the Ohio Valley and told him to get up to Indianapolis and find somebody who could look for environmental contamination. Back inside, Mel Tooley, Hal's lawyer, told her that the hearing had been

delayed again, because Cass's lawyer was still en route. Her boss
had gone out to return a few calls. Mel was checking his handheld
from a seat in one of the three rows of card chairs that had been
set out for spectators, and Evon put herself down beside him. As
a Bureau agent, Evon had known Mel mostly by reputation, which
was as another scumbag defense lawyer, smart but basically deceit-
ful. Through Hal, she'd seen Mel's better side, but she still took
him with a grain of salt. He looked ridiculous, for one thing, wearing suits too tight for his wide form and a shaggy toupee, which
he must have adopted when Tom Jones was the rage. The mess of
black curls fell all over his head, resembling the stuff he might sweep
off the floor when he took his poodle to the groomer.

She asked Mel for a better picture of what was supposed to happen this afternoon. Mel wrenched his eyes in passing anguish.

"It's just Hal being Hal," he said. He explained that family members of homicide victims had a statutory right to demand a hearing
before a convicted killer was released. There was no basis, however,
to hold Cass Gianis any longer. He had done all but six months of
good time on the twenty-five-year sentence imposed when he pled
guilty, and the only way to keep him inside would be for a serious
disciplinary infraction. Instead, Gianis had been a model prisoner.

"Here," said Mel, "take a look at his file. See if I missed something." Mel handed over a heavy redwell folder and left to return
a call of his own, while Evon sat there, turning the pages. An essential element of Cass's original plea deal had apparently been
incarceration in a minimum-security institution, treatment rarely ac-
corded a murderer, and for which she assumed there had been hard
bargaining. As a result, he had been in the Hillcrest Correctional
Facility about seventy-five miles from the Tri-Cities for more than
two decades, even turning down transfers to newer prisons where
he could have had his own room. The forms he'd filled out stated
that Hillcrest, despite its barracks, was a better location for his fam-

ily, especially his twin brother, who visited most Sundays. Tooley
had subpoenaed every piece of paper Hillcrest had on Cass, starting with his intake photo and the fingerprints he'd given when he
entered prison in July 1983, and concluding with the most recent
status report of his counselor. As Mel had said, the overall impression from the heavy file was of someone who had managed the rare
trick of being a popular figure with the administration, the correctional officers and fellow prisoners, to whom Cass taught classes
on law and GED equivalency every day. Most recently, Gianis had
finished distance classes to qualify for a teaching credential. In a
milieu in which disciplinary beefs were routine—fistfights over the
TV channel, fruit secreted from the mess that could be fermented
with a little bread into rotgut liquor, joints that relatives had smug-
gled in—Cass's record showed only a few "tickets," write-ups for
offenses no graver than reading after lights-out.

At the doorway, there was a ruffle of activity. Paul Gianis, looking
as good as he did on TV, was on his way in, followed by two
scrubbed young underlings, a black woman and a white man, campaign staffers, Evon surmised. Mayoral race or not, Paul was apparently going to resume the role he'd played from the start, as one of
his brother's lawyers. He hung his gray wool overcoat over a metal
chair and threw down a beaten briefcase on the table designated for
the prisoner's representatives.

There had been a time, fifteen years ago, when Evon would
have said she knew Paul Gianis fairly well, although she realized
that he might not even remember her now. At that time, she had
been transferred here to work on Project Petros, an FBI undercover
investigation of corruption in the state courtrooms where personal-
injury cases were heard. Paul was that rare Kindle County lawyer
who'd first had the guts to refuse a shakedown attempt by a prominent judge, and then exhibited the even greater courage required
to say yes when Evon asked him to testify about the incident after

the judge was indicted. Afterward, widespread admiration for Paul, especially in the press, had propelled him into a political career that had led him to become majority leader in the state senate. Now running for mayor, he was far ahead in the early polls due to his name recognition and the generous backing of the plaintiff's bar and several unions.

Evon nodded when Paul finally cast an absent glance her way. He seemed to register nothing at first, then looked back and beamed.

"My God, it's Evon." He crossed the room immediately to offer his hand and chatted as he stood over her, jingling the keys and change in his pocket, answering her questions about his family. Paul's wife, Sofia Michalis, was famous in her own right, a reconstructive surgeon who'd made national news twice for leading teams of doctors to Iraq to treat the victims of IEDs. Their two sons, he said, were both at Easton College.

"And what about you?" he asked. "I heard you went to work for Hal. How's that been?" The corners of his mouth peaked. Paul clearly was familiar with Hal's reputation for irascibility.

"He's not a bad guy. Bark is a lot worse."

"Hey," he said. "I've known Hal all my life."

Evon straightened up. She'd never heard that.

"The families were always like this." Paul crossed his long fingers. "His Aunt Teri was my mom's best friend and her *koumbara*, the maid of honor at my parents' wedding. In our church, that meant she was also my oldest sister's godmother, the *nouna*, which is a big deal if you're Greek. Teri was at every family celebration—Easter and Christmas and saints' days—and Hal was her favorite, so she brought him along. My Big Fat Greek Family." He smiled at his bland little joke. "Eventually my dad and Hal's got into this insane tussle about the lease on my father's grocery, but before that, Hal even babysat for Cass and me." He showed the same great white grin, engaging because it made him seem briefly unguarded. "Needless to mention, he hates my guts now."

Even leaving aside Dita's murder—a lot to leave aside—Hal hated all liberal politicians, who, as he would tell you, almost always wanted to pay for inept government services by raising property taxes, which would drive out of the city business and employment and, most important, the tenants who rented in ZP's three major shopping centers in Kindle County. Evon tended to see his point. She'd voted Republican her entire life, until 2004, when she felt like they'd closed the door on her with the national effort to equate gay marriage with leprosy.

"How's your campaign?" she asked.

"Everybody says it's going great," he said, again offering that expansive smile. He was a nice-looking man, fit, a tad better than six feet, with a mountain of black hair that gleamed like a crow, save the scattered strands gone to silver. His long face had been weighted by time in that way that somehow looked good only on men, who ended up appearing wiser, nobler and ergo more fit for power. On women, it was just age. "Can I count on your vote?"

She probably would have said yes, even if it hadn't been banter, but Paul was interrupted by the arrival of Cass's main lawyer, Sandy Stern, who, according to the prison file, had represented Cass when he pled guilty. Round and bald, with an enigmatically elegant manner, Stern demonstrated there was an advantage to looking middle-aged when you were younger. He seemed barely changed by the fifteen years that had passed since he'd first cross-examined Evon in one of the Project Petros cases. Stern greeted Paul and also shook hands with Evon with a tiny bow, although she was unsure he actually remembered her.

A skinny female clerk appeared then from the back room to announce the commissioners were ready, and Evon summoned Tooley and Hal from the hall. By the time they returned to the conference room, a deputy sheriff was steering Cass Gianis in from a side door. He moved with mincing steps, since he wore leg irons and manacles, both connected to a metal chain that circled the waist of his blue jumpsuit. Paul asked the deputy's permission before embracing his brother.

Although the Gianises were obviously identical twins, seeing them side by side Evon recognized that, like her friends the Sherrell sisters back in Kaskia, they had not matured as exact photocopies. Cass was a tad taller, and somewhat broader. The most notable difference was that Paul's nose had been broken years ago. There was a funny story about that, retold in every profile of Paul, because, during their honeymoon in 1983, his wife, Sofia, had accidentally hit him with a tennis racket when he was trying to teach her the game. His father had supposedly taken one look at the bandage when they returned and said, 'I thought I told you not to talk back.' Paul had been left with a purplish lump at the bridge that looked a bit like a knuckle. Both brothers wore glasses, Cass's simple clear plastic prison-issue frames, Paul's black and stylishly squared. By some accounts, Paul had given up his contacts to obscure his broken nose, but to Evon it made the contrast in their profiles more noticeable. The resemblance between the twins was strong otherwise, except that Cass parted his thick hair, grown out as a privilege of minimum security, on the left, while Paul combed his hair the other way.

The five members of the commission filed in from a back door, four men and one woman, a diverse racial array like a UN poster. Evon had no idea who any of them were. No doubt they were all friends of the governor, a Republican, and thus, if anything, likely to be inclined toward Hal, who, largely by himself, financed the operations of the Republican Party in Kindle County.

The chairman, a sorrowful-looking fellow named Perfectus Elder, went through a discussion of several cases that received nothing but perfunctory commentary from the assistant attorney general, a lean guy named Logan whom Hal and Tooley had been talking with when Evon arrived. While this was occurring, an elderly lady in a wheelchair was steered into the hearing room by her tiny Filipina caregiver. The woman was engaged in an addled murmur, and the caregiver remonstrated with her quietly, as if speaking to a young child. The old woman's white hair was disordered and thin, like the remains of a milkweed pod, but she was beautifully dressed, and, even reduced by age and disease, retained a look of some determination. Paul turned away from his brother to greet her and she fell upon him with sufficient desperation that Evon realized the old lady was their mother.

"Typical stunt," Hal muttered immediately, loud enough that the commissioners had to hear the remark. Under the table, Tooley grabbed Hal's hand. Evon had been around enough hearing rooms to share Hal's suspicion. Stern and Paul, an accomplished trial lawyer who'd made a bundle in the national tobacco litigation after he left the PA's office, were using the twins' mother as an exhibit, demonstrating that there was no time to lose in letting Cass out. In the meantime, Paul again awaited the deputy's agreement before nodding to Cass, who turned back to embrace their mom. She became a burbling mess, her wailing briefly filling the hearing room. Evon realized it might have been years since the old lady had last seen her sons together. Chairman Elder grimaced a bit, then called the case everyone here was clearly waiting for.

"Matter of Cassian Gianis, number 54669, objection of Herakles Kronon." Elder made a complete hash of Hal's names, not just the first, which was often mispronounced, but the last as well, which was spoken as if he were an Irishman named Cronin.

Mel on one side, and Stern and Paul on the other, met at the lectern and gave their names for the record, which was a tape recording being made by the slender young woman who was operating the machine at the end of the table. Several reporters had filed in in the last few minutes, taking the seats next to Evon in the first row of chairs, joining Paul's two staffers. Word that Paul Gianis was in the house seemed to have attracted several additional onlookers, who filled the second and third rows.

"Mr. Gianis is scheduled for release on January thirtieth," said Elder, "and Mr. Kronon has objected. Mr. Tooley, how should we proceed?"

"My client would like to address the commission," said Mel, and moved aside to let Hal take his place. Tooley was giving the wild horse its head, but doing his best not to be splattered by the mud as he galloped by. Everyone in the room, except Hal, accepted the inevitability of Paul Gianis's election.

Hal came to his feet, looking awkward, as Evon could have predicted. He had forgotten to re-button his shirt collar and his tie was to the side, and he couldn't figure out where to put his hands, which he finally folded in front of himself. Her boss, even at his best, was not a pleasing physical presence. He had a large sloping belly and an oddly lizard-like face with goggle eyes, heavy jowls, thick horn-rimmed glasses and a flattened nose. His hairline had been reduced to a few flyaway scraps.

He expressed his thanks to the board members and then began a free-form soliloquy about Dita's death. Although Hal generally avoided the unruly emotions summoned by speaking about his sister's murder, she was never far from his mind. In Hal's office, on one wall, was a small shrine to Dita, including her senior sorority picture from the Kappa Kappa Gamma house at State. She had been striking and dark, with huge eyes and a wide wry smile.

By the time Hal was a couple of minutes into his remarks, he was weeping, but he was also largely incoherent. Only one thing was clear in his presentation. Because Hal's pain remained, it seemed wrong that Cass Gianis would be allowed to walk free.

As Hal spoke, occasional loony mumblings came from the twins' mother on the other side of the room, her caregiver making persistent efforts to shush her. At the other table, Paul and Cass remained respectfully stone-faced throughout Hal's presentation.

When Hal finally sat down again, Stern rose, taking care to first close the center button on his suit coat. He still retained the faint accent of his native Argentina.

"No one wishes more than Cass, and his mother and brother here beside him, that the events of that night twenty-five years ago could be undone. It has been a source of terrible grief to their family, and they understand that their own loss has been small next to the Kronons'. But Cass has paid the price fixed by the law, a sentence that was agreed to with the consent of the Kronons at the time. The record—"

Hal could not contain himself. "It was all right with my father and mother. It was never all right with me."

Chair Elder looked even more sorrowful in the face of this outburst. He searched around for a gavel and, finding none, banged the flat of his hand on the card table as Tooley hauled Hal back to his seat. Several of the observers murmured. If Hal was hoping to agitate public opinion, it wasn't working. He was making a fool of himself.

Elder nodded to Stern, who continued for only another moment. When he was done, Elder leaned left and right to consult with his colleagues. It was unusual for anyone of stature to appear at these hearings, except when grandstanding prosecutors, usually those running for reelection, came to inveigh against the release of a particularly notorious prisoner. But that was part of the established agenda. To have influential strangers like Paul and Hal embroiled before the commission was uncomfortable, especially when there were reporters here. Elder clearly wanted to get this over with now.

"Release date to stand," Elder said. The panel then rushed out the back door, like liquid through a funnel.

Evon watched as Paul Gianis hugged his brother. The deputies took hold of Cass's blue sleeve, but allowed him to embrace his mother briefly before they steered him from the room. The reporters surrounded Paul.

Stern shook hands with Tooley and left first. Hal marched out with Evon and Mel in unhappy cortege behind him.

"Talk about wasted breath," said Hal in the corridor. The conference room door swung open a second later, and the attendant appeared, struggling to back Mrs. Gianis's chair across the threshold. Hal, who in his own way was quite a gentleman, rushed over to help. Just to prove you never knew what you would get with Hal, he knelt beside the old lady as soon as she was outside, purring to her, as if he had not just been painting her son as the spawn of Satan.

"Auntie Lidia," he called her. He rested a hand on her forearm, the brown skin mottled with age spots and a skinny white patch, shiny like an old burn. Evon was reminded of the deterioration of her mother's skin when she was dying. It had seemed as thin as paper, as if you could tear it with your fingers. "Auntie Lidia, it's Hal Kronon. Zeus and Hermione's son. It's so good to see you." He smiled at her, as the old woman looked about trying to comprehend. Her eyes were watery from age and bald of lashes. In order to help her, Hal switched to Greek. The sole word Evon understood was when Hal repeated his given name. But Mrs. Gianis caught that, too.

"Herakles!" the old lady exclaimed. She nodded several times. "Herakles," she repeated, and then brought her hand to Hal's cheek with remarkable tenderness. The door swung outward again and this time Paul emerged, followed by a trio of reporters and his two young staffers. Hal stood up, wet-eyed again, his overused hanky crushed into the center of his face. Paul surveyed all of this for a second, then spoke to the attendant.

"Nelda, I think you should get Mom upstairs. They're waiting at the home." Mrs. Gianis was still saying 'Herakles' while the attendant wheeled her away. Paul turned back to Hal with a ripe expression, something between bitterness and bemusement, his lips drawn tight.

"Don't give me the evil eye, Paul," Hal responded. "Your mother was always kind to me. *She* didn't murder anybody. Which I'd never say about you."

At the last remark, Paul's mouth actually fell open and he took a step back.

"Jesus, Hal."

"Don't 'Jesus' me. You got away with it, but I know you had a hand in Dita's murder. I've always known that."

The three reporters wrote furiously on their spiral pads. Paul's brow collapsed toward his eyes. His public image was of an eternally measured person and he was not about to let that go, no matter what the provocation. He stared Hal down for only an instant longer.

"That's nonsense, Hal. You're upset." He gestured to the two young people who'd accompanied him and threw on his overcoat as he hustled off down the corridor.

The reporters immediately surrounded Hal. Maria Sonreia, from Channel 4, who was in her heavy camera makeup, her eyebrows so perfectly defined that they could have been pasted on, asked Hal several times, "What exactly do you believe Senator Gianis's role was in your sister's murder?"

Tooley, who like Evon had stood by speechless, finally intervened, grabbing Hal by the arm and pulling him away.

"We have nothing else to say at the moment," said Mel. "We may have a further statement tomorrow."

Evon called for Hal's car on the way to the elevator, and the limo, a Bentley, whose caramel leather always made her feel as if she were inside a jewel box, was at the curb when they got there. Delman, the driver, held open the door, smiling amiably as a traffic officer in an optic vest waved her lighted baton at him and told him to move.

At Hal's instruction, Evon jumped in. Delman would drop Hal at the office, then bring Evon back to pick up her car.

"Hal, what the *hell* was that about?" Tooley demanded, as soon as they were under way. Mel was a childhood friend of Hal's. Among Hal's many myths about himself was that he was 'a city boy' who had been raised in a bungalow in Kewahnee, not the Greenwood County mansion to which his father moved them when Hal finished junior high. He had no taste for the well-heeled suburbanites with whom he'd attended high school and college, and among whom he'd now raised his children, preferring a few grade school friends, like Mel, who truth be told had probably shunned Hal back then like everyone else. Unctuous by nature, Tooley nonetheless was direct when need be with Hal, who in the right mood could tolerate straight talk.

"You know you're on page one tomorrow," Mel said.

"Obviously," said Hal. You could never forget with Hal that despite the emotional magma that frequently forced its way to the surface, he could sometimes be cunning.

"There isn't any chance, is there, that I can talk you into issuing a public statement this afternoon retracting what you just said? If we get something out fast, then Paul may not sue you for defamation."

"Defamation?"

"Hal, he's running for mayor. You just called him a murderer. He'll sue you for slander. He can't ignore it."

Hal was heaped inside his overcoat, arms across his chest, looking a little like a molting bird.

"I'm not retracting anything." Having a billion dollars had an odd effect on people, Evon had come to learn. In Hal's case, it often made him a baby. "Let him sue me. Don't I have the right to express my opinion about somebody running for mayor?"

"Even with a public figure, Hal, the law says you can't make accusations that show a malicious disregard for the truth."

"It *is* true. Mark my words. The twins were in this together. I've known those two all their lives. There is no way one of them could have done something like this without involving the other one."

Tooley shook his head.

"Hal, man, I've followed this case for you for decades. I've never seen a word that implicates Paul. And it's a ridiculous time to make the charge. After twenty-five years, you suddenly pipe up, blaming him for his brother's crime, just when Paul is odds-on to become mayor, and you're the biggest donor to the other party?"

Hal considered all of this with a sour expression, his eyes skittering about behind his thick lenses like cornered mice.

"The guy pisses me off."

Evon was in no position yet to fully comprehend the web of family resentments at play here. But at least one part of Hal's fury was understandable. Dita's murder had ended his father's political career. Zeus had abandoned his campaign for governor within days of his daughter's death. And here was Paul, scaling Mount Olympus, with the papers already saying that if he won, the governor's office was likely to be next.

"I always thought he had something to do with it," Hal said. "My parents would never hear that, neither one of them. My father kept telling us, 'This is as big a tragedy for the Gianises as it is for us,' and my mother, especially after my dad died, she just hated discussing the entire thing. And I kept quiet for their sakes. But they're gone now and I'm speaking my mind. I think I'm actually going to run ads." Hal nodded decisively. Evon was beginning to recognize that none of Hal's remarks, here or back in the corridor, were completely spontaneous. He had been considering making a scene, and the potential aftermath, when he'd arrived today.

"That'll only force him into court," Tooley said. "You go that route, big fella, you gotta have some proof."

"Evon will find the evidence."

"Me?" She couldn't contain herself. But she had spent three years now extracting Hal from the holes he blundered into.

"Call Tim," Hal said.

"Tim?" asked Evon. Hal was referring to the PI he'd had tailing Corus Dykstra from YourHouse the day before.

"Tim knows all about this case," said Hal. "He never thought we had the whole story. I bet he already has plenty of dope on Paul."

They had reached the ZP Building, and Hal, who had a conference call on the YourHouse acquisition, hopped out so he could get upstairs to his office on the fortieth floor. But he stuck his head back into the car for one second to hand over a slip of paper.

"That's Tim's cell. Find him. He'll help."

3.

Horgan—January 10, 2008

Raymond Horgan's generosity had been a fair wind at Paul Gianis's back throughout his career. Stan Sennett, Ray's former chief deputy, who was Paul's second cousin, had gotten Paul his first interview with Ray in 1982, and they had clicked from the start. After Dita's murder, Ray had held Paul's job offer open while Paul worked with Sandy Stern on his brother's defense, and that didn't change even after Cass pled. Ray said he'd always taught his deputies to ask of any decision, 'Would you think you were being fair, if the defendant was your brother?' He doubted Paul would ever need that reminder.

In 1986, Ray lost the primary to his former deputy, Nico Della Guardia, and Paul left soon after to become a plaintiff's lawyer. Even out of office, however, Ray continued to be a leading figure in the Democratic Farmers & Union Party. Horgan had helped guide Paul when he decided to turn to politics a decade ago, after two huge tort judgments, especially the tobacco litigation, basically made work a pastime for him. It was Ray who'd first introduced Paul to local labor leaders, and Ray who, four years ago, twisted the last two arms to secure the votes Paul needed as a reform candidate to become majority leader in the senate. Now Ray was general counsel to Paul's mayoral campaign.

"Not mere falsity. But reckless disregard for the truth," said Ray, reciting the standard of proof a public figure like Paul had to offer to win a suit for defamation. In his mid-seventies, Horgan was so red-faced beneath the frost of white hair that you couldn't quite suppress the thought of a peppermint stick. He was hobbled after two knee replacements, and no longer even pretended that he could recall names. Some dismissed Horgan as a barnaclized pol. But he'd retained his canniness and an air of pure delight in the sly mechanics of power.

"And can we prove that?" Paul asked him.

"Should be a slam dunk," said Ray. "What evidence do they have that you had any role in that murder?"

On the other side of the sleek conference table, Mark Crully, Paul's campaign manager, dropped his pencil.

"We have to sue," Crully said. Mark was a quiet, driven little guy, general of the backroom army you would never see on TV. He'd run campaigns all over the country for a decade, most recently winning a special election for a congressional seat in California that had been Republican for fifty years. He was good. But about one thing: winning. And he was testy now. He had no patience for lawyers. Or anyone else for that matter. "We have to sue," he repeated.

Paul decided to ignore Crully, who often seemed to have his own view of who worked for whom. Paul spoke to Horgan.

"But it'll be our burden to show I had nothing to do with that murder, won't it? It's always a bitch proving a negative. And it's not like we can do DNA on the blood at the scene. We're identical twins."

"True," said Ray. "But we'll get discovery. And the discovery will show Hal has nothing. Right?"

The three were sitting in the fishbowl conference room at the center of Paul's campaign offices, glass walls on two sides. The design was Crully's. He believed that a look of openness sent the right message, both to the campaign workers and to the press, on the limited occasions Crully admitted them. But Paul, who was accustomed to keeping his own secrets, couldn't get used to it.

Looking through the glass to the tumbling office outside, you'd think this was a campaign with no troubles. There were probably one hundred people at work at 10 a.m., all but roughly twenty of them volunteers, hustling about with purpose. The space belonged to a guy Paul had known since law school, Max Florence, who'd donated two floors. They'd bought white modular panels with big windows, and had the entire office up and running the day Paul announced. It demonstrated formidability to his half-dozen opponents.

A full half of the office was given over to fund-raising. Most of the volunteers here were at the phone bank, dialing for dollars, from the lists Paul had developed in four different campaigns. Field, the second of the three major campaign operations, was situated right across from where they sat. Jean Orange was laughing about something with her two deputies; her metal walls were covered with maps of the county, green tags showing where they had opened local offices, red tags indicating the wards where the committee-person or councilman had promised to help. Now that the holidays were over, she expected to have a thousand people hitting doors this weekend, identifying their voters. Communications, around the corner, was the place today where people were earning their keep. Tom Mileie, a thirty-two-year-old Internet expert, and his three staffers, not to mention both deputy campaign managers and the policy director, were all fielding calls from reporters who wanted to know what Paul had to say now that Hal Kronon had claimed again that Paul had helped murder Dita.

Crully interrupted once more.

"You have to sue this cracker. You gave him a day to calm down. We sent him a letter saying cut it out, and not only did he not cut it out, he repeated it to reporters this morning. So now we have to sue him."

Paul had been in public life long enough that he didn't get spooked by crises. They were, truth be told, part of the thrill. People were counting on you. Now figure it out. And he would. He always did.

"Hal's emotional," Paul said. "People understand he's emotional. If I sue him, I'm giving him a platform to keep this in the news. Our last poll said we're twenty up. With that kind of lead, you play house odds and don't gamble."

"This guy doesn't need a platform," Crully answered. "He's got a billion dollars." Crully wore a white shirt that seemed bright as a headlight, with the cuffs still linked, and a rep tie snug to the collar. Everybody else, except the Communications people who often had to put on a tie for the cameras, worked in jeans. But Crully preferred to demonstrate he was still a marine. He spoke in a low voice and tried to show no emotion as he rolled that fucking pencil in his fingers. In Paul's experience, the Crullys of the world came with two speeds. When he went home to Pennsylvania he probably spent two days crying over his mother's grave, and seething about what a drunken lout his dad had been, and hating his brothers. And then he returned to work with the bloodless air of a hit man. "And there's another problem." Mark pointed his pencil at Ray, as a cue.

"So I got a call," said Ray. "Old pal. Another *alter kocker* like me. Street-word is Hal hired Coral Glotten to design an ad campaign."

"Saying what?"

"Probably saying you murdered his sister. And it's not like you're running unopposed. Murchison and Dixon will figure out how to use this. They all will."

"Let's see the ads," said Paul.

Crully again dropped the pencil.

"Great," he said. "How much time and money do you want to spend trying to un-ring that bell? You have no choice. This is an election. Elections are about myths, about making them think you're a god, not a mortal. You know that as well as I do."

"Can Hal just do that?" Paul asked. "Spend a zillion dollars on ads?"

"Probably," said Raymond. "It's not a coordinated expenditure. Not so far as we know. He's an individual exercising his First Amendment rights. At least as long as there are five clowns on the Supreme Court who think that spending money is a form of unrestricted free speech."

"Besides," said Crully. "Suppose it is illegal. You want to go to court? Or the Election Commission? Then Hal won't need to pay for ads. He'll just hold news conferences every day about how you're trying to muzzle him. Reporters don't like muzzlers. They always figure they're next. But that's the point: You're going to court. The only question is when. So do you go now, when an innocent person could be expected to express his outrage? Or in three weeks when you're just whining about how much money Hal's spending calling you names? This isn't a close call," said Crully. He lowered his chin so that Paul could see the flat look in his fair eyes.

Mario Cuomo said you campaign in poetry and govern in prose, but as far as Paul could tell they were both trips to the abattoir, just different entrances. Governing and running were both brutal, with plenty of bloodshed, veins you opened yourself and spears in the sides from your opponents. Politics was always going to be the war of all against all—which included the people who were supposed to be with you. Crully, for example, wanted Paul to win. But only so Mark could run even bigger campaigns. He didn't really care about Paul's family or the complex accommodations they had made for decades to live with the terrible fact of Dita's murder. The truth was Crully had taken this job so he could sit out the catfight between Obama and Hillary. By May, when the runoff election for mayor was scheduled to take place, there'd be a clear winner in the presidential contest and Mark could jump onto that campaign, probably to run a swing state.

"Fine, Mark," said Paul. "I hear you, but Hal's going to use this to drag every stray dog and cat into the courtroom. I mean, am I going to be giving depositions two weeks before the election?"

"You're not giving shit," Crully said. "You sue Kronon, and then the lawyers delay everything. He'll file a motion to dismiss because you're violating his right to free speech and we take weeks to answer and then there's an election." Crully threw the back of his hand at Ray, dismissive of the law and all its routine monkeyshines and its predictable inefficiency.

Ray generally found Crully amusing, perhaps because Ray had been on the team that found him. But Horgan looked nettled. He stood up to hang his suit coat on the back of his chair. Like Paul, he preferred just to ignore Mark at times.

"Are there risks, if we sue? Sure," said Ray, as he rolled up his cuffs. "But Hal's got you pretty well cornered here. He's going to keep saying you murdered his sister to anybody who will listen. If you sue him, maybe a few more people pay attention. But there's also a chance he shuts up. Maybe the judge *makes* him shut up. Net-net, I think you have to do it, Paulie. Otherwise, you're gonna ride out the campaign wearing the collar for Dita's murder. That's a lot of weight to be trying to tote over the finish line. You need to say, 'I didn't do it.'"

"How about if I say I didn't do it."

"You need to back it up. You sue him, you have skin in the game."

Paul closed his eyes to think. Even at moments like this, he loved this life. Or most of it. The money part was horrible and getting worse. Close to unbearable. You didn't get really big dollars from anybody who didn't have an agenda and a ring to be kissed. But the rest he still relished. He knew enough about himself to admit that he liked the heat of the spotlight—Lidia had taught all her children that they deserved attention. But he still found a thrill in the magnitude of the problems, and figuring out how to get them solved. The county had been playing a shell game for a decade—there wasn't the money to run the schools or pay pensions, not if you'd passed fourth grade arithmetic. But he, Paulie Gianis, he would be the one working it out. There was no other job with this kind of impact, where the effect of your brief time on earth was magnified so far beyond your own circle. You could invent the semiconductor or make a movie and change lives, too, if people happened to bump up against those things. But in politics the effect was universal. Every person you passed on the street had a stake in what you did and usually an opinion about it. The world was what it was, full of love and cruelty and indifference. But it could get better, with less need, less violence, more opportunities. In his lifetime, black people had gone from the back of the bus to maybe, considering the results in Iowa last week, the White House. And if you put up with all the hard stuff, you could be laid to rest knowing you had helped make that kind of change happen.

"To be frank," said Raymond, "the only thing that gives me second thoughts is that he's basically daring you to sue."

"That's Hal," said Paul. "The guy's like a windup toy who turns his own key. If I win twenty million dollars in this lawsuit, he appeals for five years and doesn't even notice when he writes the check. Besides, he thinks all Democrats are socialists who want to destroy the free enterprise system that made America great. He's always been crazy-right. I remember when I was six years old, Hal had all these campaign banners for Barry Goldwater in his bedroom.

This is 1964. There weren't R's in Kewahnee in those days. Even Zeus, his dad, only became a Republican when they moved to the suburbs and he fell in love with Reagan. The hard-right stuff was Hal's defense against being a nerd. It was his way of saying he was the only guy who knew the truth."

"OK," said Ray. "But he can't really believe that any Republican is going to win in this county. If he knocks you out and the D's splinter and Flanagan gets into the runoff, he gets crushed. So if Hal's rational—"

"He's not."

"OK," said Ray, "but let's pretend. Common sense says that to go public with this kind of accusation, he has to have something to back it up. So you tell us, Paulie. Does he?"

"Not that I know of," Paul answered. Horgan, who'd done criminal defense work for decades, had asked the question so casually that Paul had responded with equal nonchalance. But Ray was still a sly cat. Only now that his steel blues stayed put on Paul did he realize that Ray had been asking the same thing for ten minutes, in hopes of an unequivocal response.

But Crully wouldn't let him answer. Mark stood up, all five-six of him, but still looking, from the hard set of his face, like somebody you wouldn't want to mess with. He was done wasting time.

"You have to sue. Period. Personally, Ray, I'm not spinning my wheels asking what Hal's got. Because if he's got anything real, Paul's not gonna be mayor anyway." Crully turned toward his candidate. "So, Paul, either quit now or sue."

Crully flipped his pencil in the air and let it bounce on the table and left the room.

4.

Tim's House—January 11, 2008

Tim Brodie lived in the same Kewahnee neighborhood in which Paul and Cass Gianis had grown up, and where Hal had started out. The little hip-roofed bungalows, all of them built of brick before the Second World War, sat squat as toads on forty-foot lots, with huge old trees in the snowy parkways. When Tim bought his house in 1959, not long after he'd made detective, he felt he'd done whatever people were talking about when they had told him to grow up and make something of himself.

Now he awoke with a start. He was on the plaid family room sofa, a heavy volume on his chest. He sat up with an ominous grunt and waited until his body and his head came back to him. His leg ached unbearably just for a moment whenever he awoke. Tim didn't know if the pain subsided or he merely got used to it. He had waited all his life for time to catch up to him and now it had.

He recognized the doorbell. When he could move, he made his way to the front door. Ordinarily, he'd expect it to be his grand-daughter, Stefanie, but he'd been over there with her and her funny little husband last night. Instead, he saw a woman on his stoop, breathing fog in the cold. She was someone he knew, he realized, but he just couldn't place her.

He opened the front door but not the glass storm.

"Evon Miller," she said, and offered her hand. "From ZP."

"Oh, hell," he answered. He stepped back at once to welcome her. He'd met Evon a few times, the first when she took the position at ZP of his pal from the Force, Collins Mullaney. Collins had liked the job, but had to fall on his sword because a ZP real estate manager in Illinois was paying bribes to lower the company's property taxes. Collins parachuted out with a big package and had no ill will toward Evon. She was a good egg, a bandy little gal, a former FBI agent who years back had busted several state court judges. She'd been in the Olympics, too. Field hockey was Tim's memory. Also didn't make any secret of the fact she was gay, which was something Tim had gotten over early in his life when he tried to make a go of it playing the trombone. What the hell did he care who you slept with, if you had good pitch and kept time?

"To what do I owe the honor?" he asked, once he had her inside. He told her to take off her coat. She was OK-looking, thick-built but with a little bit of a stylish way about her and short blondish hair. Her face was wide, and in the strong daylight, he could see she had kind of pebbly skin.

"Need to talk to you about something," she said. "I've been calling your cell for three days."

"Really?" Tim saw the contraption on the table in the foyer where he'd set it when he got done following around Corus Dykstra from YourHouse. Dead. He laughed as he slid the phone in his pocket. "I was actually wondering why my daughter called the landline yesterday. Don't get old," he told her. It was the drifting part of age, the way his mind seemed to have no home on earth, which often surprised him.

He offered Evon coffee, but she declined.

"Grew up in a Mormon town," she said. "My dad was a Jack, but I just never developed the habit. I'll take a glass of water, if that's OK."

He was in a plaid flannel shirt and twill pants and Evon could see he'd been asleep. His face was red and his white hair, some of it starting to yellow, was sticking straight up in patches where it should have been pushed over his bare scalp. He had a lumpy, marked face like an old potato, and he had become one of those elderly guys with a permanent wary expression, seemingly afraid that any second now somebody might take advantage of him. Tim handed her the glass and then led her back toward the family room, where he said he liked to sit. She had some memory that Tim was a widower, and the house probably looked just the same as when his wife passed a few years back, crowded with the relics of a lifetime. It was the kind of place where you had to turn sideways to move around the furniture. The walls were thick with photographs, both family shots and scenery, as well as children's paintings. And every tabletop was forested with objects: Limoges figurines. Little lacquered boxes. Glass paperweights. Books and more framed photos. They could have done *Antiques Roadshow* here for a month.

In the back room, a sunny add-on with tall windows, there was soft music, a swing take on "It's All Right With Me." A crooner's voice yielded to a trombone solo, and Tim stood for one second, listening with his eyes closed and a finger raised. Then he silenced the old phonograph and lifted an LP tenderly from a turntable, slipping it into a grayed sleeve. He had been reading, too, and slid a mark into a huge volume.

"Greek myths," he answered, when she asked about the book. "Once Maria passed, I figured I better get on to what was left on my lists. Said I'd read Shakespeare and got through *The Comedy of Errors*, but that's kind of a slapstick piece, you know, twins separated at birth. I can handle the comedies, but *King Lear*, whoa, that's tough. These old tales"—he hefted the book with both hands—"don't seem to put me to sleep so fast." In the light, she could see the white whiskers he hadn't shaved this morning standing on his cheeks. "So you here about Dykstra and YourHouse?" he asked.

"Not really. But Hal says you turned up a lot of great stuff following him around. Frankly, if I'd known what the boss had you up to, I'd have tried to stop him. The whole deal could have cratered."

Tim shook his head. "Nobody notices an eighty-one-year-old guy. They look right through you."

The melancholy frankness of the observation silenced Evon for a second, but Tim didn't seem to be seeking sympathy. She turned the subject and asked Tim if he'd seen the papers this week. Laughing, he pointed to a pile in the kitchen, all sheathed in blue plastic, another thing that seemed to be getting past him. Evon handed over Wednesday's front page, and he groaned at the headline: "Kronon: Gianis Part of Sister's Murder."

"Me oh my," he said, as he scanned the article.

"Paul sent Hal a letter demanding a retraction, and Hal won't budge. In fact, he repeated this stuff to a couple more reporters. And he's planning to put ads on TV saying the same thing. Gianis filed suit for defamation late yesterday."

"Oh dear," said Tim. He knew all about how people could be when somebody they loved got murdered. A brick could fall off a building and kill someone you cherished, and it wouldn't be quite as hard to accept as a homicide. When some goofed-up stranger made a conscious choice to end the life of a person precious to you, it knocked the pins out from everything we assume in living with each other. Tim had spent more than twenty-five years on the Force, many of them nodding and patting hands and telling people that they'd be best off letting it go in time. But some folks just couldn't. And Hal was one of them.

Evon said, "I didn't realize until I started reading some old news articles that you'd been in charge of Dita's murder investigation."

Tim snorted. "Wasn't anyone in charge of that investigation."

"Well, Hal says you had some thoughts about Paul and the murder, back in the day. Is that true?"

"Not how I recall," he answered. "I was never content we'd gotten answers to every question. So Hal's right as far as that goes. But how many cases can you say that about? Most of them I ever worked on. There's always some piece of it you don't have quite right."

While she'd waited to hear back from Tim, Evon had had her assistant print out everything on the Internet concerning Dita's death. The murder, when it occurred, had been a sensation. It seemed to stimulate a seething mixture of pathos and bloodlust and grim satisfaction in the public, seeing this kind of tragedy befall people so privileged, in the palace they'd fled to to avoid the troubles of the city. Instead, someone had crept into Dita's bedroom, while the other members of her family slept, and killed her, leaving a trail of blood and glass. The case topped the headlines for weeks, especially when Zeus quit the governor's race. According to the papers, there were no hard leads. And then out of nowhere, a few months later, Cass Gianis agreed to plead guilty to second-degree. But there was never a word about Paul, unless you counted the mention that Cass was an identical twin. When Paul had started his political career, talk of the murder had briefly revived. All the profiles of Paul said he visited Cass several times every month and supposedly wrote him before going to sleep each night. Paul never discussed the crime, merely repeated that he loved his brother.

"How did you even get involved in the investigation?" Evon asked Tim. "Were you detailed out there by Kindle County?"

"Nope, I wasn't even on the job any more. Hit fifty-five the year before, went into my brother-in-law's heating business. No, Zeus, Hal's dad, asked me to get involved."

"How did he find you?"

"Oh, I'd known Zeus and them forever. Kronons lived two blocks over when Maria and I moved in here." Tim hoisted himself up for a second to point out the rear window of the sun-room. "My wife was Greek. Baptized all my kids at St. Demetrios. Even spoke a couple words myself. President of the men's club four years. But she come to lose her faith, Maria did. Not her values, mind you. But she just couldn't touch her knee to ground and celebrate the Lord after our daughter died." Tim's old face grew heavy as he thought about that, then he cleared his throat again.

"The Greeks, I'm not telling anybody anything they don't know, they really don't have time for anybody but Greeks. But Zeus must have figured I was close enough. Very clubby, the Greeks. Very proud, you know. Make fun of themselves so no one else can. 'We invented democracy and been sitting on our asses ever since.' But they're a conquered people. Had the Ottomans with their foot on their throats for five hundred years. That'll take the spunk out of you, especially your men. But they don't like to admit that. Gives the Turks too much credit." His gray eyes came back to her then and lingered. She could tell he'd forgotten the question.

"You and Zeus were friends?"

Tim laughed. "Zeus, he was too grand for me. He'd glad-hand you, but he'd left the folks from the neighborhood way behind. What would you expect of somebody calls himself Zeus?"

"Wasn't that his name?"

"Oh, hell no." Tim grabbed the top of his head with his big raw hands to force his memory back into it. "Zisis," he said finally. "That's what he was baptized. But of course he wasn't in school long with American kids before they were calling him 'Sissy.' So by high school he was saying 'Zeus.' Can't blame him, I guess."

She asked again how it was Zeus had gotten Tim involved and he laughed once more, a phlegmy, geezy sound.

"See," said Tim, "that investigation wasn't any more organized than a barroom brawl. Nobody had taken control of the crime scene. Zeus and Hal and the mom had been in there twenty times before the first cop arrived. The Kronons had actually cleaned up a little bit, the mom had, even arranged the body, before anybody thought to call the police. Not that there was any real point in bringing that bunch in anyway. Out there in Greenwood County, they hadn't seen a murder in eighteen years, and probably hadn't known what to do then. Which didn't keep them from mucking around for a day or two. Then they asked for the state police, but there was too much politics with Zeus running for governor. Every trooper was out there to watch somebody else. Meanwhile Zeus is a basket case, he starts in screaming he wants the FBI. He gets them, too, for all they know about murders. So now you got three sets of nincompoops." Tim's eyes popped up when he realized who he was speaking to. "No offense," he added.

"None taken," she said. The Feds and the locals—that was like the Civil War, a battle to be fought in a different form in every generation.

"You had three different teams of evidence techs go through there," Tim said, "each with different samples. Some tests get performed three times, some don't get done at all. Everybody thinks somebody else is running leads. It was an unholy mess. So about a week along, Dickie Zapulski calls me. Zeus has asked the state police to hire me as a special to lead the investigation. Zeus got on the phone next and pretty much begged. Truth told, I wasn't loving the heating business, or my brother-in-law, but I didn't actually miss the street. But I felt for Zeus. I'd lost a daughter. So I said, OK, put me in charge. Not that anybody was actually willing to listen to me."

When Evon had found out, not long after taking the job, that Hal had a PI on retainer, she'd gone in to see Collins Mullaney, who'd stayed on a month for the transition. He reassured her about Tim, who he said was maybe the best homicide dick in Kindle County in his time. 'What was great about Timmy was he didn't get distracted,' Collins had told her. 'He didn't care who was humping who this week in McGrath Hall,' referring to the headquarters of the Kindle County Unified Police Force. 'And he didn't get caught up hating the perps either. He'd smack a kid who spit on him, just like the rest, but he always said the same thing, no matter how big a shitbum. "Didn't have a soul who cared enough to teach 'em how to behave." Kind of "there but for the grace" with him. I think he grew up in an orphanage himself.'

The crime scene, Tim said, didn't point in any particular direction. The first police to arrive had found the French door to the balcony open. It had rained hard that evening, right at the end of the St. Demetrios picnic, and there was a set of deep shoe-prints in the flower bed under Dita's window, which made it look as if somebody had dropped from above. There were some tire impressions, too, down the hill, where you'd hide a vehicle, but there'd been two hundred cars there earlier in the day, so you couldn't make as much from that. Upstairs, one of the panes in the French door was broken out between the mullions, with the glass scattered on the tiny balcony outside, and quite a bit of blood painted on the jagged glass, and the inside of the door and the carpet below. The blood trail ran into Dita's bathroom, where, by simple count, there appeared to be a towel missing, suggesting that the killer had used it to bind a wound. The ABO typing that was state-of-the-art in 1982 classified the blood in the room as B. Dita and the rest of the Kronons were O, so there was no doubt of an intruder. From the brass knob on the outside of the French door, the initial techs also lifted a good set of fingerprints, which had remained there despite the fierce rainstorm that had pelted that side of the house. No way to date prints, but the best guess was that they belonged to the intruder.

"Dita is killed in her bed," Tim said, "which is still made. Apparently she's tuckered out and watching the tube for a while, before going out to meet her girlfriends at a bar. She's in her robe and undies. No vaginal trauma, no tearing, but rape kit is positive for semen—then again, that could be from any time in the last forty-eight hours. Type B, though. Somebody smacked her first, damn hard, then grabbed her face. You could see the bruising in both cheeks. The hit on the left side made finger stripes. Meaning we're probably looking for somebody right-handed. And whoever it was had worn a ring, because there's a big circular bruise. The police pathologist's thought is our perp whacked her, then sort of covered her mouth with his hand and rattled her skull against her headboard. She dies of an epidural hematoma. Lividity and the bleeding from the scalp wound shows she wasn't dead for several minutes after she was beaten. But the pathologists can't say whether or not she lost consciousness. Probably though, since she didn't call for help." Tim recited all of this like the prayers in a breviary. The murder was twenty-five years ago, but for many people she knew in law enforcement, the details of a big case were burned onto their brains. There were few jobs more intense than having to save everybody in town from a bad guy.

"What's the time of death?"

"Well, you know, it's a Greek picnic, they're eating all day, so it's hard to tell for sure from the stomach contents, but the pathologist says 10:30, give or take. Right around ten, according to the toll records, she gave her boyfriend Cass a call. So she dies after that."

"Who found her?"

"Zeus. He wasn't much of a witness, not that I'd have done any better. Clear recollection that he heard the window break and comes running down the hall. Pretty shaky after that. Best memory seems to be that he sees Dita on the bed. The TV is on, and he asks her what's doing, but he catches sight of the shattered pane in the

door and the blood and goes straight there. Looking out, he thinks
he sees a dark figure, male, disappearing into the woods. When he
turns back to talk to Dita, she doesn't answer. So he comes over,
touches her, shakes her. It actually takes him a minute to fathom
she's dead. He calls the family doctor. Then sits with his daughter.
Can't even imagine going down the hall to tell her mother." Tim
stopped there with his own memories. When Katy passed, they'd all
known it was coming, but Maria had gone home to sleep and so he
had to call her. He still remembered the feeling. He was here, but
not really, the rest of him was still in the past when his six-year-old
daughter was alive.

Evon asked the status of the investigation when he got involved.

"They were chasing their tails. The operating theory was that the
bad guy crawled in thinking she wasn't there, caught her unaware
and he grabbed her like that to keep her from screaming, then he
took off, afraid somebody had heard the commotion. But each department had its own spin. The locals are thinking it was a burglary
gone bad. State police are talking to everybody at the picnic, hoping
somebody noticed Mr. Stranger Danger. Zeus is still pretty much
a mess, and blaming himself. Why didn't he hear her getting beat?
And he's convinced she's been killed by his enemies to get even with
him."

"Enemies?" Evon asked.

"Turned out Zeus had a passel. Pretty sharp elbows when it came
to business. There was the Greek mob, too, not to mention the hus-
bands and boyfriends of the girls he was always after. Even turned
out that some of the boys from the North End warned him not
to run against Rafe Demuzzio in the primary. FBI was looking at
that."

"And when did Cass come into the investigation?"

Tim said the police had spoken to Cass as part of the initial canvass, but he claimed to know nothing. At the start, Zeus was sure

Cass was uninvolved, and cops being cops, they were reluctant to suspect a police cadet. About three weeks in, the phone company produced the toll records from Dita's phone and Cass was reinterviewed briefly, but Cass said he and Paul weren't home and Dita had merely left a short message on his answering machine, which he erased that night.

"Cass, he would have been the last person I'd have thought of, to tell the truth. Him and Paul were in high school with my middle daughter, Demetra, and I knew them from church. Solid kids, in my book, both of them. But you know," he said, "it's the ones you think you know that fool you." Tim thought about that and squeezed his lips with his hand.

"About a month along, we had a big meeting, every investigator, just to see what we'd missed, which was quite a bit. By then two, three of Dita's girlfriends had said she'd made up her mind to drop Cass, she was sick of all the trouble with his family. So I go over and take a peek at Cass's employment file in McGrath Hall," said Tim. "Blood type B. His prints are on file, too. I ask the Greenwood PA for a subpoena and sure enough, the prints match out with the doorknob and a lot of other lifts around the room. So now we're thinking, maybe the call at 10 was to whistle his butt over there so she could tell him *adios.*

"Anyway, the Greenwood prosecutor, he wants to question Cass in the grand jury, but Cass hires Sandy Stern who won't let him talk. There's a lot of cat-and-mousing for a month. Stern is like, 'Those fingerprints mean nothing. Cass was climbing the drainpipe every night to tickle her fancy.' And the same girlfriends who said Dita was going to eighty-six Cass, when we push, they give that part up, too."

"Cass was jocking Dita right down the hall from her parents? Doesn't sound like my idea of fun," Evon said.

Tim closed his eyes and let his head revolve loosely, like a leaf in

a breeze. Who knew what folks thought of as fun, especially in that
department?

"Zeus, of course, that was the one thing he went off about, when
I told him that part. No boyo was making time with his little petu-
nia right in his *casa*. But I'm suspicioning it's probably true."

"Really?"

"Sure, cause if Cass was climbing up there to make whoopee, that
meant he knew how to get in there the night she's killed. So I get
the PA to subpoena his credit card records, and we put together a
little task force to check out every pair of shoes he bought in the
last year, and sure enough, about a week into that, we find he got
himself a pair of Nikes whose tread matches the impressions in the
flower bed. Those tracks down the hill could have come from the
Bridgestones on Cass's old Datsun, too, except there's ten thousand
cars in the Tri-Cities with the same tires.

"But we issue a search warrant, for his clothes and shoes and vehicle, and for a physical exam, to see if we can find the scar where
he was cut. We get the shoes we're looking for. Nothing turns up
with the clothes, but Luminol in the car shows blood traces, type
B again. By now, Stern won't produce Cass for the physical exam,
instead files a bunch of motions, and then when he's just about
run out that string, Sandy comes in and offers to plead Cass. He
wants manslaughter, ten years' minimum security. Zeus and Lidia,
the twins' mom, they go back to smooching in the choir room at
church, so he's heartbroken for her and is fine with whatever, but
Hermione, Dita's mom, and Hal, they wouldn't hear of ten years.
Finally, right before the PA was going to return an indictment, all
of them settled at second-degree for twenty-five years, but still minimum security. The judge gave Cass a month before he surrendered
so he could stand up at Paul's wedding."

"And were you OK with that result?"

"Depends how you mean. The sentence, I never thought that

was my business. Minimum security irritated some of the other cops, but I'm like, 'It's prison, not torture, any nice college boy would get torn apart at Rudyard, especially a former cadet.' The thing that bothered me was he wouldn't answer questions. Never did. He pled, said he done it, that was it."

"Well, what questions were there to answer?"

"The windowpane just for one. The glass is all outside, on the little concrete balcony under the French door. Meaning the window was broken from the inside. So how'd he get in?"

"You already told me. He'd climbed up there before. What was your term? 'Making whoopee'?"

"That's OK. Maybe he arrives hoping for romance, or knowing what's on her mind. Either way, she says, 'No, I'm done with this,' and he loses it and smacks her. When she passes out, he panics and flees. But if you're inside already, why not just open the latch and leave?"

"Maybe he's trying to make it look like a break-in. Only he really doesn't know much about crime scenes. So he cracks the glass the wrong way."

"Nice." Tim chuckled and pointed a thick finger at her with true admiration. The knuckle was crooked and swollen with arthritis. "Only Cass Gianis is a police cadet. And the other thing is, breaking glass, that makes noise. If you want to escape, why raise that kind of ruckus? What sense does that make?"

"So you didn't like him for the crime?"

"No, I'm not saying that. I'm saying I had a few questions. There wasn't any couch in my office for the defendant to lay down on and explain what was in his head or his heart, assuming anybody ever knows. But we had his fingerprints in her bedroom and on the door. Blood was his type. Shoes match. And there's motive because she was going to drop him. And he gave a shit-ass alibi when he was first questioned right after the crime, said he was with his twin brother—"

"Paul?"

"Right. Said they were larking around that night, drinking beers over the river. Course nobody saw them. Cass couldn't even name the liquor store where they bought the six-pack, said Paul got 'em."

"And did Paul back that?"

Tim scratched his chin while he looked at the beamed ceiling of what had once been a porch.

"Seems to me he might have, now that you mention it. You know, it was just part of the initial canvass. Troopers talked to everybody who'd been with Dita at the picnic. Report couldn't have been more than a paragraph. I would probably still have it."

"Really?"

"Down in the basement. I didn't have any staff, and I was in a different office every couple of days, so I figured I'd rather keep all the reports at home. Show you if you like." Tim used a chair arm to hoist himself to his feet and wobbled a bit with the first step. Evon watched him. He was somewhat stooped now behind the shoulders, but he remained a big man, well over six feet, with the proportions of a tight end. In the day, he must have commanded a lot of attention on the street. He motioned for her to follow, and then opened a door in the kitchen and descended unevenly toward the cellar. The old wooden steps were steep, and Tim held on to the rail and kept his other hand on the brick wall to steady himself. His twill pants were halfway down his butt.

The basement, when they reached it, was even more crowded than the upstairs. There was a distinct cellar reek, a combination of mildew and dust, and all manner of things crammed in—grimy bicycles with flat tires, garden hoses, racks of clothes, hickory-shafted golf clubs, old TVs, broken furniture. The light from a cellar window slanted over some of the mess.

"Did you ever hear of a rummage sale?" Evon asked him.

"My daughters are even worse than me. Don't want to part with anything Maria touched. Let them figure it out when I'm gone," he said, and laughed, utterly cheerful about his own mortality. He turned sideways to get past an old chifforobe and reached a metal filing cabinet, a beige box from which the paint had rusted off in uneven blots. He seemed to know at once where everything would be. He crouched over the bottom drawer and pulled out a file, then went to pull the chain on a bulb. He turned the pages with some difficulty, his fingers stiff, licking the tip of his thumb now and then.

"Here you go," he said finally. He read the report for a second, then handed it to Evon.

It was just as he recalled, too. Short interview, two days after Dita's death. Paul said Cass was with him all night after the picnic, hanging out at Overlook Park on the river. A stone lie. Cass couldn't have been with him, because, as Cass acknowledged subsequently, he'd been with Dita, punching her around and killing her.

"This is gold, you know," Evon told him.

"It is?"

"This man wants to be mayor. Leader of the police. But he lied his ass off to the cops to keep his brother out of trouble. Even after he'd been hired to be a deputy prosecuting attorney."

"Who wouldn't? I'm not sure I'd want to vote for a man who wouldn't save his brother. Besides, that's all politics. Hal can keep his crazy politics. That's not my concern." Tim waved a hand past his big nose.

"But it proves what Hal's been saying. That Paul was involved from the start. He covered up for his brother. And maybe there's more to it. Those shoes? They're identical twins. So the Nikes could have fit Paul. I bet they always shared clothes. Were they still living together?"

"You kidding? Greek family? Hal was still with his parents and he was forty. Yeah, the Gianis twins were both of them at Lidia and Mickey's. Paul, I think, was about to move out."

"What about fingerprints? Do identical twins have the same fingerprints?" Evon was feeling some excitement. She always did the job and her job was to make Hal right. She was surprised about the velocity with which she was willing to suspect Paul, whom she'd always liked, even admired. But there was an elusive quality to him that had never sat quite right with her. You could spend lots of time with Paul Gianis, as she had, and still come away feeling he was guarding something essential about himself.

But Tim moved his head from side to side.

"Seems as I remember, twins' prints look somewhat alike, but when they're in the womb and they reach out and touch the whoosywhatsit—" He stopped to find the word.

"Placenta?"

"Right. No, they have different fingerprints."

Evon absorbed that, then reread the report.

"Can I take this?"

Tim shrugged. "Public record now. PA in Greenwood did what they always do when Cass was indicted, threw all the police reports in the court file to prove the defendant had had full discovery before he pled guilty."

Evon strayed a hand to the filing cabinet.

"What else have you got in there, Tim? Any chance I can pay you to look through all your files and see if there's any more about Paul?"

He laughed. "No need to pay me. I'm on the long end with the Kronons. I've been getting a check every January first for twenty-five years."

"I know," she said. "It comes out of my budget." She smiled, though. "Nobody's ever really explained it."

"It was just Zeus's way of thanking me for dropping everything and taking over the investigation. When this here was done with, I wasn't too keen to go back to the heating business. Zeus wanted to hire me at ZP, but I'd had enough bosses as a cop to last me a lifetime. So I decided to become a PI, and Zeus was like, 'OK, we'll give you a retainer every year.' I won't lie either. Helped plenty, especially when I was getting started." Mullaney had told her that these days Tim worked principally for criminal lawyers, turning up stuff the cops had missed, and also for a number of insurance defense lawyers. Tim was the guy who'd debunk a workman's comp claim with photos showing the guy who said he was injured lifting weights. Brodie could also write a good report and was relaxed on the witness stand. He'd always had as much work as he wanted, although that had to be petering out at his age. "'Tween Zeus and Hal, they haven't called me ten times. This thing I did last week, with Corus, must have been the first in five years. So yeah, you want me to look at the files, I'll look at 'em. I'll keep track of the time, but it'll be a long while before you owe me anything."

Upstairs, she collected her parka, which had ended up on the sofa next to his heavy book. There was a faint odor in the kitchen of last night's dinner, which she hadn't noticed when she came in.

"You keep going with those myths," she said.

"Oh, I will. Was just reading about the myth of love when you rang the bell."

"Myth?" said Evon. "You mean love's not real? I wish somebody had told me that before I moved in with my girlfriend."

She rarely said anything so personal, but she couldn't pass on the joke. Not that it was all a joke in Heather's case. But Tim was mightily amused. He laughed in his husky way for a long time.

"No," he said, "Aristophanes says we were all four-legged creatures to start, some the same sex, but most half man and half woman. Zeus was afraid us humans would get too powerful so he sliced us right down the middle, and everybody spends their life looking for the matching piece. What do you think of that?" He laughed again, tickled by the idea.

"I think it makes as much sense as any other explanation."

Tim found her response amusing as well, then limped ahead to show her out. When they got to the foyer, he lingered to face her.

"You don't really think Paul Gianis had a hand in murdering Dita, do you?"

"What was he lying for?" Evon asked. "He knew what to say, and more important, he recognized that he had to lie for Cass's sake. Which means he had a lot of information by then, Tim. Maybe they *were* together that night. Maybe that's why Cass never wanted to answer questions."

Tim pondered, but an unhappy thought seemed to pull at his face.

"Don't like thinking I missed the boat like that," he said. He considered the prospect for a second, then opened the heavy door.

5.

Heather—January 12, 2008

Her given name was not Evon Miller. She had been born DeDe Kurzweil, in the Kaskia Valley in Colorado, and grew up on a family farm, where her father planted alfalfa, pinto beans and corn. He was a quiet, bowlegged man, a Jack Mormon, who'd left the church—and his parents and sibs with it—to please his wife, who said, only after their wedding, that her LDS conversion simply had never taken root in her heart. DeDe was the fifth of seven children, right about the place you'd expect the kids to start getting lost, and she was lost, aware, long before she understood why, that she did not seem to fit. She never knew when to smile, or how to make people like her, especially her mother.

But on the playing field, with a field hockey stick in her hand, she made herself real. Her father had been a baseball star, who'd signed with the Twins after his mission and played A ball until his family needed him on the farm. All her father's athletic ability had lit in her—at least that was what both she and her father believed. She fell asleep a hundred times with a stick in her hand, thinking over her moves. She was runner-up for Female Athlete of the Year in Colorado, went to Iowa on a full ride, and in 1984 was selected for the US Olympic field hockey team. She came home with a bronze medal and no idea of what would happen next. It was like coming into the daylight after a dozen years in a tunnel of ambition and competition. At a college jobs fair, she signed up to get more info about the Bureau and was at Quantico three months later. She loved the FBI, every day, for twenty years. The bureaucracy, the paperwork, the regs could make you buggy, but to a person, everyone she worked with was incandescent with pride in the mission, and gripped by a zeal to do right. It was the same kind of striving that had been so central to her life in sports.

In 1992 she'd accepted an assignment to leave the Des Moines RA, resident agency, and go undercover here, pretending to be Evon Miller, paralegal, actually serving as the watchdog over a dirty lawyer who'd turned and was secretly recording his payoffs to various judges. She chose the name Evon herself, borrowing it from a second cousin whose parents had intended a country spelling of Yvonne. But nobody, not even her cousin, pronounced the name that way. 'Like "even better," ' her cousin customarily explained. DeDe longed for the same self-confidence.

Petros, the undercover project, was a far-reaching success—six judges, nine lawyers and a dozen court clerks and sheriff's deputies were convicted—and after the last trial Evon had been called to D.C. to receive the FBI Medal, the greatest honor bestowed on agents. Even her mother sat there with her chest puffed out, accepting everybody's congratulations.

But by then, there had been a bigger reward. The chance to be someone else had made her someone else. She came out, for one thing. But far more important, she began to understand what it would feel like to enjoy being herself. The thought of going back to DeDe was as unwelcome as returning to prison. She changed Kindle County to her OP, office of preference, and received permission from D.C. to continue to be known as Evon Miller, the only name anybody here had ever called her. By now, even Merrel, the sister Evon had always been closest to, had taken to referring to her that way.

She was so much happier than earlier in her life, when she'd felt like a handball ricocheting at high speed off walls she'd never seen coming. These days her main preoccupation, in the rare idle moment when she let her mind light there, was wondering how happy she had the right to be. No one could expect perfection.

She tended to deliver that admonition to herself at moments like this, when she was holding off the familiar combination of anger and humiliation that consumed her at the prospect that Heather Truveen, her girlfriend, would disappoint her again. It was Saturday night and Evon sat in the ballroom at the Kindle County Athletic Club, a gorgeous old room, with oaken pillars three stories high, that had been beautifully transformed for the wedding of Francine and Nella, the friends who had introduced Evon to Heather. The rows of stacking chairs had all been jacketed in white satin and an amphora full of white roses marked the spot on the riser where the ceremony would occur. Beside her, Evon had saved a seat on the aisle, knowing Heather would savor every detail of the brides' attire. But any second, they would be stepping down the satin runner on the opposite arms of Nella's dad. Evon had discreetly removed her BlackBerry from her handbag to see if Heather had sent any messages, when she finally arrived.

"Made it," Heather whispered, and dropped her blonde head to Evon's shoulder and nuzzled her for a second. Heather smelled surprisingly fresh, as her scent, Fracas, briefly surrounded Evon.

They had been together a year and a half now. Heather was thirty-eight, a creative executive at Coral Glotten—funny, a little wild, clever and very beautiful. She'd been a model to start, a tall elegant blonde whose grace reminded Evon of Merrel, who'd always been the most beautiful woman Evon knew and who Evon grew up long-

ing to resemble. When Evon was eleven, Merrel gave her the Easter
dress Merrel had made four years before. Her older sister curled
Evon's hair, and shortened the hem another inch just before church.
'Doesn't she look nice?' Evon heard her sister ask their mother upstairs. 'Nice as she can,' her mother answered, 'but she'll never be
much to write home about.'

One of the many good things that had happened when she was
dispatched to Kindle County in 1992 was that she had to pretend to be the girl-on-the-side of the government's rascally lawyer-
informant and was obligated to look the part. Her hair was dyed to
a brighter shade of blonde and sheared into the hedgehog style of
the time, as if someone had taken a mower to one side of her head.
She wore four-inch heels and lots of makeup every day, and stylish
clothes, and discovered that she liked all of that far more than she'd
ever let on to herself.

But no matter how big a lipstick lesbian she was, she'd never
imagined being attractive to someone as glamorous as Heather.
Beauty came to Heather in the same effortless manner in which
Evon had excelled at sports. Heather was naturally fit, despite seldom working out, and never restricting what she ate. She was a true
ash blonde—she boasted to Evon the first time they had dinner that
the rugs matched the drapes—and was actually more beautiful with
the swollen sleepy look she had in the morning.

And Heather was fun, carefree and blazingly funny. For the first
several months, Evon found her endlessly amusing, even though
Heather's impulsiveness seldom took account of what Evon wanted.
Awake in the middle of the night, Heather became entranced by
an infomercial about Brazil and while Evon was asleep rebooked a
vacation they'd planned for months. One evening, Heather walked
into the apartment and waved her hands at the furniture she had
spent months choosing. 'This is all wrong,' she said. 'The sofa has
to go.' The sofa was crimson mohair and had been special-ordered

at a cost of several thousand dollars. Evon nearly reeled at the waste, but was delighted at the same time to have exceeded the boundaries that had confined her all her life. When Heather returned to the store, she ordered a full second living room and asked them to hold it, awaiting the day she would change her mind again. Evon had roared when she heard.

But naturally the humor faded. Watching her girlfriend toss out an expensive top she'd worn only once, Evon retrieved it from the can. 'Give it away, at least,' she told Heather, who flicked a hand at the bother. With time, Evon began to see beneath the beautiful mask. Heather worked hard on the exterior because what was inside was often beyond her control. Black funks frequently gripped her and made her impossible and bearish. She drank too much, too often, and in that state was lacerating. And she was frustratingly fickle. Their plans had been to make a day out of getting ready for the wedding, go for spa treatments and mani-pedis. Instead, Heather slid out of bed at 8 a.m. and announced she had to work. Her principal client, Tom Craigmore, ever more demanding, wanted an all-day with his creative team for the line of athletic clothing he was going to launch in the fall.

"Where did you change?" Evon asked Heather now.

"The office."

Heather had left the apartment without a bag, which meant her dress had been on a hanger at work and that she had known for some time their plans for today were doomed. Why not say something earlier, why put off being the source of disappointment? Heather was a baby that way. She'd come from a crazy messed-up home, a philandering father who'd killed himself eventually and a mother who'd never really touched the ground long enough to notice that her children were in distress. Heather as a result was afraid to face disapproval.

The ceremony began. It was a wedding with an asterisk. Francine and Nella had gone to Boston last weekend to be legally married. What was taking place here, in the presence of friends and family, was all that local law allowed, a religious commitment ceremony.

The officiant, an Episcopal priest who was a longtime friend to both women, blessed their union beautifully.

"Life," he said at one point, "is much too cruel to go through it alone." The remark pierced Evon like an arrow. Yes. That was true. She took Heather's hand and squeezed it hard.

And on the power of that observation, it turned into a great night. A few years back, at the age of fortysomething, Evon had found out that she loved to dance. The music, especially the seventies tunes of her teens—"Stairway to Heaven," Springsteen— liberated her as liquor or drugs did other people. Heather and she danced until they were a clammy mess, requesting four separate run-throughs of "Born To Run." The club personnel shooed everybody out at 1 a.m.

By the time they arrived home, Heather was caught up in the inebriated fantasy of the wedding she would make. She had a thousand ideas: walking down an aisle lit by floating candles, in doubled crystal globes also containing orchids, the ceremony conducted on a mat of fresh lavender.

"And I want Cartier," Heather announced. "My kisses do not begin with Kay, and if you come home with Zales, I don't even know your name." Heather was laughing when she said it, but there was a knife blade buried in her eyes.

When Heather left her to shower, Evon, who'd had far more to drink than usual, felt a stark mood shadow her heart. Heather's talk of marriage, her regal demands, left Evon feeling how remote the chances were. Her doubts had little to do with her skepticism about whether same-sex marriage would ever be legal in this state, or even whether she had shed enough of a closeted person's anxieties to be able to refer out loud to anyone as her "wife." Something else concerned her, even if all the champagne made it impossible for her to be more precise. It was a shock to find herself dubious, because the story of the relationship had been that she pursued Heather, put up with her, forgave her. And it was true that she still craved Heather, loved her zany side and terrific sarcasm, and had touched something strong and good in herself by doting on her. In the past several months she'd realized she was basically Heather's mother, which was not as bad a deal for Evon as putting it that way made it sound, because she enjoyed—no, relished—being a kinder, more patient and understanding person toward Heather than Evon's mother had been to her. She wasn't prepared yet to give any of that up.

But she was starting to lose faith in the myth or the legend or the fairy tale, whatever you called it, by which she'd been operating, the belief that Heather would 'calm down,' as Evon put it to herself, and love Evon as she wanted to be loved. Life was much too cruel to go through it alone. So she was here. And tomorrow when she awoke she'd believe it all again. But for now, the last glass of champagne had made her feel like a seer or an oracle who looked through the smoke called the future unable to make out any comforting shapes.

6.

Georgia—January 17, 2008

Tim saw the first of Hal's ads about Paul and the murder Monday afternoon, when he put aside his book of myths and turned on the early news at 5 p.m. He'd given up on the local TV journalism years ago—it was all about Chihuahuas hunting lobsters, or Jesus appearing on a grilled cheese sandwich—but he was excited to find himself with a role in current events. At his age, he was accustomed to feeling irrelevant.

Paul's lawsuit had made headlines for a couple of days, and now Hal was hitting back. Tim watched the commercial in amazement. A piece of paper that could have just as easily been obliterated by the seepage in his basement was now made to look like holy writ. The camera zoomed in sideways on the police report, then jumped first to the header that read "Greenwood County Sheriff's Police," then the date and finally "Paul Gianis" in the box for "Witness." The words attributed to Paul blackened to boldface and then rose off the page, all while some unseen woman with a scolding voice asked if we wanted a liar for mayor. Tonight the commercial was shown again a minute later as part of the news.

Tim turned away from the screen with a small turmoil in his gut. Not a word in the ad was untrue. But he still didn't feel quite right about it.

Tim was reconsidering all of this as he looked between the little leaded darts of stained glass in his bayed front window, already bundled in his woolen overcoat and wearing a felt hat. The BMW pulled up to the curb and he locked up and lumbered out.

"All of four blocks," he told Evon, putting on his seat belt, "but the newcomers don't shovel their front walks. I'm too damn old for mountain climbing." There had been a serious snow last week, the first in a couple of years. When Tim grew up here, it got to twenty below for days in the winter and snowed like hell whenever it warmed up. No more. Right after the flakes stopped falling, young Dorie Sherman across the street had been out with her little guy, showing him the drifts, which he'd never seen.

Evon asked for more detail on the woman they were going to see.

"Not a lot to say," Tim answered. "Georgia Lazopoulos. Georgia Cleon now. Paul's girlfriend back then. Her dad was the priest at St. D's."

"The Greek priests marry?"

"Orthodox, right. But only before they're ordained. Sometimes makes for a slow course through the seminary."

"Where I came from, the ministers' kids were mostly crazy."

"She was a nice girl, so far as I remember. Sincere. You read the report I sent?"

"I tried. But it was hard to make out much on the fax."

"She talked her head off on the initial canvass. Said Dita and Paul seemed to have words the day she was killed. That's the kind of stuff you wanted me to dig up, right?"

"Exactly. Did she tell the cop that because it seemed odd?"

"Not hardly. Cop said to tell him everything she remembered and she did, even how many pastries she ate. But I thought may as well talk to her. Given I'm billing hourly and trying to work off that retainer."

Evon slapped his hand, and Tim laughed.

"Turn here," he told her. Georgia was in the same little bungalow she'd bought with her ex-husband, Jimmy Cleon. Jimmy had been her rebound after Paul, glib and good-looking, but he'd been on drugs all along and she didn't know it until the wedding silver disappeared, not much after the honeymoon. At least that was the story. Since Georgia was the priest's daughter, everybody talked about her.

When her father had been pushed out at St. D's, he'd lost the parish house and moved in with her. Father Nik had gone odd. Brain tumor, as Tim remembered. The surgery had saved him, but he was never quite the same, and he'd had a stroke by now, too. Georgia's mom had passed while she was in high school, so it was just her and her loopy old dad, exactly the fate Tim was still hoping to save his daughters from, who were always on him to move out to Seattle where they were.

"Does she know I'm coming?" Evon asked when they parked. He'd motioned her into a space down the street, where they could maneuver over the black ruts driven into the snow. In this neighborhood, parking in the winter could be a perilous act. The city plows never got to these small streets and homeowners spent hours shoveling their spaces, protecting them with lawn chairs or those orange cones filched from road crews. The last fistfight Tim had gotten into, more than forty years ago, was when some joker pulled into his space as soon as he went to put away his shovel. But it was 3:30 and there was still a fair amount of parking here while most people were at work.

"Yeah. Said we were working for Hal. She didn't sound pleased, but then again, she didn't say no. Seemed to remember me."

"Who could forget you?" Evon asked. "Tall, dark and handsome."

He laughed. He was liking this Evon a good deal.

The woman who greeted them at the door was barely recognizable to Tim. Age had been unkind to her, had coarsened her skin and stolen the life from it, and like many of the girls in this neighborhood, she'd put on an awful lot of weight. She had been pretty, as Tim recalled, very pretty, and looking close you could see the remnants of that cheerful appealing face within a pudding of flesh. Maria had gotten pretty hefty, too, truth be told, not that he had ever thought much about that. In a long marriage, the present matters less, at least it did to him. Every day they'd been together was there in both of them, good days mostly. But he could only see Georgia as she was, and her appearance seemed to say she'd lost all connection with the girl she'd been. There was just this person who looked much shorter now, in a droopy shirt and leaving you to wonder what illusions made her put on stretch pants.

Tim reintroduced himself, mentioning neighbors he thought Georgia might recall, then asked how her father was doing. She made a face.

"You'll see," she said. "He wanders around here like he's on a treasure hunt. My biggest problem is to keep him from picking up the phone. He gets on with these solicitors from like the Police Benevolent Fund and talks for an hour and promises them thousands. I finally just had to give him a pad of checks from a closed account. He loves to write checks. The big shot."

She waved them into the dark living room. There were several beautiful icons on the wall, with their elongated flat look, and a lot of photos of Greece—the royal blue water and arid mountains—apparently taken on a family trip. Maria had wanted to go when the girls were young, but it was one more thing that got sucked under in the riptide after Katy's death.

After his own wife died, Father Nik was overwhelmed by all the work of the parish and had needed Georgia to stay nearby. He hadn't thought much of a girl going off to college anyway. She'd gotten a year of bookkeeping training and still worked in the head- quarters of the big bank where she'd started at nineteen, which was now owned by an even bigger bank. She was the chief teller, count- ing other people's money from 7 to 3 every day.

She brought them each a glass of water from the tap, then settled heavily on the print sofa. Evon sat beside her while Tim took an armchair. The TV was on and Georgia for a second couldn't look away from some account of the latest goings-on with Britney Spears, who'd been hospitalized after locking herself in a room with her son.

"What a runny mess she's turning into," Georgia said, "and with everything she's got." She continued to gaze, enthralled. Her atti- tude was just like the Greeks with their gods, Tim decided, looking in on the life that was bigger than life, these grand figures whose tri- umphs were the stuff of dreams and whose hubris led to destruction so complete it made you happy to be living small. When the show went to commercial, Georgia clicked it off. But she pointed at the TV, an old walnut console, with the remote.

"I've been watching Hal's ads," she said, and her mouth soured. "I'm sure he sent you out here, thinking I'm the bitter old witch who'll just crap on the guy who dumped her, but it's not going to happen. I'll tell you right now, I don't believe Paul had anything to do with Dita's murder." The wide figure on the sofa tightened with these declarations, gripping her arms close to her body.

"Can't say I'm surprised to hear that," Tim answered. "You wouldn't have spent all that time with somebody you figured for a murderer, right? But now and then people have another side no- body sees. Hal's got his opinions and Paul decided to sue him for speaking his mind, so here we are. None of us was there when Dita was murdered. We just want to know what you remember. No de- sire for you to make anything up."

Her brows were thick and she squinted at Tim a little, trying to figure out whether to believe him. He could see what had happened with her. Georgia was a little like a dog that had been beaten too much. She still had no idea what she'd done to bring all these troubles on herself, so she'd learned to distrust everyone.

"Well, I don't really remember much after all this time," Georgia said. "You know. The event stands out. How often are you with a girl and she turns up dead a few hours later, murdered no less? But who knows with the rest of it? What's it been? Twenty-five years at least."

"Of course," said Tim. "But memory can be funny. Sometimes you can say to a gal, just an example, but years later, do you remember what dress you were wearing that day? And they do."

"I do," said Georgia instantly. She smiled for the first time since they'd come through the door. "It was a little blue gingham sundress. I looked good in it, too." Her quick laughter drove her back into the sofa. She was, very briefly, pleased with herself.

"I'm sure," Tim answered. Beside Georgia on the sofa, Evon had relegated herself to the role of taking notes. Most of the city homicide dicks she knew weren't much on interviewing technique. They'd come in and ask a few questions with their faces turned to one side, waiting for the moment when they could say, 'Don't bullshit me, if you don't tell the truth you're going to jail.' But Tim was earnest and kind. It was like talking to somebody's grandfather who was in a rocking chair on his front porch.

"I'll tell you something else I remember," she said. "You may not care to hear it, but when I saw that commercial, saying Paul lied to the police, it pretty much came back to me. That was exactly what Paul told me that night. That he was going to meet Cass at Overlook? I can't tell you if he did or he didn't, but I remember his plans."

Evon felt jolted.

"Any reason that stands out in your memory?" she asked.

Georgia turned to her, plainly feeling challenged. "Yeah, because I was really surprised. It was a Sunday night, and my dad always went off with the men's club and that meant we had the run of the house. Guys being the way they are, Paul always liked to take advantage of that." She nodded decisively, like she'd put Evon in her place, which she had.

Behind Georgia, leaning forward in an easy chair, Tim let his fair eyes rise to Evon. He didn't want her breaking his rhythm, and eased back in.

"Did Paul say why he wanted to go out there?"

"I could guess. He needed to talk to Cass about Dita, I think. The two of them had an argument about her once a week. He was afraid Cass was going to marry her and tear his family apart."

Evon rolled over the details. It wasn't as bad as she'd first feared. Maybe Paul had met Cass at Overlook and hatched some kind of plan. But one of them, perhaps both, had left there soon and killed Dita.

"I don't want you to think I'm taking Paul's side," Georgia said. "I'm not. He was a louse to me. You know, women say, 'He took the best years of my life'? He really did. I was the girl from the neighborhood he was too good for as soon as he finished law school. And I could have had a ton of boys in those days. The way I looked? It still aggravates me. But I'll tell you the truth. I vote for him. I probably will this time, too." Georgia looked at her plump hands for a second, trying to discern the meaning of what she had just revealed.

People could get stuck in love, Evon realized, and then never recover. The best love of Evon's life had come almost a decade ago, with Doreen. They'd had six good months before Doreen was diagnosed, and another year and a half with Evon helping her die. She'd been devastated afterward, in part because the normal times hadn't lasted long enough to find out what the relationship might have been. She wondered now, if, like Georgia, she had never found her way back from mourning that lost possibility. People didn't generally think that love could ruin a life. But perhaps. Evon felt her entire body pressed down by the sheer unhappy magnitude of the idea.

"So let's go back to the day of that picnic," Tim said to Georgia. "Anything stand out in your memory about Paul that day?"

She snorted. "Well, I remember he bumped into Sofia Michalis. I could just see by the way he was talking to her something was going on. When he broke up with me, he blamed it on this whole thing with Cass being a suspect. He said he was too mixed up with all that happening. But he was married to Sofia within six months. He wasn't so confused then."

"Do you recall anything about him and Dita?" Tim asked.

She shook her full face. It wasn't clear, though, if that was a lack of memory or if she was distracted by the thought of Paul and Sofia.

"One of the officers who talked to you," Tim told her, "he said that you recalled that Paul seemed to have had words with Dita."

"Did I?"

Tim reached into his tweed jacket and pulled out the report casually, as if it were just another piece of paper an old fellow would have in his pockets, like a grocery list, or a note about calling his daughter. Georgia spidered her hands on her forehead as she read the highlighted part. Eventually, she started to nod.

"I just saw them talking. Dita went stalking off and I remember the look on his face. But that was nothing new. Paul hated Dita."

"Is that what he said that day? That he hated her?"

"I don't remember what he said. Did I tell that to the cop?" She took the report back from Tim's hand without asking and swung her head laterally as she read. "I really don't recall even talking about her with Paul that day. Except maybe when he said he was going to the Overlook, and I'm not clear on that."

"But you say he hated her?"

"There was a lot not to like. I don't want to speak ill of the dead"—she made the sign of the cross over her chest with impressive speed—"but I have to tell you the truth. Dita was just a very spoiled girl with a very sharp tongue. She was like, 'My dad is one of those guys, emperor of the universe, so I can say damn well what I please.' She was gorgeous, so there were always boys after her, the whole damned cavalry, but except for Cass, she managed to drive every one of them away after a while."

"Is that what Paul didn't like about her? Her attitude?"

"You know. He said she was wild, leading his brother astray, said his mom hated her, too, and Dita knew it and just liked egging all of them on. I don't know. You ask me?"

"That's what we're here for," Tim said.

"I think he was jealous. That's a hard row to hoe. With twins? Identical twins? He loved his brother. There isn't even a word for it really. Lidia always told the same stories about when they were little, how they couldn't stand being different. She sewed their names into their clothes and they tore off the tags. They ate off each other's plates. At night they ended up in the same bed, sleeping in each other's arms. The neighbors' collie bit Cass, and everybody swore Paul cried first, before either of them knew the dog had drawn blood. It was like they were joined at the heart. And that never quite stopped. I mean, Paul wouldn't really accept that Cass was guilty."

"How's that?"

"Well, even after Cass pled, Paul was saying he was innocent."

"Did he?" said Tim, who allowed none of the surprise Evon felt rippling through her thorax to reach his expression. He maintained a purely conversational tone. "When was that?"

"That day. The day Cass was in court pleading guilty. I was there actually. Paul and I had been broken up for months by then, but I don't know, I wanted to support the family or something. I don't know," she repeated. "Probably I was looking for an excuse to see Paul." She winced, pained by the memory and the futility of her longing. With her eyes closed, Tim noticed that her face was turning blotchy with age. "Anyway, he thanked me for coming. We went over to Bishop's, and had a beer, and he was just blown away. I mean, you can imagine, somebody's been like another part of your body all your life and they're about to lock him up for twenty-five years. He was really blue and he just said to me, 'He's innocent, you know.'"

Evon intervened. "And did you ask how he knew that?" She tried to evoke Tim's mild tone, but again, Georgia's response to her was sharp.

"Well, he was his twin brother for God's sake," she answered. Evon had Georgia's number by now. She was one of those women who didn't really like other females, while the men she'd loved—Paul who'd thrown her over, and Jimmy Cleon with his drugs, and her dad who'd kept her from college—had all done her wrong. Life had put her in quite a bind. "I suppose I figured Cass told him that. But I was trying to console him, not play detective. Paul was miserable and I was listening to him. I thought we could be friends. Does that ever work?" She kept touching the front of her short stiff hairdo to keep it in place, after every shake of her head. "And of course, right before I got up to leave, he told me he was going to marry Sofia in a couple of weeks, so Cass could be his best man before he went inside."

Tim was quiet for a second while she dwelled with that memory, which, like much of what she'd said about Paul, struck her hard.

He asked a few more questions about what had happened on the day of the murder, whether anyone else had had a visible conflict with Dita. Finally, he looked to Evon to see if she had something else to cover, which she did. She flipped back to some notes she'd made that morning.

"Thinking back, do you remember Paul having any serious cuts around that time?"

Georgia considered the question for only a second before saying no.

"Would you have been aware of any deep cuts?" Tim asked. He was as easy as if he were asking the time, but Georgia fixed him with a knowing brown eye.

"I'd have known. We dated for nine years and I was sure I was going to marry the guy. I mean, the truth is I saw him less once Dita was murdered. He was finally going to move out of his parents' after he started working, so he was looking for apartments, and then when Cass became a suspect he was completely focused on that, and we broke up."

"So are you saying you might not have known?" Evon asked.

Georgia wheeled back, remaining cranky with her. "I'm saying I saw him less. But I saw him. And I would have noticed. Everybody knew there was blood all over that bedroom. Like I said. He hated Dita. I don't think I'd have been that dense."

Evon absorbed her answer without quarreling, but these kinds of retrospective would-haves were always baloney. If the man she loved had told her he'd cut himself fixing a fence in his parents' yard, she wouldn't have thought twice about it. But Georgia was touchy enough that Evon wasn't going to argue. She looked down to her notepad.

"Is Paul right-handed?" Evon asked.

"Mostly."

" 'Mostly'?"

"Cass is left-handed. Writes lefty, eats lefty. Paul is the opposite. I always wondered when I noticed that, years ago, if that meant they weren't really identical, but apparently that happens a lot with identical twins. When Paul and Cass were little, though, like I said, they hated to do anything different from one another. So sometimes they'd both eat lefty and sometimes they'd both eat righty. They each ended up pretty much whatever the word is, both-handed."

"Ambidextrous?" Evon said.

"Right. So, for example, when they started playing tennis in high school, they used to shift the racquet, hitting forehands from both sides, but the coach put a stop to that. Paul played righty and Cass played lefty. They were both strong singles players, but at doubles no one could beat them, because basically they knew exactly what the other one was thinking on the court. They were state champions two years running. That was a big deal around here. Guys from a city school winning against all these suburban kids from country clubs? There were articles about them in the *Tribune*. And there was this one great story." Georgia fell back, smiling at the recollection.

"They were once in one of these home-and-home tournaments, Friday and Saturday, against a high school from Greenwood County, and when Cass finished his singles match the second day, the kid came after him with his racket. He was screaming, 'I didn't mind losing to you yesterday, but coming back and beating me left-handed today, that's just being an asshole.'"

The three of them all laughed hard. But even amid the levity, Evon could see Tim had reabsorbed some of his anxious aspect.

"But Cass, he did wear a big ring on his right hand, didn't he?" Tim asked.

"Oh yeah," she said. "It was one of those Easton College class rings that Paul and him both bought when they graduated."

Tim nodded, but his lips kept folding into his mouth. Evon realized he was wondering how they'd pinned a right-handed murder on a lefty.

Evon drank down some of her water, preparing to leave. They both thanked Georgia heartily for her time.

"The lawyers may want to talk to you," Evon said. As had happened before, Georgia's mood shifted sharply in reaction to her.

"The hell they will," she answered. "This isn't going to become my new profession. Tim called. I agreed to speak to him out of respect, and he said you were his boss and had to come, so I said fine to that, too. But I'm not repeating everything forty times to a bunch of lawyers so they can pick it apart. And I'm certainly not talking to any reporters. They just write what they want you to have said. This here, today, that's the end of this for me."

Tim took over again, smoothing her feathers.

"Well, no one knows anything for sure right now," Tim said. "This could all blow over in a couple of weeks. But if they go to court, it's hard to imagine you're not gonna get dragged in a little. You were Paul's girlfriend. There wasn't anybody else who'd know more about him then. You have to realize you're important."

Tim was good, Evon thought. She had never really laid aside her native awkwardness with strangers. But Tim knew intuitively what would soothe Georgia. 'You're important.'

She was not fully convinced. "Still," she said.

They were all silent a second.

"Can I suggest something?" Tim said. "Why don't I just get out my camera? It's in my overcoat and it takes video, too. And I'll record you responding to a few questions. And that will be that. At least on our side. If somebody else sends you a subpoena, then you can deal with that, but you won't have to answer about the same things for now. Just tell the lawyers or reporters, whoever it is, you aren't saying anything else."

Georgia considered this. "Can I say this how I want?"

"Course," Tim answered.

"And am I going to end up in another one of Hal's commercials, all over the TV?"

Evon had no idea how Tim could soften that. When she'd told Hal Tim might have dug up a witness against Paul, he'd danced around his office and immediately called the ad agency. But Tim didn't try.

"Probably," he said. "That's what I'd guess."

Georgia looked around the dim living room for a second, as if she were taking account of her life. Then she nodded. Tim had Georgia figured. Paul had left her behind and blasted into the firmament. But she'd been the woman with him then. It wasn't wrong if the spotlight fell on her for a second.

Georgia did two takes, the second less halting.

My name is Yiorgia Lazopoulos Cleon. I'm making this state-ment voluntarily, and I understand it might be on TV. I was Paul Gianis's girlfriend in September 1982 and had been for a long time. I was with him at our church's annual picnic the day Dita Kronon was murdered, and I do remember that Paul had words with Dita that afternoon. Paul hated Dita because he felt like she was trying to tear his family apart. I also recall that even after Cass pled guilty, Paul told me Cass was innocent. I still talk to Paul every once in a while and I've voted for him. I'd have a hard time believing Paul did something this awful, but I guess you never know for sure with people.

Georgia had added the last line on the second go-through. Evon, who was far from artsy, had learned enough from Heather that she could envision the way the director would present this, a tight shot, grainy, as Georgia spoke, all the worry and reluctance swimming through her face, even as the truth struggled to the surface. It was going to be strong.

Tim and she had just started moving toward the door when Georgia's father came thumping into the room. He appeared intent on the TV, to which he pointed with his cane in clear instruction. Georgia told him it would be a minute. The old priest looked a wreck. He wore sweatpants and a Chicago Bears T-shirt on which a long soup stain was visible. His hair was wild, and his full gray beard looked equally untamed. The frames on his heavy Harry Caray glasses might have been thirty years old. Behind them, his black eyes seemed quick and uncomprehending. Nonetheless, Tim greeted Father Nik with just the barest bow.

"Father, bless," he said, and the old man instinctively responded by raising his right hand with his thumb and first two fingers upward and making the sign of the cross, forehead to navel and then right shoulder to left. Tim reintroduced himself.

"You might recall, Father, you buried our little Kate." Standing behind her dad, Georgia tensed and shook her head sharply, indicating that those kinds of inquiries were unwise. But the old man had enough sense left to say something appropriate.

"Oh yes," he said, in his heavy accent. "Trejedy. Terr'ble trejedy."

"It was," said Tim. "Maria was never the same. None of us were."

The old man turned back to his daughter, asking a question in Greek.

"No, Dad, they know you're retired."

Georgia looked at Evon and Tim with an impish smile. "He thinks you want him to perform your wedding. Dad, they just had some questions about Paul Gianis and Cass."

The old man responded once more in Greek.

"No, Dad. It was Paul you saw on the TV. Cass is still in prison." Her tone was patient but also exhausted. She recognized the pointlessness of explaining. She added another word or two in Greek, perhaps just repeating herself, but something about her answer inflamed him. The old man was instantly furious. He turned pink as a geranium, spit flying as he began to scream. His rage filled the house. He somehow was steadier on his feet in this state, and gestured widely with one hand. Every now and then Evon heard the word "Paulos" as Georgia tried to calm him.

Tim and she had their coats on and were out the door quickly.

7.

Holes—January 17, 2008

It was a gray day, with a low, woolly sky and little light. Evon and Tim stood out on the walk for a second, trying to regather themselves after Father Nik's sudden fury.

"That wasn't pretty," Evon said.

"No. He's got something missing, you can see that."

They reached the car. Tim got the door open and turned to put his backside down first. Until Evon saw him move so stiffly, she hadn't really remembered Tim was as old as he was.

"Did you understand anything her father was yelling?" she asked once she'd closed her door.

"He didn't care for getting corrected," Tim said. "She told him he didn't see Cass on television, it was Paul, and that got under his skin. I didn't understand every word, but he was pretty much yelling that he baptized those boys and they served on his altar. There might not have been ten people in the parish could tell them apart on sight, not even their aunts and uncles, but he could, and why was she always telling him he was wrong about stuff. She was trying to convince him he was crazy so she could get all his money."

Evon groaned. "Poor Georgia." She bounced her Beemer over

the snow ruts and proceeded slowly in the clear channels carved in the street.

"Tough hand she got dealt. That husband of hers, she had to divorce him while he was in prison. Then he got out and begged her to take him back, and not two months later, Jimmy sold two hundred bottles of crack to an undercover cop. He's still inside, too, if I recollect right. But you could see how she makes her own trouble, too."

"How's that?"

"I bet if you go look, Cass *was* on TV. Don't you think with all of this fur flying, that one of the channels put on some of their old file footage of Cass being hauled off to prison?"

"Probably so," Evon allowed. "She sure didn't like me."

"Outsider. Old-timers around here are just like that. You're nobody until they say you are. Sorry to take over like that with her."

"You were great, Tim." She meant it. "What did you make of that stuff about Cass being left-handed?"

"Set me back. Sure you could see. I just went through that whole damn file cabinet and no one said a word about that. He wore that ring, though, the class ring."

"So did Paul, apparently."

"I heard that," he said. "You'd have thought Sandy Stern would have mentioned which hand Cass used, wouldn't you? Wasn't any secret we were looking for a right-handed assailant."

"Maybe his client didn't want him to say anything that might point toward his brother. Paul has to have the same blood type, right?"

Tim made a sound as he nodded.

"And why is Paul saying Cass is innocent?" Evon asked. "After he pled? What does Paul know that makes him so certain?"

A guy across the street was returning from work with an old-fashioned lunch pail, but it was Tim who had her attention, gazing

down the avenue and plainly unsettled. The shoes, the ring, the
blood, fighting with Dita, being right-handed and declaring his
brother innocent—there was starting to be a lot pointing at Paul.

"She didn't see any cuts on him, right?" said Tim.

"So she says now. But no one saw Cass's cut either. The only
thing that threw me was her remembering that Paul was going to
meet Cass at Overlook. You think that's legit or just Georgia being
contrary?"

"She sounded pretty sure."

"You know, they both could have gone from there to see Dita."

"It's only Cass's fingerprints in that room."

"But you had to have plenty of unidentified lifts, right?"

"Of course."

"And you never did a comparison for Paul, did you?"

"Hmm," said Tim, by way of an answer. His mouth squirmed
around while he pondered. She pulled up in front of his house.
"Course, he could give some excuse about being there to visit.
What would clinch it these days would be to do DNA on the
blood in Dita's room. But that wouldn't help, since they're identical
twins."

"Well, you said their fingerprints aren't the same. Maybe the
DNA isn't either."

Tim doubted that. There had been a rape case in Indiana no
more than five years ago, where the state hadn't been able to con-
vict the defendant because he had an identical twin brother. There
was DNA collected from the victim, but no way to tell which man
it belonged to. Evon remembered the case when he mentioned it.

"That science is moving like lightning," Evon said. "I dealt a little with DNA in the Bureau, and now when I read about a case in
the papers, I can't even understand what they're talking about. So
maybe there's a way to tell twins apart these days."

They talked for a second about what would happen next. She'd find a DNA expert and then would have to consult with Hal's lawyers. Tooley had brought in a big firm after Paul filed suit, although Mel was still pretty much in charge. All of the lawyers would raise hell that they couldn't talk to Georgia, but Hal would take Evon's side when he saw today's recording.

"I'll call you," she said. Tim nodded, but he was looking a little beaten up. He clearly didn't like thinking he'd missed the boat, as he'd said at his house. And that stuff about his daughter probably hadn't helped either. Evon had never thought about children until a couple of years ago, when she realized how quickly the world was changing. Now that she was fifty the moment had likely passed her by. But given how badly she occasionally missed the baby she'd never had, she couldn't imagine the pain of losing a child you'd held in your arms.

"I know it was a long time ago," she said, "but I'm sorry about Kate, Tim. I'm sure it's still hard for you."

He nodded again in the same labored way.

"Something like that," said Tim. "It just doesn't go way. It's more than thirty-five years. Katy could be dead of God knows what else by now, or had to bury children of her own. You accept that it happened. But you know that life burned this hole in your heart and it's not going to heal." She could feel his composure starting to wither as he struggled out of the car, casting his bad leg around his body as he walked off.

By the time he got into the house, the full weight of his life was on Tim. He sat down in the living room, still in his overcoat, slumped forward with his big hands between his knees, lacking the will to move any further. He didn't succumb to this very often. Everybody had things to be sad about, especially when you got to this age and carried with you the thought, only barely submerged, that the end wasn't far off. But there had been times throughout his life when a sadness thick as glue had immobilized him. As a younger man, he would drink at these moments. Older, he'd just learned to talk himself through it.

When he was born, Tim's family, the five of them, had lived in a one-bedroom third-story walk-up, about a mile from here. He was the baby, the unexpected child who came eight years after his brother, ten years after his sister. His mother was a frail woman whose nose was always running and who seemed beleaguered by her life. It was his father who held it all together. He was a big man, bigger even than Tim grew to become, who roared rather than spoke, and generally extolled life, and certainly his children and his wife. Whenever he arrived home, Tim was overjoyed.

When Tim was six, his father, a yardman on the Chicago and North Western, fell between two cars and was killed, sliced in half, according to accounts Tim heard years later. His mother was simply beyond herself, shattered by her husband's death. Tim's sister, sixteen then, left home, and his brother was parceled out to his mother's sister. But at the age of six, a bit rambunctious, and morose with the loss of his father, Tim was too much for any relative to take on and his mother deposited him with a brown lacquered valise at St. Mary's Home, telling him she would be back for him soon. She never came. He cried himself to sleep for over a year.

Most of his buddies on the Force who had Catholic educations tended to down-talk the nuns, telling stories about how the sisters rapped their knuckles with rulers, making out most of them as these dried-up, sexually deprived bitches who'd found their marriage to God as unhappy as everybody else's. But the sisters and brothers who cared for Tim at St. Mary's—and him not even born Catholic—they had saved his life. They were kind, and full of faith in the goodness and potential of every child. Even as a kid, missing his mother and his father every day, there was a piece of him that knew he was better off there. He started playing the trombone. Sister Aloysius gave it to him and he got good. "That horn, son, will get you out of here." It got him a place in the Marine Corps Band, and that in turn got him a place at City College.

He was twenty-four, playing nights in jazz clubs, when his mother walked by him on the street, her arms full of brown grocery bags. He said nothing, but trailed her all the way to a tenement. She went through the door before he could get inside, but he stood on the street and watched the lights go on in a fourth-floor window. When another tenant emerged, he went in.

His mother stood there on the threshold staring at him. Then her nose turned red, and she lifted her apron to her eyes as she cried.

'Oh, Tim,' she said. 'Tim, I didn't know what to do.' He heard a child complain inside the apartment, and a girl about ten reached her mother's side and stared at him darkly. His mother invited him in. He declined out of sheer confusion, but turned back to ask about his brother and sister. Alice, his sister, was unheard of—Tim was in his forties before he found her—and his brother, like him, had gone into the service. The next time Eddie came to town, he looked Tim up.

'I tried to tell her we had to go see you,' Eddie said, 'and she wouldn't hear of it.' Ed, a man his father's size, began to blubber. 'I was afraid if I put up a fuss, she wouldn't see me either.' It was a terrible truth, but Tim understood. He embraced his brother then, and the two were never out of touch again. Eddie called at least once a week, no matter where he was in the world, and the two fished in the Boundary Waters every summer, a place they'd first gone with their father. In time, their sons and daughters came, too. Ed had been gone six years now, dead of cancer in Laguna Beach.

Maria had invited Tim's mother and his three step-siblings every year at Christmas and they came, but Tim had no feeling for them. Instead, he regarded himself as blessed to have his wife, his daughters, and Eddie. He had people to love, who, best of all, loved him,

too. He didn't feel it made sense to waste the energy on relationships that would only pull him under some emotional waterfall in
which he'd never catch his breath.

He'd had it good in the end. They lost Katy, but there were two
more girls, good girls, wonderful girls, both now out in Seattle, who
traded off calling him every day. Maria had loved music, too—she
was a fine pianist and gave lessons to half the kids at St. D's. They'd
made a home full of music and laughter, where they all loved each
other just a little bit more because Katy's death had taught them
how precious their lives were.

When he was young, of course, sleeping in the dorms at St.
Mary's, he would wonder if anyone would ever love him, and if he
would love anybody else. He had wanted to be close to someone
and wondered what it would feel like. Even when he knew he was in
love with Maria, he wasn't certain he'd gotten it completely right.
When she turned sick, three years ago, when he began to realize he
would have to live without her, as he had lived before they met, he
finally knew for sure that he had done what he wanted to as a little
boy at St. Mary's.

Now, alone and missing her terribly, he was left to wonder if
it had been equally good for her. He hadn't been perfect as a
husband, especially at the start when the grief of his childhood
sometimes made him a roistering fool. Maria was never one to complain much, but when she did, she talked about how closemouthed
he was. He never spoke of his childhood, she said, even though she
could feel the mark it had laid on him. Had he given her enough,
shown her attention she deserved and craved, or simply been consumed with healing his own wounds? Crumbled in a defeated heap
in his living room, he was drilled by a fear that had become familiar.
Had she reached the end still longing for more he could have given,
but hadn't?

8.

DNA—January 28, 2008

"The short answer," said Dr. Hassam Yavem in his faint Anglo-Pakistani accent, "to the question you posed on the telephone is yes, in theory, given no boundaries on time and money, it might be possible to distinguish reliably between the DNA of identical twins. But you would basically be trying to thread the eye of a very, very small needle from across a football field."

Evon and Dr. Yavem, in his long white coat, sat in his office adjacent to his DNA lab. A dapper narrow gent, Yavem had a trim black moustache and a bald head that rose to a point, a bit like a hazelnut. His replies to Evon's questions were preceded generally by a brief, kindly laugh, which exposed a gold cap on one of his front teeth.

Across from him at his desk, Evon felt like she'd tightened the screws on her brain, trying to track what Yavem was saying. Hal had been in a heat as soon as Evon raised the notion of doing DNA tests on the blood found in Dita's room. She knew her boss would be frustrated if she couldn't answer all his questions.

"You can stop me when you are hearing too much," Yavem said. "One of my colleagues in Alabama is about to publish research this month showing that many identical twins are not completely identical genetically. The variations between them are very slight, but in the tens of thousands of genes there may be isolated differences."

Yavem was a famous guy, whose work concentrated on comparisons of the genomes of family members, research that had led him to establish the genetic basis of a number of diseases. He was mentioned often as a potential candidate for the Nobel Prize in Medicine. Earlier in his career, he had testified in several celebrated criminal trials. These days he referred most DNA identifications to a commercial concern he'd founded and sold a decade ago, instead applying the bulk of his time to research. The forensic cases he took on personally were few, and it was something of an honor that he had agreed to meet Evon, although Hal's name had undoubtedly carried considerable weight. The Kronons had made two seven-figure gifts to the U, Hal's alma mater, over the years.

"We've known for some time that the environment outside the womb causes some variation in gene expression, called methylation. That is why some identical twins are not completely identical in appearance, as they age. But methylation does not represent any basic genetic difference."

Evon repeated what Yavem was saying to herself, in her own terms. Methylation explained why Cass appeared just a bit taller and thicker than Paul, when they were side-by-side at the pardon and parole hearing. But that was a difference only in the way the same genes had responded to the world.

"But," said Yavem, "there are other minute differences in twins' genomes that are more pertinent to the question you asked. Those are what we call CNVs, for copy-number variations. These appear as segments of DNA that are missing, occur in multiple copies, or have flipped orientation in the genome.

"A human gene consists of hundreds or thousands of combinations of the chemical building blocks, adenine—A for short—cytosine, C, guanine, G, and thymine, T. One segment of the hemoglobin gene, to pick an example in the blood, is CTGAGG. A copy-number variation is like a typo. So CCTGAGG could be switched to CCTGTGG, with thymine substituted for adenine in the genetic sequence. CNVs probably explain why only one twin gets what we think of as a genetically influenced illness. The example I just gave you, with the A switched to a T in the hemoglobin gene, leads to sickle-cell disease.

"Most CNVs are probably benign, and some may prove positively beneficial. They occur in all individuals, not just in identical twins, probably as part of nature's great ongoing experiment. My own research suggests that about two-thirds of CNVs occur after conception, as part of fetal cell division."

"So that's what might be different between Cass and Paul?" she asked. "These CVNs?"

"CNVs," said Yavem, smiling patiently. The DNA lab visible beside Yavem's desk through a wide window was far less dramatic-looking than Evon might have expected, not all that different in appearance from where she'd taken high school chemistry, the same collection of beakers and bottles, microscopes and computers and black counters. There were rows of test tubes in blue plastic racks, capped with white stoppers. It was a small space, undoubtedly so the risks of contamination could be controlled, and the three gowned workers within were pretty much elbow to elbow. One man in a surgical mask kept removing his gloves so he could type on his laptop, before turning back to his microscope. A woman was looking at a slide with a piece of red equipment that looked for all the world like a fire alarm.

"Now the theory meets practice. My colleagues in Alabama were able to isolate identifiable CNVs only in roughly 10 percent of twins. So given where we are today, nine times out of ten, you are not going to be able to differentiate identical twins genetically. And even if you found a CNV, it does not occur in all cells of that type.

With blood cells, only 70 to 80 percent would contain that CNV, so you would need to confirm your results with a number of specimens."

"I got it," she said. There was only a 10 percent chance of success, without considering other problems. "But it is possible? You might get valid results?"

"In theory, of course. But you must understand, even if we found one or more CNVs between your twins, and even if that same CNV occurred in blood at the crime scene, that would not necessarily mean that twin was the perpetrator."

"What?"

Yavem maintained his mirthful air and smiled again.

"Imagine the CNV we detected was the one I mentioned in the hemoglobin gene. Unfortunately, *many* people have sickle-cell disease. We would know that only one twin could have contributed the blood at the scene, but *not* that the blood came from that twin. To make that conclusion, you will still need to do more standard DNA testing, which invites a host of new problems. How much, Ms. Miller, do you understand about DNA comparisons?"

"I started out in the FBI and used to know some," Evon said. "But it's a little like high school math. Every time my nieces or nephews show me their homework, it seems to have nothing to do with what I saw from the older ones a couple of years before."

Yavem loved the analogy. He laughed for some time. It was easy for Evon to see why he was in such high demand as a witness. He was charming, with no trace of arrogance. And no matter who hired him, he would get on the stand without an agenda. Everything about the man said he was above pandering.

"All right," he said. "I'll go back to the beginning. Roughly 99 percent of the genome is the same in each human. But the genes of every person contain certain regions of DNA sequences that differ from individual to individual, basically in terms of how often

they repeat. By developing a technique to examine these DNA repeat sequences—by finding an enzyme that could break them apart,
actually—Sir Alec Jeffreys in England created human identity tests
in 1984. Those tests look to a small number of loci in the genome
where repeat differences have been studied and cataloged so we
know how often they occur. With matches at some or all of those
loci, we can then say statistically that only one person in a million,
or even a billion, has the same DNA repetitions."

Trying to take this in, Evon looked up to the acoustical tiles on
the ceiling. This was basically what she'd first learned at an in-service
at Quantico, when she went back for further training in the early
nineties.

"But that's not hard these days, is it?"

Yavem smiled. "That depends. Do you know how these specimens you want to test have been stored?"

"Not yet." The truth, which she wasn't ready to confess, was she
didn't even know if the evidence still existed. Tim had dug up the
inventories recorded by the state and local evidence techs, so she
knew what had been collected originally. As far as Evon could tell,
after making a few phone calls, the state crime lab tended to preserve evidence in murder cases as a matter of protocol. But that
was a rule with many exceptions. Exhibits frequently were never
retrieved from the court file, or after a case ended. Rather than
retransmitting the evidence to the records section, troopers and
deputy PAs frequently dumped it in a drawer, where the specimens
moldered until they were thrown out. But the prominence of the
Kronon case, with a gubernatorial candidate's daughter as the murder victim, made it more likely things had been done by the book.
If so, the blood by the window, which had to be from the murderer,
would be of special interest.

"You can be all but certain," Yavem said, "that evidence gathered
in 1982 was not stored in a way designed to preserve DNA. No

fault of the techs for not being mindful of a technology that didn't exist. But DNA breaks down over time, just like any other cellular material. Blood specimens might have been refrigerated. But we can also extract DNA from fingerprints—since they're really sweat residue—but no one really practices precise temperature control in storing prints. Then there's the issue of contamination. No one knew that they should be careful about shedding their own DNA—skin cells, for example—into the specimens they were collecting.

"Given the risks of degradation and contamination, your best option is the most widespread form of testing today, STR testing—short tandem repeat testing—and in particular Y-STR testing, which focuses on the Y chromosome. Y-STR is discriminating with very small specimens and the Y chromosome, due to its structure, does not degrade as quickly. And, of course, you don't have to worry about contaminating cells contributed by females, because only males have a Y chromosome."

"And what's the chance that Y-STR works?"

"Fairly high," Yavem said. "But the problem of degradation and contamination would exist not only in doing the Y-STR examination. It would also be a significant factor in applying the two tests used to prospect for CNVs, processes using technologies called 32K BAC and Illumina BeadChip."

Yavem then outlined a full testing protocol for Evon, mostly so she understood everything Hal would have to pay for. First, they would examine the DNA to determine that Paul and Cass really were identical twins, hatched, as it were, from the same egg. There were thousands of pairs of twins around the world who had learned in recent years, after the discovery of DNA, that they were fraternal, not identical. Second, Yavem would do Y-STR testing to establish that the blood at the scene had come, to an overwhelming degree of probability, from Cass or Paul. Third, they would do these two other tests hoping to find a copy-number variation between the twins. And then, fourth and last, they'd try to find the CNV in the same genetic location in a number of blood specimens collected at the scene.

"That's why I would say," said Yavem, "at the end of the day, the chances of getting a scientifically reliable result are no better than one in one hundred. A long shot in anyone's book. Yet we would be most happy to try. It would be a very interesting project, and one with some obvious research implications."

She reviewed the last details with Yavem about cost and timing— the CNV tests were proprietary and would have to be performed at the facilities that owned that software, meaning the process all told would take at least three weeks. She thanked him lavishly and asked him to invoice her for his time, then headed back to the office to try to explain all this to Hal.

9.

Knowing—January 28, 2008

Hal was pretty much as Evon had left him that morning, canted back in his desk chair in his huge office, amused by what he was seeing on a large plasma screen on his wall. He might as well have had a bowl of popcorn beside him.

When she'd gone in to tell Hal she was on her way to see Yavem, Kronon had been reading his employees' e-mail. Every company these days informed workers that they could not expect e-mails on the company account to remain free from internal inspection. But Hal took that as license for occasional surveillance. Originally, the feed had been set up so Evon's staff could catch a little jerk in the leasing department who was peddling the names of potential tenants to a competitor. But Hal never turned off the stream. He liked to see who was passing links to porn sites or saying critical things about him, or to pick up office gossip. As far as Evon knew, he did nothing with the information, which he digested like a disinterested god entertained by the foibles of the mortals below.

Now, Hal was turned toward the screen and chewing on his

thumbnail as he viewed the finished version of the commercial featuring Georgia. Evon hadn't seen the completed ad and watched it straight through with him. It was very strong.

"It goes on the air tonight. Let's see his poll numbers after this," Hal said.

Hal's vast office was paneled in a richly grained pale wood, sycamore, Evon believed, with built-in cabinetry to match. On the far bookshelf, he maintained his little shrine to his sister—replete with her college yearbook photo, a piece of childhood pottery, and pictures of Dita beside his parents or his favorite aunt, Teri. A nearer shelf was set aside for photos of his mother and father. In fact, an oil portrait of Zeus, one of several in the ZP offices, hung outside the door. The credenza under the TV, by contrast, was dedicated to a three-deep forest of pictures of Hal's own family. Say whatever you might about Hal, but he was a dedicated father and husband. He boasted too much about his kids, but that was due to a radiant love. Mina and he had four children, the eldest two boys done with college. Hal hoped they might be lured into the business, but they were both committed to humanitarian projects. His older son, Dean, was doing AIDS work in Africa. All of Hal's kids, even the two girls, who were still in high school, regarded their father's political views as antediluvian, and Hal tolerated their opinions as an amusing failing of youth, even though he would have chewed through the throat of anyone else who said such things. As for Mina, he doted on her. He called his wife three or four times a day, and was invariably gentle with her, and happy to follow her directions, which he accepted as a sign of love. She laid out his clothes every morning. He was, truly, one of the most happily married people Evon knew.

"One in a hundred, huh?" he asked, following Evon's summary.

"And at least a quarter of a million dollars."

Hal pondered. "But he said he'd do it, right?"

"We can make the motion to Judge Lands. Yavem will give us an affidavit saying that he believes it's possible to get valid results. But it's new science, Hal. The *Frye* hearing to establish the reliability of the test could go on for a month, just by itself."

Hal was thinking, but his heavy face was bobbing agreeably as he considered the prospects. Evon wanted him to sort through the potential results before he made up his mind, which would then be permanently set like concrete.

"Look, Hal, I've been thinking about this, and we need to consider what happens if it goes the other way. We may thread the needle, as Yavem puts it, and find that the blood is Cass's. In fact, if we get a positive result, that's still the most likely one, when you remember the guy pled guilty. That's a big risk. Your reputation will never be the same. And Paul would become a giant martyr who could just start moving his furniture into city hall."

Hal listened to her attentively, as he generally did, his goggle eyes clearly focused behind his dense lenses.

"Do it," he said then. "I realize this could boomerang. But they killed my sister, and as sure as I'm sitting here, I know Cass and Paul have been hiding stuff all these years. I *know* it. And I want the truth. I owe it to Dita."

Back at her desk, Evon called Yavem's lab, then settled in with everything that had piled up, most of it concerning the YourHouse deal. ZP's investigators had discovered that decades ago there had been a small paint factory on part of the site in Indianapolis, which explained what Tim had overheard when he was tailing Dykstra. But the soil borings so far had turned up none of the expected contamination. Dykstra had feigned outrage and was demanding that Hal sign the letter of intent this week or call off the deal. Hal could not demand a price concession yet—ZP was supposed to pay 550 million dollars, four hundred of it in cash to be raised by cross-collateralizing the equity in the shopping centers—and as a result,

Hal was whistling Evon down to his office five times a day, demanding a report on literally every new hole that was dug.

She did not get out of the office until well past 8. As her BMW 5 Series ascended from the garage under the ZP Building, Evon called Heather and received a text in reply. "Workg late. Crap More." 'Crap More' was Heather's code for Craigmore, the demanding client.

The condo they shared was in a new building, thirty stories of glass. They had chosen the apartment together, although Evon had paid for everything—Heather basically wore every dollar she made. Heather had furnished, twice now, with the same spare elegance with which she dressed. There was a full wall of windows over the river, and a lot of tidy minimalist furniture that required the place to be neat as a pin to achieve the desired effect. It was beautiful in the perfect way Heather was beautiful, but Evon never felt fully at home. Left to herself, she'd prefer overstuffed chairs and a couple of dirty socks on the floor amid a scatter of magazines. Her discomfort was greater when she was here by herself.

She went downstairs and worked out for an hour, then, still in her sweats, turned on SportsCenter and ate a Lean Cuisine. As usual, work was on her mind. She remained impressed by the commercial featuring Georgia and continued to suspect that Hal, in that goofy intuitive way of his that often served him well in business, might be onto the truth.

But eventually, something bigger began to force its way on her. You couldn't be a trained investigator and play dumb forever. And a fatal recognition had begun to form a few weeks ago, when they returned from Francine and Nella's wedding. Heather had departed with Tom Craigmore too often on last-minute trips, had been gone on too many late nights with Tom, after which she seemed to return trailing the fresh scents of a shower. Evon knew she should have suspected long ago that Heather was sleeping with him.

When they had met, Heather had confessed that every once in a while, when she wasn't in a relationship with a woman, she'd have sex with a man. Heather was insecure enough to think she had to do this to cement her place with the client. But Evon couldn't pretend any longer that it wasn't happening.

Love was the biggest thing on earth. But it seemed almost inevitably to end up twisted and bleak. Was that the truth? That this feeling everybody longed for and believed in and wrote songs about led nowhere good, down this sinkhole into the blackest part of yourself, into screaming battles and hearts that would have hurt less if they'd been split with an ax? Was that the truth of love? That it was the surest way to end up hating someone else?

By ten o'clock, Evon was in bed, and fell asleep with a book about Sandy Koufax on her chest. She woke again near midnight and snapped off the light, and roused once more two hours later when Heather arrived. Evon's girlfriend was clearly drunk and blundered around in the bathroom, knocking things over, the steel cup by the sink and, from the sounds of it, some cosmetics. In the dark, Evon said, "Hi," and reached for the light.

Heather stood still with a hand drawn over her chest, her eyes startled and large. She was otherwise naked, lovely with her long slender shape.

"You scared the shit out of me," Heather said. "I thought you were asleep."

"Not really. Sort of restless. How was tonight?"

"I can't make up my mind about whether Tom is a total hoot or a complete asshole."

And what kind of fuck is he? Evon nearly asked. There was a time, years ago, when she would have done that. But anger no longer accumulated in her until it became potent as a bomb. Instead, she was willing to experience the welling force of her own hurt.

"I can't do this any more." Evon thought she had said that to herself, until she observed the way Heather again stopped mid-motion, standing over an open drawer in the Eames wardrobe, a nightshirt in her hand.

"And what is it that you can't do?"

"Watch you stumble in here after you let some guy paw you or screw you or God knows what else."

"Oh please."

"I think that's my line."

"I mean," said Heather, who was crying instantly, "you don't know what you're talking about. I mean, accusing me."

She didn't bother to answer for a second.

"You've basically admitted it to me half a dozen times when you were blitzed. You've laid in that bed when I've asked where you were and said, 'It doesn't matter.' How many times is that? I was just willing to pretend I didn't know what you meant."

"It *doesn't* matter," Heather cried. Evon knew how Heather would explain herself, because Evon remembered what Heather said she got out of her occasional dallying with guys in the past. She liked to laugh at them, Heather claimed, and she probably meant it. She wanted them to see that they couldn't have her, didn't reach her. But that didn't mean it didn't matter to her. It just mattered in a different way from when she lay in Evon's arms. That was screwed-up stuff, but it was how Heather was. With sex, everyone was screwed up, or at least a little different in their secret treasure chest of wishes. But whatever her behavior meant to Heather, it mattered to Evon. That was the only issue. She told Heather that again.

"You want me to stop seeing the men I work with?" Heather asked. She was being dramatic now, crossing the room while she spoke and sweeping her arms about. "Is that what you want? I will. I mean, this is just batshit-crazy lesbian bullshit, but I won't hang out with the people I'm not attracted to."

"I don't think you'll stop. I think it's important to you. I think you don't know why, but you won't stop. And you're tearing my heart out, and so *we* have to stop."

"I love you," Heather said. "And you love me."

Now that Evon was fully awake, she realized how close to the surface this had been, how thoroughly she'd considered the alternatives and made her plans.

"I'm going to sleep at Janet's tonight. And tomorrow. A few nights. You'll have to be out of here by the end of the weekend."

Heather dissolved. She cried with total despair. Her nose ran. She left her beautiful self behind. She'd been too drunk to remember to take off her makeup and the muddy streaks ran from her eyes to her chin.

"I can't leave here. This is where I live. This is my house. I love you. Please. I'll change. Rebecca has a shrink. I'll see a shrink. I will, I'll change. I swear, I'll change. Please." She began shuffling toward Evon on her knees, with her arms outstretched. It was wrenching to see, in part because of the little secret piece in Evon that gloried in Heather's debasement. Heather had been hurt back, she'd been destroyed almost. She reached the bed and clutched Evon by one calf. I love you, she said. Please, she said. Evon now was crying, too.

They had done this before, three or four times, albeit with different provocations. Each of them had played her part now, Evon angry, Heather abject. Evon had scared her, Heather had promised to repent. They could resume, with the hope that it would be better.

There was a richness to that, to hoping. Evon had always been desperate with hope when it came to the people she loved. But by now, she realized her optimism would shatter. The drama that engaged both of them—I love you, I hate you, I want you, I don't—would start again, only to lead back here. Evon knew enough about herself by now, had been taught enough by good therapists, that she realized this was a piece of her, too, wanting someone, like her mother, who would never fully accept her, for whom she would never be good enough. That was the mythology the old Evon believed in, the resident programming. And to step away from it, she had to wrestle herself. It was like she had to hold the old Evon—the DeDe piece—right down on the bed and rise up out of her body like the filmy spirits that levitated from corpses in old-timey movies. It took a strength that seemed almost physical. But she knew what was right. She knew what was needed. She wanted to be happy and the first responsibility for that fell to her.

She was packed and dressed and out of the apartment, and away from Heather's high-pitched clamor, in another ten minutes. She sat in her car in the garage under the building, waiting until she felt ready to drive. It had been such a long road for her, just to face what she wanted, which had seemed so frightening and shaming and, worst of all, alien. She had hated being different, feeling different, and having to take that on for life. But she had. And now, at the age of fifty, there was something else to face, something worse: that she might never be loved at all, never, not in the unburdened, lasting way she still hoped for. She sat in her car in the dark garage at 3 a.m., with her arms wrapped around herself.

10.

On the Trail—January 30, 2008

It was 7:30 a.m. and he stood in the light-rail station in Center City, one glove on, his right hand bare as he extended it to commuters. He was positioned in the lower level, near the bank of doors, so he could catch both the inbound and outbound rush, but there was no heat here and the temperature could not have been more than ten degrees. The young interns who had accompanied him were stomping their feet and walking in circles, but the rush of engaging with so many people distracted him from the throbbing in his ears. Since John F. Kennedy abandoned the formal top hat for his inauguration, it had been the preferred political style in the US to greet voters bareheaded.

"Paul Gianis, hoping for your vote for mayor on April third." He must have said that five times a minute, never varying more than a word or two.

He loved the meet-and-greets, but not for the reason most might suspect. They taught him humility, for one thing, a trait their mother always commended, even if she practiced it rarely. In today's world only athletes and entertainers were real stars. Paul had been majority leader of the state senate for four years, but people still registered his as no more than a familiar face, figuring they'd met him someplace unrecalled, like their cousin's wedding. When they heard his name, the commuters' reactions varied. Most smiled tepidly and shook as they passed by. Some stopped to tell him they'd shopped in his father's grocery, or that they'd voted for him in the past. There were always a few who wanted a picture, particularly if they were with their kids. Plenty of folks breezed by coldly, R's or, more often, people who regarded politicians as a plague, especially ones making it harder to get to work. Of course, people he'd known for years—lawyers on the way to the office, most of them—would stop to say hi. And there was also one great Latino guy who, by sheer coincidence, he'd run into at four or five of these stops around the Tri-Cities, who opened his arms and hugged him this morning, shouting, "Pablo, *amigo*!"

Occasionally, commuters wanted longer conversations. Moms tended to ask pointed questions about schools and the Rec Department, both perilously underfunded, and younger people who were engaged in what used to be regarded as a reverse commute, going from their Center City apartments to jobs near the airport, would sometimes tarry to find out his plans to make the county more energy-efficient or to feed start-ups in the tech sector. Doing this day in and day out—and he was at a different bus stop or here every workday, and in grocery stores all over the county on the weekend—you could get a feel for the issues. There were still too many black folks moved to complain about the police force's excesses, particularly in the North End. And inevitably he heard stories that broke his heart—today it was the dad of a gravely disabled son who couldn't get adequate help from the schools or county agencies, but who refused to institutionalize a boy whose mother had abandoned him long ago. There was also comic relief—morning travelers who expected him to do something on the spot about their neighbor's barking dog, or the zeta beams from Mars, or, very often, the judge hearing their divorce case, whose rulings against them were a sure sign of ingrained corruption. But he loved it all, the meeting, the wooing, the listening, telling his staffers to write down ideas and plans and names. This was the open heart of the city, full of need.

"So like what's with this murder thing?" a young man in a stocking cap and overcoat asked now. It was the third time this morning someone had referred to Hal's ads. He had practiced an agonized look and a toss of his head, as if it were beyond comprehension.

"This dude's an asshole, right?" said the guy. His skin was spotty and he had probably experienced a miserable adolescence, but now he was clearly not lacking in confidence.

"Your words," he answered.

"Yeah, but it sounds bad, man." With that the fellow was gone.

At 8:45, he and the two aides left the station. He had a breakfast at the Metro Club, a fund-raiser with trial lawyers. He'd lost some support there because he'd been willing to discuss damage caps as part of a failed effort at health care reform last year, but most of the attorneys attending had been colleagues forever, and he was still their guy, especially since he'd be controlling the County Law Department from the mayor's office.

When he opened the back door of the campaign car, a red Taurus a couple of years old, Crully was in the back seat. Mark leaned out and asked Kim and Marty, the interns, if they'd mind grabbing a cab. That could not mean anything good. Mark would only have come out in the cold because he had to brief the candidate in private on something he needed to know about before he ran into any reporters. Sure enough, Crully handed over a fistful of papers. Discovery motions from Hal's lawyers.

"No motion to dismiss?"

"Huh?" Crully answered.

"You said they'd file a motion to dismiss our complaint on First

Amendment grounds and we'd be briefing it until the election. But they've skipped that stage and gone straight to discovery. Right?"

Mark shrugged, indifferent to the fact that he'd been flat wrong. Hal and his lawyers had outflanked Paul and wanted Judge Lands to order production of all the evidence that the state and local police still had on hand, and to direct Paul to give saliva and fingerprints. They were going to try to do DNA tests. He read over the attached affidavit from Hassam Yavem, a couple of times. It was shocking, actually. He'd had an idle worry about DNA testing once or twice over the years, but one thing he'd been told repeatedly was that there was no way to tell his DNA from his twin brother's. Yavem was a real scientist, though.

Crully could tell what was on his mind.

"Ray already talked to Yavem. It's like one in two hundred the test will actually work."

"And is all that stuff even around?" he asked.

"Apparently the blood is. They found it in the state police fridge. They actually have a ten-year retention policy and then they *adios* it, but not this."

"And why was I so lucky?"

"AIDS," Crully said.

"AIDS?"

"It's from 1982. They didn't do routine AIDS screening on blood in 1982. So when they got to 1992, nobody wanted to touch it. It sat there."

"Great."

Crully didn't like what he was seeing in Paul, and he was seeing it every time this subject came up. Crully had been running winning campaigns long enough to be able to pick his races. And he chose them on two bases. First, he wanted to win. Occasionally, just for money, he'd work a stone loser in an off-year election for some Democratic gazillionaire who thought she or he was the new face of democracy. But Mark had tasted ashes often enough, and if he needed money, he could move back to D.C. and lobby. So he wanted winners, one. And two, he wanted a hardworking candidate. People would never believe how many of these men and, more rarely, women didn't want to put in the time. They liked getting up in front of cameras or an adoring crowd, even if it was half relatives of the campaign staff. But they didn't care for eighteen-hour days. And they wanted to pretend that the money grew on trees, that George Soros or someone was going to take a liking to them and pour down millions out of a pillowcase. They thought it was degrading or embarrassing to ask people to make their support tangible. Gianis was a pro. And tireless. Two days ago, he'd told Mark that Crully could begin adding campaign appearances in February, three more every day. And Paul still had a law office, not to mention that the state senate would go back in session next week. Gianis wasn't going to get more than four hours' sleep a night until May.

Crully had met Paul three years ago when he was weighing a run for Congress. Crully had made a conditional commitment to a race in California, and ended up having to decline. But he had attended college at Easton, same as Paul, and while still a student, Mark had worked local races here, so he knew the right people to hire now. He welcomed the challenge of a big-city mayor's race. And he liked Gianis. Straight shooter. Progressive. Could take advice. And believed in more than his own election, although they all believed in that first and foremost. Paul understood the metrics—how many volunteers, how many dollars. The guy, Clooney, who was running finance, gave Paul ten names to call before he went to sleep, and he'd have his cell out and the list in his hand as soon as the car door closed when they finished an event. Often, he'd be done by noon and ask for ten more. He didn't whine about needing to see his wife and kids—everybody on the flipping campaign needed time with their children or girlfriends—and he didn't come out of a church whispering about what a narcissistic asshole that preacher was. He knew you didn't find shy types in the pulpit. This thing with Kronon was the first time Gianis seemed to have lost his usual discipline. He was acting scared was what bothered Crully. You could never win scared. Everybody—the press, your opponents, your staff—felt it. A leader always acted like a leader. Paul seemed anguished by this whole deal with his brother.

"This is out of control," Gianis said. Crully watched Paul stare out the window at the big buildings and crowded streets of the city he hoped soon to govern. "And what do you want me to do about this?"

"What do you mean, what do I want? You do the obvious thing. Cooperate. Stick out your chin and say, 'I've got nothing to fear. He can have my prints. He can have my spit.' This isn't about what happens in the courtroom. You're fighting a war of impressions. I've said that before."

"We don't want that test. We're not going to get good results," Gianis said.

Crully thought his heart had stopped.

"What the hell does that mean? Are your fingerprints there? Or your DNA?"

Gianis revolved toward Crully, his mouth crimped sourly.

"What do you think, Mark?"

"So what do you mean 'bad results'? That's a good result, isn't it, if your shit isn't there? I'd roll up my sleeve and ink a fingerprint card in front of two dozen cameras. And I'd do it today."

"I can't do it today."

"Why?"

"I need to talk to my brother. I need to talk to Sofia. This is hard on my kids. I need to prepare them all." Gianis continued to roll his tongue around inside his mouth as he turned back to the window. He removed his glasses, as he did frequently, to rub at the lumpy bridge of his nose. "And the bad result, in case you haven't figured this out, Mark, is that Yavem won't be able to tell whose DNA it is, and Hal and his ad team will twist that as proof I could be the murderer. And the only thing I'll have is what I had to start, namely saying I didn't do it. This thing is a trap."

Crully took some time. Gianis had a point.

"This whole suit is becoming a train wreck," Gianis said. "You told me I had to sue, just to make a statement, and that the lawyers would tie everything up until the election."

"Yeah, and you told *me* there was nothing to worry about. Now Kronon's got you lying to the cops. And your sad-sack ex-girlfriend, who has the fact you ruined her life just about tattooed on her forehead, is saying you told her your brother was innocent. Don't fuckin blame this on me. The ex, hell hath no fury, OK. But the cops?"

"I forgot about it."

"Well, that was unfortunate," Crully said.

"I didn't lie to the cops anyway. Not that it makes any difference."

Crully hadn't talked with Paul about any of this in detail, and he wasn't sure he cared to now. Even when shit came bubbling out of the earth like a clogged septic field, he never went back to the candidate to ask about the hot little thing on the side or the no-bid deal for a big contributor. Because he wanted to be able to tell reporters with a straight face that there was no truth to the charges, so far as he knew.

"You didn't lie to the cops?" asked Crully. "How is that? You told the cops that you and your brother were out drinking beers over the river when it happened. And your brother pled guilty to the murder, so unless Cass had a chat with Einstein and conquered the laws of space and time, he wasn't with you when the woman was killed. Right?"

Gianis assumed that agonized look Crully hated and gazed through the window again, shaking his head unconsciously at the magnitude of the complications.

"I never told the police we were together all night. They must have misunderstood me. I said that after the picnic we went out to the Overlook and had a few beers."

"Do we want to go with that? A misunderstanding? Will Cass back that up?" They had said nothing in response to Kronon's commercials, citing the ongoing litigation. Ray had filed a good motion with Judge Lands, asking him to set ground rules: Could the parties talk or not? It was a complicated issue, apparently, because Paul was a lawyer and legal ethics prohibited attorneys from making statements outside of court about a case while a lawsuit was pending. Judge Lands had scheduled a hearing for next week.

"Of course Cass would back it up."

"And your brother didn't tell you he'd killed the Kronon girl by the time you spoke to the police, right? So you didn't recognize the significance of the timing."

"He's never told me that, frankly."

"He didn't tell you he was going to plead guilty?"

"Of course he did."

Crully felt himself squint. "Are you splitting hairs?"

"You could say that, I suppose."

Gianis was hiding something. That was the real problem. You could bad-mouth the press, and the campaign finance laws, and say politics was all flimflam, and be right 90 percent of the time, but hard truths, big truths about candidates, often emerged in campaigns. It was like performing brain surgery with a jackhammer. But it was getting clearer every day that there was something Gianis wasn't telling.

"Look," said Crully. "Is there anything else?"

"Like what?"

"Come on, Paul. Who the fuck am I, Carnac? I don't want to have to figure out the right question. You know what would sink the ship. Is this ship sinking?"

"No." Gianis slowly turned back to face Mark. Paul had those mystical black Greek eyes, so dark you couldn't really see into them. "You want to hear me say it?"

Crully didn't know for a second. "Yes," he said finally.

"I didn't murder Dita Kronon. I didn't have a goddamned thing to do with it."

A good politician was always a decent actor, so Crully had learned to take everything with a grain of salt. He knew a guy whom Clinton had dragged into a quiet corner in the White House so POTUS could assure him, strictly between them, that he'd never even coveted Monica Lewinsky. But Crully couldn't help himself: He believed Paul and felt relief wash through his entire upper body.

"My brother thinks we should dismiss this lawsuit," Gianis said.

"Fuck," Crully said. "You can't dismiss the lawsuit. It'll be a disaster. It will look like you're guilty."

"I'm not saying I agree with him, Mark. But I take his point. It's just a tar baby, this thing. Unless we agree to that test and hit the bull's-eye. But it's 199 out of two hundred we don't. It'll all get murkier. You'll forgive me, but I should never have listened to you guys."

"OK. Blame me. You want to, go ahead. But you can't dismiss now. You dismiss and I have to quit."

Gianis tilted his chin down so he could give Mark a hard look. "Threat?" he asked.

"Call it what you want. We have to play this out in court and hope for the best. Maybe Lands imposes a gag order and makes Hal take his ads off the air."

"He won't. I wouldn't if I were the judge. You can't let a politician file a lawsuit and silence his critics. And Du Bois Lands is a good lawyer. I used to work with him."

"I didn't know that," said Crully. His heart perked up. "Why didn't somebody tell me that?"

"Because it's a long story," Paul said. They were at the Metro Club and Paul opened the door, but before he slid across the seat, he patted Crully on the shoulder and smiled for the first time on the trip. A real smile. "Buck up, Mark. It's actually a great day."

"It is?"

"My brother gets out of prison." He looked at his watch. "In fact, he's out."

At 8:30, the correctional officers would have fingerprinted him in the administrative center, to be sure they were releasing the right guy, and let him put on the old blue jeans and the sweatshirt in which he'd surrendered. Hillcrest looked like a ranch in a cowboy movie, surrounded by a low white fence. Not even barbed wire. They called it the Honor Camp, meaning there wasn't anyone in there who hadn't figured out he'd do really hard time if he was caught after running off. This morning the guards would have shot the bolts on B gate, which was opened solely to release prisoners and receive deliveries from sixteen-wheelers, and swung the two sides wide. And his brother would have walked out on the frozen dirt road alone. Sofia had left before six to drive him back.

Kim and Marty, the interns, were already under the Metro Club's green awning. The constant pedestrian rush had ground the ice and snow of a few weeks ago into a charcoal mush that had limed over in a few stubborn clumps that still clung to the cement with the tenacity of a living creature. How much salt could the walks stand, he wondered, before they pitted and would need replacement? He'd never wondered about that in his life, but it would be a preoccupation if he became mayor. Every screw and nut in the structure of the Tri-Cities would be his concern.

His cell vibrated just as he reached the two aides. It was his personal handheld, not the mobile from the campaign. He thought it might be Beata, who'd called once already, but he hadn't found the kind of complete privacy even a whispered conversation with Beata required. The number was blocked.

"Paul Gianis," he said.

"Says who?" his brother replied. The two of them both laughed like seventh graders, laid out by some idiotic joke. His brother was on Sofia's cell, on which the number was always withheld so she could talk to patients on her own schedule. The twins hadn't had a phone conversation in God knew how long, probably close to twenty years, when their dad died. The lines inside the facility were all recorded and they therefore preferred to talk face-to-face.

"All OK?"

"A-OK."

"So," he said, "we're free."

"We're free," his brother answered.

"I still wish we'd been together." Cass's release date, an item every prisoner could remember instantly even if it was eighty years off, had always been January 31, 2008. But somehow Corrections had recalculated it as today in the course of the pardon and parole hearing.

"We talked about it. Couldn't blow this breakfast off, not when the group set the date four months ago. But I'll see you for dinner?"

"Still the plan."

They hung up. He was crying, of course, and groped under his topcoat to get his handkerchief out of his back pocket. The thought of sitting down to a meal with his brother, sleeping under the same roof for the first time in twenty-five years, still seemed beyond easy imagining. They had made no extended plans for the future, purely out of superstition. The idea, as it had been for a quarter of a century, was to get through it, all the way to the end, one day at a time.

Twenty-five years. The immensity of the time settled on him. He could remember the guilty plea, and the day a month later, right after Paul's wedding, when Cass's sentence started. Both events retained in his mind the clarity of things that had happened last week, and that of course made the passage of time seem less consequential, especially now that they'd survived it. But twenty-five years was a literal lifetime for each of them when the sentence began. Saying good-bye at that gate, he'd had no idea how he would ever bear it. A year after Cass's time inside started, he was still jarred every day by the reality that he couldn't just call his brother, and his heart sparked when he woke up Sunday mornings, anticipating their visits. You had to be a twin, an identical twin, to understand how cruel their forced separation had seemed to each of them.

And now it was over. He closed his eyes and breathed deeply, still not sure he'd regained his composure. The penetrating cold reached all the way up to his sinuses. Then he set one foot in front of the other and entered the club. His life, he realized, in the elemental way he had known it at its beginning, had started again.

II.

11

Cass—September 5, 1982

Cassian," says Zeus, showing off as usual, by utilizing the name Cass was given at birth. "So pleased you are with us. Did I see your mother? I must say hello."

Zeus delivers a tight handshake, briefly summoning all his power and charm as he levels his black eyes. Behind him, Hermione, Dita's mom, thin and simple like a piece of blank paper, passes by without the pretense of a smile. She has little use for Lidia—and Mickey—and thus for Cass.

Zeus is warmer, although he would never stand to see his treasured daughter with a cop, whatever Zeus might be required to say in public these days. But Zeus is a fake. His genial manner can bloom into bouquets of compliments, but the man Cass occasionally sees with a glass of whiskey in his study is insular, calculating and dark.

Dita is fearlessly outspoken about everyone else in her family. Her mother is "a twit," consumed by appearances, and she calls her bawdy Aunt Teri, who most people think is responsible for Dita's own outrageous manner, "entertaining." As for her older brother, Hal, Dita sees him as basically clueless, but loves him nonetheless.

Yet about Zeus, she says very little. Love and loathing. You can almost hear it like the hum of power lines whenever she is around her dad. Dita says her father has told her one thousand times in private that Hal takes after his mother while she is more like him, an observation Dita clearly relishes. But the looks she aims at her father's back roil with contempt for his unctuousness and grandiosity and limitless ambitions.

In his white suit, Zeus this afternoon more resembles a pit boss in Vegas than a political candidate, leaving aside his stars-and-stripes tie. Pausing to greet other guests, he is nevertheless headed toward Lidia, who is beside Nouna Teri, with her bleached hair, stiff as straw, and her piles of jewelry. Like his brother, Cass is faultlessly attuned to the nuances of his mother's moods, and even at fifty feet he catches the baleful look with which Lidia registers Zeus's approach.

Neither Paul nor he fully understands his parents' grief with the Kronons. Now that Dita's dad is on TV so often, Cass's father, Mickey, won't turn on the set, even to watch the Trappers. It's mystifying because their elder sister, Helen, insists that before they were born, Zeus was regarded as the family's savior. In the mid-1950s, Mickey was so totally disabled by a leaking mitral valve that he could not work, and Teri prevailed on her brother to hire Lidia in his office. She remained there for two or three years until she was pregnant with the boys and the invention of the heart-lung machine allowed Mickey to have valve-replacement surgery. With Mickey good as new, Papou Gianis helped their father open a grocery. Paulie and Cass worked there from the time they were five, when they began stocking shelves, and Cass still recalls the day his father, who always held his temper around customers, threw his white grocer's apron from the cash registers to the dairy case and yelled out that the store would be moving. He was furious about his lease, which was now held by Zeus, who'd bought up most of the commercial property in the old neighborhood.

"OH GOD!"

Across the lawn, despite the music and loud conversations, Cass suddenly makes out a startled yelp that he knows automatically is his brother's, and he dashes toward the sound. Arriving, he sees his twin laid out on the lawn with Sofie Michalis hovering over him, both of them laughing like children. A hunk of barbecued lamb and some macaroni are on the ground beside Paul's ear, along with an oval paper plate. Several dozen people, most old neighbors, have circled around his fallen brother. Once it's clear that Paul is fine, a number turn away and greet Cass, inevitably asking, "Which one are you?" That question always leaves Cass feeling as if a wire has shorted somewhere in his chest.

The deepest secret in Cass Gianis's life is how infuriated he is that he does not really match his brother. While Lidia was pregnant, she took great heed of the story of Esau and Jacob, and as a result, instructed Dr. Worut before she was etherized for the delivery to tell no one, not even her, which baby had been born first. Presented with the boys afterwards, she named them simply from left to right, Cassian and Paul, for her father and Mickey's. No one has ever known who is older.

But Lidia's intent to be rigorously evenhanded was taken by the twins as an instruction to remain the same. They shared a room, friends, books; they could not turn on the TV without deciding beforehand what they would watch. Every year, they fought off the principal's well-intentioned effort to put them in separate classrooms, even while they mocked the teachers who thought they cheated because their papers ended up so similar. Their life was like an apple, cut into precise halves, until Cass, in high school, began to suspect that Paul preferred it this way, because it worked to his advantage. The differences between them, no matter how trivial they seemed to everyone else, subtly marked Paul as better—more appealing, smarter, more adept.

Paul was always the more competitive one. Running laps with the tennis team to build endurance, Paul would continue after the session. Cass can remember his fury. Because he had no choice. Paul knew when he set off that he was essentially dragging Cass behind him. In tournaments, Cass always had the better head-to-head record with shared opponents, but he refused to play Paul, even in practice, knowing he would lose.

By college, he was slightly furious every time his brother came into the room. It was very confused. Because he loved Paul so intensely, and longed for him at times every day, once he had moved in his own direction.

Now Cass has been in an extended conversation about the academy with Dean Demos, a sergeant on the Force in Property Crimes, when he sees Dita steaming in his direction.

"Your brother is really a total jag-off," she says, loud enough for Dean to hear, and adds, as if that weren't enough, "I just can't handle your entire fucking family." She is drunk of course although the real problem, Cass suspects, is that she dropped a 'lude before the picnic so she would be able to get through it.

"Yeah, well," he says, and instead of getting into it, simply slips his arm around her waist and leads her slowly across the lawn, away from the crowd and toward the river. He understands that her anger flags quickly, and after a minute, she sags against him as they walk.

His family thinks he loves Dita because she is the worst woman in the world for him, as if his passion is for sheer contrariness. But Dita is like no other female he has ever known, potty-mouthed, brilliant, fearless, screamingly funny—and, her secret, profoundly kind. Not fifty people at this picnic realize Dita works her butt off every day as a social worker in the Abuse and Neglect Division of the Kindle County Superior Court. Cass has watched her with those kids, to whom she gives her entire heart.

She is, no question, the most complicated person he knows, with vices everybody sees and strengths she keeps hidden. She is certainly the greatest ever in bed. She has sex—'fucks' is the only real word for it—as if she invented the activity. She comes more quickly and more often than any other female he has ever heard of, a quaking, gasping, sweating, moaning heap, who says as soon as she finally has her breath again, "More."

They do it most often right here, in her bed. It's a weird turn-on for her to be down the long hall from her parents, bucking and carrying on at volume, albeit with the door locked. She has sneaked him up the stairs on occasion, but most nights, he just climbs to the tiny second-floor balcony outside her window, ascending on the hooks driven into the brick wall to hold the phone wires.

His mother hates Dita, probably because she is as strong-willed as Lidia. But that makes Dita a perfect ally for Cass. Dita will never succumb to convention. She will never say 'OK, that's what Paul would do.' She will demand that he—and they—be different, and that is an assurance he requires, because the tidal pull his brother exerts will last forever.

He wants to marry Dita. That is another secret, because her response, especially initially, is bound to be harsh. 'Me? Marry a cop?' Or more likely, 'Me, fuck just one guy for the rest of my life?' He cannot imagine how horrible it would be to have her actually laugh in his face. Paulie smolders, but Cass has absorbed all of Lidia's quick temper. That is the one piece of Dita he still does not know how to contend with, the part that dislikes herself and tries to drive everyone away. The risk of loving Dita is that she will hate him for doing it.

Around six, when it is just about time for the picnic to end, the sky darkens and opens, drowning them all in rain. Dita, predictably, stands out in the downpour until her blouse is soaked through. He finally takes a tablecloth and throws it around her and shepherds her inside. She tries to drag him upstairs, but there are too many people in the house, and he whispers that he will be back later.

Near seven, Paulie, who has hung on with Cass and the members of the picnic committee to clean up, has had enough.

"Let's get a couple cold ones and sit out by the river."

"No hokey-pokey while Father Nik is playing pinochle with the men's club?" Nik would lose his entire salary if the men didn't take turns throwing hands to him. His parishioners feel obliged to take care of Nik now that Georgia's mom is gone and the father's priestly vows require him to remain alone.

"Not tonight, Josephine," Paulie answers. He actually looks troubled.

"Where's Lidia?" Behind her back, they have called their mother by her first name since they were in grade school.

"She's gone. She said Teri was going to drive her home so they could visit." The boys meander across the lawn.

"What was up with Sofie Michalis?" Cass asks. "Were you guys going two falls out of three?"

Paul explains a bit, but concludes, "Can you believe how good she looks?"

"Uh-oh. Paulie has a crush." It's been years in fact since his brother indicated interest in any woman besides Georgia. In college, Paul and she agreed to date other people, but it was halfhearted. He was still on the pay phone in the dorm lobby, pouring in quarters and talking to Georgia at least three times a week. They clung to each other, as to life rafts in the tide of growing up. But that time has been over for a while now. Georgia isn't dumb. She'll be good at all the stuff women once were supposed to do, having babies and keeping house, but Jesus, it is 1982, and being with her would be like an endless loop of Father Knows Best. *The slim chance that Paul might actually escape her lifts Cass's heart. In the meantime, his brother crumples up his chin and wheels to look around.*

"Jesus, Cass. Cut the crap. Georgia'd be crying for a month."

Instead Cass whispers the same thing in a singsong several times until his brother slugs him in the shoulder. In reprisal, Paul asks, "Brewski or not? Or are you just going to hide in the bushes until you can climb up the drainpipe?"

This effort to get even is so simpleminded but inevitable that Cass breaks into loud laughter. The night is ripe. After the rain, the air has become cool and clear. There is a slice of moon over the river, and the water rushes below. Cass has a full sense of life's possibilities and the joy of loving certain people. Paul. And Dita. He loves Dita. He realizes he has decided.

He will ask her to marry him tonight.

12.

Aunt Teri—February 1, 2008

In prospect, Evon had regarded retirement from the FBI as some-thing akin to dying. She had her twenty in more than three years ago, but was required to wait until age fifty to claim her retirement benefits—about half her salary for the rest of her life, one of the big selling points of the Bureau to start. Within the agency, the standard advice was to go as soon as possible, when you were young enough to establish yourself in another career, but she'd thought she had time to figure out her future—until a local headhunter called. With the headlines then about ZP employees in Illinois bribing tax asses-sors, Hal and the board had decided to replace Collins Mullaney as head of security with somebody who had shining armor and a crime-buster reputation. The fact that Evon had also done an MBA in the weekend program at Easton—a way to stay busy after Doreen died—and had management experience as deputy special agent in charge of the Kindle County RA made her a perfect fit, and one to whom Hal made the proverbial offer she couldn't refuse.

So here she was, the senior vice-president for security at a publicly traded company. But the most unexpected aspect of the job was how much she loved it. Heather, who could be astute about everybody else, had sized Evon up accurately one night when she said, 'You're just one of those people who loves to work.' True, but the challenges were intricate in masterminding security for a company that owned 246 malls and shopping centers in thirty-five states, with over three thousand employees. She basically confronted the same issues as a suburban police chief, with far less authority. There was a big-league felony on one of their properties every day—serious drug deals, truck hijackings, shootings. Terrorism preoccupied her, since the haters could make quite a statement by, for instance, blowing up a mall during Christmas season. Over two thousand security guards roamed their sites, most rented from an outside vendor, but they became her problem when they stole from tenants or, like one creep, raped somebody in a clothing store dressing room. Every day she had to deal with reports of road rage in the parking lots, vandalism somewhere, kids caught smoking pot on the security cameras, slip-and-falls, and six-year-olds getting their sleeves snagged in the escalator. Who would have believed that so many protest groups would desire to make their case in the local mall? And none of that considered internal operations, where she was responsible for computer security and investigating the astonishing range of misbehavior your own employees could think up, everything from sexual harassment to a guy in Denver who was pocketing the proceeds when he rented out the far side of the company parking lot for football games at Mile High Stadium. Not to mention compliance issues, which brought the never-ending grillings from the lawyers. Often, she was still at her desk at ten at night and back at seven, with not much time in between when her brain went into neutral.

Her days, of course, were frequently prolonged by hours listening to Hal. Apparently, a session was about to begin. His slender assistant, Sharize, appeared in Evon's doorway to tell her she was needed immediately. In Hal's vast office, she found him seated on the beige ultra-suede sofa near the windows beside his elderly Aunt Teri. A desperate look emanated from amid the dark rings that often made Hal's brown eyes look like caves.

"Aunt Teri is giving me hell about taking our licks at Paul Gianis."

Evon had known the old lady since coming to work here. Childless, Teri had always been close to her only nephew, and now that both his parents were gone, Hal spoke to her at least once a day, often in marathon conversations that made him late for meetings and conference calls. Evon admired the old woman in a way, although she frequently had the sense that Teri had become a prisoner of her own outrageousness, the foul-mouthed, razor-tongued spinster who'd toughed her way through the world, and by now was a self-conscious imitation of the gutsy and shameless old broad everybody expected. Hal took great pleasure in recounting their adventures together. Teri, for example, had taken Hal bungee jumping without his parents' knowledge when he was sixteen—he admitted she virtually cast him off the bridge—and flown him to see the monuments at Mount Rushmore, piloting the plane herself, not long after she'd gotten her license. Hal loved to burnish her legend, speaking of the men she drank under the table—starting with him—or the way that Teri would routinely announce at family dinners that she was taking a trip the following week, usually to Manhattan or Miami, to get laid. There had apparently been only a few serious boyfriends, and none of them able to keep up with her.

"This serves no purpose," Teri said to her nephew, largely ignoring Evon. She had a hand on her gnarly cane, which looked to be an old shepherd's crook, undoubtedly Greek, and half her face was covered in large turquoise-framed sunglasses. Macular degeneration had left the old lady legally blind. "I've never liked vengeful people, Herakles. Never. Paul had nothing to do with that murder. And you know it."

Evon had met a few folks approaching ninety who retained considerable physical grace, and Teri might have been one of them if she had ever been persuaded to give up alcohol and cigarettes. Sometimes Hal let her smoke in the office, but she hadn't lit up yet, a sure sign that he wanted to get her on her way. Teri's appearance was, to be honest, about as trashy as a half-blind octogenarian could get away with, with giant rose balls of rouge inflaming her cheeks, dyed shoulder-length blonde hair resembling a pile of hay, and crimson fingernails grown out like talons. Beneath the rouge and powder—and a full daily baptism in perfume—she seemed to have shrunk inside her own skin, which hung in folds from her forearms. She wore lipstick the color of a fire hydrant, and gold jewelry by the pound, huge pieces clanking on her neck and around her wrists. She was seriously bent and one hip was terrible. But she remained willful and cagey, and except for occasional difficulty remembering names, her intellect was largely undimmed. The reverence she was automatically due as a person of advanced age made her a tough customer, and she knew it.

Hal continued to resist.

"The hell I do. Have you been watching TV?"

"Georgia Cleon is a jealous twat," said Teri. "She's bitter. Nobody told her to marry Jimmy. I'm sorry it turned out bad for her, but that wasn't Paul's fault. She's just mad because"—she was briefly stumped for a word—"because Paul dumped her. Or dumped on her. However they say he broke her heart. Isn't that what they say now?" She finally turned to Evon, but only for brief clarification.

"Dumped her," said Evon quietly. That was the term Heather used in her messages on Evon's cell. She talked until the allotted time ran out, bouncing between extremes, raging and then begging for another chance. 'I can't believe you dumped me. I deserved so much better from you,' last night's barrage had started. Evon had no explanation for why she listened to every word until the message was cut off. Because you love her. Because you are hoping in every syllable to hear some semblance of the beautiful girl you fell in love with—beautiful and graceful, and sane.

"Evon talked to Georgia, Aunt Teri. Evon, tell my aunt. Did you think Georgia was just making this up?"

Evon told Teri that Georgia actually appeared reluctant to share her information, but Teri wasn't hearing it.

"Sorry, girlie, but I've known that woman her entire life. I'm sure Georgia has convinced herself about some of this. But Paul telling her Cass was innocent? She just wants everybody to know how close she was to Paul."

"She was," Hal protested. He had removed his suit coat and his tie and sat, with an arm on the sofa back, close to his aunt, his large belly looking a little like he'd strapped on a flour sack.

"Georgia was old news the day Paul saw Sofia at that picnic. Everybody knew it but Georgia. Dora Michalis told me that Paul started showing up at the hospital to have coffee with Sofia the very next week."

Evon was impressed with the old lady's recall of events twenty-five years ago, although Dita's murder had probably kept many details from that period fresh. Even Hal seemed to realize he'd been trumped.

"These families were together always and were then torn apart," Teri said, "and I grant you that had started before Dita's murder. But that is nothing to revel in. Lidia has been my best friend for eighty years. Your father would have hated this, Hal." She said something in Greek and Hal, although clearly displeased, translated for Evon.

"'He who respects his parents never dies.'"

"Don't make faces," said Teri. "From the day Cass was arrested Zeus said the same thing—"

Hal interrupted, his lips indeed pouched in distaste. "'A tragedy for both families.' I know."

"Your mother, I grant you, she wanted Cass strung up at first, but after your father passed she took his point of view. When Paul first ran for office, I heard her hush you a hundred times when you carried on the way you've been doing now. You just never liked those twins."

"That's not so. I babysat for them, Aunt Teri."

"And complained afterwards. Lord only knows what it was that bothered you."

Hal took in the point for a second, but refused to give ground.

"I respected my parents when they were alive, Aunt Teri. And I treasure their memory." He pointed to the shelves holding their pictures. "But I'm not letting them run my life from the grave."

The old lady was still shaking her head so that her layered gold necklaces rattled.

"I'm telling you, it's disrespectful to use your father's money to punish Paul. Zeus wouldn't have stood for that."

Hal recoiled. Teri had hit the sorest point, and Hal, being Hal, endured an instant when his eyes appeared to water. As far as Evon could tell, the biggest issue in Hal's life was his father, even though Zeus had been dead since 1987, killed accidentally on a trip to Greece. But as someone put it to Evon when she was considering coming to ZP, 'Hal is trying to walk in his father's shoes in feet half his size.' Zeus had been a force, smart and magnetic and handsome, who would probably have been governor of this state had grief not driven him out of the race. Hal was none of those things and he knew how often others made the unfavorable comparison. As a result, his life, in considerable measure, was dedicated to a losing competition with his father's ghost. Hal never spoke ill of Zeus. In fact, he quite often described his father as 'a god,' for whom he genuinely seemed to hold limitless affection and respect. But he was determined to prove that his own success was not due to what he had inherited. The principal evidence was relentless expansion of his father's shopping center empire. In the early 1990s he had taken ZP public as a REIT, and since then he'd made a number of strategic acquisitions like the YourHouse deal, which was close to being publicly announced. Hal himself was now worth more than a billion dollars. But his nails were still bitten down to ragged stumps, and so he tended to speak with his hands in fists, to avoid displaying the manifest evidence of everything that nibbled at him from inside.

With Teri's last remark, it was apparent he was losing his sense of humor with her.

"Knock it off, Aunt Teri. It's not Dad's money, it's mine. I've made twice what he did."

Even Teri knew she'd gone too far. She threw a wrist and her bangles at him but said nothing more. Instead she thumped her cane on the floor and tried to pull herself to her feet. Hal, ever loyal, clambered up to grab her by the elbow. Her hand groped in the air until she caught him by the cheek and kissed him, leaving a vivid imprint.

"You're a good boy, Hal. My number one nephew." An old joke, of course. She had no other nephew. She reached after Evon. "Here. You walk me out. He's too important." Evon substituted her arm for Hal's, despite his mild protests.

They were no more than thirty feet from Hal's door when the old lady stopped. She averted her face, trying to find the little fragment of sight she retained so she could see Evon.

"You have to make him stop this. This will come to grief for everyone."

"Ms. Kronon, I'm an employee. No one tells your nephew what to do."

"So you say, but he likes you. He values your judgment."

"Well, so far, there's been more to his suspicions than I would have guessed. I have no basis to tell him to stop at this point."

Authoritative as always, Teri said, "Paul had nothing to do with killing Dita. Aphrodite wasn't just Hal's sister. She was my niece and I loved her. Don't you think I'd be the first to want Paul punished, if he had any hand in her murder?"

Evon walked Teri to the ZP reception area, where German, who served as both her caregiver and her butler, was waiting. When the elevator arrived, he stepped inside and held the door for Teri, but she didn't move, angling her head again to see Evon.

"You're the lesbian, aren't you?"

Evon still didn't like being known that way. It said both too much and too little. But Teri was an old lady. Evon managed a polite nod. Teri stared a second and took a step closer, so that Evon noticed how thick the powder was in the channels engraved in Teri's face.

"Wish I'd been born in your time," she said quietly, then felt with the crook to make her way into the elevator.

13.

Du Bois Lands—February 5, 2008

D u Bois Lands had been hired in the PA's office about three years after Paul, and ended up as the junior prosecutor in the courtroom where Paul held the first trial chair. D.B. was a good lawyer—exact in his thinking, a better writer than most of the deputy prosecutors, and a passionate and charming courtroom advocate. Paul and he enjoyed working together, and spent time outside the office. Sofia was particularly fond of Du Bois's wife, Margo, a pediatrician, and even after Paul left the PA's office, the couples saw each other once or twice a year.

Then in 1993, D.B.'s uncle, Sherman Crowthers, had been indicted for extracting bribes as a judge in the Common Pleas section of the Superior Court, where personal-injury lawsuits were heard. Judge Crowthers was an American tragedy. An all–Mid Ten tight end at the U, who had grown up picking walnuts on a plantation in Georgia, he became one of the Tri-Cities' premier criminal defense lawyers and a leading figure in the civil rights movement. His first triumph was successfully representing Dr. King, who was arrested here after leading open housing marches in 1965.

No one ever really understood why Sherm had fallen under the venal spell of the chief judge in Common Pleas, Brendan Tuohey. Sherm lived high—the black nouveau riche thing, not much different from the Greek nouveau riche thing Paul saw growing up—but he'd made his fortune before going on the bench. One friend said Sherm's explanation was twisted but simple: 'Mama didn't raise no fool.' He refused to be a black man who got less while many of the white judges around him turned their seats on the bench into ATMs.

As a plaintiff's lawyer who made his living in those courtrooms, Paul had heard the same tales as everyone else. Appearing before certain judges said to be part of Tuohey's ring, Paul worried that the defense lawyers might slip something into the judge's drawer, but he figured he would be OK if he got to a jury. And he was—more than OK. He got good cases, usually through his Easton Law School classmates in big firms who wouldn't soil themselves with contingency matters, worked the files carefully and rang the bell hard, several times.

In 1991, Paul won his first big verdict, eighteen million dollars in a trial before Sherm Crowthers. Paul represented a concert violinist who lost an arm on the light-rail when the doors closed on his Stradivarius and dragged the musician several hundred yards down the track. Days after the jury had come back, Paul was in the courthouse and bumped into Sherm, who more or less steered Paul, with an arm like a tree branch, into the private corridor outside his chambers. Post-trial motions were still pending, in which the defense was trying to overturn the verdict, but Paul assumed that the judge wanted no more than to offer congratulations on a job well done, until he pushed Paul into the small clerk's alcove in his chambers and closed the door. Sherm was huge, six foot six and well over three hundred pounds by now, with a storm of overgrown gray eyebrows and intense yellowed eyes.

'Motherfucker,' he said to Paul, 'you don't seem to understand what's goin on here.'

Paul, who didn't think he scared easily any more, was too terrified by what was happening to answer. The judge then told Paul that he had to try the food at Crowthers's sister's restaurant in the North End.

Quietly asking around afterward, Paul learned that Judith Crowthers reputedly bagged for her brother, tending the cash register at her thriving soul food restaurant in her abundant purple eye shadow and dangling earrings, and accepting without comment the envelopes certain lawyers handed over as they paid their lunch checks. Paul had no thought of dealing with something like this without talking it over with Cass. They met two days later in one of the tiny whitewashed attorneys' rooms at the Hillcrest Correctional Facility. By now, Paul understood the grim operating mode of the whole corrupt system in Common Pleas. His fee on the case was close to four million dollars—the ten or twenty thousand he was expected to hand over was next to nothing. If he refused, he had no doubt Crowthers would set aside the verdict, reversing key evidentiary rulings, and order another trial, which Paul almost surely would lose. If he reported Sherm to the authorities, it would be Paul's word against the judge's, who would claim he had done no more than recommend his sister's restaurant. Worse, Paul would be a marked man whom Chief Tuohey and his cabal would do their best to drive out of the courthouse.

'Fuck him anyway,' Cass concluded. After years in Hillcrest, they both knew the perils of kowtowing to bullies. It never ended. You stood up. But didn't snitch.

Paul filed a motion the next day, asking Judge Crowthers to disqualify himself from presiding further on the case, because of 'inappropriate ex parte contact,' which went otherwise unexplained. There were half a dozen people who'd seen the judge with his arm around Paul, drawing him toward his chambers. If it came to a showdown, Paul would get some backing. Rather than go through that, Crowthers withdrew from the case, but for the next two years, whenever Paul's firm filed a new lawsuit in the Common Pleas section, it ended up before one of Tuohey's judges who, without exception, granted the defendant's motion to dismiss the complaint. Eventually, they referred out any new matters in Kindle County and began trying to develop their practice in the outlying counties.

And then Special Agent Evon Miller of the FBI arrived in Paul's office. The government's undercover investigation of Common Pleas judges, Project Petros, was all over the news. Evon had a copy of Paul's motion in her hand and wanted to know exactly what "inappropriate ex parte contact" meant. Paul stalled until he could get to Hillcrest the next Sunday. Cass and he, as usual, saw this the same way: It was time for this shit to end. Paul told Evon the story on Monday, and agreed to testify. Crowthers, it turned out, was on tape, but the government informant who'd made the recording had died, giving Sherm a shot at trial. But with his placid recitation of the shakedown, Paul appeared to be the emblem of everything good in the law, and a potent contrast to the deeply compromised sleazeballs who were the government's other witnesses. The trial was over, in effect, as soon as Paul left the stand.

Du Bois Lands was Sherman Crowthers's nephew, the child of his wife's sister. D.B.'s mom was a schoolteacher who ended up with a drug problem and, in time, a prison sentence—for black folks it was still the case that when they stumbled they had further to fall. D.B. had lived off and on with Sherm in his huge Colonial home in Assembly Point and regarded his uncle as his idol. When Paul entered the federal courtroom to testify against Crowthers, Du Bois was in the front spectators' row. He had striking grayish eyes and they bulleted Paul. Du Bois would never say a word, but Paul knew what D.B. was thinking: 'You didn't have to do this. You could have said it was all too vague by now, that you just couldn't recall.' The two of them never exchanged another word.

These days, Du Bois had sat on the bench five years. He'd been promoted to Common Pleas a year ago, and was assigned to the same courtroom his uncle had occupied fifteen years before, where Paul and Ray Horgan now awaited the start of proceedings. The courtroom was Bauhausy and functional, with all the furnishings, including the paneling and a low, squared-off bench and witness stand, formed of yellowing birch. Kronon and Tooley sat across the courtroom at the other counsel's desk, and there were dozens of reporters and sketch artists in the front rows of the straight-backed pews. The benches behind them were thick with civilian onlookers.

When Du Bois had been assigned to the suit against Kronon, Paul had taken it for granted they would move to disqualify D.B., but Ray was adamantly opposed. He didn't want to take the risk of antagonizing black voters, of whom Paul still had a fair share, despite the presence in the race of Willie Dixon, the county councilman from the North End. Beyond that, D.B. had a sterling reputation. And when he'd run for the bench, Ray had been one of his three campaign co-chairs.

Now the elderly clerk bellowed out the case name, "Gianis versus Kronon, Number C-315." Tooley in his silly shaggy toupee arrived first at the podium and introduced himself for the record, while Ray rolled forward, his gait halting given his rickety knees. With heat, Tooley began to explain his new motions related to fingerprint and DNA testing, but Du Bois cut him off.

"I've read all the papers, gentlemen. I always do." By reputation, D.B.'s in-court demeanor was serious, even stern. But his tone never changed. He treated everyone who appeared before him with civility, tinctured by an undercurrent of skepticism. He was also said to be great at the basic job of a judge: deciding. He ruled after appropriate reflection, but without wavering, unlike others who dithered or tried to force the parties to settle even trivial disputes. "Let's take the motions in the order they were filed," the judge said.

"First, Mr. Horgan seeks guidance about what public comment the parties may make concerning the subject matter of this lawsuit."

D.B. treated the motion seriously, but as Paul had expected, refused to gag either party, even though the lawyers litigating the case would have to adhere to the rules about comments outside court. Since Paul wasn't acting as his own counsel, it would be unfair, the judge said, to restrict him, especially in light of the campaign. Paul wondered if D.B. was going to kill him with kindness.

Lands turned then to Tooley's motions related to the crime-scene evidence and to compelling Paul to give fingerprints and a DNA specimen.

"Mr. Horgan, what do you say?"

To craft their response today, Paul had called a big meeting two days ago in the fishbowl with Crully, Ray, half a dozen campaign officials, even Sofia, who was getting increasingly concerned about the way this run-in with Hal was playing out.

At the podium, Ray still radiated charm and the authority of someone who had been an important figure in these courts for fifty years.

"Your Honor, let me say to start that Senator Gianis will take every reasonable step to prove that Mr. Kronon's allegations are ill-motivated lies."

The judge interrupted the grandstanding.

"The motion, Mr. Horgan."

"Judge Lands, I told Mr. Tooley last week that assuming we get equal access to the evidence, we had no objection to him serving his subpoenas on the authorities in Greenwood County related to public documents in the court file or the fingerprint evidence collected at the scene. They've hired Dr. Maurice Dickerman as their fingerprint expert, and I see Dr. Dickerman in court today." Ray turned from the podium and lifted a hand like a ringmaster. On cue, Mo Dickerman, the so-called Fingerprint God, stood for just a second in the back of the courtroom, in his dark suit. A skinny angular man, Mo used a finger to push his heavy black frames back up on his nose. Dickerman was the longtime chief of the Kindle County Unified Police Force's fingerprint lab. Like all police employees, he was permitted to work after hours on his own. "Senator Gianis will produce his fingerprints to Dr. Dickerman whenever the court orders, even today."

Ray stopped there.

Du Bois nodded, as if to say, 'Reasonable enough.' Now in his late forties, Judge Lands remained handsome, with close-cropped hair, a mid-tone complexion and those startling gray eyes.

"Your Honor," said Tooley, "we still haven't heard any answer to our request for DNA."

Du Bois raised his hand toward Ray, who responded.

"Judge, we're eager to come forward with all probative evidence, but this request for a DNA test is clearly a bridge too far. In order to be entitled to discovery, a party must show that there is a reasonable likelihood that whatever proof is sought is potentially relevant. Dr. Yavem concedes that there is no better than a one in one hundred chance that an examination of DNA will lead to admissible evidence in a case like this with identical twins. So that part of the motion is little more than an effort to embarrass and harass Senator Gianis."

"Your Honor," answered Tooley, "this is not a matter of percentages. And even if it were, why wouldn't Senator Gianis want to take a test that has a 99 percent chance of not incriminating him?" This was a non sequitur, an answer aimed only at the reporters. Du Bois, nobody's fool, understood the posturing and had heard enough. Up on the bench, he dropped the pen with which he was taking notes and pushed aside his papers.

"Here's what we're going to do," the judge said. "Some of what's been requested doesn't appear to be at issue. So, Mr.

Tooley, I'm going to grant your motion in part and approve these subpoenas you've served out in Greenwood County on the police and the court related to the police reports and the fingerprint evidence, with the proviso that the full return on the subpoenas be shared at once with Mr. Horgan. Second, because the fingerprinting doesn't seem to be in dispute, I'll allow you, Mr. Tooley, to issue any other subpoenas directly related to the issue, and the court will accept Senator Gianis's offer to provide fingerprints, and I will direct that he do so."

"We'll do it right here, right now in open court, Judge," said Ray. The intention was to play to the press and it worked. The journalists in the front row were tapping away or scribbling as fast as they could.

"Thank you, Mr. Horgan, but I don't think we need to turn my courtroom into a crime lab." There was a riffle of laughter.

"Then we'll go right down to the lobby to do it with Dr. Dickerman."

Du Bois moved the back of his hand as if to say, 'Whatever.'

"I did have a thought about Dr. Dickerman," the judge said.

Mo stood up again in the back of the courtroom and walked toward the bench. No one had ever accused Mo of being reluctant about attention. The judge proposed that Mo be appointed the court's expert, with the parties splitting his fee. Mo was renowned around the world, probably the most widely respected print expert in the US, outside the FBI. No one was likely to contradict him, anyway. Ray agreed immediately, fulsomely praising the judge's idea. D.B. acted as if he hadn't heard.

"So I'll direct that whatever fingerprint evidence is found be delivered to Dr. Dickerman," Lands said. "If the fingerprint lifts from the scene remain in a condition where current comparisons are likely to be probative, then he should compare those prints to the ones he gets from Senator Gianis today."

"And the DNA?" asked Tooley yet again. Clearly, Hal was hot to do that test.

"Well, you know, Mr. Tooley, Mr. Horgan may have a point. I'm not sure you get to run a test that your own expert says is overwhelmingly likely to be unproductive. But I'll withhold my ruling. I'll give Mr. Horgan a week to file a written response about it; you, Mr. Tooley, will get a week to reply. By then, Dr. Dickerman may have the fingerprint results, and those may inform my ruling on the DNA. So let's meet again then. Mr. Clerk, please give us a date."

"February twentieth at 10 a.m."

"That will be the order," said Du Bois. Watching from the plaintiff's table, Paul thought he would not have ruled differently. Du Bois had been fair and savvy and measured.

The judge called a recess and rose on the bench, which brought everyone else in the courtroom to their feet. From that vantage, D.B. looked for the first time directly at Paul. The glance was fleet, but seemed to have been accompanied by an expression somewhere between a grimace and a smile. 'See?' he seemed to say.

14.

Dickerman—February 5, 2008

It had been years since Tim had entered the Temple, as the Kindle County Superior Court Law and Equity Department was known. Constructed of buff-colored brick in the 1950s, the building had the proportions of an armory, with a dome above bleeding weak light down in the central rotunda, through which at 9:00 a.m. a determined crush swirled. Tim's natural terrain had been the Central Branch courthouse a few blocks away, where criminal cases were heard. In here, he still felt like a tourist, and after he passed through the metal detectors, he found a uniformed security guy to direct him to Du Bois Lands's courtroom on the fourth floor.

Tim had known Du Bois's uncle well, but only while Crowthers was an attorney. Nonetheless, the impression Sherm had made remained vivid, since there was no defense lawyer whose cross-examinations Tim liked less. Sherm tended to terrorize a witness, yelling in that booming voice, mocking and badgering, looming over the witness box so that his sheer size was yet another instrument of intimidation. In one murder case, Sherm had taken the weapon found at the scene and pointed the pistol at Tim for a good ten minutes as he questioned him, before the deputy

PA finally responded to Tim's pleading looks and objected. Like everybody else in the courtroom, the prosecutor had been mesmerized by Sherm.

Tim had come to court today at Mel Tooley's request, so he could go at once to serve any new subpoenas the judge approved. With Ray Horgan's agreement, Tim had already dropped off other subpoenas last week out in Greenwood County, and yesterday had brought the fingerprint lifts and reports produced in response to Mo Dickerman's office.

Tim was sitting in the back of the courtroom when Dickerman came in and caught sight of him. He slid over on the bench to make room. Tim had been through God knew how many cases with Mo, who was just coming up when Tim was already a detective lieutenant. He had probably been the first dick to recognize how exceptional Dickerman was—a great witness and unusually learned in his field. Eventually, Tim recommended Mo for promotion over several guys senior to him. As a result, Mo had always been somewhat in Tim's debt, and Tim had gotten along with him as well as anybody did. As a guy, Mo would never really pass as warm, and he was so up on himself these days that he had fewer friends than ever in McGrath Hall.

Mo was past seventy now—around seventy-two, Tim thought, which made him the oldest employee of the police force. Yet he was too famous to be forced into retirement, and the County Board grandfathered him every year. He was one of those thin guys who didn't age much, but you could see some wear on him, more weariness in his long face and plenty of gray now in his thinning hair. Around the eyes there was a sad gathering of puffy, wattled flesh. Like Tim, Mo was now a widower. His wife Sally had died only a few months back and you could see the evidence of that, too, in a watery vacancy that had replaced Mo's prior intensity. Tim grabbed Dickerman's knee as he sat.

"How is it with you, boyo?" Tim asked. "You OK?" Dickerman had been out when Tim dropped off the subpoenaed evidence yesterday.

Mo made a face. He knew Tim was talking about Sally's passing. For Tim, Maria's death fell into the broad category of things you couldn't do anything about, and he usually spoke with great reluctance about those years—shuttling her for treatments, shopping with her for wigs, sitting in the waiting room with his insides scoured by worry during the course of three lengthy surgeries, his daughters' weeping as soon as they caught sight of their mom, whenever they came to town. But Mo clearly was of the other school, talking about Sally constantly so he could believe it himself. Telling Tim the story now, Mo leaned down in the yellowish courtroom pew, ostensibly to keep their conversation private, but it looked as if the memory had doubled him in pain.

"When they found the lump, I was thinking, 'Oh, Jesus Christ, she's going to lose her tits,' and then after we saw the big-deal specialist at the U, I'd have gotten on my knees for him to tell me that was all there was to it. There was nothing to do. They tried, but they just made her miserable. At the end she begged me not to ask her to do anything else. She didn't last eight months from diagnosis to the funeral."

Tim very briefly covered Mo's hand with his own. You live with somebody, peaceably, dreaming beside each other, sharing meals, making a family, but there seems no special excitement to it, even though you know, as Tim did, that you're living with a person of exceptional kindness. And then she's gone and the depth of the loss almost surpasses understanding, even when you realize you're also mourning your loneliness, and the inevitability of it.

Judge Lands came on the bench then and they both stood. The clerk called Kronon's case first.

Tooley and Horgan strolled forward from their respective tables, two stout fellows looking a bit like a bride and groom as they met in the center of the courtroom before Tooley preceded Ray to the podium.

Du Bois was one of those judges who knew his business and didn't waste time. As a cop, Tim had never been all that keen about judges. Many just seemed to get in the way, with a fair number of them thinking the whole case was about them. Whoever went to a baseball game to see the umpire?

At the front of the courtroom, the lawyers bickered while Lands kept control. A couple of times, Mo was mentioned and he popped up beside Tim. Eventually, the judge asked Mo to step forward. He moved toward the bench stiffly. He'd been a basketball player years ago, as Tim recalled, and he was clearly having trouble with his knees.

When court broke, Tim made his way up to the defense table where Tooley, as usual, had his hands full with Hal. Kronon had realized that Paul and his team had gotten exactly what they wanted. TV cameramen were barred from any other part of the courthouse, except the rotunda. By going down there to give his prints, Gianis would be able to mount a show for the evening news.

"Fucking publicity stunt," Kronon said.

"Hal," Tooley said, "he was going to get to do this in front of the cameras, no matter what. It's a public proceeding."

Horgan's associate came by and asked if they wanted to witness the fingerprinting, and the three made their way downstairs. Dickerman had set up shop on the stone ledge that decorated the Temple's central hallway. At Dickerman's instruction, Paul had gone off to wash his hands, and he returned now, striding through the lobby, several steps in front of Ray Horgan, as the xenon beams of the cameras came on simultaneously, flooding the hallway with their glare. Gianis slid off his suit coat, handing it to one of the young campaign aides, then removed his cuff links and rolled up his sleeves.

In Tim's day, Mo would have taken the prints by inking Paul's fingers and palms and rolling them on a piece of stiff paper called a ten-card. That remained the procedure in most police stations, but Mo preferred a digital impression, called "live scan." For his private consulting business, Mo owned his own equipment, and he had his assistant, probably a grad student from the U where Mo taught, bring the metal jumpkit from which Dickerman extracted the scanner, which was about the size of an adding machine. Mo connected the scanner to his laptop and took several different versions of Paul's prints. The first was a four-finger slap, then Dickerman bore down on each of Paul's fingers, rolling it across a white band beneath the scanner's platen. The images popped up immediately on his computer screen, as the camera guys fought each other for close-ups. For safety's sake, Mo also took impressions on paper, using one of the new inkless pads.

Hal had seen enough and drew both Tim and Tooley aside.

"He'll never match anything," Kronon said about Paul. "His prints won't be anywhere in that room. That's why he's making such a show of it. He looks like a vaudeville magician rolling up his sleeves."

"That was always the risk, Hal," Tooley told him.

"We should withdraw the motion."

"It was just granted. We can't withdraw it."

"He won't match. And because he doesn't match, and the DNA is no better than one in a hundred, his asshole buddy, Du Bois, will then deny the motion for the DNA, too. I want the goddamned DNA."

Accustomed to Hal's pique and the irrationality that was often part of it, Tooley remained silent for a second, before venturing the obvious.

"It means something, Hal, if his fingerprints aren't there. We can't pretend it doesn't."

"It doesn't mean crap."

Tooley rolled his eyes at Tim and announced he was going back to his office. Hal's Bentley had rolled to the curb. Alone, Tim returned to witness the last of the fingerprinting, but Gianis was already slipping his cuff links back in. Fitting the scanner into the foam cushion inside the metal case, Mo caught sight of Tim and gestured for him to wait. It was another ten minutes because several of the reporters wanted to talk to Mo, too. By the time Dickerman came over, Tim and he were alone in the marble hall.

"I meant to tell you before," Mo said, "but I got distracted about Sally. You're gonna have to get your rear end back out to Greenwood County."

"And why's that?"

"I'm gonna need Cass's fingerprints, too, and they weren't in that mess you brought over yesterday."

"Cass?" Tim asked. "I thought he has different fingerprints from Paul."

"No, that's true. But telling them apart in a situation like this—it's not that easy." As he often did, Mo reverted to a lecture, explaining that most of what showed up in twins' fingerprints, the basic skin patterns of loops and whorls and ridges, was identical, the product of shared genes. Subtle variations emerged during development, when the fetus touched the uterine wall, or itself, causing differences in what print examiners called 'the minutiae,' the areas where skin ridges ended or branched or ran together.

"Don't misunderstand," said Mo. "If I give any decent examiner ten-cards from Paul and Cass Gianis, they'd see enough to distinguish. But you know better than I do that latents at a crime scene don't come in ten-finger sets. You get partials, a couple of fingers, whatever. You understand all that. And with, say, a partial print, you may not be able to tell which twin it's from.

"So you know, the best way to do this kind of comparison is to start out with the ten-card from each man and isolate the differing points. When I didn't get Cass's prints from Greenwood, I called Tooley to get him to call the PA's office. In the meantime, he sent over Cass's intake prints from Hillcrest, which I guess he got when he subpoenaed Cass's file for the pardon and parole hearing. It's a laser copy. High-res, but it's a copy. Nobody can testify from that. Which is why I need you to go back out to Greenwood and make them find Cass's ten-card."

"Got it, Boss," said Tim. He thought calling Mo 'Boss' might get a smile, but Dickerman stood there, looking nettled instead. Something was weighing on him.

"There's one other thing," said Mo. "Which maybe you can help me figure out."

Tim shrugged, feeling somewhat flattered. Generally, Mo didn't think he needed any help figuring out anything.

"When I got that copy of Cass's prints," said Mo, "I decided I could use them at least to do some prep. I've got to go over to Italy for a week to give a lecture—"

"Poor soul," said Tim.

"Yeah, it's tough. But I wanted to get a head start. I had Logan Boerkle's report from 1983 where he identified Cass's prints. I figured I'd see what part of each print Logan had relied on, and then when I got Paul's card today, I'd have someplace to start the comparison."

Tim nodded. It made sense.

"Logan was barely sober in those days." Logan had been the head of the fingerprint lab here whom Mo had displaced. He got hired in Greenwood County, but that was like going from the big leagues to A ball.

"Logan's the one who died of exposure in his own cabin, right?" Tim asked.

"Right. He had some place up in Skageon with just an outhouse and he got drunk and went out to take a piss, and passed out in the snow and died there. Back in '83, when he made Cass's prints, he was already a shambles. Most of the time when he showed up for work, he didn't know one end of a microscope from another. And damn me, when I start comparing his report and the lifts from the scene to the prints I got from Hillcrest—they don't match. Close. Very very close. But in several cases, they display just the kind of minute differences you'd expect with a twin."

"Which Logan missed?"

Mo hitched his shoulders. "Possibly."

"So you're telling me the wrong brother is in the can?"

"I'm telling you what I'm telling you."

Tim considered this at some length, then shook his head.

"Paul Gianis is too smart to think he'd get away with that twice. He's a former PA. The way he went strutting around that lobby—he knows his prints weren't at the scene."

"Or he thinks no examiner would bother to look again at the lifts identified as Cass's in '83," said Mo. "Maybe Paul figures I'd confine my new examination to the unknowns. There's plenty that would do it like that. But either way, I need Cass's original prints. Maybe when I compare them with Paul's, this will make more sense. Maybe I'll see what Logan was talking about. But I'm buffaloed now." He peered at Tim again.

"This stays right here," Mo said. "I don't want anybody hearing this, and then in two weeks thinking I'm a world-class bonehead."

Tim agreed. He couldn't make any more sense of this than Mo. They parted, joined in a weird compact, two old guys afraid they could be slipping.

15.

The Scene—February 9, 2008

Heather hadn't moved out when Evon returned to the condo, last Sunday. She had opened a suitcase on their bed, but had gotten no further than that. In her nightgown, Heather was sitting on the covers in a butterfly pose, soles of her feet pressed together, her blonde hair flowing smoothly over her shoulders. She began weeping as soon as Evon appeared at the door to the room. Evon had no doubt that Heather had staged the whole thing, laid the case out and dressed herself in a casually revealing way.

'You have to leave,' Evon told her.

Heather begged, repeated her pledges of love, but ended up enraged. Evon couldn't throw her out of her own home, she said. Heather was ignoring many facts—that Evon had paid every penny for the place, that the title was solely in Evon's name and that Heather hadn't contributed her share of the assessment for months. Evon had told her she had until next Saturday to go.

Now, on Saturday morning, Evon arrived at the condo, full of resolve. She knocked but of course Heather didn't answer. When Evon tried her key, she found Heather had changed the locks. Evon hammered on the door for only a second, then called a locksmith and the head of the condo association. In the meantime, she went to her safe-deposit box to retrieve the deed to the place to establish ownership. Evon had the smith drill out the cylinder while Rhona, the association president, and her husband, Harry, both of whom lived next door, came into the hallway for a second to watch. She could hear Heather on the other side, threatening to call the police. When the drilling didn't cease, Heather opened the door, just as the tradesman had bored through. Heather was in a negligee again and offered Evon both keys.

"I would have given them to you. All you had to do was ask."

Evon didn't bother responding. Heather would say anything at this point, no matter how obviously untrue. Evon left the locksmith at work on a new dead bolt, and drove to Morton's and bought the biggest duffel bag they had in the store. Back at the condo, she started packing Heather's stuff in front of her. Evon slammed Heather's dresses, still on the hangers, into the bag, knowing that Heather, who treated every garment as if it were made of Venetian glass, could not bear the sight. When Evon was done, she took the duffel down to Heather's car and hoisted it onto the hood. Heather followed her, weeping and screaming, which gave Evon the opportunity she needed. She flew up the stairs—she could still outrun most people she knew—and closed the new click-lock. Heather was now on the other side of the door. She phoned Evon inside more than forty times in a row. Evon answered once: "If you don't go away, I will have no choice but to call the police." Half an hour later, while Heather was still calling every five minutes, Evon opened the door to toss out Heather's purse. Once the pounding and the texting and phone calls had ceased, once the woman was finally gone, Evon sat on the living room floor in the space that had been happily theirs and howled.

When Evon opened the door for the Sunday paper, Heather was

asleep in the hall, still in her negligee, using her handbag as a pillow. Evon called mutual friends and watched from the window as the two guided Heather to their car across the street. One had her by the waist, one by the shoulders. Heather was hysterical and they were nodding at every word. Evon was able to do nothing all day but talk to Merrel and watch the Pro Bowl. She was right, she knew, had done what she had to. All she needed now was someone to explain all that to her heart.

She was not much better when she went to work Monday morning. The loss, the drama, the sleeplessness had hollowed her out, made her feel as if the only part of her left intact was her skin. The vast entry of ZP's headquarters was five stories high, glass on three sides, with giant seamless sheets of taupe granite cladding the only wall, which contained the building's central service corridor. There workers in gray jumpsuits were on a lift hanging a huge crimson heart of woven roses as a Valentine decoration. It was too much for Evon. She barely made it into her office before closing the door so she could cry privately at her desk. She was still blubbering when Mitra, her assistant, buzzed to say Tim Brodie was here. Evon had totally forgotten the appointment. Tooley had copied all the old police reports for Ray Horgan, then handed the file back to Tim, asking that Evon and he, the ones with law-enforcement training, review the materials to determine if there were other leads they should follow.

Now she blew her nose and went to her purse for makeup. She looked horrible in the mirror of her compact. Crying with her contacts in had left her red-eyed, and the inflamed ridges of her nose made her resemble Rudolph. Tim took one glance at her once he came through her door and asked, "What happened?"

She tried to stiffen herself, but it didn't work. She dropped her face into her hands.

"I've got girlfriend problems," Evon said.

"I kind of took that from what you said when you were at my house. Anything requiring an old man's advice?" You couldn't resist Tim. There was a calm understanding that seemed part of his expression. Her father was this kind of man. Not as brainy. But centered. And thoughtful. And loving at the core. She needed to talk to somebody. Most of her friends knew Heather, too, and were caught in the middle. She'd largely been keeping all of it to herself.

Evon told him the story in short strokes.

"The worst part," she said, "is me. What was I thinking? What was I doing with somebody like Heather? A model. A former *fashion* model. I just wanted to believe that somebody that beautiful could care for me. It kind of made me beautiful by association, I guess."

"There's nothing wrong with beautiful," Tim said. "Not in and of itself." Maria had been one of the most beautiful girls he'd met, with wide-set features and a perfect mouth. He'd loved her almost at once, because she seemed to take no notice of how pretty she was. "It's kind of like money. It's what it does to the people who have it or want it that's the bad part."

"How stupid can I be? I'm fifty years old."

"People see what they want to see. You care to skip psychology class, then just remember that. Every time somebody falls in love, they create their own mythology to go with it. Don't they? About her. And you. It makes it all bigger than life. Has to be, doesn't it? To be so special. So this gal, used to be she was a goddess and so were you, and now she's mortal."

"Mortal? She's crazy. Seriously disturbed. People warned me, too. And I didn't listen."

"Think you're the first?" Tim had been standing in front of her desk, still in his overcoat, with his stocking cap in his hand. Little tufts of hair stood straight up on his head from removing his hat. He pushed the outerwear aside and fished around in the pocket of the brown Harris tweed jacket he always had on and came out with a piece of paper. "Copied this down a few months ago from *A Midsummer Night's Dream*." He read it out.

Love looks not with the eyes, but with the mind;
And therefore is winged Cupid painted blind.

He handed over the torn scrap of paper, where he'd printed the quotation out in block letters. You had to love Tim. Eighty-one and studying Shakespeare and understanding it, too.

"You just happened to be carrying that around in your pocket?" Evon asked.

"Naw," he answered, "I copied out a couple of passages from the plays I read that I've been looking at whenever I get to thinking a lot about Maria. Somewhere in fifty years, Cupid loses his blindfold. That's the part I wonder about. I wonder how badly I disappointed her."

"I can't believe you weren't good to her, Tim."

"Tried to be. I just never was the kind to talk about my feelings. So she was never completely sure I had my whole heart in it. Looking back I think I did. But then again, you wonder if it's just stuff you're making up so you feel better."

It was easier in some ways to cherish the dead. He knew, with more than a little remorse, that the Maria he mourned was not quite the woman he'd lived with for more than fifty years. He lacked her sharp tongue, for one thing, and thus he couldn't really summon the angry words that escaped her every once in a great while, words that made his deflated hopeless heart flounder in his chest. But he remembered something that was not as clear in life—who she was to him, the casting that could be made by the needs she filled, the zones of need and pleasure. In memory, he did not deal with her full complexity. But he felt what their love meant to him.

"Still, it was worth every second," he told Evon. "At least for me. I can only say what I used to tell my daughters when some boy would break their hearts. Can't be that something makes you feel so good without it making you feel bad, too, now and then. It's how life is."

She took that in for a second and came around her desk. She thought she was going to pat his shoulder or touch his hand, but he opened his arms to her and held her against him. She realized she'd been desperate for that hug.

"I think we have work to do," she finally said.

"More and more," he said. He removed his coat, plopped himself down on her sofa, and handed over a thick file. It turned out there was a problem already. He explained why Dickerman was in a heat to get Cass Gianis's fingerprints, but Greenwood County maintained they no longer had his ten-card. Like Cass's blood specimen, the card had been obtained from the Kindle County Police Academy, to which Greenwood returned it after Cass's guilty plea. Those prints in turn had been trashed when the county automated its fingerprint system a decade ago.

"Didn't Greenwood print him again when he was arrested after the indictment?" Evon asked. She was back behind her desk, an inch of plate glass marked with a translucent green rim. Ramparts of paper rose there, with photos of Merrel's kids in nice leather frames in a row on the far corner. Pictures of her other nieces and nephews occupied a shelf in her bookcase, and her awards from the Bureau and a color courtroom sketch of Evon on the stand during one of the Petros trials hung on the walls.

"You'd have thought," Tim told her. "The best anybody can figure is they didn't print him when he came in to surrender on the indictment, because they already had the other ten-card from Kindle County. They'd promised Cass's lawyer, Sandy Stern, it would be a quickie deal, no more than an afternoon and Cass would be out on his own recognizance. They promised to keep looking, but I doubt anybody out there is gonna stay late to do it.

"Anyway," he said, "I've been over by Tooley this morning. He gave me a subpoena for Cass to give fingerprints and whatnot. But I'm gonna have to chase around and find him. Ray Horgan already told Mel he won't accept service on the subpoena. Said Paul just about busted a gut when he heard. Wants his brother left alone, after all Cass has been through. Sandy Stern won't cooperate either. I get the point, but we gotta do what we gotta do."

"Cass is living with Paul, right?"

"That's what the newspapers said. Supposedly he wants to work on opening a charter school for ex-cons. But he's kept a low profile. I talked to Stew Dubinsky and he says he hasn't heard of any reporter seeing hide nor hair of Cass since he came home."

"Maybe he went on vacation," Evon said. "That's what I'd do after twenty-five years inside."

"I hope not. Dickerman's ornery already."

Greenwood County had also produced the color photographs the techs had taken in Dita's bedroom the night of her death. Evon got up from her desk to examine them beside Tim. She had never really developed a taste for crime-scene photos. It wasn't the blood and guts that bothered her. Playing field hockey at a world level, she'd seen more than her share of scalp wounds and teeth flying like popcorn kernels as the result of a misdirected stick. But the pictures always seemed undignified and voyeuristic. Here was someone, like Dita, who'd come to a tragic end, and you were looking at her as an exhibit, a collection of visible trauma, with no sense of the life that had animated her.

Tim on the other hand seemed to confront the photos with sad determination. There was nothing about it he liked either, she suspected, except its importance to the job. As she watched him and the intensity that still gripped him, she recalled a story Collins Mullaney had told her.

'Timmy taught me a lot,' Collins had said. 'I remember, we pulled some floater out of the river near Industrial Pier. Gang thing, and Jesus, what they'd done to this boy. It took a lot to make me sick, but this did. "What're we doing here, Timmy?" I asked. He didn't take one second to answer. "Helping the rest of them be good. Proving to them that this here won't be tolerated. So they know there's reason to mind their p's and q's, and do unto others. Because you and I are out here rounding up the ones who don't. That's what we're doin." That was quite a speech. It never left my mind,' Mullaney had told her.

The shots of Dita's face and neck were revealing. Blood had co-agulated in a thick clump at her crown and rusted the mass of black hair for several inches below. The scalp wound at the back of her head, portrayed in a close-up, was a smile about an inch across, the laceration bloated by the walnut-size hematoma beneath it. It looked like Cass—or Paul—had had one hand over her mouth, gripping damn tight, as he rattled her head back and forth against the headboard. On the right side of her jaw, just at the point where it met her skull—"mandibular condyle" was the term, she believed—there was a faint oblong bruise. And Cass or Paul had given her a solid whack across the left side of her face. Rich with blood, Dita's rosy cheeks had bruised easily and the strafing of an open hand was clear, with three streaks left by the fingers. The low-est of them disappeared into a whorl of color and in a close-up, you could see a tiny break in the skin from which a trickle of blood had browned.

"That's how you knew about the ring, right?" said Evon, point-ing at the bruise on Dita's cheek.

"Those clowns out there in Greenwood, they looked at me like

I was the Wizard of Oz when I told them that. They'd been figuring she'd been punched. Shouldn't be so catty about it. They were smart guys and all, just took a fat paycheck and a quiet life. But clueless totally."

"Tooley and the other lawyers have been telling me we have to prove that Paul owned that ring, by the way. They'd rather not just go by Georgia, especially since we promised her we weren't going to question her again."

Tim nodded, but he was preoccupied by something else. He shuffled through the photos.

"You know," he said, "seeing these, I recall I got into a little something with the police pathologist out there in Greenwood. She was the same as the county sheriff's police, not accustomed to homicides, and a little prickly about it. Wasn't real happy to be getting pointers from an investigator. Looking at all of this, I wanted to say that slap on Dita's cheek came several minutes before she got the wounds on the back of her head. Look here. See the difference in the color of the bruises. Bruising doesn't continue long after death." He flipped between the mark along the jaw, contrasting it with the reddish-purple circle on her cheek. "Look at this, too." He pointed to the photo taken of Dita's left hand. She had long, elegant fingers, admirable even after the purplish pooling of blood at the sides, which occurred postmortem. But that wasn't what had Tim's attention. There was a rusty smear on the left knuckle.

"Tech put a hemastick on that. It was her blood. And there were traces on the left side of her face. So my thought was that Dita wiped off her cheek, when that little cut started in bleeding. But that's the only blood on her hands. She never reached back to touch her scalp wound. Must have passed out before she knew she was bleeding."

"So what was the issue with the pathologist?"

"Seemed to me like Dita was with Cass or whoever for a while.

He smacked her on the cheek, they talked, she wipes that little faint trickle of blood from the cheek, and then he wallops her against the headboard, maybe ten minutes later. Dr. Goren, she agreed that the slap came first. But she wasn't with me about the color of the bruises—said that could have been related to the closeness of the vessels to the skin. And that tiny little cut would have been stanched when the assailant grabbed her."

"The blood on the knuckle?"

"Goren said maybe Dita did reach back to her scalp before losing consciousness, just grazed the area. I say that would have been her right hand. Truth, of course, is it could have happened either way. So we never had a meeting of the minds about the timing. Pathologist thought she gets slapped and is just stunned by that when he grabs her again and pounds her head back."

"Why stunned?"

"Well, there's no sign of a struggle. Didn't even turn her head as he's bouncing it off the furniture—blows are more or less in one place. And look at her right hand. You'd have thought she might have fought back and he would have grabbed it. No bruising at the wrist. Same with the left hand. And there weren't any foreign skin cells under her fingernails. DNA these days might show something different. But we all figured he caught hold of her pretty fast. Strong guy, though. Try grabbing my head to push it back." Evon did. "Not so easy. There's some natural resistance," Tim said, "even if she didn't have time to lift a hand."

"And what was the significance of the timing? What did it mean to you if there was a lapse between the blows?"

"Well, hell, if she's slapped and sits there with the assailant for ten minutes, instead of screaming for help, it's got to be somebody she knew."

"Maybe an intruder held a knife or a gun on her."

"And then beat her to death, instead of using the weapon?"

"A gun makes noise."

"So does breaking a window. More likely someone she knew."

"That all fits Cass, right?"

"Or Paul. Sure. Like I said, Zeus was so hysterical, putting on so much pressure for results, it was hard for anybody to think straight."

His remark reminded Evon of something.

"You said last month that Zeus thought Dita had been killed by his enemies."

"The Greek mob."

"Right, but I didn't understand that."

Tim laughed and sank back into the sofa cushions. This was going to be another one of his stories.

"Around Athens, there's a bunch called the Vasilikoses. Started out running a pretty big protection racket in the twenties. Smart guys. Their motto is 'Not a lot from a little, but a little from a lot.' Twenty-five drachmas a week. Who can depend on the police anyway? Nikos, Zeus's dad, he's here but kind of a wannabe who's got some connection to a lot of these big-time Athens gunslingers. During WW Two, Zeus gets sent as a translator to join the Allied forces in Greece when they arrived in October 1944, once the Germans took a powder. Apparently, Nikos has his son check in with his pals. Zeus was there until May 1946, and he comes home with his pretty young wife, Hermione, whose maiden name is Vasilikos, and baby Hal, who's a year then, and a duffel bag full of cash and booty that the Greek mob wanted out of the country, before the civil war starts and the commies win and take it all away from them."

"Zeus told you this?"

"A little. He didn't need to say much. This was pretty much common knowledge around St. D's."

"And what's with the duffel bag?"

Tim laughed the same way, made merry, like most cops, by the eternal oddities of the way humans behaved.

"Zeus builds his first shopping center in 1947. You know, he's a genius. He figures out Americans want to shop. But where's the do-re-mi come from to get started, he's just some mustered-out soldier boy from Kewahnee?"

"The duffel bag?"

"So they say. So Zeus gets rich, but you know, back in Athens, there's kind of a dispute. Cause nobody there seems to have thought their money was going to be Zeus's bankroll. He's like, 'This is America, you don't hide money under the mattress, besides it worked out.' To Zeus's way of thinking, he got a loan which he paid back with big-time interest, and in Athens they're thinking, 'No, guess we made an investment and we want a piece forever.' And Zeus is like, 'Go jump.' And they're like, 'We'll see.' Hermione's dad, Zeus's protector, he'd kicked the bucket the year before Dita was murdered. So it fits. Even the way Zeus died. You ever hear that story?"

She knew Zeus had died in an accident in Greece. No more than that.

"The Greeks," said Tim, "they're always running back to the homeland, but Zeus, because of the bad blood, he never wants to go. From the day Dita dies, Zeus had this notion to rebury her on Mount Olympus and finally, on the fifth anniversary of her death, Hermione agrees. Some of her Vasilikos relatives come up for the ceremony. And the next morning, Zeus goes out for a walk, to meditate over the grave, and he never returns. They find him five hundred feet down the mountain." Tim shifted his big shoulders. "Around St. D's, there weren't many who didn't think he was shoved."

Evon had never heard a word about Greek gangsters from Hal, even though he often spoke about both of his parents when he had a drink in his office at the end of the day. What did they say? A vast fortune washes away the sins of prior generations. To Hal, Zeus was an Olympian figure, the embodiment of the pure genius of entrepreneurship. Hal probably knew no better, either. Or didn't ask. Tim had already explained it to her.

People believe what they want to believe.

16.

Sofia—February 11, 2008

The same afternoon, Tim drove out to Easton University. It was not forty minutes this time of day, when the traffic was good. Easton was what people thought of when they talked about college, rolling hills and redbrick buildings with classic white gables and Doric columns, the oldest private university in the Midwest. It wasn't all rich types any more. All kinds of parents and their kids—Indian and Vietnamese and Polish, black and brown—had figured out that a school like this was the ticket for life. These young people, all of them, when you got their attention away from their damn cell phones, shared the same alert, confident look, so different from that of the poor kids Tim had encountered when he was on the job. These youngsters met your eye and smiled; they had nothing to fear from grown-ups. Demetra, Tim's middle daughter, was an Easton grad. She'd attended with the benefit of a substantial scholarship, and Tim and Maria had both loved visiting, seeing their child strolling around among all these young people, radiant with their prospects in life.

He found the Alumni House, a small brick building with a white wooden arch over the doorway. He had a cock-and-bull story ready for the woman who greeted him at the reception desk.

"My nephew was at my house and lost his class ring down the drain in the sink. Thought maybe I'd contact the company that sold it to him and see if they could replace it. Any chance somebody here knows the outfit?"

"What class?"

"Seventy-nine."

Even after close to twenty-five years as a PI, Tim still had a hard time with the fibbing, a frequent occupational hazard, since he liked to believe that his whole professional life had been an effort to get at the truth. But when he was carrying a badge, he gave a lot of defendants a line about how much better it would go for them if they just puked up all the ugly details of a murder, when he knew for a stone fact that many of those kids might walk away, if they just shut up. Every job required some white lies now and then to do it right. And he knew how far he could go. He never said anything that would have gotten his wrinkled old ass arrested.

The woman was gone a long time, but came back with the name of a company in Utah. Apparently they'd been doing business with Easton College for half a century.

He then crossed the campus to have a look at the law school's yearbooks. Easton University School of Law was a big gray stone Gothic hunk with a large central courtyard. The dorms, the class-rooms, the law library were all in here. Kids from all over campus came to lounge on the huge lawn in the spring.

The yearbooks, he discovered, were stored in the library. What a gorgeous place that turned out to be, three stories tall, with long oak tables that looked like there should be armored knights surrounding them, and oak wainscoting clear to the ceiling. The bal-cony level was rimmed by a polished brass rail. One of the research librarians retrieved the 1982 volume for Tim without any ques-tion, even though he was prepared with another story about how he wanted to get a photocopy of his nephew to use for his fiftieth-birthday card. The yearbook for 1982 contained two photos of Paul Gianis, a head shot, like the ones for the other 160 graduates, and a group pose of Paul among the members of the law review. Seated with the editors in the front row, Paul had a hand on each thigh. And no dang ring visible, not on either hand. The picture had to have been snapped only months before Dita was killed. The photos of Paul in the 1980 and 1981 volumes were no help either.

There were two computers near the front desk for general use, mostly so kids could check their e-mail, and no password was needed to access a Web browser. Half his work as a PI could be done on the Internet these days, and for a person his age, Tim thought he could handle a computer reasonably well. Nothing fancy. He was way out of his league with cases involving computer security breaches. But he could type a name into a search engine.

There were hundreds of images online of Paul Gianis, most from the last decade. Tim examined them one by one, but whenever Paul's hand was visible, the only ring he wore was his wedding band.

Driving back to town, with the rush hour starting, he called the company that manufactured Easton's class rings.

"Oh dear," said the woman he got on the phone. "We'll have to get the records from the warehouse. And I don't know if we can replace it. Styles change, you know."

"Love to surprise him if I can."

"We'll check."

His last stop was to try to serve Cass with the subpoena Tooley had drafted. Sofia and Paul lived in Grayson, an area at the western edge of the county that had long been home to teachers and cops and firefighters who were forced by residency requirements to remain in the Tri-Cities. It was a neighborhood of tidy three-bedroom houses, one step up from the bungalows of Tim's neighborhood in Kewahnee. On the corners there tended to be larger houses with sloping lawns, usually owned by the doctors and lawyers, bankers and insurance agents who served the locals. The Gianis house was one of the very nicest, built, according to what Tim had read in the *Tribune* archives, near the turn of the nineteenth century by the Morton family who owned the department stores. The newspaper referred to the architectural style as 'Romanesque revival,' ochre brick decorated with lots of concrete festoonery in the shapes of laurels. It had a green tile roof, and copper gutters that had taken on that seafoam patina. There were lights on upstairs but no cars in the driveway. He focused his binoculars on the house for several minutes, but he saw no sign of movement. Both of Paul and Sofia's sons were in college at Easton, according to the papers.

By now, he needed to pee again. There were times he felt the urge the minute he walked out of the john. Going tinkle every ten minutes was just part of being an old guy. Sometimes, he'd study his body with amazement at the damage time had done, all the sagging and the pallor of his flesh, white as a fish belly. There was so much that didn't work any more. Sometimes it seemed to take a minute just to pick up a coin. And his mind often reminded him of a car in which the shifter just couldn't find the gear. But occasionally there were pleasing surprises. Yesterday morning he woke up with a hard-on and considered it like a visitor from another planet. He'd thought he was pretty much dead in that area and felt good about himself for hours afterward.

There were so many retired police officers out this way that the Fraternal Order of Police lodge had bought up the VFW hall several years back, when the veterans' group pretty much went broke. The yeasty odor of spilled beer greeted him as soon as he opened the door. The big hall on the first floor was empty, but he could hear noise above and took the worn stairs.

Up here, there was a long old-fashioned mahogany bar with mirrors behind it. The rest of the room was occupied by a few eight-sided card tables with green felt. It looked like nobody had taken a mop or broom to the pine floor in several years. A crowd of old-timers were around one of the tables, with several onlookers as the players tossed around quarters and cards. Tim wasn't three steps into the room when he heard his name called at volume.

"Jesus Christ, I thought you were dead. I really did." It was Stash Milacki, who had a seat at the table, laughing so hard his face was bright red. Stash had a brother, Sig, who was crooked as a stick and got Stash made detective, but Stash wasn't bad on the job, although he never reached Homicide, which was what everybody wanted.

Tim laughed at the sight of him, but went off to do his business before returning to shake Stash's hand. Stash must have put on fifty pounds since Tim saw him last, and he was no lightweight back then. Now he was an old guy with a red face who had to spread his legs on the barrel chair to make way for his belly.

"Talk to him and don't talk to me," someone said. Tim only now recognized Giles LaFontaine on the other side of the table. With his trim gray moustache, Giles looked twenty years younger than Stash. Tim had shared a beat with Giles when he first was on the street. "So you just another broke old bastard like the rest of us, can't afford to go play golf in Florida?" Giles asked.

"Eh," said Tim. "I been lucky. Still work now and then as a PI."

"Really?" said Stash, like he didn't believe him.

"Do some stuff for ZP, for one," said Tim. It was the only one at the moment, but no point being precise.

"Now what kind of piece of shit is that?" Giles asked. "Those commercials? I had my grandson with me the other day and one of these ads come on, the one with the old girlfriend, and the grandson he's sure it's a joke. 'No,' I tell him, 'this crazy man, Kronon, he really thinks Paul Gianis killed that girl.' That's true, right?"

"That's true."

"I owned the TV station," said Giles, "I wouldn't let him put that shit on the air." Paul lived in this neighborhood for years and people here were proud of his prominence and success. There were a couple of fellas around the table who didn't appear as vehement as Giles, but he wouldn't back down. "The brother done his time, that oughta be the end of it. It's twenty-five years later and now all the sudden this crackpot says Paul was in on it. That doesn't wash, not with me."

"What's the brother up to now?" Tim asked.

Giles shrugged as he peered at his cards. A guy next to him, Italian or Mexican from his looks, said, "Didn't the papers say he wanted to teach ex-cons? Like what he'd been doing inside?"

Another fellow, sitting behind the players, spoke up.

"Bruce Carroll lives right next door to the Gianises. You know him?"

Tim didn't.

"Bruce said he and the missus are home most days and they haven't caught sight of him. Cass. That's the brother, right? He's probably hiding out from the reporters, but they haven't seen him go in or out, except the day he came home from prison."

"Did he leave town?" Tim asked.

The man who'd been speaking just shook his head. "Might be. But if I spent twenty-five years in the can, I'd want to hang out with my family. Paul's his identical twin, isn't he? Close, right? For years, I been reading how Paul and him wrote each other every day."

"Me?" said another man. "Twenty-five years inside? I'd get four girls and a bottle of whiskey and tell them to see how much I could take."

The men around the table all laughed.

For the most part, Tim didn't spend much time with ex-cops. There were three former Homicide dicks he'd played golf with every summer Saturday for at least thirty years, but that had stopped for him when Maria took sick. That proved to be the end of the game, too. Dannaher's back was too bad for him to swing much, and Rosario couldn't see where the ball went. Carter could see fine, but forgot where the ball had landed by the time he left the tee. Leaving aside the golf buddies, Tim's closest pals were all former musicians. Some still played and Tim loved to hear them, but his hands were too stiff for him to do much with a trombone, and his embouchure was gone. Mostly he and his friends listened to music, grunting at the best passages, telling stories of old gigs and good players. His best friend, Tyronius Houston, had moved out to Tucson and begged Tim to visit. There were a couple of others who'd be show-ing up around here again in April, once the weather improved.

Tim used the john again before he departed, then drove back to the Gianises' house and sat across the street. Near six, a car finally pulled into the garage. When the door went up, he caught sight of another vehicle parked inside, a gray Acura. These days, Paul was probably being driven around by his campaign staff. Given the dark-ness at 5:30, when the lights came on in the first floor of the house, Sofia was displayed as clearly as if she were on a stage set. With his binoculars, Tim watched her whisk through the kitchen in her green surgical scrubs. He put his car in gear and pulled into their round driveway.

Sofia Michalis had been one of those kids who stood out from the time she could talk. Maria was friendly at church with Sofia's mom, who, with four older kids already, tended to act like her baby was possessed. Sofie could read, literally, not long after she was up-right, and started school a year early. But unlike some other kids Tim had seen who were isolated by phenomenal intelligence, Sofia always seemed outwardly normal, with huge intense black eyes, al-most like a cartoon character's. She'd been a classmate of Tim's middle daughter, Demetra, and Sofia was one of those little girls you couldn't have in the house too often. She'd play jacks with De and then, if Tim was at home, would stop off in the kitchen to ask him about his latest case. By the age of seven, Sofia was reading the newspaper cover to cover every day. She was preoccupied frequently with questions about the methodology of detection—how did fingerprint powder stick to the ridges? How could you tell for sure what a person reduced to a skeleton had looked like? It was all he could do at times to keep from answering, 'How in the hell do I know?' But then, after mulling over his answers, she would turn back into a kid.

'There aren't any bad people like that around here, right?' she asked him about one of Tim's goriest cases, a serial murderer named Delbert Rooker who'd killed several young women.

'Not a one,' Tim had told her. Even at seven, Sofia, he realized, was too smart to fully believe him.

One of the games Sofia and Demetra played was doctor and nurse, Sofia the doctor, De the nurse and a bevy of dolls as the patients, and darn it, if that wasn't exactly how it had turned out. De had done a PhD in nursing eventually and was chief nursing supervisor at Hutchinson out in Seattle. And Sofia had rocketed through med school and residencies and was now chief of plastic and reconstructive surgery at U Hospital.

Sofia also was one of two or three neighborhood girls who helped them with Kate when she turned sick. Sofia would come over and read to Kate, or babysit for an hour while Maria ran to the grocery at times when Tim's daughters couldn't be there. Sofie wouldn't take any money, not that they didn't need it in her house. You could just never forget a kid like that.

Tim always felt a tinge of parental pride in Sofia's achievements. If you were anywhere in the US but Kindle County, Sofia was probably better known than her husband, after leading teams of reconstructive surgeons to Iraq. Tim had seen her several times on CNN, talking about the horrible toll IEDs were taking both on our soldiers and on many Iraqis. It was a horrible thing about hu-

mans that as much as we had achieved in helping people thrive—in
medicine, and agriculture and technology—we'd so magnified the
malevolent force of a single bad actor. Sofia and her colleagues
helped turn that around miraculously, grafting burns, getting shredded limbs ready for prosthetics and crafting the missing pieces of
faces out of silicone.

Tim rang the bell of the Gianis residence and could hear footfalls
down the stairs. The door swung open and Sofia stood stock-still.
He had no intention of reminding her who he was, but with a brain
like that, she likely forgot no one, and given her profession she
probably could reimagine any face she saw without the wear of time.

"Mr. Brodie?" she asked.

He couldn't keep from smiling. She surged forward to hug him
and held him for several seconds.

"It's so wonderful to see you. Come in, please. Come in."

He shook his head. "Wish I could, sweetie, but I'm here on business."

"Well, come in anyway. How are Demetra and Marina?" Tim's
oldest daughter was a musician who played French horn in the Seattle symphony and taught the horn players at the U. She'd started
out in rock 'n' roll and collected her share of bummy fellas along the
way before finding Richard, a bassoonist. They'd never married—
Richard was against it in principal—but they had two terrific girls,
including Stefanie, who'd ended up moving back here.

One thing you knew for sure about Sofia, even when she was little, was that she wasn't going to have the looks to be Miss America.
But she kept herself nicely, wearing makeup even for the surgical
theater. Her black hair was still shoulder-length, and showed the
smoothing hand of a professional. Her fingernails were bright red.
And you could still swim in those eyes. Her nose remained too
much for her face, but even that was an impressive statement of self-
acceptance, given her line of work.

Tim refused to take off his coat, but he stood under the brass chandelier in the entry and they talked a solid ten minutes about his family and hers. Behind Sofia a baronial central staircase with a beautiful walnut balustrade rose to a window of stained glass on the landing. A dog penned up in the kitchen was barking forlornly and scratching the finish off a door. Sofia knew about Maria—in fact, she tried to remind Tim that she'd been to the wake, but that whole time to Tim had been like getting dragged under a tide, hoping you lasted long enough to get back to the air.

"And you say you're working?" she asked. "I thought you retired ages ago."

"I did. But I work some as a private investigator. Do some things for ZP, I'm afraid."

"Oh dear," Sofia answered. She laughed. "Now I understand why you didn't want to come in."

"Sorry to say it. I've got a subpoena for Cass. Just to get his fingerprints for the present. DNA later, if the judge ever allows it."

"I'm so sorry, Mr. Brodie," she answered, "but that's for the lawyers."

"Well, if you tell me he lives here," he said, "I can just drop this and we can be done with it." He'd drawn the papers out of the pocket of his overcoat.

She smiled with the same warmth but shook her head.

"I can't say anything, Mr. Brodie. I hope you understand."

"Course I do. Here's my card. If you happen to see him, maybe he can give me a call."

"I'll keep the card," she said, "but only so I know where you are."

She asked him for Demetra's current e-mail address before he left.

The next morning, he was outside the house by 5:30 a.m. The garage door went up no later than six. There was only one car now, and Sofia, in scrubs again, got in it. She backed out and zoomed down the street, then jammed on the brakes just as her older gold Lexus went past him. She backed up so she was abreast of him. Her window went down, and he lowered his.

"There's still hot coffee in the house," she said. "Can I get you a cup?"

"You were always too nice," he answered. "I'm fine here. You go put some people back together."

She waved, happy as a schoolgirl, and drove off. He knew for sure Cass was gone.

17.

The Ruling—February 20, 2008

Today is the turning point," Crully told him. It was 9:15 and the morning throng, many transported by earbuds to some electronic wonderland, stomped through the winter streets of Center City.

Mark and he were on the way back from a breakfast with the Fraternal Order of Police Leadership Council. The cops were going to endorse Paul eventually. They had nowhere else to go, but Tonsun Kim, the newly elected union chief, wanted to dance a minuet to the tune of his standard demands. More cops. Bigger raises. Larger pensions. Less oversight. But they liked Paul. As a former PA, he understood what it was like out there, and he reflected a natural affinity for these audiences. He was one of those kids who said from the age of six that he wanted to become a police officer. As a result, they heard him when he preached that street justice only made their jobs harder. If there was less hostility in the black and Latin communities, the police would hear less bullshit and more applause and get more assistance. He loved selling people on win-win approaches.

"With the cops?" he asked in response to Crully's remark.

"No, with the lawsuit." They were walking toward the Temple now. Afterward, he was going to have a long day on the phone, dialing for dollars. Hal's ads had definitely slowed the flow of contributions. At some point, he also had to sneak off to call Beata about meeting him at the apartment tonight.

In the midst of a campaign, when you were like a tin duck in a shooting gallery, vexations were often shelved for a while, as if they were an itch you didn't even feel until you had time to scratch it. But he remembered what was bothering him now that Mark mentioned court. The *Trib* headline this morning read, "Fingerprint Report Clears Gianis." The story detailed Dickerman's findings, which were not supposed to be public until Mo announced them to Judge Lands today. The hard spin on the facts would signal to anybody who knew about this stuff where the report had come from.

"I didn't like the *Trib* headline," he said.

Crully smirked. He thought Paul was posturing. Almost certainly, Crully had leaked the report, in order to produce two days of favorable headlines rather than one. But he'd done it without asking, because he wanted Paul to be able to say, 'I had nothing to do with it.'

"I mean it, Mark. The judge will be pissed."

"The judge is a big boy. He knows it's an election. And you're dodging Scuds from a billionaire crackpot. He knows you have to make news." This was typical Mark, thinking he was an expert, even about an environment where he was actually a novice. Crully was caught up in his own slipstream. "Big public announcement that your prints aren't at the scene," said Crully. "Lands is going to say no DNA. That's the end of the line for Kronon. And just in time."

He asked what "just in time" meant. Crully tried to hold back for a second, then spilled.

"Greenway did some polling for Willie Dixon." Dixon was the strongest black candidate, a city councilman from the North End, smart, but sometimes too strident for his own good. Still, Willie was running a strong campaign on a shoestring, punching way above his weight. There were two other African-Americans on the ballot, including May Waterman, a friend of Paul's from the senate, who was in the race because Paul had told her several months ago that he wouldn't mind at all if she ran. The same paid petition handlers had gathered signatures for both of them, and as Crully had predicted, no one had noticed. "You know there's a guy over there with Willie playing both sides."

In a campaign, there were always staffers who were looking over the hill. The mayor's election would run in two stages, the first trip to the polls April 3, and then another ballot in May between April's two highest finishers, assuming neither of them had reached a majority in April. If Willie didn't make the runoff, some of Dixon's people would want to jump to Paul and they were building their cred with Mark now.

"Anyway," said Crully, "my guy says we're only up six."

Six. He nodded, holding back any panic. Crully was actually making sense. They'd absorbed Hal's onslaught, the fingerprints would clear him, and the lawsuit, without the DNA test looming, would no longer tantalize the press. Today would be a good day.

Lands strode onto the bench with his face rigid. He knew D.B. well enough to see the judge was put out. Lands asked Mo Dickerman, who was seated in the first row of the courtroom, to step forward, and Mo limped up in front of the bench.

"Dr. Dickerman, I've seen your written report. Would you agree that what I read on the front page of the *Tribune* this morning is a fair summary?"

The courtroom filled with laughter, but Du Bois's gray eyes shot toward Ray for just a second. He didn't allow his gaze to drift to Paul, but there was no doubt where D.B. was placing the blame.

It was part of this life that you often took a pasting for stuff you'd never wanted anybody to do.

"It seemed fairly accurate," Mo said. "I could not identify any of the latent prints accumulated in 1982 in Ms. Kronon's bedroom as being from Senator Gianis. There were a few about which I could not reach any conclusion without also seeing Cass Gianis's prints, which I've suggested to both sides they might want to obtain. But the senator was otherwise excluded on any identifiable print from the scene."

There was a little riffle from the spectators and the journalists' row.

"Well," said the judge, "I'm going to place your report in the court file, so it's available to everyone else who may not have seen a copy in advance." Du Bois was laying it on thick.

"Judge, I would just like to say—"

"No need, Mr. Horgan. We all know how this goes. It might be your side, it might be your opponents, it might be someone else whose agenda none of us understands. So I make no assumptions. And even though this was designated as a report to the court, I realize in retrospect that I didn't explicitly advise the parties against premature disclosure. But let me be clear now. There will be a full investigation of any similar incident in the future. Understood?"

At the podium, Ray nodded several times, virtually bowing, his whole stout upper body canting from the waist like a knight's before the throne.

"Judge," said Tooley, "we'll cooperate in any inquiry you want to make right now."

"All right," said Du Bois, ignoring Mel. Like many other people in this courthouse, the judge didn't seem to hold Tooley in high regard. "So the pending matter is Mr. Kronon's request to enforce his subpoenas to obtain the blood standards and the other evidence that remains in the hands of the state police, with the express intention that defendant Kronon can attempt to do DNA identification on the blood and any other genetic evidence from the crime scene. In addition, Mr. Kronon asks me to order Senator Gianis to provide a DNA sample by way of an oral swab."

The judge looked briefly at a folder he had with him, then webbed his hands to address the courtroom.

"I've given this a great deal of thought. We know from Dr. Yavem that the DNA results are very, very likely to be inconclusive. And the fingerprint report of Dr. Dickerman reinforces that estimate. I agree with Mr. Horgan that at some point a chance of success that ends up getting measured in basis points makes a test burdensome and oppressive. But that's not really the problem here. The question I have been wrestling with is whether inconclusive results could be relevant in any way to this proceeding.

"Now, in pondering this, I need to remember that this is Senator Gianis's case. He sued Mr. Kronon, and in this lawsuit, like any other, it's the plaintiff's burden to prove that it's more likely than not that what Mr. Kronon said on several occasions—namely, that Mr. Gianis was involved in the murder of Dita Kronon—is false, and, further, that in saying that, Mr. Kronon acted with reckless disregard for the truth. If we put the standard of proof in mathematical terms, it's Mr. Gianis's burden to prove that as a jury weighs the evidence, 51 percent goes his way.

"It's also important to reflect on the meaning of the results Dr. Yavem might report. Yavem says that there is no better than a one in one hundred chance that he will get a positive result for either twin. Yet Dr. Yavem's inconclusive finding won't be a determination that the DNA present could come from anyone in the world. A result like that would be truly irrelevant. But when Yavem says his test is inconclusive, he is very likely to mean that the DNA might be Senator Gianis's or it might be his twin's. Talking only about that result, he'll be saying it's 50 percent either way."

Sitting at the plaintiff's table, studying Du Bois, he suddenly knew where this was going. He felt the alarm, like sudden nerve damage, rocket to his toes.

"So in trying to prove that 51 percent of the evidence shows Mr. Kronon's accusations are false, by definition a 50 percent chance that the DNA is the senator's *is* relevant. It's an inconclusive result for the plaintiff, because it doesn't further his goal of proving that the accusation was false. But for Mr. Kronon it's quite pertinent to his defense. Because for the defendant to prevail in this lawsuit, a jury need only conclude there is a fifty-fifty chance that what he said was true.

"Now, as a citizen, I will say that I have some strong personal views about the underlying events. But my opinions have no place in this courtroom. I can only follow the law. And following the law carefully, I conclude that the DNA test is relevant to this proceeding. So I will authorize a subpoena to the state police and to the Greenwood County police for any genetic materials they have retained, especially all blood evidence, and I will allow Dr. Yavem to test those materials. And I will order Senator Gianis to produce a DNA specimen by way of oral swab to Dr. Yavem. Mr. Horgan, will you retain your own expert?"

Standing at the podium, Ray seemed unable to move. His suit jacket, buttoned to address the judge, strained over the full contours of his torso, and shock had straightened him up.

"I'm sorry, Your Honor. I'll advise the court shortly, but with no criticism of your ruling intended, I hope you understand that I was not expecting to be crossing this bridge today."

Du Bois nodded. He seemed faintly pleased that he'd been a step ahead of everyone.

The judge said, "I'll give you three days to retain your own expert, and I'll stay production until then. That will be the order of the court. Gentlemen, I'd like to see a full discovery schedule in a week. That will be all."

Du Bois again declared a recess to give the courtroom time to clear. When the judge rose, Lands once again glanced toward the plaintiff's table. In listening, he'd gradually realized that Du Bois was right. If he'd thought about this as precisely as D.B. had, if he hadn't looked at this with the rosy view of a partisan, he would have understood that what he'd realized to start—that the DNA test was a trap that ninety-nine times in a hundred would serve Hal's ends—also dictated the legal and evidentiary conclusion. He stood up and caught the judge's eye and nodded slightly, out of respect.

Crully and Horgan and he went straight across the hall to the attorney room to figure out what Paul was going to say to the media in the rotunda downstairs. There were a few beaten wooden chairs in here and one worn oak desk like the ones his teachers sat behind when he was in grade school.

"Can we appeal?" Crully asked. "I don't like the optics, but I just want to know all the options."

Ray was shaking his head. "Waste of time. We could file a mandamus, but no appellate court will supervise a discovery motion. They'll dismiss our petition out of hand and we'll look worse."

"I think we make the best of it, now," Crully said. "Say there will be no ID of Paul. Say it's a technical ruling. Emphasize the print report. Does that sound right, Chief?"

He had always been the more temperamental twin. His brother smoldered, but he occasionally felt anger fill his veins like lava. He struggled now for self-control. You chose this life, you walked a tightrope with only gumption and a parasol, the chasm chanting its siren song below. But there was no point in daring when the only outcome was bad.

"Nothing is right," he said to Crully. "This whole lawsuit is a fourteen-car collision. I listened to the two of you, and now I'm getting my keister tattooed on a weekly basis."

Horgan muttered, "Paul."

"No," he said. "That sounds like I'm blaming. And I'm not. You both gave me your best advice. And I made the decision. But I've been in enough courtrooms to know once you file, you lose all control. I should have laughed it off and called Hal a right-wing goof."

Ray lifted one shoulder. In retrospect, Paul might be right.

"So what comes next?" he asked Ray. "A dep, right? Hal will depose me for three days."

"We can set limits," said Ray. "Maybe even put it off until the election."

"No, we can't. Because it'll be the same logic as giving fingerprints. Or DNA. I can't hide. I've got to look forthcoming. And they'll want to depose my brother next. They've already got some old dick hunting around for Cass with a subpoena. Maybe they'll want to question Sofia after that."

"They won't get Sofia," said Ray softly. But that was no more than a confession about Cass.

"We're going to dismiss this lawsuit today," he said.

Crully sat back with his nasty little eyes narrowed.

"Fuck that," he said. "I already told you what I'll have to do."

"Frankly, Mark, it's probably time for a change anyway. You've set up a great organization. You're a great field marshal. But you've swung and missed on a couple of big things. Leaking that report was not smart. Du Bois, you know, he'd probably have done the same thing. Probably. But it was the wrong time to piss him off."

Crully simmered without words, but his face against his white shirt was noticeably redder. From down the hall outside echoed the sound of a woman who'd come out of another courtroom wailing. Mark was a veteran of these moments, when a campaign like a tank went over a grenade and the finger-pointing started. He wouldn't comment about the leak and hand Paul the truth, especially in the presence of a witness, because Paul would have that to hold over him forever.

"You'll lose," said Crully instead. That was the ultimate revenge for firing him. "You dismiss, you'll lose."

"It won't be any worse than what's coming next. I've got the print results. I've shown I wasn't there that night. I'm not going to let Hal use the blood to say there's a 50 percent chance I was. That's a lie. Or let him keelhaul my brother. I always promised myself, *always*, that I'd never sacrifice my family for my career. Cass has spent twenty-five years in shitsville and has the right to rebuild his life. And instead, he's getting filled with buckshot five times a week on every channel, and the whole county is talking about a story that should be dead and forgotten. My kids are reading that I'm a murderer—not the usual political horse-hockey, but somebody who supposedly killed a woman with his bare hands. This isn't worth it to me, Mark. If I lose, I lose."

"And let a right-wing nut like Hal Kronon run you off the cliff?" That came from Ray. His sad blue eyes and ruddy face were set to the question, which was a serious one. Ray and he had lived by the same credos, and believed that the people with money didn't get the right to own the democracy, too.

"I didn't say I'd drop out. I said I'm going to dismiss the lawsuit. I'll fight the good fight. I won't give up. And I'll talk about the Big Lie. Because that's what this is. But the lawsuit is over. No DNA or deps or ring-around-the-rosy."

He stood up to show he'd decided.

18.

Objections—February 20, 2008

The morning showed the faintest signs of spring. The temperature was in the mid-twenties, but there were no clouds, a wonderful improvement over the usual low-hanging sky of steel wool. On warmer days when Evon had no meetings outside the office, she walked the twelve blocks to ZP from her condo. In the winter when she didn't need to drive, she most often risked what she privately called "Demolition Derby," otherwise known as the Grant Avenue bus. In the Tri-Cities, the bus operators were a law unto themselves, bullies in the traffic, who veered from the curb to the left turn lane with no concern for other vehicles. The transit unions had insulated the drivers from much responsibility, except in the event of homicide.

As soon as Evon stepped off the bus, a block from ZP, she saw Heather across the street. Her former girlfriend was wearing a head-scarf and Ray-Bans, and was wrapped in an oatmeal-colored wool Burberry coat Evon had bought for her, but Heather had no desire to conceal herself. Evon looked in her direction for a second and then began walking double time. She could hear the click of

Heather's heels on the pavement as she ran to catch up, arriving breathlessly at Evon's side.

"You love me," Heather said. "And I love you. This makes no sense. I'll be better. I promise. I'll make you happy. I'll make you completely happy. Just one more chance, baby, please. Just one."

Evon had actually hoped Heather had given up. There had been no communication in a week. Now Evon never looked up, never slackened her pace as Heather followed along, elbowing aside the pedestrians coming in her direction, elaborating on her soliloquy. She meant all of this, of course, about love and devotion. She knew so little about herself that she actually believed what she was saying.

Evon hated bringing her shit into the office—Heather knew that, too, which was why she'd been so confident she could corner Evon out here. But there was no choice. Evon headed into the ZP Building. Heather not only followed her through the revolving door but managed to squeeze herself into the same sealed quarter compartment. Heather tried to embrace Evon—she seemed intent on a kiss—and in the close confines of the glass panels they had a brief struggle as Evon, much shorter but far stronger, held Heather off. But still the woman pleaded.

"How can you be so heartless? How can you treat me this way? I don't deserve this, Evon. I love you. I was good to you. How can you do this?"

Finally, Evon pushed out of the revolving door, which Heather was trying to obstruct, and burst into the open air of the lobby. She hurried off, but Heather called after her.

"I'm pregnant," Evon heard her say, and wheeled. They had talked about that. At the best moments, lying in each other's arms, they had shared that fantasy.

Evon waited a second to gather herself.

"That's crap."

"I am. I did it for you. Evon, I want to do this. A child needs a family. We can be a family."

That was a frightening thought, really, this bag of loose nuts and bolts that was Heather as somebody's mother, even with Evon to deflect a bit of the damage. But that was not where Evon's heart ran. Her heart ran to the cruelty of this, of probing every soft spot, each of the many festering regrets. This was how cruelty was done, Evon thought, when someone needed something so much that they became indifferent to the pain they were inflicting.

The security guard, Gerald, sat at a desk built of the same taupe granite as the rest of the vast lobby. It was his job to record IDs and issue passes so visitors could move through the turnstiles to the elevators. He was in Evon's department and called her "Boss."

Hurrying forward, Evon hooked a thumb over her shoulder and told Gerald, "Keep her out." She proceeded past him while Gerald, quick off his seat, snagged Heather by the arm.

"Whoa, lady," he said.

Heather called after Evon.

"If I don't hear from you, I'm going to have an abortion on Friday." Her voice was piercing. There couldn't have been a soul in the lobby who missed it.

Upstairs in her office, Evon closed the door and sat alone. She didn't cry, but she was shaking. Fortunately, she had no time for her own agonies, with a conference call beginning in moments. Dykstra had finally agreed to a twenty-five-million-dollar price concession for the Indianapolis brownfield—he blamed underlings for failing to disclose it—and the deal had been announced yesterday in the *Journal*. The closing was scheduled for next week. Evon's call this morning with her counterpart at YourHouse was to discuss how to meld operations. Twelve people ended up on the line and she wasn't done until after 11:30. When she finished, Evon's assistant informed her that Tim Brodie was waiting to see her on an urgent matter.

"I called you," Tim said when he came in, "but you were on the phone, so I figured I better walk over and deliver the news. Paul Gianis just announced he's dismissing the lawsuit." He described Judge Lands's ruling, and Paul's press conference in the Temple rotunda, which ended with a pack of cameras and reporters running after Paul as he exited the courthouse.

A part of her was still recovering from Heather, but even so Evon was astounded.

"Does Hal know?" Evon asked.

Hal had run off with Tooley as soon as court ended to meet with a business reporter to discuss the YourHouse acquisition. About fifteen minutes later, as soon as Hal had returned, she and Tim went down the hall to Hal's sycamore redoubt. Tooley was still with him and neither of them had yet heard the news.

Hal was furious. "How can he do that?"

Tooley explained the law. Until the start of trial, every plaintiff was allowed to dismiss the suit he or she had brought.

"Just like that?" Hal asked. "Doesn't he even have to say I'm sorry?"

"We could ask for costs."

"What are costs?"

"About two, three hundred dollars," said Mel. "Filing fees. Witness fees on the subpoenas."

"I don't want two hundred dollars," Hal said. "I want his DNA. He's hiding something."

"You can certainly say that. Scream it out loud. I'm sure Cia over at the agency can design some great ads that make that point."

"I'm not letting him get away with it."

"With what?" asked Tooley.

"Hiding whatever he's hiding."

"Hal, what could he be hiding if the test is 99 percent likely to be inconclusive? Don't smoke your own dope."

Hal's bulging eyes ran back and forth behind his glasses as he considered his friend's advice.

"I want the DNA."

Mel dropped his glance to his hands, then tried another approach.

"Hal, you won. Don't you see this? You won this motion. You made a convincing case that this guy knows more than he's telling. And Paul said uncle. Accept victory, Hal. Celebrate for a second."

"This isn't a victory," Hal insisted. "I want to know what Paul Gianis had to do with my sister's murder. I want the DNA. You should do something. I'm the client. Those are my orders. Do something."

"Maybe I can think of something after the YourHouse closing."

"No, now," said Hal. "This is even more important than YourHouse. The corporate lawyers can fill in for you."

Tooley and Tim left Hal's office together. Evon stayed behind to brief Hal on her progress with her to-do list for the YourHouse closing.

"Jesus Christ," said Mel, as soon as the door was closed. "Hal's been my friend since we were six years old, but he's never known when enough was enough. I swear to God, in high school, he'd ask the same girl out six times and be surprised every single time she said no."

"The only part I don't get," said Tim, "is that dropping the suit seems sure to do Paul more damage than the test probably will. It's just strange thinking."

"Maybe Paul's like me," Tooley said. "And Hal's made him crazy."

Mel shook his head again and advanced to the elevator.

Du Bois Lands's gray eyes rose from the paper he was holding on the bench. The rest of his body did not move. The judge read aloud:

"Defendant Kronon's Emergency Objection to Plaintiff's Motion for Voluntary Nonsuit."

It was the morning following Lands's ruling, February 21.

"Yes," replied Tooley from the podium. Ray Horgan was beside him, elbow to elbow with Mel. From behind, both men seemed to have the solid, indifferent mass of cattle. In the rows to the rear of Tim, the courtroom was full, although not with the same swarm of spectators that the lawsuit had been drawing. Everybody here today was in a gray or blue suit. They had to be lawyers.

"Explain," said the judge to Tooley.

"Your Honor, Mr. Kronon is objecting to Senator Gianis's efforts to avoid taking this critical DNA test. We think the Court should hold his motion to dismiss in abeyance, until he has provided DNA and the test has been performed as the Court ordered. He's trying to thwart your ruling."

Horgan started to bluster, but the judge calmed him by raising a hand.

"Mr. Tooley, Senator Gianis is doing what the law allows, isn't he?"

"He's hiding something," said Tooley. Tim saw Hal pump his fist beneath the counsel table from which he was watching eagerly.

"That's your interpretation. There are other interpretations as well. I don't care about interpretations. I'm just the umpire. I'm calling balls and strikes. The law is the law, Mr. Tooley. If you have a problem with the senator's motion to nonsuit this case, take it up with the legislature. Your objection is going to be denied."

"Well, Your Honor, before you rule, we're also seeking alternative relief."

"Which is?"

"We would like enforcement of the subpoenas which were stayed pending your ruling on the DNA motion. Once you ruled, those subpoenas became enforceable and we'd like the evidence produced."

This time Horgan succeeded in butting in.

"Judge, that's ridiculous. If there's no lawsuit, there are no subpoenas."

The judge took a second.

"No," he said in reply to Horgan. "I get what he's arguing. It's timing. The subpoenas were enforceable before your motion for dismissal. What evidence are we talking about?"

Tooley had a list. First, there was the subpoena to Paul to produce a DNA specimen; second, to Cass to produce fingerprints; third, to the state police to produce all physical evidence in their possession, most of which had been collected at the crime scene, including the blood spatters by the French door and the blood standards taken from various people. There was a similar subpoena to Greenwood County, in case anything had been missed in the production they'd already made.

Ray interjected. "Judge, they're just trying to do the same test on their own."

Du Bois cracked the slightest smile at the caginess of the ploy.

"Again, Mr. Horgan. It's just balls and strikes to me. What does the law require? All I want to do is answer that question. That's why I get the big bucks." In a world where some of the lawyers who appeared before the bench made multiple millions, judges frequently offered ironic remarks about their salaries, which seemed picayune by comparison.

Du Bois sat a second longer as he pondered.

"OK, here's what's going to happen. We're going to finish up this lawsuit. But not today. If you gentlemen look behind you, you will see that there's a courtroom full of lawyers here for my Thursday motion call. And many of those attorneys have clients who are paying them to sit here. So we're not wasting any more of other people's time or money. We're going to set this over for a week. I want all of the addressees of those subpoenas, or their representatives, in court, with the evidence Mr. Kronon is seeking. And I want simultaneous briefs from plaintiff and defendant on the issue of whether those subpoenas can be enforced as a matter of law. And we'll thrash all of that out next Thursday. If the subpoenas, any of them, remain valid, the evidence will be handed over right here. And then, Mr. Tooley and Mr. Horgan, much as I have enjoyed visiting with both of you, we are all going to be done with this lawsuit, and I will look forward to seeing you both on other occasions."

The judge banged his gavel and told his clerk to call the next case.

19.

Her Ring—February 22, 2008

Shirley Wilhite," said the voice on Tim's cell phone, the next morning. "Bet you thought I forgot about you." It was about 11 a.m., and Tim was settled in the sun-room, reading more of his book on the Greek myths, while Kai Winding tooted along from the phonograph. His first thought was that Shirley had to be another widow—they phoned all the time with every imaginable angle, anything from a casserole too delicious not to share or women who claimed they were returning *his* call. "They took forever getting those records from storage. Everybody thinks they have too much to do. That's what's wrong with this country, if you ask me."

He talked to her another second, feeling, as he often did, that he was playing from behind. Then it came to him: She was from the ring company in Utah.

"Lucky we were still using paper back then," said Shirley Wilhite. "Five years later, we had everything on floppy disks. Remember them? Try finding somebody who can make sense of those things. Easton College, right? What was your nephew's name?"

"Gianis." He spelled it. In Utah, Paul's name meant nothing. "Not really my nephew, by the way. I just call him that."

"Oh sure. I'm Auntie Shirley to half my neighbors' kids."

"Exactly."

"OK." She took a second. "We got two of them."

"Twin boys. I'm looking for Paul."

"OK. All right, well, he bought two rings."

"Two?"

"Let me look here. Yeah. One a man's, one a woman's. Same model. The J46 with emblem. Now I need the catalog." He heard her clattering around. "No, we don't make it any more. I think the K106 might look the most like it. I'm going to send you pictures. You use a computer?"

"Some."

"Well, the current catalog is online. But I'll send you copies of the old catalog, so you know what he had. Got a fax number?"

"Can you give me pictures of the woman's ring, also? Maybe he'll want to replace both. And if it's not too much trouble, send the order form, too. Maybe he'll want to make a claim for insurance."

"Not a problem. Happy to help."

Two rings? He considered that. Late in the afternoon, he was on his way into Center City to pick up the faxes, which he'd directed to ZP. He passed Georgia Lazopoulos's house and on impulse parked and rang the bell.

She stared at him through the storm door. Her dark raccoony eyes and the rest of her heavy face instantly took on a glum reproachful weight.

"You said you wouldn't bother me again." Her voice was muffled by the glass, but clear. She was dressed as she had been when they'd been here last time, in pink stretch pants and a dowdy ruffled top.

"I just need to ask you one question about that class ring Paul wore."

"Paul didn't wear a class ring," she answered, and closed the door.

She had been a sweet-natured young woman, at least as much as Tim had seen of her. It was a wonder sometimes what life did to people. He started down the stoop, then reconsidered, and climbed back up and rang again. Nothing to lose.

"You told us he wore a class ring," he said, as soon as the door opened.

"No, I didn't. And frankly I wish I hadn't told you anything. You made a fool out of me, you and that woman who was with you. There isn't a person around here that doesn't think I was crazy to let you make that tape. I sound like a vengeful old witch."

"I don't think that's fair," said Tim, "not to us. Or to you for that matter."

"Everybody's mad at me. They think I went out of my way to do Paul dirty. Even Cass showed up here to give me a piece of his mind."

"Cass did?" It was the first Tim had heard of anybody seeing Cass since the day he'd left prison. "When did that happen?"

"Oh, I don't know. A few days after the ad went on television. He wanted me to talk to their lawyers, and I said I wasn't making that mistake twice. He just stood where you're standing and said, 'There's nothing for him to say, Georgia, except that he's sorry you're still so hurt.' He made me feel this small." Her hand came up for a second.

"But he didn't say anything on that commercial was untrue, did he?"

She didn't answer, but brooded. Her fingers had never left the knob to her front door and now she started to close it again.

"Wait," said Tim. "I don't understand about the ring." He was afraid the confrontation with Cass had turned her around. She would disavow everything she'd told them before. "I know he bought one."

"That's what you asked me—did Paul buy a ring like Cass? And I said he did."

"Seems he bought two, actually. I thought he must have given you the other one, because the second was for a woman."

"No, that was Lidia's. She'd always sworn her sons were going to be educated, even though there wasn't anybody in her family or Mickey's who'd been to college. She never made any secret that she wished she'd gone. So the twins thought it would be sweet to get her a class ring. They knew their mom. I think Lidia showed the damn thing to every person she met for the next ten years."

Georgia, of course, hadn't gone to college either. Tim couldn't guess if it was Lidia, always a strong personality, or the ring that spurred her bitterness.

"And Paul wore the other one, right?"

She looked through the door with a purely hateful expression for one moment and then turned away without a word, leaving Tim on the cold concrete. He more or less thought he was expected to go, but she'd left the front door open, and so he waited in the freezing air, hoping she might return—which she finally did. When she arrived, she snatched the storm door open and reached out to drop something in his palm. It was the ring. There was a large red stone in the center, with the numbers 19 and 79 raised from the embossed design on either side.

"See? You can have that for all I care. Paul gave it to me when he graduated. I wore it around my neck on a chain. Remember when girls used to do that? It wasn't the ring I wanted, but it was a step in the right direction, I thought. Stupid me."

"So he didn't have the ring when Dita was killed?"

"Jesus, Tim. Are you listening? I had the ring. I was wearing it. I wore it most places and I sure as hell was going to wear it to the church picnic with all those other girls sniffing around Paul. As far as I know, Paul has never had that ring on his hand in his entire life. He didn't like rings or jewelry. He thought that kind of stuff wasn't for guys. I could barely get him to wear a watch."

Tim looked down at the ring, then back at Georgia, whose face had darkened again. She heaved a great sigh and opened the storm door once more, but only briefly enough to snatch the ring back. With that, she wheeled and slammed the door behind her.

"No ring," said Evon. They sat in her office. She had one shoe on a trash can as a footrest. "Didn't she tell us Paul wore a ring?"

He told her Georgia's version and she nodded. "She's right. She said Paul bought a ring like Cass. But you'd have thought she would have told us what became of it."

Tim looked askance at her. No woman he knew was going to volunteer that a fella had kept her on the string three more years with a class ring instead of a diamond. Evon got his point.

"Besides," Tim said, "she probably didn't understand the significance. As loose as that investigation was, I don't think there was much in the papers about Dita's bruise pattern or what it meant."

"So Paul didn't wear a ring, and Cass did," Evon said by way of recapitulation.

"Right. So it appears."

"And Paul's fingerprints aren't there, and Cass's are."

"Right."

"I think the boss may want to think twice about opposing Paul's motion to dismiss the lawsuit."

"Maybe. There is one other thing." He'd been sitting on what Dickerman had told him about Cass's print card from Hillcrest not matching the lifts from the crime scene. Tim had given Mo his word not to repeat that, but by now Dickerman had had the time to reconcile the discrepancy and Tim had heard no more about it.

Nonetheless, at the outset, he warned Evon that Mo sometimes viewed things in his own way.

"There's a story about Mo, not sure it's true, but somebody's sister swears she saw it happen. You know the light-rail, how you buy a ticket, purple inbound, white outbound? So Mo is headed out to the airport and he gets on with his white ticket and sticks it in the little ticket holder on the back of the seat in front of him. And he sees everybody else has got a purple ticket, and he actually turns to the lady beside him and says, 'Look at all these idiots on the wrong train.'"

Evon laughed hard. "That can't be true," she said.

"You get the point." He explained what Mo had concluded from looking at the photocopy of Cass's prints at Hillcrest.

"That can't be true either," she said. "How could it? He said in court that Paul doesn't match any of the lifts from the scene. So what is he saying now? Neither of them were there?"

Tim shrugged. He had absolutely no answer.

"We never got Cass's fingerprints, did we?"

"Never came close. That's another weird thing. Supposedly even the neighbors don't see hide nor hair of Cass, but Georgia told me he came right to her door to read her out for making that commercial."

"So he's not on vacation?"

"Apparently not."

Eventually, Tim asked how she was doing in her personal life, and she answered with a bitter little smile.

"I spent most of last night researching how to get an order of protection."

He groaned.

"It'll be a long time before I go down this road again, Tim. I can't stand the disappointment." She smiled ruefully and asked him, "What does Shakespeare have to say about that?"

He didn't answer but started rummaging in the inner and outer pockets of his sport coat. Finally, he found what he was looking for folded in fourths in his wallet and held it out.

"Are you kidding?" she asked.

"Read it. That's from *Comedy of Errors*."

It was another scrap of ruled paper with a quotation written out in block letters, about being a drop of water in the ocean, looking for another drop.

"Now what does this mean?" she asked, after she'd read it over several times. When she handed the scrap back, Tim studied it again.

"I'm not so sure," said Tim. "Except everybody finds all this confusing at times. And disappointing. But there's an ocean out there. You shouldn't stop. Not at your age. If Maria had died when I was fifty, I'd have thought, 'I'm too young to be alone.'"

"But not now? You know what they say, Tim. A man your age who can still drive can get the former Miss Universe." He laughed about that, even though it was a tender spot. He couldn't see much at night any more and tried to avoid driving after dark. Pretty soon, his sight wouldn't be adequate for daylight, either. That meant he'd have to go to Seattle. One of his daughters or the other begged him at least once a week to make the move. But he wasn't ready for that. Not yet. He wasn't ready to leave his house, and his things, and the life he'd had with Maria.

"Not now. No appetite for it. I have my folks to love. Daughters and the grandkids, and the ones I still hold in my heart, Maria and Kate. They're all precious to me, each of them, they taught me who I am. But at this age, you're just holding on to that, enjoying it. But fifty? I'd say, 'I can do this again, learn more, change more, love more.' I really would."

She looked up at him from her desk, still not sold. When he reached the door, he turned back.

"You can't tell anybody that stuff about Dickerman. That's simply on the QT."

"They call it the DL these days, Tim," she said, smiling. "And that's too goofy to repeat to anybody. Did you ever talk to Dickerman after he analyzed Paul's prints?"

"Tried, but I haven't caught up with him." Mo had been on the West Coast lecturing at several police academies, and then, believe it or not, in Hollywood, where he was a consultant for a TV show. Now that forensic science was hot stuff on television, you could barely hit the clicker without seeing Mo poking his heavy black-framed glasses back up on his nose on one true-crime show or another.

"Circle back when you can," Evon said. "Just so we can cross that one off the list."

He wished her a good weekend, which was meant in jest. She'd be here both days doing compliance stuff for the YourHouse deal, which would finally close on Monday.

20.

Win or Lose—February 28, 2008

The final proceedings in *Gianis v. Kronon* had drawn a herd of spectators and the well of the courtroom was also crowded. Horgan had been accompanied by two associates, and Hal's big law firm had sent three lawyers to sit by Mel. There was an assistant attorney general, an Indian woman who headed the appellate division, along with two troopers from the state police, one of whom was carrying a steel box, which presumably contained some of the blood. Two deputy PAs had come in from Greenwood County, and Sandy Stern had shown up, too, to represent Cass. The only person not present who might have been expected was Paul Gianis, who, as he had last week, was skipping the session, in accord with his position that the lawsuit was over. His absence also prevented him from being forced to give a DNA specimen on the spot, if the judge ruled he was required to do that.

The spectators' pews were almost completely full. Evon sat with Tim in the front row, along with reporters and sketch artists. When the case was called, all the lawyers gathered in front of the bench, looking a little like an a capella group ready to perform. Each gave his or her name. Sandy Stern said he was making "a special appearance."

"It's always special when you're here, Mr. Stern," said Judge Lands, who seemed positively lighthearted knowing that he was about to escape this bramblebush of a case. "Any problem with Mr. Stern's appearance, Mr. Tooley? He's telling us that he's going to speak for Mr. Cass Gianis, but won't accept your subpoena if I rule against him."

Mel argued halfheartedly that Stern was trying to have it both ways, which was exactly what the law allowed, and the judge overruled him.

"OK, let's find out what we're fighting over," said the judge. "Ms. Desai, tell us if you would, please, what evidence the state police have in their possession."

It was mostly blood—the spatters from the window, the blood specimens that had been taken from the members of the Kronon family at the time, and Cass Gianis's blood, which had been obtained from the Kindle County Police Force fortuitously, because Cass had done a draw for a drug test in preparation for entering the academy. The state cops had retained plaster castings of the shoe-prints in the flower bed, and the tire prints collected down the hill from the house, and glass shards from the broken French door, which had been maintained in order to compare the refractive index of any traces of glass recovered from the clothes or other effects of an eventual suspect. Finally, the state police also had sealed envelopes containing evidence collected from the person of Dita Kronon: fingernail clippings that the techs had taken from Dita after her death, and six different hairs that had been gathered off her body, as well as several fibers, all of which proved to have been from her clothes. Even in 1982, when crime-scene forensics was in the middle ages compared to now, the lab had been able to say that

there wasn't a concentration of foreign skin cells under Dita's fingernails, which tended to show she hadn't fought off her assailant,
and thus presumably knew him. As for the hairs, at the time of the
guilty plea, two were said to resemble Cass's, but DNA testing over
the last twenty-five years had shown that the supposed science of
hair comparison was no more valid than detecting character from
the bumps on somebody's skull, which had passed as courtroom evidence in the nineteenth century.

The Greenwood County PAs spoke up next. They said they'd
produced everything already, except they'd finally found Cass
Gianis's ten-card, which they'd sent to Dr. Dickerman on Friday in
compliance with Judge Lands's prior orders. The need to account
to the judge for the missing prints, with reporters present, had
clearly inspired a more thorough search than the clerk's office and
the sheriff had bothered with previously.

"All right," said Judge Lands, "I'm going to hear from the attorneys. Who would like to address the present motion?" The two
prosecutors' offices both said they had no position. Tooley, the pro-
ponent of the motion, was allowed to argue first. He was brief. It
was all chronology, Mel said. The subpoenas were validly served.
Their enforcement had been stayed pending the ruling on the DNA
motion. The motion was allowed and thus production of the evidence was called for at once. Whether the case was over or not, Hal
was entitled to get what he'd subpoenaed.

"That's preposterous," said Horgan when it was his turn to talk.
"The case is over with the motion for nonsuit, which the court
must allow. The force of the subpoenas ends with the dismissal."
Ray mentioned several cases that said that, and then talked about
Paul, who he said was being harassed by Hal. Stern added similar
thoughts, and said that after twenty-five years in prison Cass was entitled to be left alone. As usual, Judge Lands looked thoughtfully
at all of the lawyers as they addressed him, even though he un-

doubtedly would have known what each was going to say if they'd reduced their presentations to pantomime.

"All right," he said, once Tooley had finished a brief rebuttal, "this has been an interesting exercise, although my wife would probably tell you it shows what's wrong with me, that I enjoyed passing a Sunday afternoon thinking about the essential nature of a subpoena." Everyone in the courtroom was chuckling. Judge Lands was rarely this expansive.

"To state what we all know, a subpoena is a command from the court to produce evidence for the purpose of a lawsuit. In that sense, Mr. Tooley, the evidence gathered doesn't belong to the party who requested it. Legal title to that property belongs to who-ever produced it in the first place to the court, or, in a case like this, to law-enforcement authorities. The court—or the police—borrows that material, as it were, for the purpose of the proceeding. When that case is final and fully exhausted, the parties to the suit have no further right to the property in question, unless it happened to have been theirs in the first place.

"Now, I have made it clear that Senator Gianis is going to get to exercise his right to end this lawsuit today. But there are a cou-ple of preliminary questions in deciding the fate of these subpoenas. The first is whether the evidence ought to be preserved for the sake of any other legal proceeding. Let me direct a question to the representatives of the prosecuting attorney's office from Greenwood County and the attorney general." Both women rose. "Are there any pending investigations in your office related to this crime?" The judge was asking delicately if either office had reopened the investi-gation of Dita's murder to consider Paul's role.

"None," said the assistant AG. The attorney general of the state, Muriel Wynn, was an old friend of Paul's and a strong political supporter. She'd been unequivocal when the press had asked about Hal's suit, referring to it as 'drivel.'

"None at this time," said the PA from Greenwood, being a tad more lawyerly. They were Republicans out there, but they would not be naturally attracted to thinking they'd missed something a quarter of a century ago. Prosecutors, like everybody else, liked to believe they'd done a good job to start.

On the square bench, which reminded Evon of the boxy sedans of the 1950s, Judge Lands made notes. He had the full attention of the big room, which had been rendered silent because no one seemed to understand exactly what he was thinking.

"Next question. Is either of Mr. Kronon's parents still alive?"

Tooley's mouth fell ajar before he answered no.

"And who was the residual heir to their personal property, after satisfaction of specific bequests?" asked Judge Lands.

Mel, a criminal lawyer and litigator by training, looked as stunned by this detour into probate law as he would have if the judge had propounded questions about the chemical composition of distant stars. He finally turned to Hal, who stood up at counsel table and tried to close his suit coat as he'd watched the lawyers do. It didn't quite fit that way and so he ended up holding it closed with one hand.

"Me," said Hal.

"No other living children?"

"No, sir."

"And if you know, Mr. Kronon, who was your sister's heir? Was that you, too, or your parents?"

"No, my dad had set up trusts, usual estate planning stuff. Everything of Dita's became mine."

Lands again scribbled notes.

"Fine then, I'm prepared to rule. All of Mr. Kronon's subpoenas may be enforced, but only to the extent they pertain to evidence originally obtained within the four walls or grounds of Zeus Kronon's house. That would include evidence taken from the body of the decedent, Dita Kronon. I have reached this conclusion because the law is very clear that even today Mr. Kronon would have the right to appear in the original criminal case against Cass Gianis in Greenwood County and make a motion requiring all this property to be returned to him. As a result, I've determined that I will not be abusing my discretion by ordering that property turned over to him now.

"But that, Mr. Tooley, is as far as you may go. The subpoenas directed to both of the Misters Gianis are quashed. No DNA, no more fingerprints."

"What about the fingerprint card Greenwood County just sent to Dr. Dickerman?" asked Mel. "Can we have that?"

"Nope," said the judge. "I was about to get to that. The fingerprint lifts from the house are encompassed by my ruling, and Dr. Dickerman should turn those over to Mr. Kronon. The fingerprints Senator Gianis gave for purpose of this lawsuit belong to him and should be returned forthwith. The fingerprint card of Cass Gianis belongs to Greenwood County, since the county is allowed by law to maintain a database of fingerprints for future criminal investigations. Cass Gianis's blood will be returned to him, after proper notice to Kindle County, which is the only prosecutor's office for fifty miles with no legal representative here at the moment."

Everybody in the courtroom howled at the small joke. Evon had noticed long ago that any effort at humor somehow seemed side-splitting when it came from the bench.

"And with that, Mr. Horgan, Senator Gianis's motion for voluntary nonsuit is granted and this case is dismissed. Good day, all of you, and thank you for your presence."

The judge left the bench.

Tooley motioned Tim to come forward to receive the evidence the judge had just ruled belonged to Hal. Tim signed the receipts and marked the envelopes and containers with his initials and the date and time. Sandy Stern had caught sight of Tim doing this and stepped over to pay his respects.

"This was the finest detective any of us ever saw," Stern told Evon, who'd come forward with Tim to help him keep everything straight. She still wasn't convinced Stern knew who she was.

"So I've heard."

"That's why old folks hang on," Tim told them both. "To hear all those compliments they didn't deserve in the first place."

All three were still laughing when Mel Tooley approached Stern and took him by the elbow.

"What the hell was that?" Mel asked.

Stern smiled in his serene, enigmatic fashion.

"Well," said Stern, "the judge is supposed to be the smartest person in the room. It's satisfying when it actually happens, no?"

Tooley did not appear convinced.

For once Mel had no trouble convincing Hal not to speak to the press, since he appeared, just like Evon, utterly befuddled. Along with Hal, Tim and Mel and Evon squeezed into Hal's Bentley to go back to ZP. Tim kept all the evidence in his lap. He wasn't sure if he was supposed to take it to Dr. Yavem or not.

"Did we just win or did we just lose?" Hal asked as soon as Delman, the driver, closed the door, which shut with the padded sound of a jewelry case.

"You just watched the baby get divided," said Mel. He clearly lacked Stern's appreciation for the judge's performance.

"I think we may be OK," Evon said. She'd been thinking about all of this for some minutes.

"Really?" Hal was eager for any good news.

"The idea was to do the DNA testing, right? We have the blood evidence from the house, right, from the French door? That's clearly the murderer's."

"But we don't have the DNA from either brother," Mel said.

"We got the fingerprint lifts from the house. Lots of them were identified as Cass's. You can extract DNA from old fingerprints."

"You can?" Hal was delighted to hear it.

"It's not for sure," Evon said, "but we can try. I mean, Yavem can. I know it's been done. It only takes a speck. With that many prints, he's bound to get something."

"What about Paul?" Mel asked. "Dickerman has to give back his fingerprints."

"You can get DNA off the bone from a chicken wing somebody ate. Or a cigarette they smoked. If Tim follows Paul around for a couple of days, I'll bet he can pick up something."

"Great," said Tim, who'd said nothing to this point. "Paul knows who I am. Our paths have been crossing since Cass and him went to grade school with Demetra. And he's seen me in court. They'll throw my butt out wherever I turn up."

"Maybe not," Evon said. "You're the one who's always telling me old men are invisible. And if they throw you out, you just refer the assignment to a buddy you trust who works as a PI. You must know a hundred old codgers who'd be good."

Tim didn't smile, but Hal said, "Fabulous." Even Tooley had brightened a little, less chagrined by having been so far outflanked by the judge.

Tim drove the evidence to Yavem's lab, then returned to the cubicle he'd been given at ZP to use the computer to study Paul's daily calendar, posted on his campaign website. Gianis's schedule seemed superhuman, when you remembered that he had stiff legislative duties and still kept a law office. He was shaking hands at bus stops and train stations during the morning and afternoon rushes. He attended fund-raisers at breakfast, lunch and the cocktail hour, and convened press events several times a week, at which he announced policy initiatives. There was one at a fire station today, where he was going to discuss his proposal for the future of the department, a tender subject, since over the last thirty years better building techniques had made as many as a third of the firefighters here and elsewhere in the country redundant. In the evenings and weekends, Paul tended to do town hall meetings in community centers or local places of worship. Out of curiosity, Tim had compared Paul's schedule to that of his top three opponents, none of whom appeared to be exhausting themselves the same way. It just made you wonder what could possibly be worth it. And there wouldn't be any letup if Paul got to city hall. That wasn't a 9-to-5 job either.

That night Tim attended Paul's town hall at the JCC in Center City. Gianis drew a small crowd, no more than seventy-five people, but he looked enthusiastic as he charged up the stairs to the stage in the center's auditorium. He was wearing a camel hair sport coat but no tie and began by speaking on his own under the lights for about fifteen minutes. Paul was charming and relaxed as he talked about his campaign's three s's—schools, safety, stability, meaning stable finances—and growing up here in Kindle County. He'd worked every day in Mickey's grocery until he started college. He told funny stories about putting price stickers on canned goods, from the time Cass and he were five years old.

"In my family," Paul said, "the invention of the bar code was a bigger deal than landing on the moon."

As soon as he turned to the audience for questions, there were several about dismissing his lawsuit against Hal. Occasionally, as he was pondering his answers, he removed his heavy glasses to rub the purple bump on his nose.

"To be blunt," he said about the lawsuit, "we made a mistake. I was upset that someone was saying these kinds of things about me, and I wanted to take a stand. But at a certain point, when people become obsessed you have to accept that they're not rational. They're going to believe what they want to, no matter what you do."

The explanations seemed to go down well with most of the small crowd. An old fellow in a flannel shirt stood up then and gave a long tirade about bullies like Kronon, swinging their billions like truncheons. If rich people could spend without limit trying to decide elections, we were basically back to where we started, when the only voters were white men with property. The audience applauded. Eventually the questions turned to school funding and the quality of lunches.

Midway through the evening, Paul opened a bottle of water that had been left on the podium and drank deeply. Tim kept his eye on it after that.

When Paul left the stage, Tim was at the back of the line of five or six people waiting to speak to the candidate personally. Standing on the last stair, Paul took a long draught from the water bottle and emptied it while he was conversing with an elderly woman who had a pointed question about the crumbling county hospital. Up close, Paul looked tired, with ashy marks under his eyes that seemed to have appeared since Tim had last seen him in court.

During his years as a PI, Tim had collected a set of disguises he used on prolonged follows—silly wigs, secondhand work jumpsuits, even a couple of dresses he wore in desperate moments. It was impressive, really, how unsuspecting people were in general. For this event, he'd stayed simple, shedding his old topcoat in favor of a parka. He put on the glasses he wore to drive at night, and got another stocking cap that he tugged all the way down and kept on all evening. Now, Tim stepped up and reached for the bottle after Paul screwed the top back on.

"I'll take care of that for you, Senator."

Gianis handed it over, careful to say thank you, before turning to the next person in line. Moving off with the water bottle, Tim thought he could feel Paul do a double take, but Tim feigned dropping the plastic container in a trash bin, and pushed it up the sleeve of his parka while he had his hand in the can. He sealed the bottle in a plastic bag as soon as he got to his car and took it over to Dr. Yavem's office first thing in the morning. The doctor's young colleague told Tim that they expected the DNA results to be back in three weeks.

21.

Name Day—February 29, 2008

February 29, Cass's name day—not the make-do event they normally observed on March 1 when they were young, but his real name day, the birth date of St. Kassianos, which rolled around once every four years. In the last month, there had been far more tension with Cass than Paul had ever anticipated, and hoping to smooth things over, he'd planned a grand celebration. It would be the first name day party for Cass in twenty-five years, an open house for relatives and neighbors so they could get acquainted again. Then Tim Brodie had started sneaking around with that subpoena, like a cat after a bird, and the party had to be scotched. Sofia called the guests and blamed the cancellation on campaign emergencies. Even now, when the lawsuit had been dismissed, it seemed to make more sense for Cass to lie low. There was no telling exactly what Kronon was going to attempt next, but he was virtually guaranteed to try to drag Cass into it.

So their celebration had ended up decidedly more restrained. Earlier in the day, the twins went to St. Basil's Home to see their mother, then continued separately to a round of evening campaign events. Back here at 9, they carried in from Athenian

House, and were joined by a few guests. Sofia and Paul's sons, Michael and Stephanos—Steve to everyone—had driven in from Easton to congratulate their uncle, but stayed only briefly. Both boys still seemed nonplussed by the sight of the twins together. Beata Wisniewski had come for dinner, but left immediately afterwards, with a 6 a.m. flight to visit her mother in Tucson.

Beata had first come into their lives in 1981 as Cass's girlfriend, his passion before Dita. A big gorgeous blonde, nearly six feet tall, Beata was an eighteen-year-old cadet in the police academy who had encouraged Cass to apply, too. But even before Cass was accepted, they had flamed out. Beata fell for one of her training officers, Ollie Ferguson, whom she married almost immediately. Cass, more disappointed than heartbroken, had gotten involved with Dita several months later. As it happened, neither choice of partners had worked out particularly well for either of them. These days, Beata sold real estate, mostly commercial, but she'd found them this apartment overnight when they'd realized that Tim Brodie was on Cass's trail. She had even placed the lease in her name. She, too, seemed uncomfortable with the new order of things, of being with the family with secrets to keep, and looked relieved to depart.

Now Cass sat beside Sofia, across from Paul at the round dining table that had come with the furnished apartment. Sofia had stayed up all night, baking baklava, loukoumades and diples, and the vinylized mahogany veneer was dusted with flakes of phyllo and a scatter of crushed walnuts that had fallen off the pastries as they were consumed. A small pyramid of opened store boxes, Cass's presents, was at the far end.

The apartment was, in a way, a cheery place. The living space faced the river and had good early light through the broad windows. The floor plan was open, without walls between the kitchen, dining room and living area. There were two small bedrooms behind the west wall. Sofia had brought lots of family photos so the feel was less sterile. But it still was basically a hideout. Cass usually came and went in disguise, and Paul had to be careful to coordinate his arrivals so they were not seen together.

Following Beata's departure, Cass removed the blue cashmere sweater she'd bought him, so that the twins were again dressed identically. Looking across the table, Paul felt almost as if they'd retreated to being six-year-olds in the same sailor suit. Each wore a white broadcloth shirt and the pants from one of the blue 140-weight suits Paul's tailor had made. The same Easton rep tie was in the pocket of each man's jacket, hanging on the back of his chair. The only real difference was that for the evening, Cass had shed the black glasses. He rubbed the bridge of his nose and, with the celebrating over, reached into his suit pocket and tossed down the new nasal prosthetic Sofia had had crafted at the end of January. The little knot of silicone resembled the bent joint in somebody's finger, leaving aside the transparent wings meant to make the piece blend into Cass's skin. The coloration was so precise it looked as if Cass had dumped a living thing on the table. He could pass easily without makeup, but especially with the heavy powder they both wore every day for the cameras, the prosthetic was indetectable.

"This thing is still killing me," he said. He'd removed his glasses apparently because of how much the bridge of his nose hurt. Cass sounded put out, which, so far as Paul was concerned, was becoming his regular tone. Sofia picked up the prosthetic and went to the kitchen behind them to hold it under the hot tap.

"You're not getting all this new adhesive off," she said. "You have to make sure it's removed every day from the piece and your skin. You know that." She told him to apply an antibacterial ointment to his nose every night for the rest of the week. There were other surgical adhesives without the same history of irritation, but they'd chosen this one, newly on the market, thinking it would make the prosthetic more secure in the prolonged heat of the camera lights.

An empty bottle of retsina, and another they'd just opened, sat in the center of the table. Paul removed printouts of tomorrow's campaign schedule from his briefcase and tossed them down next to the bottles. For a few minutes they discussed who would go where, how the calls and e-mails on legal cases and legislative business would be handled. Sofia had the best mind for timing all of this. The twins could not be in public at the same moment; Paul's arrival at any event had to occur after sufficient travel time from wherever Cass had last appeared. As the last work of the evening, Sofia went online with her laptop and put dozens of reminders on the calendar that Paul and Cass shared. Paul was thinking what he thought every night: they could not keep this up.

Paul was ready to go, but Cass held up a hand.

"I've thought this over again, and I really think we should appeal Du Bois's ruling yesterday," Cass said.

Paul couldn't believe they were going through this again. He had waited twenty-five years for the day when Cass and he could dwell together in free space, but like most of what you looked forward to in life, the reality since the end of January had been more challenging than he'd envisioned, and far crazier than anything that had gone on before. Singletons could never understand what it was like to look across at someone who was basically you, experiencing the tide of love and resentment that inevitably came with the sight. After Cass was sentenced, Paul was in actual physical agony for weeks at the prospect of their separation. But they had adjusted to life apart. People adjust to loss. And now he found dealing with Cass every day, and the similar ways their minds worked, with the same lapses and backflips, often unsettling. He had forgotten this part, how it inevitably felt like they were like opponents on an indoor court, basketball or squash players, throwing their back ends at each other as they fought for position.

"Cass, nothing has changed. We can't appeal. On top of everything else, Du Bois was right."

"I think Du Bois did that to fuck us. He's just been waiting for the chance. Tooley hadn't figured out that that stuff was legally Hal's property."

"You know what I think? I think he's a great judge, better than I ever believed he'd be, and I always thought he'd be pretty good." The problem in assessing who'd make a good judge was that the job called on a set of skills less important for practicing lawyers. Smarts served you well in both lives. But patience, civility, a sense of boundaries and balance were more dispensable for courtroom advocates.

Cass laid his plastic fork across the top of one of the black takeout containers. Paul had discovered that his brother got somewhat grouchy with a glass of wine. There were, in fact, all kinds of things he didn't know about Cass after not living with him for a quarter of a century. His twin was more strong-minded and stubborn than he'd been as a younger man. It had taken Paul a while to realize that he could not simply concede, as he once might have, knowing Cass would defer to him next time. Because Cass no longer easily gave in ever.

"Subpoenas enforced *after* a case," Cass said. "That's murky enough. We can appeal."

"Cass, there are already a ton of people who think we dismissed the suit to hide something. If we come back and start fighting Hal on a motion that he's got every right to win, it's going to reinforce that impression."

"How about saying, It's twenty-five years, Cass did his time, this thing should be over and done with, and we're being harassed by a rich lunatic?"

"Do you really think the average Joe is going to side with us if we try to keep Hal from recovering the relics of his sister's murder? It's not my idea of family memorabilia, but people will understand if he wants to have it, rather than let the police throw it away."

Sofia, who in the last couple of months had tended to retreat from the brothers' collisions, especially when there was an edge to them, had sided on this issue with Cass, rather than Paul and the lawyers. Like Cass, she was still not content with the decision not to appeal.

"We're making it easier for him to do the DNA," she said. "That's the problem."

"True, Sofie, but he doesn't have a good specimen from either of us."

Cass said, "We've asked about that. They'll extract my DNA from the fingerprints that were identified as mine."

"They'll try. That's no slam dunk, Cassian. And they still won't have my specimen."

"They'll get it. You know that. They'll pick up some tissue when you blow your nose. Or a pencil you chew on. Or they'll do a lift from the cheek of some woman you kiss at a fund-raiser."

"Well, that could screw them up then, right? At least half the time."

"That might not matter, man. Not if they do the test. That's why the only alternative is to stop them."

Paul put his forehead against both of his palms. It was this circle. It had been for months, this tension between preventing the test and winning the election.

"If we could stop them. But we can't," Paul said. "Every court will decide against us, and they'll do it quickly with a month to the election. It'll be a parade of bad rulings accompanied by a barrage of bad publicity, and each one will say, in effect, Gianis is hiding something. So we hunker down. If Hal comes up with a result we don't like that he tries to publicize, we deal with it then, depending on what he's saying. But at least there's no nightmare scenario. No prosecutor will touch this case, because Hal's broken the chain of evidence. He's too much of a zealot for anybody to believe beyond a reasonable doubt he didn't tamper with the specimens."

"That's still not the best alternative," Cass said.

"You're right. The better alternative," Paul said, "is for me to drop out." He put his head back in his hands, but he could feel both his wife and his brother staring. "There are ten times a day," Paul said, "when I'm ready just to announce that."

For a minute, Cass looked like he was going to come over the table.

"It's not simply your decision."

His brother's statement, uttered so baldly, inflamed Paul.

"The fuck it isn't, Cass. That's how it is."

Cass struck the table with both of his palms, which jumped the opposite edge into Paul's ribs. The moment of bright pain brought him to his feet, and Cass followed, both with closed fists at their sides. The last fistfight they'd had was at age seventeen, but Paul could still feel the primacy of those struggles, as he'd tried for a second to obliterate life's most central, and often troubling, fact, his brother. If it was true, as some psychs said, that their connection was more intense than anything other humans experienced, then the same had to be said about their anger. In twenty-four years, he had never really raised his voice to Sofia in their occasional quarrels.

Sofia had popped up, too, and had imposed herself in front of Cass, taking him by both of his shoulders.

"Don't be juvenile," she said to them.

They stared at each other, in animal posture, nostrils flaring and breathing hard, just one more second. Sofia pressed Cass back down to his chair.

"Paulie," she said, "we can't give in to Hal Kronon. You've promised Ray, and everyone who works for you, that we won't."

He was exhausted. A campaign was vitalizing when you were winning, but at low times, it felt like you were undergoing a form of ritual sacrifice.

"We're going to lose anyway."

"The hell," his brother answered.

"I told you. The *Trib* is going to publish a poll on Sunday where we're running third now."

"I told *you* that," Cass said, "and it's thirty, twenty-nine, twenty-eight. We could still be first given the margin of error. Their story is going to say tie."

"We were twenty points ahead two months ago. And inside the campaign people understand trends. The troops were restless anyway, now that you fired Crully," Paul said.

Cass looked stricken. "You agreed Mark was a pain in the ass."

"I'm not blaming you. I said that the wrong way. I think it was the right move on balance." They had resolved long ago that they would never second-guess one another on decisions that had to be made in the moment. And they'd talked a dozen times about what to do if Du Bois gave Hal the DNA. They had agreed that it would be best to dismiss the lawsuit, which made it inevitable Crully would quit. It was better for Mark, anyway. In another week or two, he'd have been looking for a way to jump off the sinking ship, blaming Paul for the hole in the hull. Mark was not the kind to hang around and keep bailing. He'd already been hired by Hillary to take over in Pennsylvania, where he was from. "I'm not blaming you. I'm just saying the direction is obvious. Hal's going to keep hammering us. He may never have anything more than Georgia, but she'll be a household name with the media buy he's made for that ad."

Peering at Georgia Lazopoulos every time he turned on a TV

filled Paul with clotted emotions, mostly horror and guilt. The brute fact that clobbered him was that she would have been someone else if he'd made a different choice. Sofia had added to his life as much as he'd subtracted from Georgia's, if not more. But romance wasn't ordinarily a zero-sum game.

"Cass, it looks bad. That's all I'm saying. So why hang in and worry about the test?"

"Dropping out won't stop Hal. It'll motivate him, in fact. Hal would do the DNA even if you announced tomorrow that you were leaving the US and becoming a citizen of Belarus. And besides, now that Camaner has taken over, he'll get his arms around the campaign, and we'll win, once the focus is back on the actual issues."

"We're running out of cash, Cass. The crowds are thinner at every event, especially the fund-raisers. You're seeing the same thing. And we agreed when we started that we're not running this campaign on debt."

"I don't think we make this decision now. Camaner has to get a chance. A campaign is a rodeo ride. We both know that."

Paul nodded. He was ready to sleep. He stood up and hugged his brother. "*Hron-yah poh-lah,*" he said in Greek as he held him. 'Many happy years.' This was still one of the greatest feelings he knew, hugging Cass, lingering with the solid fact of his presence.

Sofia and he went to the garage, where her Lexus was parked.

"You're trashed," she said. She took the car key out of his hand.

"No," he answered.

"You're trashed," Sofia repeated. When they came up to the street, there was a sleety rain falling and the asphalt reflected the lights, making it feel as if it were Christmas again.

"You know the basic problem, don't you?" Paul asked. "He likes being me more than he likes being himself."

"God, Paul. That's a hell of a thing to say."

"I should never have agreed to this. The fact that he can pass himself off as me doesn't mean he has the right to do it. I should have drawn a line. It was crazy."

"Are you forgetting the last twenty-five years?"

"Hardly. That's why I said yes. It was a horrible, hard time and we hung in together, no blaming or recriminations, and I couldn't imagine ending that period with all-out war. But truth? I was shocked that he didn't want to go back to his own life."

"That's naïve, isn't it? You're one of the most important men in this county. This state. Cass Gianis is an ex-con. And a convicted murderer."

"But you know, as adults, when the world went to hell, he'd become so determined to be himself. He was proud of all the differences between us. He was funnier and more spontaneous than I was, less disciplined. That was the whole thing with Dita. Even if it was stupid, he insisted on making the kind of decisions I never would have. I'd always taken it for granted that come January 31, 2008, he'd be in a heat to get on with his life, have kids, all of that."

"You liked this idea, Paul. When we first discussed it."

"Because I thought it meant time off. Instead, Cass has added events to the schedule and we're both working like we're in chains."

"It's been incredibly convenient at times. You can't deny that. He loves the fund-raisers, squeezing dollars out of every handshake. And you can't stand them any more."

"I can't stand any of it," he said. "I can't. If we lose, this is the end."

"Wanna bet?" When she sneaked a glance his way, she was smiling.

"You haven't heard me say this before. Hal has changed my perspective. Politics won't be the same. I'm not the first. This is just a grander version of what they did to John Kerry with the Swift Boat thing. So now the rich nuts call you a murderer. But what I believed in, building coalitions and organizations, is out the window. It'll all be about how fast you peddle your ass to some billionaire, so you can counteract the guy on the other side who's done the same thing. A pox on all of it. Honestly, when I think of the future, I'm more excited about the idea of working with Cass on that charter school for ex-cons—something simple and within our control, where I can be sure I'm actually leaving the campsite a little cleaner than I found it."

"Paulie, we just need to get through the election. That was what we all agreed to start. You'll be less exhausted and you two can figure it out."

"What is there to figure out? Something has to give, baby. You got two guys and one life. I love Cass, but I can't put up with this a lot longer. My mother always worried about the brothers in the bible, Jacob and Esau, and Cain and Abel. Cain is always the bad guy, but I'm beginning to feel for him, with his brother moving in on him."

"What do you mean moving in on you?" Sofia asked. The light from the streets was on her eyes when they shifted briefly in her husband's direction.

"You know what I mean," he answered quietly. There was so much he had failed to anticipate by living one day at a time until Cass's sentence was over. He never had to weigh his relationship with his brother against his marriage. Now the geometries seemed confusing to them all. In the month before they rented the apartment, Paul had returned home frequently from late-night events to find his brother and his wife together, padding around the house in their socks, still lingering over a meal, or side-by-side watching TV or a movie. Their familiarity with each other, and especially the physical aspect of it, which he had somehow never imagined, had been disquieting. The speed with which Sofia placed her hands on

Cass to restrain him tonight, and even the way his brother received it, had troubled him again. Why hadn't he realized what would confront him?

He was too tired for all of this. His mind was spinning down to dark places. It was past midnight and he'd be up at 5:30.

"I'm trashed," he said.

22.

The Results—March 6, 2008

The young colleague of Dr. Yavem's with whom Tim had deposited the evidence surrendered by the state police left a message on his cell saying that they had concluded the tests and wanted to talk to him or Evon at 2 this afternoon. Tim met Evon at ZP and they taxied to the hospital. They were at the U in ten minutes and then walked in circles on their way through the med school to Yavem's lab. The hospital, famous as a cancer treatment center, had itself grown like a tumor, spreading in all directions. Sometimes you had to go half a block to find an elevator. All in all, the hike to Yavem's lab was longer than the drive out here.

Dr. Yavem emerged to greet them and brought both back to his small white office, with its long window into his laboratory. Tim realized that he might as well be looking through the glass at something occurring fifty or one hundred years from now, because the work taking place there was that far beyond what he would ever comprehend. DNA identification had not even been invented when Dita was killed in 1982. He'd heard the term because of Watson and Crick, and a book he'd read. Tim thought for a second about his father's father, a sour, silent man who'd been born on a

farm near Aberdeen and hadn't even seen a railroad train until one
started him on his journey to America. The old man lived to the
time of television but refused to watch the set, convinced it was possessed.

In the taxi, Evon had described Yavem as a merry little guy, but
to Tim he seemed pretty grave behind his spare moustache. There
was barely room for two of them on the other side of Yavem's
desk, which ironically made Tim like him more. It meant Yavem had
given up the space to his lab and his research and not his ego.

"I have quite a bit to tell you," Dr. Yavem said, "but it will probably make the most sense if I explain my results in the order in
which I performed the tests.

"Remember, Ms. Miller, I described a very basic testing protocol.
The first step, in order to do things properly, was to confirm that
the blood at the Kronon home had come from one of the Gianis
twins. Then, assuming that was the case, we needed to confirm that
they were identical twins. If so, we'd employ two different tests to
prospect throughout each man's genome for so-called copy-number
variations. If we were successful in identifying a CNV, we'd then
analyze the blood from the crime scene to see if we could find the
same one at the same locus.

"Step one was the well-accepted part of the testing regime. Given
the age of the specimens and the likelihood of contamination, we
said we would try Y-STR testing first." Clearly a practiced teacher,
Yavem, as he spoke, turned now and then to Tim, who finally
pointed back at Evon.

"Tell her, Doctor. She's going to have to explain it all to me later.
Very, very slowly." Yavem laughed just a second before reverting to
a somber expression.

"We had DNA specimens from a number of sources. There was
the original blood from Hal and Zeus Kronon. I had a very good
specimen from the water bottle that you told me Paul Gianis had

drunk from. And I had fingerprints that had been positively identified as Cass Gianis's.

"I began by analyzing the Kronons' blood."

"Why Zeus and Hal?" asked Evon. "Weren't they excluded by blood type?"

"Yes, but in this case, specimen contamination was a considerable risk. That's one of many reasons to look first at the Y chromosome. Because females at the scene present no chance of contamination. But we knew that both Hal and his father had spent quite a bit of time in Ms. Kronon's bedroom before the police closed the scene, so I thought it would be helpful to have their Y chromosome sequenced. When you do a DNA analysis, you don't know precisely what cells you're analyzing. It may look like a blood drop to the naked eye, but even a single skin cell from someone else can show up in the results. So if we have a specimen large enough to test in several regions, it's very helpful to understand what the DNA of a possible contaminating cell looks like, so you can understand a variation in results. With a father and son, you expect the same Y sequence, but we did both, basically as a way to validate ourselves. And that proved fortuitous because Hal and Zeus are not in fact genetically linked."

Evon had one of those moments. The veins at her temples throbbed and her vision wavered. She understood why Yavem wasn't smiling.

"Hal is not Zeus's son?"

"Not genetically."

Tim grabbed her arm now that he understood. His gray eyes, clouded and marked by age, swung her way and he made an indefinite sound with his mouth in a tiny o.

"I'll flip you," Evon said.

"Uh-uh. I ain't telling him," said Tim. "There's not enough money, not in the whole entire world."

"God," Evon said. She took a deep breath and said, "OK," meaning Yavem could go on.

"I then moved on to the Gianis twins. We got very good sequencing off the water bottle on Paul. So we then tried to extract DNA from some of the fingerprint lifts that were identified as Cass's, and we succeeded at that. We didn't get as complete a result, but there were still identifiable short segments at a number of loci."

"What about the copy-number variations?" asked Evon.

"We weren't looking for them at this point. That's a whole different array of tests. We certainly confirmed that Paul and Cass are in fact monozygotic twins—identical twins from the same embryo."

"No surprise there," answered Evon.

"Yes, well," said Yavem. A brief smile escaped him and he looked downward, seemingly to suppress it. "Forgive me," he said. "Because once the Gianis Y was sequenced, there was another unexpected result. I actually hadn't noticed. Teresa called my attention to it." He gestured through the window toward a figure in a white coat in the lab, the woman Tim had met with.

"I hope it's better than the first surprise," Evon said.

"Of the same nature. Zeus Kronon was the father of the Gianis twins."

Evon felt her jaw hanging. "Fuck," she said, a word she spoke aloud in conversation no more than once a year.

Tim actually laughed. A few drunken wags at St. D's had asked how Mickey Gianis, who could barely get out of bed, had fathered more children. Tim recalled one Sunday evening when Father Nik tore the head off someone at the men's club for speaking such a malicious slur.

Evon was looking at him.

"Did you know that?" she asked.

"Of course not."

Evon in the meantime had taken a moment to calculate.

"So that would mean that Zeus and the Gianises all share a Y chromosome?"

"Correct."

"So the blood at the scene might have come from Zeus, too?"

"Looking solely at the Y chromosome we'd get that result. But we know there are other genetic differences between Zeus and his twins. Because Zeus is a different blood type than those men. They're B. He's O. Their mother must be type B. But if the twins' Y chromosome matched the blood, we'd know it was one of theirs. We quickly concluded, however, that was not the case. Like Zeus, the blood could not have come from the Gianises either."

A quick fear withered Evon's heart.

"Please tell me it's not Hal's."

"By all means. It is surely not Hal's. Or Zeus's. Or the Gianises'. Nor Hal's mother, Hermione, for that matter."

"The *mother*?"

"Yes, none of the blood collected at the scene contains a Y chromosome."

Evon stopped for a second, before asking how that could possibly be.

"You can be sure that we examined a dozen of those blood spots to be certain. But we got the same result each time. All the blood on the walls and window came from a woman," said Yavem.

III.

23.

Lidia—September 5, 1982

L idia Gianis walks the contours of Zeus's sloping lawn with care. *She has not attended this picnic in more than twenty-five years, having sworn never to return. In Lidia's life, there are few vows she does not adhere to. She believes in will—ee thelesee in Greek. Spirit. Will cannot turn snow to rain, or roll back the sea, but it can keep you from being simply steamrollered by fate.*

Now and then Lidia reaches out to Teri for support because she has chosen a pair of wedged espadrilles. That is more heel than she is accustomed to, since Mickey, two inches shorter to start, does not care to feel as if he were a child being led around by the hand. But she approached this gathering intending to look her best, which has proven a vain effort in the breathy Midwestern heat that has left her flushed, and damp with sweat. Preparing this morning, she examined herself solemnly as she applied her makeup. Not an old lady yet, she decided, but further on the way than she would prefer. The sturdy and abundant body of her girlhood was surrendered in the course of three pregnancies, especially the last one with the twins, and her wide figure is better concealed beneath a floor-length shift. The coils of black hair, pushed back from the brow by a discreet band to create a leonine rush, are now overgrown by wires of gray that she regards like weeds. What she practiced in the mirror was the piercing black-eyed look, clever and determined, by which she knows herself.

Now, treading carefully, she carries her head high on her long neck, even though her upper body is weakened by a seasick feeling of high anxiety. The nausea reminds her just a little of the mornings during her first two pregnancies with Helen and Cleo. With the boys, she was healthy as a horse—except for the fact that she thought of killing herself every day.

"My brother does it right," says Teri, "but I sometimes think, when I watch him gliding around like a swan, that his pride will kill him." Teri adores Zeus, even while she mocks his excesses. He sports the same white suit he dons every year, preening as he greets his guests. It sometimes seems that Teri and she have been talking about Zeus their entire lives—the adolescent kisses Lidia and he shared, his marriage, his children, his feud with Mickey, his titanic success. If you asked, each woman would claim the other one raises the subject.

There are some friendships that pass into permanency due solely to an early start. Choosing today, Lidia might not welcome the company of a woman so profane and odd. But Teri is central in her life, like a stout tree you watched grow from a slender stick in the ground, a physical marker of the mystery of time. These days, Teri and she seldom meet face-to-face. The Gianises moved to Nearing a few years ago, when Mickey opened a second grocery there. And Teri refuses to visit Lidia's home, rather than tolerate Mickey's inevitable rages about Zeus. Instead, the two women babble to each other on the telephone at the start of every day, often for as long as an hour. A few minutes afterward, neither can recall what they discussed, except on the frequent occasions when one has slammed down the handset due to a comment too unkind to be tolerated.

It falls to the offender to call back first, most often the next day, at which point the disagreement goes entirely unmentioned. In a relationship so old, rebukes are pointless. Years ago, Lidia stopped asking Teri to curb her vocabulary, instead bringing up her children to understand that no one else on earth was allowed to talk like Nouna Teri. And decades have passed since Lidia last encouraged Teri to accept one of the many men who courted her. Teri prefers to believe she is too much for any male. 'I don't want one,' she will tell you to this day. 'Cold feet in bed when you don't need them and a cold dick when you do.'

Suddenly, there is a commotion. People surge forward and Paul's name is on the air, accompanied by laughter. Lidia leaves Teri behind, until she sees her son struggling back to his feet, laughing with a girl who looks somewhat like Sofia Michalis. The young woman is holding Paul's elbow as she hands him an empty paper plate. Paul's focus on her is intense—as the song says, eyes only for her. Watching, Lidia feels a surge of hope. Georgia Lazopoulos is an empty vessel, entirely incompatible with the huge hopes she holds for both her sons. Paul probably would have proposed to Georgia long ago if Lidia had been at all encouraging. Even Father Nik, who is as dumb as his daughter, has begun to figure out that Lidia is the problem and has been increasingly cold to her. But she is unconcerned. It has been her longtime belief that these boys, conceived and carried in agony, must in some recompense from God be destined for greatness.

As she returns to Teri, Lidia feels her stomach suddenly lurch into spin cycle. Zeus is coming their way.

"Lidia, agapetae mou"—'my dear'—he says and throws his arms wide in triumph. The vast history between them reveals itself in not so much as a flicker in his broad expression. She tolerates only a quick kiss on her cheek, but he grips her tightly for one second—he is still hale and strong—then turns to wave over Hermione, who not

surprisingly has already headed this way to insert herself between Lidia and her husband. "Look who is here," he says in English. Hermione does not bother with a welcoming word, and merely extends her hand, beset with a diamond-circled Rolex that cost more than the house Lidia lives in. "We enjoy seeing Cassian," says Hermione, "ena kala paidee"—'a nice boy,' almost as if Cass were a child who'd come over to play. Hermione is beautiful but dull. She is slender—why are rich women so often thin as wafers?—with her hair expensively colored the shade of weak tea and swept up in a beehive. She has mastered an elegant smile, but they both know she has never cared for Lidia, who is far smarter than Hermione, and once enjoyed a troubling emotional proximity to her husband.

"You have stayed away too long," Zeus tells Lidia, "and I cannot imagine why."

That is too much. She manages no more than a stiff smile and turns heel, with Teri trailing after her. Zeus's sister grabs Lidia's arm again after another ten yards.

"A lease on a grocery store? Lidia, really. It's twenty years."

"I had stopped coming before that," Lidia responds, but curbs herself there. Sometimes, when she is alone in the house, and Zeus appears on the living room TV, which she has left on for company, she will slip into the room and marvel. He has grown to be so smooth—the younger man made no secrets about what he wanted. Now his ambitions are concealed like a dagger in a jeweled sheath. Back then, there was no denying her attraction to Zeus. He was her best friend's older brother, big and good-looking and full of some- thing she found irresistible—Zeus believed that greatness was his fate. Because of that, he was the only man she ever met who felt like a true match for her and her belief that her spirit should fill the world. She has always hoped, most secretly, that her sons have some of the same quality.

When Lidia was sixteen, her fascination with Zeus—and his with her—brought them to an evening that even now she recalls as one of the most fateful of her life. In those days, boys and girls would slip off from the Social Club at St. D's to the choir room to kiss. Everybody tried it, pairing off almost at random. Zeus was nineteen by then, a little old for Social Club, and Lidia realized eventually he was there only for her. Each week, they stayed in the choir room longer. People were beginning to joke. And then one night he put her hand in his lap. 'Do you know what this is?' he asked. He pulled it from his trousers. She stared, horrified but wildly pleased. 'Touch it,' he said, 'please.' She did, and he touched her, unleashing a tide of pleasure that felt at first as if it would stop her heart. But she would not allow the last step. 'I must be married,' she told him.

'Then I will marry you,' he answered. It seemed like comedy. She actually laughed, but Zeus was ardent. 'No, I mean this. Truly. Let us go now to speak to your father.'

Zeus took her hand and pulled her toward the door, almost before she was dressed again. Her father was in the front room of their apartment in a sleeveless undervest. He had been drinking beer and listening on a large console radio to baseball, a game for which, although an immigrant, he had developed a great fascination. As she stood, hand in hand with Zeus, she could still feel what had gushed from her wetting the inside of her thigh.

'I wish to marry Lidia,' said Zeus.

Her father looked at Zeus coldly and then snorted as he turned back to the radio.

'No daughter of mine will marry into a family of hoodlums.' Lidia, he said, came from honorable people, farmers in Greece who made their way here honestly, selling produce. The Kronons at home were sheep rustlers and blacksmiths, which was another word for thieves. These days, Nikos, Zeus's father, translated for the mafiosi when they shook down the Greek restaurant owners, reiterating the Ital-

*ians' threats, which were often carried out, to break windows or
sabotage the plumbing.*

*The next night she met Zeus under the streetlight in front of her
house.*

*'Marry me anyway,' he said. He had made a plan to run off. But
she could not go against her father. She had cried most of the day,
but she knew which man had to command her loyalties.*

*She went back inside, and for years after barely spoke to Zeus.
To avoid humiliating him, she told no one about his proposal, including Teri, who would have been enraged that Lidia's father had
said such things about the Kronons to her brother's face. The moment receded as if it had never occurred. Zeus enlisted in the army
the week after Pearl Harbor, nearly dying at one point in a mil-
itary hospital, but he returned, married to Hermione, with Hal,
a babe in arms. Lidia by then had wed Mickey, the son of her
mother's best friend, before he left for the service in 1942. Mickey
was nice-looking, and worked hard, and wanted to be a good husband, which she knew even at sixteen was not likely to be true of
Zeus. Mickey lived by a narrower compass, but that didn't matter
because she took it for granted, when she kissed Zeus good-bye
under that streetlight, that she would never feel the same way
about anyone else.*

*Mickey was an uncomplicated person, but he was everything he
promised to be. Then he took sick. He had rheumatic fever as a child
and the mitral valve in his heart did not close properly. In her mind's
eye, Lidia saw the blood spurting past the structure, as if it were
a finger in a dike. There was no way for the doctors to operate.
Mickey took medicine, but he declined. By 1955, he could no longer
go to the produce market and remained at home. Soon he was in
his bed, drowning in his own body. Lidia tried her best to believe he
wouldn't die.*

Teri arranged a job for Lidia in Zeus's office. Zeus knew her, knew how bright she was, and his business was erupting like a volcano, with shopping centers spreading around the Tri-Cities like a lava flow. And Lidia's family needed money. As for what had once happened between them, it was a lifetime ago. She did not imagine that she would be attractive to Zeus any longer. She was becoming matronly, and he was, in his sister's own words, "Sir Lance-a-lot," a nightly visitor to the bars on Street of Dreams, from which he frequently extracted some little trinket half his age whom he bedded in one of the swank hotels nearby.

Yet Zeus was wooing Lidia from the first moment he saw her there.

'Your father spoiled not only your life,' he told her the first time he was alone with her. 'He ruined mine.'

Sometimes, he came up behind her chair, when no one else was around, and sang a Greek folk song, "S'agapo," 'I love you,' in a whisper. If there was not time for the entire tune, he sang one of the lyrics:

> *Your window which is closed*
> *Your window which is shut*
> *Open, open one panel of it.*

She answered with a hundred remonstrations. That is the past. Our lives are what they are. I am married, Zeus. She avoided his office if she could, and if not, told her colleagues to call her there in five minutes. He tried each time to take her in his arms as she wriggled free.

Along with most of her coworkers, she attended this party twenty-six years ago, the first of the Labor Day picnics. Zeus had bought the house only eighteen months before and offered her a tour. Another couple was with them, but when her eyes adjusted to the change from the brilliant sun, the other two had been way-

laid, perhaps at Zeus's instruction. He had been drinking, as had she. Finding they were alone, he drove her into one of the servants' bedrooms right off the kitchen. It was a small room with narrow windows like a prison cell and a simple chenille spread on the twin bed. She did not cry out, because the consequences of that, for her life and his, for her job, were beyond quick calculation. But she resisted fiercely, holding him off. 'No. Zeus. This is craziness. Zeus, I am saying no.' But he continued bearing down on her. 'Please,' he kept saying. 'Please.' It was as if what had begun in the choir room had taken place only a minute before. Familiarity with his physical presence had never left her, and her body, largely unused in this way for years, rose to him, no matter what she wanted. But she stopped saying no and fighting him off only after he had entered her and she had begun to weep in hopelessness and shame. She dressed and left the room without a word.

Out on the lawn he found her again. 'I am so sorry,' he whispered. 'I will marry you,' he said, 'I will still marry you,' as if two decades, two marriages, had not intervened. At that moment, she learned everything about Zeus she needed to know. Not that he was a liar, although she did not think for a second that he would leave this mansion, and his son and his wife. But rather, that he believed what he was saying. Like someone in Galaxy magazine, Zeus wanted to live six or seven different lives at the same time. She knew then that Zeus probably would not have married her either when she was sixteen. His greatness, if you could call it that, was that he did not accept human limits.

She turned away, still with no idea what to do. There was no one to tell, not her husband, who quite likely would die on the spot, nor even Terisia, who was loyal and old-fashioned enough to side with her brother: What else was the man to think, after all his overtures, when you snuck with him into the house? It had not happened, Lidia decided. That was the only way to live her life.

It was more than three months before she accepted that she was pregnant. She hoped at first that she would miscarry. Her faith was of her own construction, but as a mother, she would not even contemplate forcing a child from her womb. Finally, when she realized she would be showing soon, she laid down in Mickey's bed and wrapped him in her arms. 'We are going to have a baby,' she said. 'Soon I will have to quit work.' She did not know then or now what Mickey believed. In every marriage there are subjects that are unapproachable. Even then, sick as he was, he could, every few months, get up like a whale breaking the surface for a moment to spurt, declaring afterward each time that it would have been a fine way to go. But Lidia's impression at that moment was that Mickey was simply too sick to care. He knew he was dying, that his wife, the mother of his daughters, was loyal in her care for him and would be beside him when he passed. Eventually, his great joy at the birth of his sons, who could carry forth his name, was the final antidote to questions.

In 1958, the year after the boys came, U Hospital had purchased a heart-lung machine, one of the first, and Dr. Silverstein told Mickey they could save his life. It was a miracle, of course. It was like watching a man stand up out of his own grave.

His grocery was open soon after. Seven years later, the lease came up for renewal. They had always known the terms were favorable, but believed that Old Man Kariatis just wanted someone he would never have to chase around for rent. But Mickey's lawyer discovered that Kariatis was a straw man; he had sold long before to ZP. Mickey's rent was barely half what Zeus was charging on the adjoining properties. Zeus's generosity drove Mickey into a fury. She never dared ask why, although she was certain what inference her husband was drawing.

Yet to this day, she never believed Zeus suspected the boys' paternity. The story of Mickey's episodic potency was well circulated

at St. D's. Zeus merely meant to do Lidia a favor as a shabby recompense for his behavior.

As for Mickey, his rage at even the mention of Zeus's name was
the only disruption. Whatever had occurred was otherwise a piece
of the discarded past, part of Mickey's illness, which they saw now
as a distant sea, remote and unthreatening when considered from
the cliff known as good health.

And then she heard that Cass was romancing Dita. She waited for
the relationship to pass, but it was clear that Cass was smitten. The
jeweler, Angelikos, has told Lidia that in the last two weeks Cass has
been in to look at rings. She has sat up nights in despair. How could
it be that the damage of a single moment can spill through time to
endanger another generation?

Lidia would tear out her tongue before confessing anything to
either of her sons. Nor can she approach Zeus. There is no telling
what the man's grandiosity would impel him to do, but Zeus's ac-
tions were certain to show no regard for Mickey. Teri is a possibility,
but she might doubt Lidia after all this time, especially knowing
how deeply Lidia disapproves of Dita. Worse, Teri might feel obliged
to involve her brother. The best alternative is to go directly to Dita.
If she will not promise to give up Cass, then Lidia will have to try
Teri next.

Close to 6 p.m., just as the picnic is scheduled to conclude, the
skies open. The guests run in all directions, but many, hoping to
wait out the worst of the pelting downpour, crowd through the
rear door of Zeus's house, which is open so the guests can use
the bathrooms nearby. Knowing this, Lidia has already planned
to hide inside. She has told Cass that Teri will drive her home
and said just the opposite to Teri. But now, as dozens crowd into
Zeus's rear hall, she takes advantage of the confusion to slide past
the velvet rope looped between two brass stanchions that closes
off the upper stories. Dita's room is the first door she opens on

the second floor, with a collection of paper dolls pasted to the walls, bizarre decorations Lidia thinks for a girl of twenty-four. She finds a magazine and takes a seat in Dita's bathroom on the commode, then stands for a second to consider herself in the mirror, summoning again her dark-eyed look of imperial strength. She believes in will.

24.

Family Tree—March 10, 2008

Zeus had left his sister a considerable bequest, and Teri had been a shrewd businessperson in her own right, often investing in real estate with her brother. Her condo occupied far too much space for one person, especially somebody who had trouble seeing or getting about. Yet Aunt Teri was basically trapped here by her treasures, which she'd accumulated around the world and with which, Hal said, she would never part. He claimed she was like one of the pharaohs who would prefer to be entombed with all the stuff.

The condo was in one of the lavish old Art Deco buildings constructed in the 1920s on the river's edge, not far from Center City. It sported fancy limestone arches and decorations on the exterior, and a red tile roof. Teri's apartment had the feeling of a Fabergé egg, every inch elaborately decorated and ribbed in gilt. Each object was gold—the picture frames, the table legs. Even the many glass display cases for her various collections were etched in gold leaf. Within the boxes were the eclectic range of things that fascinated Teri—African jewelry, buttons of whalebone, antique children's toys, and of course erotica. An entire case, a yard square, was dedicated to phalluses—a Greek tradition, she pointed out, but one that nonetheless sent her nephew screaming. Hal walked in with a scarf and covered the case the minute he arrived.

Teri had welcomed Evon's request for a meeting without any questions. Tim had wanted to come, too, but Evon told him without further explanation that she felt Teri and she had a rapport.

"So, what's up?" Teri had a highball that her servant, old German, had poured for her without apparent instruction, and she settled herself on the large chesterfield with a flowery pattern, her cane at hand almost in the manner of a scepter. Even at home, Teri was in her heavy makeup and jewelry. Seated ten feet away, Evon could smell the old lady's perfume. On the gold-leafed wooden coffee table in front of her, Teri had everything she might need positioned precisely so she could find it—the remotes for the TV and the audio system, a cordless telephone, her drink and a golden bell, presumably used to summon German.

"We got some surprising results from our DNA tests," Evon told her.

Teri screwed up her stoplight-colored mouth and made no effort to contain herself.

"Fuck," she said. "I was afraid of this."

"Is that why you wanted Hal to stop the investigation?"

Teri didn't respond, just shook her head of broom-straw hair from side to side.

"What a goddamned mess," she finally said. "All right. Tell me."

Evon tried to explain the DNA testing protocol and how it had inadvertently turned into a paternity test, but Teri interrupted.

"Don't beat around the bush, dear."

Evon sensed already that she wasn't the one holding back information.

"Well, Hal isn't Zeus's son. Not biologically."

"Fuck," Teri said again. "You're not going to tell him, are you?"

"That's why I'm here. Tim and I—we don't think it's a good idea."

"That's for damn sure. It would break him in two. Definitely not."

"If worse came to worst, we wanted to be able to say we talked to you and that you agreed it wasn't in Hal's best interest to share that information with him."

"Scapegoat, right? That's what you're looking for?"

"I wouldn't put it that way."

"Put it however you want. You can't tell him. Period." Teri frumped around on the sofa, agitated by the notion, and unconcerned about the crossed obligations Evon felt. "I suppose you're wondering whose he is?"

"I'm not sure it's my place."

"Well, I'll tell you. Just so you understand how it happened. And why Hal can't find out. Did you ever hear that crap how my brother was a big hero who nearly died in an army hospital during World War II?"

"Hal talks about that all the time."

"Well, it was true, in a way. But Zeus wasn't overseas. He was in basic training. And he got the mumps."

"Like kids?"

"Pretty serious with a grown-up. Especially a man. It nearly did him in. One of his senior officers was a Greek and he called my father and we all took the train down to Fort Barkley in Texas. Zeus was pretty fuckin' sick, I want to tell you. Fever of 106. Face was the size of a watermelon and his balls had swollen up, they looked like a couple of damson plums. Took a peek when my folks weren't looking. Quite a sight. Anyway, he made it. But the doctors told us at the time, there wasn't much chance he was going to be able to have kids.

"So when he mustered out and comes back with Hermione and Herakles, I knew something was up. He kind of dripped out the story over the years. Hermione, you know, she was a Vasilikos. Did you hear that?"

"Greek mobsters, right?"

"Right. Yeah, my dad—what a dickhead that man was—he was a big Mafia wannabe. And he had the wrong kind of acquaintances in Athens and Zeus went to pay respects. Hal was just a newborn, a month or so old. Family was telling some fairy tale that the father was a dead Resistance fighter, but apparently she'd spread her legs for some German colonel, who'd skipped town when the Americans kicked the Nazis' brown-shirted behinds. My big brother was the kind to see an opportunity. And Hermione, no way around it, she was a piece of ass in those days. So he came back here with a wife and an heir and a duffel bag full of money. And in some ways, it all worked out.

"My brother held Hal close always, because Zeus knew he was the only child he'd ever have. Zeus took some tests, but it was as the army docs had predicted, a sperm count close to zero. He always made out like it didn't bother him, but a Greek guy, one like Zisis? Everything he did in life, I think, came from the fact that his nuts would have been more useful making noise in a couple of maracas."

"Something to prove?" Evon asked.

"Exactly. Building all of these vast shopping malls, remaking the landscape. And naturally he fucked every woman he could find to say yes, and a few who may have only been thinking about it."

Evon still marveled at these stories of Zeus as mob crony and philanderer. The Zeus she knew originally was the myth Hal created, undoubtedly with his father's influence. That Zeus was not merely the kind of man Hal aspired to be, but someone to whom he would always rank second. The irony, Evon was realizing, was that no matter how much of a brat, Hal probably was the better person.

If money hadn't magnified his worst traits, people would even have described Hal as a good guy.

"Well, what about Dita?"

"Oh, she was Zeus's. I don't know exactly how they did it. I think the doctors sucked him out with a vacuum or something several times and saved it, and then turned Hermione upside down and shot it into her from a fire hose."

"Really?"

"Of course not." Unseeing, Teri still looked around to enjoy her laugh at Evon's expense. "It was some fertility treatment. What had happened was our dad was diagnosed with lung cancer in the early fifties. And even then the doctors, the ones who knew anything, blamed cigarettes. We all smoked like we should have had brick chimneys on our heads, Zeus and my dad and mom and me, and Zeus took it in mind that if he stopped cold my dad would, too. Our dad, he was way too big an asshole to do something like that, even for his son, so he croaked himself instead. But apparently, smoking can also fry your nuts. Who knew? But some little cupcake Zeus had been balling comes to him about 1956 for money for an abortion. He was sure she was running a scam, but rather than tell her the truth, he goes off for another test, and lo and behold, there are quite a few little beasties swimming around in his spunk now. So that's where Dita comes from, eventually."

"Well, she's not Zeus's only child," Evon said.

In her big turquoise glasses, Teri looked through the haze of her own smoke trying to make out what little she could of Evon.

"I figured that had to come out in the wash, too."

"And how did that happen?" Evon asked.

"Well, dear, I think he put his nasty where it didn't belong." Teri got another good chuckle over herself. "You know, you look back, you're always amazed by what went past you. I always knew Zeus and Lidia took quite a shine to one another when we were all kids.

Not that anything could come of it. There was always one of those burning-hot old-country grudges between the families. Lidia's people, they didn't have the spit to wet their palms, but they still took some pride in looking down on the Kronons. I was sixteen before I set foot in her house. Lidia and me, we just all the time met up at the library." 'Li-berry,' Teri pronounced it.

"At church with the youth group, the priest, Father Demos, he was sweet-natured but not up to these city kids. He'd be talking to himself and one couple or another would sneak off to the choir room. We all did it some. It was sort of like playing spin the bottle. I took my turns, too. That was how I started to figure I was barking up the wrong tree. The boys just left me cold." Teri laughed out loud at the memory, proud of the defiance if nothing else. But Evon knew that for a woman of Teri's age to say that, even to herself, had taken considerable courage.

"Anyway, Zeus and Lidia, I knew they were taking more turns than others. But twenty years later, I figured everybody had grown up and moved on, and my Lidia, she needed a job. You got more use out of a spare tire than anybody could of Mickey with his messed-up heart.

"Lidia, when I finally heard the story from her, many years on, she made it sound like Zeus had his way with her, but I never got an answer when I asked how many times exactly she got herself taken advantage of." Teri cackled for a second. She loved the way sex made idiots out of everybody. She was on her brother's side in a determinedly old-fashioned way. But Lidia was the sole support of her family, without any choices. Zeus was, politely put, a complete asshole. "Anyway, she got herself knocked up and never said a word to Zeus, or me for that matter. Probably didn't want to turn me against my brother."

"And what about Mickey, her husband? Did he know?"

"Well, sick as he was, everybody kind of took it as one hell of a surprise when Lidia got pregnant, but he always acted happy about it. Course after I knew the real story, it made me wonder how big a cluck he could have been. While she was pregnant, she was always whispering to her closest friends how he could still manage about a minute's worth, but even then I wondered. But she must have convinced him. You can never tell what people will choose to believe.

"Right after Mickey's surgery, it was like the twins' second birthday party, and Mickey was drunk, and started in how they were no children of his, and Lidia, who usually would go crazy angry when she was upset, she just got weepy on him. 'Don't say that, Mickey. Why would you say something like that? They're yours and you know that. You can't be saying things like that.' Pretty soon he was bawling, too, and begging her to forgive him. Even when he started breathing fire about Zeus a few years later, he never said anything about my brother touching his wife. That's another thing you can't tell Hal—that those boys are Zeus's. Can you imagine? They are, he isn't. You'd have to post guards at the windows."

Evon's instinct was the same as Teri's. Not only would Hal be devastated, he was likely eventually to go into one of his bewildering tailspins, obsessing over the legal complications that might entitle the twins to some share of Zeus's estate. Evon and Tim had agreed that the best solution when they finally spoke to Hal was to stay on the subject—the tests showed the blood at the scene was from neither of the Gianis twins. That might be shock enough to keep Hal from asking his usual sideways questions. Hal was preoccupied anyway these days, inasmuch as his bankers were raising questions about the YourHouse deal that Hal and his lawyers felt should have been posed before the closing.

"If we end up having to tell him the blood is a woman's," Evon said, "he's not going to leave it at that. He'll want to know who killed his sister—and what Lidia had to do with it."

Teri shifted back among the silk pillows, trying again to get an eye on Evon.

"And why say that?"

"It has to be Lidia's blood at the scene. The twins have a type-B parent, and it wasn't your brother. Lidia wore an Easton class ring on her right hand that would have left that circular bruise on Dita's cheek. And you can see now why she was desperate to stop Cass's relationship with Dita. Tim and I are beginning to wonder if Cass pled guilty to keep his mother out of prison."

Teri pursed her bright mouth and shook her head adamantly.

"Lidia didn't kill my niece."

"And Cass did?" Evon asked.

"Hon, I'm just like you. I wasn't there. But I've known Lidia Gianis my entire life, and I've heard all of her secrets by now. And she didn't kill my niece. Worse comes to worst, I'll tell Hal the same thing. She'd say it to you herself, if she could, poor thing. I still go over there to see her, when I can stand it. The caregivers, they dress her up and move her around as if she was a doll. But her brain is like the stuff you scrape out of a cantaloupe. Breaks my heart. She can still talk some, if you don't mind hearing the same thing five times in a minute. But she didn't kill Dita."

Evon struggled with this a second. Teri had clearly not reached the end of what she knew, but the old lady wasn't going to share the rest, and Evon had no place to demand it.

"You know," Teri said, "I didn't think this was why you were calling. Hal said your girlfriend did you wrong and then went all batshit crazy on you. Thought you wanted advice, one old dyke to another."

Evon laughed out loud at Teri's boldness, but she was embarrassed that Heather had made her the talk of the ZP Building. Hal hadn't heard about Evon's domestic problems from her.

"She showed up at my apartment building last night and I swore out a protection order at the police station."

"Oh dear," Teri said. "Doesn't sound like a good time."

"It hasn't been. I may be off relationships for the rest of my life. You seem to have survived."

"I don't know," Teri said. "I always had my doubts about that stuff from Aristotle, that love is one soul inhabiting two bodies. But if you think I'm sitting here by myself with a highball and a cigarette because I wouldn't prefer some old biddy coming in to nag me to get rid of both of them, you're wrong. Here's another saying." She reverted to Greek.

"Meaning?"

"That's Socrates. 'Find a good wife and you'll be happy; if not you'll become a philosopher.'"

Evon was laughing when German came in. Teri apparently had been ordered by her doctors to take an afternoon nap. She fussed at him but got ready to say good-bye. Evon walked around the coffee table to hug the old woman and Teri brought her face and her powerful scents to Evon's cheek.

"Oh, you're such a nice girl," she said.

Hal was screaming at somebody on the blower when Evon and Tim were shown into his office the following afternoon. It sounded from all the talk of collateral that it must have been one of his bankers. Tim went to the window for a minute to enjoy the view from the fortieth floor. He'd lived his whole life pretty close to the ground, no more than two stories for the most part, four if you counted his time in McGrath Hall. He felt excited as a country boy by the chance to stare through the wall of glass at the full stretch of the Tri-Cities. From here, you could see the River Kindle, a satin ribbon in today's sun, cutting the municipalities apart. Within the embrace of the river's branches sat block upon block of his city, the perfect squares that looked from this vantage like the pieces in a children's toy, but which were actually full of all that throbbing life. The feeling welled into Tim again that had come to him as he aged: All in all, people were a whole lot of fun.

Evon moved over to stand beside him. Eventually she pointed, with a grim chuckle, to a bug that had somehow worked its way in between the two layers of glass in the double-paned window. It was some kind of beetle that had gotten flipped onto its back. With the bug unable to turn itself over, its six little legs were churning wildly.

"Talk about a design flaw," Tim said.

"Right," said Evon. "And humans have heartbreak."

For a second, Tim hugged her to his side.

Hal slammed down the phone.

"There have to be plant forms that have more brains than bankers," he declared, and directed Evon and Tim to his sofa. They took their places dutifully. She spoke.

"I know your hair is on fire with the bankers and YourHouse, so we'll make this fast. The DNA came back early. The blood isn't Paul's."

Hal gasped, winced, and dropped the pen he'd been holding.

"Damn," he said, and repeated the word a few times. "So it *is* Cass's?"

"No," Evon said. She sat forward in a locker room posture, her elbows on her knees. It was game time for her, Tim realized. "It's not from either of them."

Hal's full face went still, and his eyes flicked around under the weight of a fact neither he, nor anyone else for that matter, had imagined.

"Neither?"

Evon nodded.

"You're saying that Paul dismissed his lawsuit to keep us from doing a test that shows that his brother and him, they're both innocent?"

"We didn't say they're both innocent," Evon answered. "That's possible. But you still have Cass's fingerprints, shoe-prints, the tire tracks, the sperm fraction. It's hard to say he wasn't there."

"But whose blood is it?" Hal asked.

"We don't know for sure. We had specimens from your family and Paul and Cass and it doesn't belong to any of those people."

"That's it? Yavem didn't say anything else about whose it could be? There's no other identifying trait?"

Evon looked at Tim for a second, then faced her boss.

"He said the blood is a woman's."

"A woman?" Hal slammed back in his chair, his mouth wide open. "A woman? And do we have any idea who?"

"Best guess is Lidia Gianis." She took Hal through the reasoning—the blood, the ring.

"Auntie Lidia killed my sister?"

"It's possible," said Evon.

"No, it's not," he answered. "Let me tell you something. My Aunt Lidia was strong and tough, and she was old-school enough that she'd have whacked my sister a good one if she got fresh. But banging her skull on the headboard a few times? No chance. And even if you made me believe that, there is no way she'd let her son go to prison for her. That's the standard-issue Greek mother. She'd put a dagger in her breast for her children."

"It's what we have," Evon said. "Maybe Cass and she did it together, and he pled by himself to make the best of it."

"Why would my Aunt Lidia want to kill my sister? OK, she doesn't want Cass hanging with Dita. How about smacking her son upside the head instead? This is ridiculous. And there's nothing at all on Paul? Paul's been taking his mother's punches?"

"We don't know, Hal. The one person against whom there's no physical evidence of any kind is Paul."

"Except the bullshit he told the police, covering for his brother."

"If Lidia killed your sister by herself, then even that statement was true."

Hal sat back again in his big leather chair and turned from both of them. He reached to his desk and tossed a pen at an empty corner of the room. Finally he revolved back, seized by a new idea.

"But there's no physical evidence against Aunt Lidia, right? I mean nothing definitive. We don't know for sure it's her blood. She's not the only person in the world who's type B. Can we get her fingerprints?"

Evon looked at Tim. He just shrugged. He couldn't imagine how, but there was no point saying no until he thought about it.

"OK," Hal said. He waved his hand, letting them go.

Evon checked with Hal in an hour. His door was open. He was canted back in his chair, his hands behind his head as he stared solemnly into space. She grazed a knuckle on the door. His large eyes, surrounded by purplish flesh, briefly revolved toward her, then, after the briefest effort at a smile, he looked again to the place where the wall and ceiling met.

"I was just thinking back to when we were all kids," Hal said. "When I used to go over to Lidia's with Teri. A lot of the time I ended up looking after Paul and Cass. I always envied the two of them, to tell you the truth."

This confession, not atypical of Hal when he grew reflective, alarmed Evon for a second, until she reminded herself that Hal had no reason to know how much jealousy he should have felt. Then again, there would never be any telling what part of the truth he had sensed.

"They were fifteen years younger than me, and used to follow me around like ducklings. But sometimes I'd look at them, the way they were with each other, and I was jealous. 'They're never alone,' I'd think. 'Never.' It seemed like a wonderful thing. When I was their age, I was this fat weirdo that nobody wanted to talk to at school." Hal smiled ruefully at the recollection of the child he was, although Evon doubted that the pain of that past was fully sub-dued. "And I wished I could be like them. With a twin. Somebody who'd never hate you, or look down on you, because he was just the same, somebody who'd never turn away from you. It still seems like a blessing to me. Crazy?"

Two nights ago, Evon had returned home on the bus in the midst of an unpredicted rainstorm, the drops, big as grapes, pelt-ing down with assaultive force. Heather was in the doorway of the building, huddled under the cantilever close to the glass en-try, but the overhang had not offered her much protection in the high wind. Her hair had been reduced to waterlogged strands and her hat and coat were soaked gray. As a result, it took Evon a moment, as she continued striding toward Heather in rage, to recognize what she had done. Her hair had been dyed to match Evon's murkier shade, and she'd probably swaddled herself in bulky sweaters to make it appear she'd gained some weight. If Heather could have chopped six inches off her legs, she might have been a better copy of Evon, but the imitation was nonethe-less careful. She wore a slouch hat Evon owned and that Burberry coat Evon had bought for both of them. At a distance, Evon was suddenly and irrationally afraid that Heather might even have sacrificed her looks with cosmetic surgery to create some resem-blance. As Heather started forward, Evon could see that she had studied Evon's posture and her jocky, slightly bowlegged stride. Evon was stunned but also infuriated. Did Heather think this was love? Apparently so. Or was it, as Evon suspected, the most abject confession of dependence? Perhaps Heather thought this was what Evon wanted from her, to erase herself completely. Was that love, reducing two to one?

Evon had told Heather that she was going to the police station to swear out a protection order and went at once before she could change her mind.

"I don't know," Evon said now in answer to Hal's question. "It must make them crazy with each other at times."

"Sure," Hal said. "But they're tight for the most part. They always were. Must be nice. Me?" he said. "I don't even have a sister any more."

He shook his head about that, then they both went back to work.

25.

St. Basil's—March 12, 2008

St. Basil's Home for the Aged was operated by the Greek Orthodox Archdiocese and had the reputation of a first-class operation, as these kinds of places went. It looked like an old school, a broad three-story structure of red brick, surrounded by precisely landscaped grounds. Whatever the irony, Lidia Gianis's place of final residence was supported largely through the generosity of the Kronons and a few other wealthy Greek families. Over the years, Tim had had several former neighbors move in here, with no complaints from any of them, except for the obvious one, that their move out was likely to be in a casket.

Evon had talked to Tim for a while to convince him to do this. Whatever the Gianises' motives, she said, they had hidden the truth, from the Kronons, and from Tim and the other investigators. There was nothing disrespectful or cheap about getting answers to questions that should have received more forthright responses a long time ago. It was a good sales pitch, but the idea of trying to take advantage of an addled old lady still didn't sit well with him.

"Came to visit Lidia Gianis," he announced at the reception desk. The young woman, a college volunteer by the look of her, had a spray of turquoise in the front of her short hairdo. With the phone to her ear for another conversation, she asked, "You are?"

"Tim Brodie. Old friend from church."

She gave him the room number and pointed the way. Tim limped down the corridor wondering how soon his moment would come for a place like this, with the sprightly odors of disinfectant and air freshener not quite hiding the more unsettling smells of defecation and death. But it was a fine-looking place, decorated Colonial, with wooden pilaster strips in the corners of the hall and heart-backed chairs and comfy sofas in the reception area, all the furniture done in tasteful small prints, Martha Stewart on a tight budget. He passed by the chapel, fairly good-size, with white pews and a lovely dark walnut altarpiece. Three icons, elongated medieval figures on gold fields, were set on each side of the opening to the altar table, the crucifix and the stained glass window.

Clomping further down the hall, he heard live music and couldn't resist following the sound to the door of the dayroom. The old faces, mostly women's of course, were raised to the strains of a cello as if it were a sweet breeze. The young Asian woman with the instrument between her knees was quite talented, judging from her tone and bowing. Her music, Brahms, was offered as a gift, a reminder of the eternal and evenhanded power of beauty, a thought that stirred him deeply. He actually found himself wiping one eye as he moved on.

Once he reached Lidia's door, he asked for help from one of the staff members circulating in their bright smocks. She summoned Lidia's attendant. A stout black lady with short straightened hair, she approached, smiling broadly. She had a bad hip and rolled her body around it as she moved. He introduced himself and she shook with both hands, a kindly soul.

"I'm Eloise," she said. "Take care of Lidia most of the time."

"She decent for a visitor?"

"Oh yeah, we pretty her up every day and she just love it." Eloise waved him behind her, but stopped with her hand on the silver doorknob. "If she get nasty, don't mind her. Them dements are like that, you know." She put her good hip to the door.

Lidia's private room had the ambience of a decent chain hotel. The decorating scheme was all pastels, with plush carpeting and sheer curtains under the opened drapes, and a flowered print spread on the twin bed. Lidia sat in a beige recliner. A broad window behind her admitted a comforting rush of daylight, but her face was raised to the gray glow of a TV, from which Tim recognized the voices of *Law and Order*. A blanket rested on her lap. Lidia looked, for lack of any other term, hollowed out. She was far thinner than the woman he recalled, and beneath the makeup, her cheeks were now bunkers in her face. The black eyes were worst, clouded and shifting. Her entire head seemed compressed by whatever damage was occurring in her brain. It made his heart sore to see it, but it was what happened, what was happening to him. Rise and fall. The circle turns. His granddaughter, Stefanie, had called yesterday to say she was pregnant and Tim was still aloft on that news.

"Hey now, Lidia," said Eloise, "Mr. Tim here come to see you. And you look so nice today. Don't she look nice, Mr. Tim?"

Tim could only nod, still shy of paying compliments to a woman who was not his wife.

"See," said Eloise, "you wearing that bracelet your sons brought you on Valentine's Day. She always looking at the jewelry she got on."

Lidia's vague eyes turned to her wrist, which she studied as if she were surprised to find she had one. When she glanced back, she cast a cold look at Tim.

"Is he my husband?" Lidia asked Eloise.

"Oh no, honey. He just a friend." Eloise propped Lidia up in the leatherette recliner. "You all go head and visit. I'm just outside, case you need me."

Tim sat down in a wooden-armed chair a few feet from Lidia.

"Do I know you?" she asked Tim.

"Tim Brodie, Lidia. We met a million years ago at St. D's."

"I don't know you," she said. "I had a stroke and my memory is not so good."

"Yeah, well, my memory isn't what it once was either."

In thirty years on the Force, and twenty-five-plus as a PI, he'd done lots of interviews under daunting circumstances, questioning children and the mentally handicapped, and naturally enough, the desperately bereaved. But this would be a new chapter and he had no idea how to start.

On Lidia's bedside table were photographs of her two daughters and the twins and a passel of kids.

"Now who are all these folks?" he asked her.

"I don't know. The girl just put them there. But they're all nice people."

Tim picked up one photograph, a group shot of her grandchildren, Paul's two boys and her daughters' daughters.

"Now these grandkids of yours, they're a good-looking bunch." Tim meant it. The Gianises were always a handsome family.

Lidia was frowning. "Is that who they are?" she asked.

"Beautiful," Tim said. "All of them."

"My daughter is a movie star."

"I know." She was referring to Helen, who was still maybe the most gorgeous woman Tim had ever met face-to-face. She was said to be a handful, personally, and never got further than a brief role in one of the soaps. According to the local gossip, she was on husband four or five by now, a strumpet by the straitened standards of St. D's.

"Yes, I think they're all nice people. I have a son, did you know that?"

"Two, I believe." He tapped the picture of the twins, a recent one, Paul with his lumpy nose and Cass beside him, just a tad bigger.

"Identical twins," she said. "No one can tell them apart."

He agreed.

"My sons come here all the time. One of them is a big deal, too. Is he an actor?" she asked Tim. "People just love him. They tell me so all the time. Everyone here knows who he is."

Tim said he knew Paul, too, then asked about Cass, hoping for any information. Cass seemed to be some kind of shapeshifter, materializing, then disappearing.

"Oh yes. They are such good boys, both of them."

"I thought the other one, Cass, didn't he have some trouble?"

Lidia pondered a second and shook her head. "I had a stroke and my memory's not so good." She raised her hand again and stared at the bracelet, which, by whatever logic was left to her, once more brought her attention to Tim. "Who are you? Do I know you?"

"Tim Brodie, sweetheart. I thought maybe we could play a little game, you and me. See here?"

He reached into the pocket of his overcoat and removed an inkless fingerprint pad and several pieces of eight and a half–by–eleven copier paper. He showed her how it worked, putting her whole hand on the pad and the way the impressions magically appeared on the page. She was childishly amused by the process, and they continued for several minutes. Lidia offered no objection when he bore down on her fingers to roll the print onto the sheet.

Being with Lidia couldn't help putting him in mind of Maria's last days, when she was mostly gone and couldn't speak. All in all, his wife was the kindest person he had ever known—love seldom left her and she had filled their house with love like light. But in dying she became ornery and sharp-tongued, and frequently raised her voice to him, telling him that whatever he did was not right. It was a grief impossible to bear at the time, the raw unfairness that she had to die and leave as final memories ones of her being somebody else.

Nothing was fair, when you got down to it. People tried to be fair and made up rules about what was fair, but those laws didn't have much to do with what really happened, if you were willing to notice. Here he was, no more than eight years younger than Lidia, playing with her like a child. He was still mostly himself, and she was just a little fraction of the proud, regal soul he'd observed from a distance. You couldn't help but pay attention to Lidia in those days. The power of life swelled through her—it was like the swirling red lines on an old barber pole, no start or end, but you had to stare.

"Are you my husband?" Lidia asked as he was putting the papers and the pad back into his coat.

"No, Lidia. Just a friend."

"I don't see my husband much. I think he may still be mad, you know." Mickey had been dead twenty years. As Tim recalled the story, Mickey had been terrified of the initial open-heart surgery in 1959, when it was a recent innovation, but he came through like a champ. A little less than thirty years later, the pig valve had to be replaced, an act of routine maintenance, but Mickey stroked out on the operating table.

"And what would Mickey be angry about?"

"He never really said, but I knew he was always mad about Zeus."

"What about Zeus exactly?"

The question stopped her cold.

"Some silliness," she said. "I don't really recall. You must forgive me. I had a stroke and my memory's not so good."

Tim nearly laughed out loud. She was all but gone but she remained crafty.

"But why would Mickey be mad about Zeus?"

"Mickey?" she asked.

Tim considered his options.

"Lidia, did Zeus ever know he was the father of Paul and Cass?"

"Oh no," she answered, and clapped a hand straight to her chest. Some thoughts seemed to tumble through her head, then slide away like the rush over a waterfall. She looked again at her wrist. It was her right hand she kept gazing at, Tim realized.

"That's a beautiful bracelet," Tim said. "Mind if I see it?"

He took her hand. Doing the prints, he had noticed the Easton College class ring her boys had given her. It was quite loose now on her finger. The top of the ring, with the crest and the stone and the raised numerals of the year, hung down toward her palm. But forty pounds ago, it would have fit well and was substantial enough to have left that bruise on Dita's left cheek.

Yet what he'd missed before was the scar. Beneath the bracelet, reaching from the back of her wrist upward a good six inches, there was a line of shiny, whitish flesh. The scar looked like a river running through a topical map, wiggling a bit within neat margins. It was the scar, he suddenly realized, not the bracelet, that preoccupied her.

"Where did you get that mark on you, sweetheart?" he asked.

Lidia slowly raised her arm to study it.

"Oh, that," she said. "I cut myself."

"How? You recall?"

She contemplated, then repeated her mantra about her stroke. But she never lowered her arm.

"And who sewed it up for you?" From the even look of the scar, and the faint little puckers on either side made by the sutures, it appeared that a surgeon had closed that wound. When Zeus brought Tim on to the investigation of Dita's killing, the investigators, in the midst of their infighting, still hadn't checked the ERs for cut cases the night of the murder. Tim spread the canvass to every hospital for thirty miles. Naturally they discovered several bad lacerations treated that Sunday night and the next morning, but none of those patients proved to be of any interest.

Tim touched the scar gently.

"Sure looks like you had a doctor for that."

"I think it was that girl," Lidia said, the limb still aloft. Tim took her hand and lowered it, before her arm started to hurt.

"Which girl is that, sweetie?"

"You know her." She smiled at Tim, as if he were playing a game. "So smart. Such a nice girl. She became a doctor."

Tim tried to recall when Sofia Michalis got back to town after med school. Then he remembered Georgia's complaints about the attention Paul had paid Sofia at the picnic.

"It turned out OK for her," Tim said. "Was that who did your stitches there? Sofia?"

Lidia tried to hold the thought, but shook her head.

"I don't know anyone by that name," Lidia said. She apologized again about her stroke.

"Sofia is the woman Paul married."

"Oh yes. Paul is a big deal. Everyone loves him."

"Any chance, Lidia, you got that cut at Zeus's house?"

She looked again and this time touched the patch of smooth skin.

"Did I?" she asked. The idea seemed to make sense to her. From the dark contraction of her irises, he could see her struggling. "My memory is not very good."

"Did that happen before or after you hit Dita?" he asked her.

In response to the question, a slim fragment of mental agility again returned to her, just long enough to set something off, some kind of alarm perhaps. She reared back, then began rotating her head and her thin floss of gray hair.

"Did you hit Dita?" he asked her.

"Who is that?" she asked.

"Zeus's daughter. The girl Cass was seeing. Did you end up hitting her, Lidia?"

Her head went side to side for quite some time, more in sorrow, it seemed, than disagreement.

"I really can't talk about that," she said.

"And why not?"

"Oh, it's such a long time ago. Do I know that man?" She was pointing at Sam Waterston on the TV.

"Did you hit Dita, Lidia."

"I don't know about that," she said. "You should ask my sons. They know better than me."

He was going to quarrel with the evident logic of that—how would her sons know better than she whom she'd walloped?—but there was a more focused manner in the way she was shaking her head around, determined, as it were, to let go of the bad thought. He'd promised himself he was going to treat Lidia with dignity and avoid upsetting her. He was nearing the end of what either one of them could tolerate.

"Lidia, did you kill Dita Kronon?"

She stared at Tim. "Do I know you?"

He reintroduced himself and she explained about her stroke.

"Who killed Dita Kronon, Lidia?"

"Oh, that was all so sad," she said. For a moment, worry consumed her time-whittled face. "That girl was no good."

"The daughter? Dita?"

"She had a terrible tongue in her mouth."

"And did you kill her?"

"Oh no," she answered, as if the idea were as laughable as if Tim had asked if she'd made a recent visit to Jupiter. She stopped for some time, turning her wrist as she sorted through the strange rush of ideas.

"You sure you didn't kill her, Lidia?"

The question this time brought about a mercurial change. Her brow closed and her look became sharp, even fierce, as that lingering remnant of the darkly determined woman of decades ago once more asserted itself.

"They just never believe me," she said. "They never believe me."

"Who doesn't, dear?"

"You can just go away. I'm tired of all of this. I don't know who you are, and you're just asking all these questions to embarrass me. You can go away. Who are you anyway?" She cast a look at the door. "What is that girl's name?"

"Eloise?"

She shouted for Eloise. When the attendant didn't appear promptly, Lidia, with no warning, grabbed the remote for the television and threw it at Tim. He got a hand up partially, but it clipped his scalp. In the meantime, Lidia leaned over her chair and swung at him with a closed fist. She didn't come close. Shocked, he'd risen to his feet and was backing away. Lidia was screaming that she didn't like him when Eloise finally came through the door.

"I don't like this man and I don't know who he is."

He fled the room and waited in the hall while Eloise summoned another attendant, a little Filipina who couldn't reach five feet with a hand over her head. She seemed to have a good way with Lidia and Eloise left the two of them while she walked Tim out.

"She get like that some, but she is really such a sweet lady mostly. Funny thing, though. Must have been she had a little of that in her somewhere along. The doctors all say they just don't know. Some of them, those bad traits come out, some the Alzheimer just change them completely."

"No worries," said Tim. "She kept looking at her right wrist."

"She do like that, hundred times a day. Them boys always giving her jewelry, so she got something to see."

Tim nodded. The twins gave her the jewelry so people would think Lidia was fixated by the gems, rather than the scar.

"She ever say where that scar on her wrist came from?"

"Broke a window, she said once. You know, they tell you one thing one day and something else tomorrow."

"But she is right-handed, isn't she?"

"Oh yeah. Some of them dements, they forget so much they don't even know which hand to use to pick up a spoon. But she ain't like that. She use that right hand for everything."

"How long have you taken care of her?"

"Lidia? Oh, it's three, four years at least. She wasn't so bad when she come in here. Only thing was she could never keep those boys straight. Sometime she tell me Paul was here and sometime she call him Cass. But these days she don't hardly recognize either one. Lots of times she call them something else entirely once they gone."

"And what might that be?"

Eloise stopped. "What is that name? She's sayin it all the time." Eloise touched the wooden support rail that ran along the wall as if it might help her recollection. "Brings me in mind of something whenever she do it." One hand shot up when her memory finally sparked. "Oh, I know. It's one of them cartoons my grandkids watch. Fella always got lightning in his hand, this character."

Tim got it quickly. "Zeus?"

"Zeus!" She beamed. There was a good deal of gold in Eloise's mouth. "That's who she tell me come visit. More than once. Must be they resemble him some to her mind."

Once he was home, Tim paged through his files until he found the bundle of clippings from Dita's murder. There were photos of Zeus in nearly every story. Then Tim called up Paul's campaign site. It was ridiculous, frankly, when you looked at it, the resemblance he and so many other folks never saw, let alone remarked on. The shape of the face differed a bit but the three men shared the same nose and hair and mouth and eyes. What had Mickey made of their looks? Probably nothing. People didn't see what they didn't want to. Was that the hardest part of life, to look at it fresh and without preconceptions? Or would it just be unbearable chaos that way?

The next morning Tim went out to McGrath Hall to deliver Lidia's fingerprints. McGrath had been the police headquarters since 1921. The red stone heap might have passed for a medieval fortress, with stone arches over the massive planked oaken doors and notched battlements on the roof. When Tim was on the Force, he had hated the place, because he only got called down for somebody to bust his chops over something he could do nothing about. Then his last year and a half as a cop, they made him acting chief of Homicide, a job he never asked for, and gave him an office here. The gossip and intrigue that swirled through the halls was like a maelstrom that was just going to suck him down, and he often wished he could come and go in disguise. The milieu of the place became a big part of what had driven him into retirement.

Dickerman's office was in the basement of the building. If the brass had their way, Mo would have been situated halfway to China. They hated him, because Mo was always using his eminence to bend them backward with threats to raise a public ruckus if they wouldn't buy a new piece of equipment or software he wanted. The higher-ups thought, often with good reason, that the money could be better spent on other aspects of policing. But on a force that like most urban departments was frequently mired in controversy, if not scandal, Mo and his worldwide reputation were assets they could not afford to dispense with.

"How was Hollywood?" Tim asked when he arrived. Mo's lab down the hall was huge and state-of-the-art, but his small office was barely big enough for his desk and his metal filing cabinets. His garden windows were half-height and emitted only the barest light through the wells.

"Those people," Mo answered, but said no more.

Mo had retained possession of the original lifts from Dita's room, because Mo's travel schedule had kept Tim from picking them up. He handed over Lidia's prints now. Mo had insisted on negotiating a new contract with Tooley, which acknowledged that this examination wouldn't utilize any of the prints Judge Lands had ordered returned to other parties. Mo was a stickler, knowing that there were plenty of people in the county who'd use any controversy, especially in his outside employment, as a reason to oust him. He promised to begin the print comparison that night. He was one of those widowers who minimized his time at home.

"You know," Tim said, "I never got to ask you about that thing with Cass's prints from Hillcrest. Last time we talked, you were wanting to get a look at Paul's ten-card, because you thought Cass's intake prints at Hillcrest didn't match the crime scene."

Mo looked through his heavy frames for some time and then got up to shut the oak door. It had an old-fashioned frosted wired pane in the middle on which Dickerman's name was printed in block letters.

"You remember that day last month when Lands whistled me up to the bench to report on my findings about Paul's prints?" Mo asked.

"Sure."

"I nearly wet my socks. I was just waiting for him to ask me the wrong question and I'd look like Ralph Kramden. You know, 'Humanah humanah.'"

Tim laughed. It wasn't a bad imitation of Jackie Gleason.

"I thought you said Paul's prints didn't match the crime scene."

"They don't. Now that I've finally gotten a look at Cass's ten-card, I can exclude even the inconclusives."

"And what about Cass himself?"

"You remember a few days after Greenwood finally found Cass's prints and sent them over here, Lands said I had to give them back. Stern had an associate hie out this way to carry the card back to Greenwood County that afternoon. What does that tell you?"

"Maybe there was something they didn't want you to figure out. Maybe Cass's prints don't match the crime scene either?"

"They do. With all the craziness in this case, that wouldn't have been a complete surprise. But the minute I got that card, I looked at everything. Cass's prints were all over Dita's room, just the same as Logan said back in 1983, including the outside knob of the French door."

"So what was the big deal?"

Mo looked away and poked his tongue to his cheek.

"It's been a while, I'll tell you, since I was sitting up at night thinking about a case. I was ready to hire a brass band when Lands finally entered the dismissal."

At his age, Tim now and then found himself having unpredictable lapses, where he simply couldn't follow the loops of an ordinary conversation. That seemed to be happening now.

"I'm not catching the drift, Mo. Cass's prints are all over Dita's room and Paul's aren't. What's strange?"

Dickerman wiped his lips with his whole hand.

"It's that print card from Hillcrest."

"What about it?"

"Well, as soon as I got Cass's original impressions from Greenwood, I compared them to the prints from Hillcrest, and I know that's a laser copy, and there's no evidentiary value, but those are not Cass Gianis's fingerprints—the ones from the institution? They look a lot alike, but in the minutiae, there are distinct differences."

"Are you saying they're Paul's?"

Mo took quite some time before saying yes. "From everything I could see, the answer is yes."

Tim felt his mind spinning like a tire trapped in the snow.

"What the hell?" Tim finally said.

"I know. I was standing right there. I was looking Paul Gianis in the face when I took his fingerprints. You saw me do it. But the prints I took in the courthouse match the prints from Hillcrest."

"Jesus," said Tim.

Mo pointed. "Same rules: Not a word to anybody. If this ever got out, Horgan and Stern would have to come after me. They'd make a stink that I was looking at stuff I should have returned, and they'd say my opinion is a sign of incompetence. I don't need any of that."

Tim promised. He knew Mo had arrived at the wrong conclusion about Paul's fingerprints, he just couldn't figure out why. You could see even Mo was of the same mind.

26.

The Deal—March 20, 2008

Marlinda Glynn, a sharp young woman who'd taken a semester off from the University of Iowa to work on the campaign, was holding out his cell phone when Paul reached the backstage area at the West Town Community Center. They'd tried a morning town hall, but there couldn't have been more than twenty-five people here, most of them elderly folks who'd arrived largely to alleviate boredom. He was hoping the call was from Peter Neucriss. Peter was an old friend, and the most successful plaintiff's lawyer in this part of the world. Paul was going to beg him for another hundred thousand. Peter had already produced close to two fifty, bringing in checks in the names of every member of his family and his firm. When Peter said no, as Paul expected, he'd know for sure what was written on the wall.

"This guy says he's Hal Kronon," said Marlinda.

"Joke?" Paul asked.

"I don't think so. It really sounds like him." Marlinda had been there the day of Hal's tirade at the pardon and parole hearing. "And his secretary was on the line first."

Paul took the phone as he walked to the car.

"It's Hal," said Kronon, with an easy tone that made it seem as if the intervening decades of nastiness were simply stagecraft meant to obscure the fact that they were actually the best of friends.

"So I was told. Mind if I ask how you got my cell?"

"I have people who can get that kind of information in five minutes. There's this thing called the Internet."

Paul smiled in spite of himself.

"I'd like to have a sit-down with you," Hal said. "Just the two of us."

"Are we going to discuss the size of the contribution you're planning?"

Hal laughed, which Paul might not have expected.

"Not exactly. Take the meeting, Paul. I won't be wasting your time."

They agreed on 2:30, after lunch. Neither wanted to be seen with the other, so Hal suggested the building office at West Bank Mall, Zeus's original shopping center, and still one of the most successful in the nation. The place covered a square mile, the white brick buildings connected by networks of open walkways. To compete with the indoor malls, Hal placed heat torches outside in the winter and misters for summer's dog days, and even hired kids to escort shoppers under umbrellas when it rained. And the center thrived. You were lucky to find a parking space within four blocks of the store you wanted to visit.

Paul was still bewildered about why mall shopping had emerged as Americans' most thrilling pastime, as if coming back with several bags full of soft goods were the equivalent of big-game hunting. Whenever he was at a place like this, he wondered what we'd done wrong as a nation to make acquisition seem pleasing to so many. There was a kind of resignation to the activity that bothered Paul the most. He had nothing against leisure. It was a proud achievement that we'd given people time away from labor. But why shop, instead of garden or ride a bike?

He might have questioned the lines of folks passing by, if he thought they would have answers. He was wearing sunglasses, but was often recognized. People stared for the most part, but two couples stopped him, one to encourage him, the other to have their picture taken, much as they would have if he'd been walking along dressed up as Donald Duck.

He found the building office, a low freestanding structure. A young woman showed him back to a conference room with a cheap table and a few chairs. Hal was sitting on one of them. He rose and offered his hand for the first time in twenty-five years. Paul took it after some hesitation, then both men sat down.

Paul put a small digital recorder on the table and turned it on.

Hal's eyes ran back and forth to it.

"I told you this would stay between us," Hal said.

"Right. But I'd rather not pat you down for a wire or try to figure out if this room is bugged. I'll have my own copy, in case you ever go back on your word."

Hal's look darkened. Paul wasn't sure Hal was a secure-enough guy to deal with the open distrust, but he was the one who'd asked for the meeting.

"I'll just get to the point," Hal said. "I wanted you to know that I'm going to pull all those ads about you. I told the agency to get them off the air, even the ones where we've paid for the time already."

Paul nodded, trying to show no other reaction. There was a "but" coming.

"I suspect Georgia will appreciate that," Paul said. "I saw her a few weeks ago, and she thinks her hair looks like it was done by the serial killer in *No Country for Old Men*."

"Nobody tricked her."

"I'm sure."

"She wasn't lying, was she?"

Paul moved a hand to suggest that wasn't worth a response.

"What can I do for you, Hal?"

Kronon had a heavy, unhealthy look. He was heading into his late sixties now. His hair was fleeing and age was overtaking him quickly. Zeus looked like a movie star at Hal's age. Those recessive genes were a bitch.

"I'm considering making a public statement," Hal said.

"You've already made a few."

"This one will say I'm convinced you had no role in my sister's murder."

Paul's heart spurted, much as he wanted to contain his reaction. They would have a chance, if Hal did that. He still wouldn't bet on himself—too many voters just had a bad taste in their mouths at the mention of his name, and some by now were unsettled by the thought that his identical twin, a person with the same DNA, was a killer, even if he wasn't. But still. They might crawl back to second by the time of the first election in two weeks.

"That's a rather substantial change of heart," Paul finally said.

"Well, we've learned some stuff."

"Like?"

"That it was your mother's blood in my sister's room. Not yours or Cass's. Lidia's fingerprints are there, too. I have the report from Dickerman in my pocket, if you want to take a look."

Paul inhaled a few times to still the combination of fear and rage that flushed through him.

"How in the hell did you get my mother's fingerprints?"

Hal shrugged. "I already told you. The Internet. Everything's out there."

Paul took a second. The last thing he could tolerate was Hal Kronon in the role of wise guy.

"What do you want, Hal? I know you want something in exchange."

"Nothing complicated. I want to know what happened," Hal said. "I've spent twenty-five years sure you and your brother shorted my family on the truth. So I'd like to hear the whole story. And if you tell me, assuming it's true, I'll make that statement."

"Who decides if it's true?"

"Me."

Paul smiled.

"I don't know what happened, Hal. I wasn't there."

"But you know what you've been told."

Paul thought for a second. This was always a tale like the shell of a snail, whorls on whorls, and one that he'd known for a quarter of a century could never be shared. Back in the day, his mother always repeated a Greek proverb. 'He who reveals his secret, makes himself a slave.' Hal Kronon was the last person in the world to whom he'd make himself or his family a slave, especially after the sacrifices of the last twenty-five years.

"I'm not talking about that with you, Hal. And if I did, you wouldn't believe me anyway. But I'll tell you this one thing as a favor. Even today, I'm not sure who killed your sister. And I never have been. All I know for certain is that it wasn't me, and that I didn't have anything to do with it."

"That's not enough."

"That's all I have to say, Hal."

"You'll lose the election."

"Thanks to you." Paul was in fact increasingly at peace about losing. He'd turned fifty nearly a year ago. This was a good time to pull back and think about his life and what he really wanted, instead of capitulating to momentum, like a kid flying downhill on a sled. He was sick of meetings like this, with people begging or bullying, or trading favors. He'd longed for power for some good reasons, but also because that was what his mother always wanted for them, and because after Cass's guilty plea, he felt more obliged than ever to redeem their lives. But he'd done it and discovered power was a trap. You controlled less than you thought, and got beaten on like a piñata, and never escaped watching eyes, except at home. He could stand losing. The one who would be inconsolable was Cass. Paul wondered for a second if Cass would have taken Hal's deal. Probably not. But Cass wasn't here.

He webbed his hands tightly before he spoke, hoping to contain his anger.

"You know, Hal. I need to be honest. You have a lot of nerve. You're pulling those ridiculous commercials off the air? Great. You think I don't realize your lawyers have advised you that if you leave them up now, knowing all this, that I can re-file for defamation and clean your clock? Those ads always were a bunch of malicious lies, and you've been promoting them for months. Which is the real point. Any decent human being, having learned what you have, would come here to say one thing: 'I'm sorry. I'm going to the top of the ZP Building to scream to the world that I was wrong and that I'm sorry.' Instead, you're trying to hold me up, and to get me to sell out my family as the price of what even a modest respect for the truth should require you to do anyway."

Hal leaned over the table, coming perilously close. Paul could feel the heat of his breath when he spoke, and took in the beefy odor of his person beneath his cologne.

"You talk to me about respect for the truth?" Hal asked. "Your family has been hiding it for decades. My parents lived with Dita's death every day until they died. And I realized all along that none of us knew what really happened. And you think I owe you something, out of duty or honor? Excuse me, but somebody in your family killed my sister."

"Somebody in my family went to prison for twenty-five years.

And frankly, as I told you before, even today I don't know what happened. Maybe nobody in my family killed your sister."

"Then why did Cass plead?"

"We're done with this conversation." Paul stood up and grabbed his recorder. "I think your political views, Hal, are goofy. I always have. And I think your tactics are low. But I always thought you had some limits, that in your own cockeyed way you were a decent guy."

Ever a baby, Hal looked for a second like he was going to cry. Then he stiffened himself with a comforting truth.

"You're done for," he told Paul. "You'll never be mayor."

Paul answered from the door.

"So what?" he asked.

IV.

27.

Dita—September 5, 1982

*D*ita Kronon sheds her wet clothes and heaps them on the floor, where Tula, the maid, will deal with them in the morning. After grabbing a short pool robe from her closet, Dita crashes on her bed and clicks the TV remote. She told Greta she might slide by for a drink at 10:30, but she's shredded now that she's down from the 'lude, and Cass will be here by midnight.

It's been a long day already. She nearly did a dance when the rain sent all those shrieking greaseballs back to where they came from. Her parents are all the time telling her to embrace her heritage, but she has been explaining to them since she was about twelve that she is an American. Period. She's called Dita because that was as much of Aphrodite as she could pronounce at the age of two, but she's clung to it, rather than be known by a name so foreign and weird.

Hal, naturally, loves all of the Greek stuff, but he was born over there and still speaks the language. He's into all the rigmarole at church, the pained figures on the walls and the incense and chanting and the priest shoveling out the so-called Holy Gifts to everybody in the room from the same fucking spoon, all of which to *her feels like a really bad Halloween party. But Hal is a dork, who sometimes seems to embarrass her parents simply by breathing. Dita loves him anyway. Whenever she gets ready to marry somebody, she might look for a man a little like Hal, at least somebody as devoted and kind.*

But she won't marry anyone right now, which she's been explaining to Cass for weeks. She's gotten herself into a bad thing with Cass. She met him Memorial Day weekend at the club, where he was working as a lifeguard for pocket money, while he waited for the police academy to start.

'Watch this,' she told Greta, as soon as she found out who he was. The whole concept was to see the look on his face when she told him her name. She's gone out with plenty of guys, even done a few, purely on a bet or because it will make a good story. She was wearing a two-piece her parents had forbidden her to put on at the club under any circumstances, and she motored over to where Cass could see her, and smiled up to the chair while she squinted in the sun. And of course, as soon as it was his turn to climb down, he came over. He was good-looking, you had to give him that, very hunky, all that great Greek hair. That was one thing she liked about being Greek. The hair. And the food. That, too.

Cass is a good person, for sure, nicer, smarter, funnier than she expected. And it always thrills her when a guy falls as hard as he has, even though it also seems to paralyze something inside her. Cass truly gets a lot about her. He understands what she's doing at Jessup, how deeply she connects with her clients, these beat-up kids who everybody wants to act normal after there hasn't been a single normal fucking thing in their lives. But Cass seems like he's on this big mission with her, as if he's such a prize that she'll like herself better, just because. And with all his good intentions, Cass is becoming a pest.

She is pondering all of this, when, like a ghost, Mrs. Gianis steps out of Dita's bathroom. Her heart turns to a fist for a second, while she assures herself that she's not tripping. Dita grabs her robe around her and pulls herself up on an elbow.

"What the fuck?"

"I came in from the rain and the washrooms downstairs were occupied."

"That was four hours ago."

"Once I was here, I realized that I should take the chance to speak to you, Dita."

Dita is the only person in the house who can lock her door. Her mother found one of those tarnished old brass skeleton keys and gave it to Dita when she was thirteen, telling her to turn the key every night. That was a very, very fucked-up period around here, which nobody ever speaks about, and which Dita does her best not to recall. Every now and then, especially when nightmares wake her, memories float back at her, shapes in the darkness and the sensation of weight upon her and the suffocating aroma of her father's cologne, and the severe look from her dimwit mother when she handed Dita the key, as if it were all Dita's fault. But her room as a result has always been Dita's sanctuary. Once she turns the key, neither of her parents will do any more than timidly knock, which is why she loves to ball Cass—and several before him—right here. And also why Lidia's presence is so wrong.

"Well, I was fucking standing outside for about six hours."

"We need to talk privately. Like two adults. And I was afraid, Dita, if I asked you to do that, you would never agree."

She is right about that, for sure. Dita has more need of a third tit than a heart-to-heart with Mrs. Gianis.

"So you broke into my bedroom instead? I think you better go."

"I need to talk to you about Cassian." In her silly floor-length muumuu, Mrs. Gianis has crept close to Dita's bed. Her long fingers are webbed in front of her heart, in an aspect of prayer.

"Sorry, Lidia. That's none of your business." The Gianises are old-world and Dita knows calling Mrs. Gianis by her first name will seem impudent.

"I need to ask you, Dita, to stop seeing him."

"Ditto. MYOB."

"Dita—"

"Look, Lidia, right now I'm just fucking your son, so don't worry about it."

Mrs. Gianis slaps her. Hard. Dita's cheek erupts in pain, almost as if it's been skinned. The old woman has advanced on Dita so quickly she barely has had time to react, and in the process of drawing back, or maybe in recoil from the blow, she's whacked the back of her skull against the mahogany headboard. In the meantime, Lidia has retreated at least twenty feet, obviously shocked at herself, and is suddenly crying, an act that seems as unlikely as if a stone statue were standing here shedding tears.

"Oh my God," she keeps saying. *Lidia had been doing her in-charge thing, her favorite routine, but now the old lady has lost it and grown frantic. She presses a hand to her forehead, like it will hold in her brain.*

"I am pleading with you to act like an adult, Dita. To listen to me."

Dita tenderly touches her cheek and tells Mrs. Gianis to fuck herself.

"You cannot marry Cass. Or, God forbid, have his child."

"'God forbid'? Is that this old crap? The Gianises against the Kronons? You and your feuds. My father always says your family are like hillbillies."

"He never said that."

"I'll call him down here."

"He would not speak about me or my family that way."

"'Just a bunch of sheep-fucking hillbillies.' That's a quote."

"Dita, Cassian is your father' s child."

"Bullshit."

Lidia reacts as intensely and unpredictably as before, throwing her hands wide in rage and striking a pane of the French door. The resonant thump of bone against the glass sets off a cascade of remarkable sounds, a shriek from Lidia, and a pop like a muffled gunshot as the window breaks, followed by the wind-chime tinkling of the shards showering onto the concrete balcony outside. Lidia is looking down in amazement as blood bubbles from the back of her wrist. That sight, which Dita hates, as well as what Lidia has said—that her father, Captain Wanderdick, fucked her, too—is dizzying to Dita. It seems to unravel the loose knot that holds the different parts of her together. She needs to scream and she does.

"Get out!" Her head is starting to hurt as much as her cheek. *"Get the fuck out of here! Or I'm calling the police."*

Crazed and overwrought, Lidia moves one way, then the other, dashes to the bathroom and reappears with her arm wrapped in a towel. She starts to speak, but Dita grabs the phone beside her to dial the cops.

Crying fiercely, Mrs. Gianis struggles with the door. A little star of blood has already reached the outer layer of the towel swaddling Lidia's forearm. Finally Dita tells her to turn the key.

Once Dita hears the front door slam, she dials the phone in her hand. It keeps ringing until she gets Cass's answering machine, on which she leaves a message.

"You better get your ass over here. Your fucking mother just beat the crap out of me, and I'm totally going to call the police." Dita is astonished to find herself crying, perhaps only over the indignity. One thing is for sure—she is done with Cass and his lunatic family. She touches the back of her head. The fucking bump is starting to swell.

28.

Changing Partners—May 14, 2008

The Kindle County Tribune

WEDNESDAY MAY 14, 2008

Local Roundup

Just When He Thought It Couldn't Get Any Worse: Gianises Split

The office of state senate majority leader Paul Gianis (D—Grayson), 50, who last month failed to qualify for yesterday's runoff election to become Kindle County's chief executive, announced late Tuesday that the senator and his wife of nearly 25 years, Dr. Sofia Michalis, had agreed to divorce. Dr. Michalis, 49, who heads the Reconstructive Surgery Department at University Hospital, plans to marry the senator's identical twin brother, Cass. Cass Gianis was released from the penitentiary on January 30, after completing a 25-year sentence for the 1982 murder of his girlfriend, Dita Kronon.

It has already been a turbulent period for Senator Gianis. He was the initial favorite in the mayoral race and led by as much as 20 points in some early polls. His slide followed an intense negative advertising campaign funded by the real estate mogul Hal Kronon, CEO of ZP Properties, headquartered in Center City. Kronon alleged that Senator Gianis also had a hand in the murder of Dita Kronon, Hal Kronon's sister, charges Gianis furiously denied. Days before the April election Kronon pulled his advertising off the air without explanation, but the change came too late for Gianis, who missed the runoff by about 3,000 votes. Following his loss, Gianis endorsed yesterday's winner, North End councilman Willie Dixon.

Disclosure of the Gianises' impending divorce seems to have been timed in the hopes it would be lost amid election coverage, but the news became the subject of comment, much of it humorous, across the country, where the effect of Hal Kronon's ads on Gianis's campaign has already attracted substantial attention. The *Tribune*'s Seth Weisman, who frequently writes about Kindle County's political oddities in his nationally syndicated column, commented immediately on his blog.

"At least Paul has a chance to retire his campaign debt now," Weisman wrote. "Who wouldn't buy a ticket to that Thanksgiving dinner?"

On the sofa in his sun-room, Tim read the *Tribune* item over at least three times. His first thoughts were for Sofia, who, Tim felt, would be devastated to find herself the subject of scandal. He watched as much as he could stomach of the smirking coverage of the divorce on the morning news program, then finally called Evon about 9.

"I was just going to pick up the phone," she said. "Hal's already airborne, asking if this could have anything to do with Dita's murder."

"I can't see how. Can you?" Tim had never told Evon he suspected Sofia had sewed Lidia's wounds the night of the murder. There was no way to prove it. And his loyalty to Sofia made him reluctant to see her put through Hal's wringer.

"Do you have the time to nose around a little? Just to be sure. It'll keep Hal off my back."

"Hell yeah. I admit the whole thing eats at me."

With all the unfinished business in life, all the crimes where ancillary questions went unresolved, it surprised him that he remained preoccupied by the killing of Dita Kronon and the many pieces that didn't quite fit. He had thought for a quarter of a century that Cass Gianis committed the murder, and perhaps he had. But for Tim the case had been safely filed under "Jobs Done Right." At eighty-one, it was unsettling to see your supposed accomplishments unravel, since it left you to wonder how many more would come apart over time.

"Hal's still pissed that Paul wouldn't tell him the story," Evon said.

"Guy spends two years running for mayor," Tim answered, "and then won't recite a little piece of ancient history to get himself a better shot at the job? Whatever tale he has to tell has gotta be worse than what people were already thinking. Or at least as bad."

After much thought in the booth, Tim had still punched his ballot for Paul. In his concession speech, Paul said Sofia and he were going to take some time to consider the future, but until now Tim had not realized that meant their relationship. It was one of the truest adages he knew that you could never tell from the outside what was happening in a marriage. Sometimes inside, as well. All in all, it sounded like the Gianises had themselves one hell of a mess.

He told Evon he'd poke around a little more to see if recent developments had shaken loose something new. Evon asked him to check back before taking on any big expenses.

Tim didn't expect any of the Gianises to be more inclined to talk to him, but there was no harm in asking. Sooner or later, he might wear one of them down. He phoned Sofia at work, but it went straight to voice mail, where the message said Dr. Michalis was out of the office. Naturally. There were slimers from all over America who wanted an interview. Tim took an old-fashioned approach and wrote a letter, addressed to Sofia at the house in Grayson, saying he was thinking about her and needed a few minutes.

Around eleven, he went out to the Gianises' house, joining at least six different TV vans with their potato-masher antennas on the roof. A county cop was in the driveway to keep the reporters from acting like jerks and creeping up to the windows. Tim caught sight of a cameraman he used to know just a little, Mitch Rosin, sitting on the back of his van, enjoying a cigarette in the mild weather. The flowering shrubs were in bloom, and the trees had exploded into green overnight a few weeks ago. At Tim's age, there was a special pleasure in spring.

Rosin squinted through his own smoke as Tim gimped up.

"Brodie, right?"

"Right."

"How the hell have you been?" Rosin worked as an independent and had produced some documentaries for the cable networks. His shoulder was a mess, he said, from carrying the camera for forty years, but otherwise it had been a great life, as a professional voyeur. The rear doors of the van had been thrown open and Tim sat beside Rosin on the dusty bed of the truck. They gabbed a good twenty minutes, laughing about old cases. Like a lot of people, Rosin remembered Tim from Delbert Rooker. Delbert had killed six schoolteachers and tried to abduct at least four more. He actually rented space in a meat locker along with the deer hunters and had the six bodies wrapped and hanging right there. Except for being a homicidal maniac, Delbert could otherwise have been Mr. Peepers, right down to the pocket protector. Worked for the state Department of Transportation approving truck licenses.

"I take it," said Rosin, "that he didn't have a positive experience in grade school."

"So it seems. Guy never explained, though. We went in the apartment with a SWAT team. Here he is in a three-flat and he's grabbing these poor women, sticking them in his trunk, and then dragging them up the stairs to a third-floor apartment in the middle of the night, wrapped in a tarp. No one ever hears or sees anything. And of course, he's just inside his own sick world—not only took pictures but made audiotapes so he could relive each kill. And never cleaned up. There's blood and hair all over the living room rug. We had him sitting in the kitchen, handcuffed to the radiator while we searched. I says, 'Delbert, didn't you know you shouldn't be doing this stuff?' I was just trying to knock out the insanity defense. But he shrugs. 'Had it coming,' he says. 'All of them?' I ask. 'Had it coming.' OK, well then that's how he saw it."

Tim eventually asked what was up with the Gianises. Rosin told him that Paul's and Sofia's offices said each was on vacation. No one had a clue about Cass, whose latest whereabouts once again were unknown. There was no word on when any of them would be back, but the gossip shows all wanted the first footage of the new couple whenever they appeared, so Rosin was sitting here.

While Tim was talking to Rosin, the mail carrier arrived in her little truck and took a trip to the house next door. A tiny dark woman wearing a pith helmet and PO-issued shorts, she clearly didn't like doing her job on-camera and virtually dashed up to the neighbors' mail slot.

Tim tried not to react. He stood up and stretched and said something about moving his old bones. He drove around the block and ended up following the mail van for an hour, until the carrier stopped for lunch in a little Bibimbap hole-in-the-wall. She was jawing in Korean with the owners when Tim sat down beside her at the counter on one of the vinyl-covered round backless stools. She was a small woman, maybe fifty, with a beautiful coppery color and a wide sunny face. Her knotty little calves were displayed beneath the hem of her shorts with their maroon stripe down the seam. A large wooden cross hung from her neck, which Tim didn't take as an especially good sign.

He picked up a stray copy of the *Tribune* for a second, then put a hundred dollars in twenties down at her elbow.

She stared at the money.

"No way," she said.

"Just need a conversation," he answered. "How long is the Gianises' mail held?"

She ate for some time, using her sticks, her face close to the bowl.

She never looked down when she swept up the money and put it in her left pants pocket.

"Monday."

"And have you delivered mail there for Cass? Cassian?"

"Couple things."

"Any forwarding for Paul?"

"Start last week."

"Where to?"

She laughed. "I not the phone book." Still she closed her eyes. "Center City. Tee hun-rat on Mo'gan."

"Three hundred on Morgan," Tim repeated delicately.

She nodded. He couldn't think of anything else.

Thursday morning, Tim decided to see if he could find Cass. There was a guy he used now and then, Dave Ng, who could get social security information. Tim never asked how, but over the years he took it that Dave had somebody—or somebody who had somebody—in Baltimore in Social Security HQ. This was too far over the line for Tim, except when he was desperate. Ng charged five hundred bucks that Tim would have to bury in his gas and mileage expenses for Evon. Ng called back in an hour.

"Zero," he said. Tim had never met Ng face-to-face and for all Tim knew, he was really a black guy named Marcellus. In payment, Tim mailed two blank postal money orders to a PO box in Iowa. "Last job was at the Hillcrest Correctional Facility downstate. No employment this year in either quarter."

He might have thought Cass was a phantom, but both Georgia and Eloise, the attendant at St. Michael's, had seen him in the last few months.

On the way back to the Gianis house, he stopped at the FOP lodge hall. There'd been a jar of pickled eggs on the bar he'd been thinking about for two months at least. It had been an entire era since he'd eaten one. The same bunch he'd encountered last time was playing pinochle, Stash and Giles and the guy who'd told him he was never going to find Cass, and three more. There was a pile of quarters in the center of the table.

"God oh mighty," said Stash at the sight of Tim. "Here comes the walking dead."

"Greetings from zombie land," said Tim. He pulled a chair up behind Stash and said, "Jesus, you wasting all that money on a hand like that?"

Stash turned full around and Tim laughed merrily.

"I don't even know the rules of this game," he confessed. "Far as I know, you win with petunias."

"You still chasing around for Kronon?" Giles asked. "I'd have thought he'd have declared mission accomplished. He sure sank Paulie's ship."

"Just some loose ends I'm trying to tie up, more for my own sake than anyone else's," Tim answered.

He went to the bar and laid down two singles and ate two pickled eggs, then returned to the table to ask the guy who knew the Gianises' neighbor if there was any news about Cass.

"I actually talked to Bruce, after you were here. Told him you were on Cass's trail."

Tim nodded. He hadn't expected to fool anyone. Still, you could tell from the deliberate way the man didn't look up from his cards that he thought he'd gotten the drop on Tim. He was a fair-size guy, basically bald but wearing the fringe of hair he had left long enough to overflow his collar. Man seemed decent enough, but Tim sensed he hadn't actually been a cop, more a wannabe, probably welcome here because he lost a lot more than he won.

"He said no sign of Cass," the man said. "The wife saw Sofia in the driveway a couple months back and asked how it was all going and she just says, 'We're all so happy he's home.'"

"Yeah," said one of the guys on the other side of the table, "apparently she was *real* happy." A chorus of lurid laughter circled the table.

"They were bound to hit the rocks anyway," said Stash. "Paulie, he's been catting around for years."

Tim had learned a long time ago not to say never. A dick could make a fool out of a lot of men. But still.

"Now what kind of bullshit is that?" asked Giles, who'd been quick to defend Paul last time, too.

"No bullshit to it. You know Beata Wisniewski?"

"Any relation to Archie?" Tim asked.

"His daughter." Archie had been a captain who ran the Eighteenth District in the North End. There'd been stories for decades about drugs and cash disappearing from the dope-slangers out there. Plenty of defense lawyers told the same tale: A client who'd been dealing a pound ended up getting charged with selling six ounces. That was still enough to catch real time, but none of the dealers complained in court that the coppers had pinched their coke and were selling it themselves. If that was what was going on out there, and the PDs were pretty much sure of it, the captain figured to be getting some. Otherwise, he'd have gotten rid of the bums long before. But that was the days of yore by now.

"She become a cop, too?" Tim asked.

"Got into the academy straight out of high school, on some kind of waiver," said Stash, "long time after that was supposed to have stopped. Good-looking girl, too. Big but fit. She rode with me right after she started on the job. About six months in, Cass pled guilty and she was freaked out about it. Apparently, Cass and her, they'd been tight at one point."

On the other side of the table, a dark guy circled his thumb and forefinger and poked his other index finger through, as if he knew something. Stash shook his head uncertainly.

"She left the job after a few years when she got pregnant," said Stash. "Married to a training officer, Ollie Somebody, who had a big bottle issue. Guy used to try to smack her around and of course she's sober, and trained, and big, and apparently she put the asshole in the hospital twice. But finally she decides life's too short. Anyway, Roddy Winkler's got a son used to live in the same building she moved into. This would be just after Paulie started making real dough. And the kid, Roddy's son, he was also a lawyer, and he said he saw Paul leaving her place in the early a.m., more than once."

"Jesus," said the Mexican-looking character on the other side of the table, "I'm liking this story less and less. Not only is Paulie steppin out, but he's poking his brother's old girlfriend."

"Brother had to say go for it," said the guy who knew the neighbor.

"Weird shit," said the man next to Tim. There was a brief discussion then about the number of guys who wanted a chance with the Doublemint Twins.

"Early a.m.?" said Tim, going back to Stash's story. "Don't you think Sofia would notice the other side of the bed was a little cool?"

"Fuck do I know?" asked Stash. "Wifey must have been traveling."

"There's two kids at home."

"I'm just telling you what Winkler's son said. You know, I bumped into him at Roddy's and he says, 'I got something'll tickle you about your old partner.' He said Paul was turning up every once in a while until she moved out two or three years ago."

"Like for a decade?" Tim asked. This was cop truth, third-rank hearsay which was valid until it was disproved.

"So Paul's president of the state senate by now," Giles said, "and the press never picks this up?"

"Everybody likes Paulie. They only throw mud on the ones they don't care for. 'Sides, for all I know, they looked and never got anything they could print."

"What line of work was she in, this Beata?" asked Tim. "She go back on the job?"

"Too smart for that. Sells real estate, I'm thinking. Commercial property."

The hand was over and Stash looked at Tim and just heaved his thick shoulders. Don't blame him, he meant.

Tim went back to use the facilities, as usual, then stopped at the bar and had one more pickled egg. The heartburn would be hellacious later, but you had to live a little.

This business about Paul was a surprise, but it made the end of the Gianises' marriage make a little more sense. On the one hand, it really had nothing to do with what Tim was up to. On the other, you could never tell what got passed along as pillow talk.

He went to the public library in Grayson. They were closing libraries all over town, but this one was still bustling, patronized by lots of folks in his age range, and moms with kids too young for school. It had the sterile functional look of a lot of stuff built in the sixties, modern without a lot of frills. He found Beata Wisniewski's business address on the Internet, and a smiling photo of her on the real estate brokerage's website. As advertised. Good-looking girl, blonde with a little help for Mother Nature, but Tim never met a woman, his own Demetra included, who was blonde at age sixteen and didn't regard it as her God-given right to maintain the same hair color for the rest of eternity. He called the brokerage. The secretary said Beata was out on a showing until 3, and Tim went over to the office, which was right on the east side of Center City near the U Hospital. This was an area where Tim wouldn't go without his sidearm when he was a cop, and now it was all hip young folks. The real estate agency had apparently been situated here for a while, a three-story building with a gated lot. Ng could have gotten him the make of the car she owned, but he figured he knew who he was looking for, and as it turned out, it wouldn't have been hard to spot her anyway. A big black Audi with the vanity plate BEATA pulled into the lot about 3:45. He got out of his car, limping toward her. The spring day had gotten windy.

She was pretty much a Brünnhilde type, just big everything, not overly heavy, still nice-looking with her blonde hair upswept for a professional effect, and more than six feet tall in her high heels. She was wearing a light coat and had her briefcase under her arm, but she troubled herself for a quick smile when he came toward her. He extended his hand.

"Ms. Wisniewski? Name is Tim Brodie. Knew your old man a little bit."

She stopped moving and her bluish eyes approached absolute zero. Her jaw set like a linebacker's.

"This is private property," she said. "Next time you show your face here, I'll call the cops and you can tell them about the good times you had with my father."

Driving away, Tim tried to rewind the interlude frame by frame, hoping to determine when the ice storm had set in. Was it mentioning her dad? But he was pretty sure it was his own name that had chilled her. Which meant she knew who he was. Which meant in turn that the story about Paul and her had to be true.

Just on a hunch, he decided to sit on her house. Given how unstrung she'd appeared, she might need some smoothing.

He returned to the library. He put the cell phone listed on the brokerage website into a reverse directory, but the billing went to the office. The Tri-Cities' white pages online showed a T. Wisniewski on Clyde, which was about three blocks from the realty office. He used the street maps on the assessor's website to get the property identification number for that address, then confirmed with a different listing that Beata Wisniewski received that real estate tax bill. By 5:30 p.m., he'd driven out to the string of three-story row houses. Daylight saving had started and the young inhabitants were strolling in the mild night, a good half of them walking their dogs.

He circled for quite some time. About 6:30, he saw the Audi go down the side street, and he reached the alley soon enough to see the vehicle pull into a garage. He drove past slowly and glimpsed a splinter of Beata through the rear fence. It took a while until somebody pulled out of a space within sight of her front door, but Tim parked then and waited. He had no idea where Paul had camped out. But he'd seen lots of guys chucked out by their wives, and most didn't go far from home, not so much to be contrary as to consolidate whatever they had left. About half an hour after the sun had gone down, a little past 8:30, a light popped on in what he guessed was Beata's living room. Seconds later a car pulled up a few spaces in front of him. It was a gray Acura like the one he'd seen in

Sofia's garage back in February. Leaving the vehicle, a man actually ran the first couple of steps as he made his way down the block. Tim thought he recognized who it was as the fella passed under the streetlights, but the guy was on the move, and Tim saw poorly in the dark. He took a few photos during the instant the man appeared again beneath Beata's porch light. He was in her house only a second before emerging, lugging a huge suitcase, with Beata right behind him. They jumped in the Acura and were gone.

He tried to follow them, but given his vision, he had little chance. He lost the Acura as it mixed into the swirl of traffic close to the Nearing Bridge.

Tim pulled over to study the photos he'd taken, just to be sure he'd gotten it right. Enlarged, the digital photos turned grainy. Still, they confirmed what he thought.

He'd finally found Cass Gianis.

29.

One Man—May 18, 2008

On Sunday night, Tim drove back to Grayson and parked kitty-corner to the Gianises' orange-brick house. The newsies and the cop stationed in the circular were all gone, probably because their various employers didn't care to pay double overtime. But the mail carrier's information meant that Sofia might return now. And there were indeed lights on. He kept his binocs on the place until he saw Sofia move through the kitchen, then he walked across and rang the bell. In a minute, he could hear somebody behind the heavy varnished oak door, and a face flashed in the little viewing panel on top. The dog he'd heard last time was yapping indignantly.

Sofia opened, dressed in blue jeans, the dog bounding beside her. She didn't look especially well. Without makeup, her skin was lumpy. Her lip actually trembled as she stared at him with her giant eyes.

"Mr. Brodie, please. Please. Can't you respect our privacy? *Please.*"

The dog, a young lab, just old enough to have grown into her paws, reared up and clawed the screen. Tim put a hand forward to quiet her down.

" 'Tim,' " he said. "Think you're old enough to be calling me that."

"We've been through hell and back for twenty-five years now. We're just trying to put things back together. Don't we get peace at some point? Hal Kronon is crazy."

"I hear you, hon," he said. "I do. Truth is, figuring it all out may mean more to me than it does to Hal at this stage. Here it is, twenty-five years later, and I'm finding out I didn't do much of a job."

"I'm sure that's not true, Mr. Brodie."

"You know, Lidia's fingerprints were there in Dita's room. And what looks to be her blood."

Sofia didn't answer. She looked down at the tile floor of the entry.

"Sofia," Tim said, "I'm thinking you stitched up Lidia's arm after Dita was killed."

Her face jerked up like a marionette's on a string.

"Who told you that? Have you tapped our phones? Would you actually do that?"

"Of course not, Sofia."

Behind her, Tim noticed a man on the landing of the house's broad central staircase. It was Cass. Tim hadn't been in the same room with him for twenty-five years and by now, without that lumpy nose, Cass had become the better-looking brother, a little more vital than Paul had appeared in the latter stages of the campaign. He descended the stairs quickly and circled his left arm around Sofia to ease her out of the doorway.

"Good night, Tim," he said, and used his free hand to close the door.

On Monday morning, Sofia and Cass were all over the news. Some PR adviser had convinced them to do the equivalent of a perp walk in front of the vipers' nest of lenses. The Kindle County all-news cable channel covered the event live, which Tim watched from home. The pair emerged from the house shyly, standing together with uncertain smiles, their hands a hairsbreadth apart. The cameras swirled around them, while reporters shouted over each other with questions to which the couple didn't respond. In the midst of all of that, the dog escaped from the house and Cass had to chase her, whistling and clapping. The pup was a bit wild and raced around for a second, but finally returned, lying at Cass's feet to avoid further scolding, her tail flapping on the driveway. Cass led her inside by the collar, then exchanged a chaste peck on the cheek with Sofia before raising the garage door with a key. Each departed in a different car.

And where in the heck would he be going anyway? Tim wondered.

Paul, too, was back at work. The cameras got him pushing through the revolving door of the LeSueur Building about 9, smiling but shaking off the requests for comment as he made his way through the Art Deco lobby with its artful brass decorations. Building security guards held back the cameras as Paul reached the elevators.

On Wednesday, Tim went out to Grayson at 5:30 a.m. Whatever deal Cass and Sofia had made with the press seemed to have stuck. The camera vans were all gone. Around six, Sofia in her older Lexus rolled out of the garage, undoubtedly headed for surgery.

Tim stayed put to see if Cass's Acura would emerge, as it did around 8. It was clear to Tim after following Cass about five minutes that he was looking for a tail. He'd go two or three blocks, then back into a driveway and come out going the other direction. Tim avoided Cass the first time he used the maneuver, but when Tim turned the corner moments later, the Acura was at the curb, facing the other way beside the heavy old trees in the parkway. Cass actually smiled at Tim and lifted a hand to wave.

Tim called Evon.

"I'm gonna have to rent a new car every day," he told her. "I'm curious as hell to know where Cass is going."

"Do we care?" she asked.

"Maybe it's just because I don't have something better to do, but I look at all these stories about Cass and Sofia. You see one that says what kind of job he's got?"

"He's opening a charter school, isn't he? He's trying to get an exemption from the state Board of Education, because he has a felony record. Didn't I read that?"

"Where's this school? When's it open? And what kind of schoolteacher gives a damn about being followed?"

"I don't know. Maybe they're just sick of the reporters. Hal hasn't asked me anything for a week. He's in a big melee with his bankers." Apparently, within days of the YourHouse closing, Hal's lending consortium had decided to mark down the portfolio of unsold single-family houses ZP had just bought. The lawyers on both sides were fighting like minks, and negotiating around the clock.

"I'll pay for the rental cars myself, if you want," Tim offered.

"No, he still wants dirt on the Gianises. There are columnists and bloggers all over the country writing about getting 'Krononed,' meaning having some big-money maniac destroy you politically with phony charges. He'd be happy to have any information that shows there's something fishy with Paul. And what about Brünnhilde? Any sign of her?"

He was driving by Beata's house on Clyde every day, but the mail was piled up on the concrete lip under the mail slot in her front door, so much of it that the winter storm door was ajar.

On Thursday morning, in a rented Ford Escape, he lay two blocks off the Gianis house, but still lost Cass in the traffic as he headed into Center City. With no better alternative, Tim went down to the three hundred block on Morgan, where the letter carrier had said she was forwarding Paul's mail, to see what he could suss out.

Two new high-rises took up the block, here on the edge of Center City. When Tim was in the orphanage this part of town was all industrial, with huge square warehouses of unfaced brick and factories with looming smokestacks. It was a big trip in those days to come into DuSable. Each class went once a year, riding in on the Rock Island Line. He remembered the excitement, feeling queasy on the rolling carriages, then frightened by the size and might of the city, but the sight that most amazed him was at the other end, where a railroad turntable spun the locomotives around in the days before the engine cars were built to run backward.

Both new buildings had large banners in the windows, red lettering three feet tall, offering units for sale and rent. He entered each to see if there might be a directory of residents, but doorpersons were stationed at security desks in both lobbies, and he decided to wait before calling any notice to himself. Sooner or later, the Gianises were going to accuse him of stalking and seek an order of protection. He spent the day eyeing the doors and driveways to the buildings, listening to a tape he'd gotten at the library of the same book of Greek myths he'd been trudging through.

Friday morning, he was there again early, hoping to catch sight of Paul leaving one of the buildings on his way to work. Instead, he saw Cass's Acura arrive at the 345 Building about 8:45 and slide down the ramp into the private parking garage underneath. Tim left the blinkers on in his rented Corolla, and dodged traffic to cross the street, thinking it might be worth it now to check the directory. He had just opened the outer glass door to the lobby when a blue Chrysler convertible came up the same driveway. The vehicle was no more than thirty feet away, and he got a good look at the driver, who stopped at the top to check the cars in the street coming from both directions before turning right onto Morgan. It was Paul.

Tim limped back across the avenue to the rental car. He was lucky. Paul got caught at a light two blocks down and Tim managed to follow him all the way to a seven-story concrete parking structure across from the LeSueur Building. Paul soon emerged with his briefcase as he headed in to work.

Tim drove back to 345. When he'd wandered by yesterday, he'd seen visitors poking around at a small screen built into the security desk, using an attached telephone handset. The guard was gone for the moment and Tim lifted the receiver and followed the instructions on the screen, pressing the pound key to bring up a listing of residents. There were no Gianises, but he scrolled through and found T. Wisniewski in unit 442. He called for the hell of it, but there was no answer after eight rings.

He stood there sorting out the possibilities. Beata had a house, so she'd probably rented this place for Paul, but that had to be before he split with Sofia. There wouldn't be much point to putting things in her name now. Paul was still a famous face and word that he was living here would get around. Maybe it had been what the rogues would call their 'stabbin cabin,' although it seemed to Tim that Paul would have risked a lot less attention going through the back door of Beata's house. And what all was Cass doing here? The two brothers didn't figure to be on the best terms right now.

"Help you?" asked a portly middle-aged lady, who'd emerged from the package room and resumed her post on a high swivel chair behind the rosewood security desk. She wore a sport coat with *345*, the building logo, emblazoned above her heart. He could see from her squint that she'd been warned to watch out for somebody like him.

The 345 building, like the competitor down the block, was developed to meet all the needs of a busy urbanite. Here on the first floor, there was a gym and an overpriced organic grocery, and a couple of other small shops behind them.

"I was just looking for the dry cleaner," Tim said, expecting her to direct him to the cleaner whose sign he'd seen next door. Instead, it turned out there was a dry cleaning establishment here, too.

"Right down the hall." She pointed to the granite corridor. He could feel her watching as he gimped off, and for safety's sake he entered the store with its steamy smell of starch. An Asian lady asked if she could help. She had quite an accent, and he needed to get her to repeat herself twice, what with the noise of the pressing machine behind her. In the interval, an idea came to him, just a way to confirm that Paul was living here now.

He turned every pocket in his sport coat inside out as the lady watched.

"Supposed to pick up my boss's dry cleaning. But I don't have the ticket."

"What name?"

He told her Gianis and spelled it. She looked in her receipts and then threw the switch to start the merry-go-round of garments shimmering in their plastic wrappers. So Paul was here. Tim was about to go through the routine of telling her he'd forgotten his wallet, too, but she hung two suits from the hooked stainless arm that extended over the counter.

"You forgot one suit t'ree week," she said.

"Really?" He looked at the second garment. It was exactly the same as the one in front of it, a lightweight blue wool with a faint herringbone. He hoisted the plastic sleeve for one second, as if trying to be sure the suit was his, and looked inside to see the label of a bespoke tailor, Danilo. If it was the guy Tim was thinking of, Danilo made clothes for athletes and mobsters, a clientele for whom he kept his mouth shut.

He took both suits off the hanging arm and held them out in front of himself, trying to make out the difference. He moved them from hand to hand a few times and finally hung both on the stain-

less steel arm again, so the shoulders were fully aligned. Now he
caught it. The second suit, the one in back now, was probably half
a size larger at the shoulder, and the sleeve was a micrometer longer
as well.

"Three weeks, huh?" he asked her.

"Yeah." She showed him the receipt. Written on it in marker was
"442," but that show-and-tell exhausted her patience.

"You pay now," she said. So he opened his wallet and went
through the whole act, cussing himself out and asking her to point
him to an ATM.

Monday was Memorial Day. Tim was going to his granddaughter's
for a picnic with her husband's family later in the day, and he had
looked forward to that all weekend, sharing the young couple's excitement about Stefanie's pregnancy, and getting congratulated for
having hung around long enough to see some of his DNA arrive
in another generation. With nothing better to do until then, he decided to park across from 345 for a few hours that morning. Cass's
Acura appeared close to 10 a.m. Just as on Friday, roughly five
minutes after Cass arrived, Paul pulled out in the Chrysler. Tim
followed Paul to his senatorial office, and then to a parade in his district.

On Tuesday, Tim was at 345 at 7:30 a.m., wearing the twill
navy-blue uniform from the old heating and ventilation business
he'd briefly been in with his brother-in-law twenty-five years ago.
Both the waist-length jacket and the matching billed hat sported the
shield of Bob's company, which he'd sold off a decade ago. These
days, the pants didn't quite close over his belly, but he made it look
OK with a belt and a safety pin.

He stood outside the 345 garage on the concrete divider that
separated the incoming from the outgoing traffic. As soon as a car
pulled out and sped into the street, he ducked under the closing

door and continued down the ramp into the garage. A Cadillac heading up honked and Tim raised his hands in protest, pretending that he had every right to be here.

There were two floors, smelling unpleasantly of oil and engine fumes. The best he could do was lurk near the bottom of the ramp, sucked back against the cinder block wall. When the Acura came in, it circled straight down to the lower level. Tim took the stairs and waited until he saw the Chrysler head back up. He walked around the floor several minutes before finding the Acura, the engine still warm.

He was stationed on the bottom level of the garage Wednesday. He knew there was a fair chance he was going to get his elderly butt arrested for trespassing but curiosity had a serious grip on him. He had five hundred dollars cash on him for bail and had alerted Evon.

Cass pulled in at about 8:55, and spent a minute jogging cars. He moved the Acura into the space the convertible had been in, then returned with his briefcase to the Chrysler he'd left running across the row.

Inside the Chrysler, Cass disappeared from view. Tim walked by at about fifty feet. He didn't risk more than a quick look, and thought Cass was peering down at a computer, his shoulders shifting slightly. Tim walked up to a meter on the wall, pretended to monkey with it, then limped back in the other direction at the leisurely pace of a man getting paid by the hour. This time, when he passed by he could see clearly that Cass had his face in his hand, gripping the bridge of his nose, as if he was suffering a sinus headache or had come to grief over something. Afraid to stare, Tim went up one floor and stood beside the garage door, thinking he'd get a better look at Cass in the break of light when the door rose. And he did. But the driver was Paul.

"There's just one man," he said as he sat in Evon's office Thursday afternoon.

"Give me a break."

"Cass leaves the house. And Paul goes to work. I've been down in the garage three times now. Cass is living with Sofia, but once he leaves the house, he's pretending to be Paul. He's putting a prosthetic over the bridge of his nose every morning."

Evon couldn't keep from laughing.

"Come on. A fake nose? Does it have a Groucho moustache attached, too?"

"That's how he's getting away with it. Because nobody would ever believe it."

"I'll say."

"No, listen." Tim waved at her with both hands. He was quite excited and pleased with himself for figuring this out. "What does Sofia do for a living? She remakes faces all the time, and uses all kinds of prosthetics as part of it. You can go on the U Hospital website for the Reconstructive Surgery Department and see them—prosthetic noses and ears and chins and jaws and cheeks. Whole features or a piece of them for people who've lost, say, their nose to disease or accident or surgery or gotten it shot up or blown off. She's been doing it twenty-five years. There's a gal they call an anaplastologist who actually fabricates the prosthesis to Sofia's specifications. I've been reading all about it. The prosthetic is silicone and hand-painted with all kinds of pigments to be an exact match for the skin—freckles, veins, whatever is on the rest of the nose, and the edges are feathered so thin it blends right in, especially under those glasses Paul wears. I mean they use 3-D cameras and computers to make an exact casting. Look on the Internet. Close-ups like you were kissing the person and you can't tell. It's amazing."

"Come on," Evon said again.

"Yesterday when I saw him put it on, he must have been late, and he did it in the car. I figure he was painting on the surgical adhesive they use, cause it's got to cure in the air a little before it works. Today he had more time and went up to the men's room on the first floor. I'd put on a wig and a dress so I could follow him close and got in the elevator with him when he headed back down to the garage. He'd recombed his hair so the part was on the other side, and put on black frames like Paul, and fixed up his nose. I was standing right next to him. I'm telling you, you absolutely couldn't tell."

"A dress? How much do I have to pay for a picture?"

"It's not in the budget," he answered.

Evon looked down at her desk.

"How could that possibly work, Tim? I thought you said you followed him to court yesterday."

"I did."

"A man spends twenty-five years in prison and then knows how to practice law?"

"You think it's that hard? Most of it's just common sense."

"Never seemed that way to me," Evon answered. "OK. And where's Paul?"

"There is no Paul. I'm telling you Cass is being Paul."

"So there never were twins? I was just seeing things when the two of them were standing side-by-side at pardon and parole?"

"Well obviously there used to be two. I just don't know about now."

"And where did the real Paul go?" Evon asked.

"I'm trying to figure this out. There were identical twins in California. Sisters. Good seed and bad seed. And the bad seed started living her sister's life. Hired a hit man to kill the good sister, but the hit man narced her out and the bad seed is in San Quentin for life."

"So Cass covets Paul's wife, kills Paul and takes over his life. Right?"

"He's already been convicted on one murder," Tim said.

"And he committed this one with Sofia's agreement? This is the Sofia you've known since she was born?"

"It's just one idea."

"And why bother announcing that Paul and Sofia have split up? Why doesn't Cass just go around with his fake nose pretending to be Paul?"

"Cause there's supposed to be two of them."

"So say Cass has gone to Iraq. Or Alaska."

"I don't know. He needs to air his face out with that adhesive. You can't wear it too long. So maybe that's why he wants to play both of them. It's just crazy is all."

"And what about Brünnhilde?" Evon asked.

"Beata? Maybe Paul's hiding with her."

"You said it was Cass who drove her away. Right? You took pictures. And why would a man who's spent the last decade in the public eye want to hide from anything?"

Nothing ever added up in this case. Cass was sentenced to prison, but Paul entered the facility and was standing in the courthouse rotunda twenty-five years later. Lidia had been with Dita the night of the murder, bled all over the room, but her son pled to the murder.

"And not that Hal will care about paying these expenses," Evon said, "but what does any of this have to do with who murdered Dita?"

Tim's mouth soured as he thought.

"Something," he finally said. "I can't tell you how exactly, not yet. But if we figure this out, we're going to get to the bottom of Dita's murder, too. I have that feeling."

"OK, but how are we going to do that, Tim? You can't just go up to the guy and yank on his nose. What if you follow him into the men's room and confront him?"

"It's a single pew, for one thing. And he'd probably have me arrested for stalking, call me crazy, and lob a couple of mortar shells at

Hal, too." Tim sat thinking. "Maybe there's another way to smoke them out. You think you still remember how to follow somebody?"

She straightened indignantly in her large desk chair. The stuff you learned on the job, in situations when lives were on the line, was etched onto the fibers of your nerves. The skills were always there.

"Brodie, I could get inside your jock and you wouldn't know it. Especially if I got a little assistance."

He answered, "Let's see."

30.

Follow—May 30, 2008

Friday morning, Tim arrived at U Hospital. At the information desk, he asked directions to the office of Dr. Michalis. He knew she'd be here; her voice mail said she booked patient appointments Monday afternoons and all day Friday. The reconstructive surgery group had a little alcove of its own on the surgical floor. Tim took a seat in the sunny reception room. Sooner or later, Sofia would emerge. He was hoping it would be by lunchtime.

About two hours later, she swung out the rear exit in her long white coat, heading a few steps down the corridor to the ladies' room. He was waiting for her when she reappeared.

Sofia stopped dead and gasped and covered her heart with her hand. She spoke to him slowly, her face averted.

"Mr. Brodie. Tim. You know how fond of you I've always been, but if this continues, I'm going to follow my husband's wishes and get a restraining order."

"Your husband," said Tim. "Which one would that be? The one you're divorcing or the one you're going to marry? Although, so far as I can tell, the same fella's playing both parts."

Sofia, God love her, would never make any kind of liar. Her head whipped up, pretty much as it had when he suggested she'd stitched Lidia's arm. But this time, she was angry. He could see a hardness in her he'd never witnessed. Not that it was a surprise. Sawing off wrecked limbs required some flint.

"Hon, we don't mean you any harm," Tim said. "Or the rest of your family. Hal, he wants to know who killed his sister. Me, too. The rest of this costume party—I don't care why Cass is sticking a phony bump on his nose every morning, I really don't. Hal doesn't know about that. Nor does he need to. Just sit down with me and tell me what happened when Dita was killed. I know you wouldn't lie to me."

She seemed to consider the offer for one second, then her small cut-off chin shook minutely.

"Excuse me," she said, and shoved past him.

"He'll be moving any second." Evon saw the text pop up on the screen of her handheld. It was a few minutes before eleven in the morning.

From 345, she had followed Cass, disguised as Paul, as he drove in the blue Chrysler to the parking lot across from LeSueur. She slid into a space a floor above him. After trailing Cass into the office building, she spent two hours in a coffee shop off the lobby, getting some work done. On sight of Tim's message, she headed back to the garage. While she was still paying for parking at the automatic machines, she saw Cass push out of the LeSueur's revolving doors, with their brass fleur-de-lis grilles. He had a cell phone pressed to his ear, and a vexed narrow look on his face.

Tim had taken Cass's measure well. He was in a blue suit, as Tim had predicted. Brodie had discovered that was the only attire the Gianises wore on business occasions. Far more important, Tim had correctly foreseen that as soon as he confronted Sofia, Cass would run. He had to. He couldn't wait for the police to show up and ask him for fingerprints. Impersonating a lawyer was still a crime that the bar associations, with their influence, insisted be prosecuted.

In her Beemer, Evon was waiting for Cass as he ran to the Chrysler. She let one car get between them on the ramp down and called Tim's cell to tell him they were on the move. He was six blocks away.

The Chrysler exited onto Marshall Avenue and headed north in the thick Center City traffic, where the buses and double-parked trucks and jaywalkers created an obstacle course. She'd always been great at the follow, in her own humble opinion. At forty miles per hour, she could fit her car between two others with no more than four inches' leeway, and she'd always relished the occasional need for speed. Stock car racing went on the long list of things she wished she had tried.

Nonetheless, given what Tim had just told Sofia, Cass would realize he'd been shadowed, despite his morning evasions, and he'd respond accordingly. When he'd driven six blocks, he pulled into the valet area at the Hotel Gresham, and stood outside his car for a good ten minutes. As Evon passed him, Cass was chatting with the valet and checking his cell phone. When she looked back in her side view, she realized that Cass was photographing the traffic with his phone. Given that, she did not double back. Instead, she let Tim settle into position around the corner. He called in a few more minutes to say that Cass was under way again.

When she took over the tail, Cass was circling blocks. She and Tim alternated until Cass pulled into another parking structure by the Opera House. While Tim continued driving around, Evon stopped in a loading zone, left her flashers on, and hiked back to the parking lot. She took the elevator to the second floor, then walked down. Crouched on the ramp above, she saw the Chrysler pulled over in a handicapped space, right past the gate where entrants drew tickets. Cass had his cell phone out. She figured he was comparing the incoming cars with the photos he'd taken earlier.

About ten minutes later, a young man came out of the elevator lobby and approached Cass. They spoke for a second, during which she placed him: Paul and Sofia's older son, Michael, whom she recognized from the happy family scenes in Paul's campaign ads. The two men hugged quickly, and from the way each of them shuffled his hand in his pocket, she took it there had been some kind of exchange. After another hasty embrace, Cass walked away. When Michael opened the door of the Chrysler, Evon realized Cass had given his nephew the key. Evon panicked because she lost sight of Cass behind a van entering the garage. She was afraid he'd taken off on foot. As she was racing back toward the elevator, she recognized Cass from behind, walking placidly up the ramp. On the third floor, he got into a vehicle.

She phoned Tim as she watched Cass pull out of the lot.

"They switched cars. You're looking for a little red Hyundai two-door. Orange New York State plate."

Tim had picked up the coupe by the time she'd run back to her own car. Not long after she'd exchanged places with Tim on the tail, Cass suddenly gunned the Hyundai and streaked straight down Grand Avenue.

"He thinks he's clean," she told Tim on the phone.

She followed Cass over the Nearing Bridge. When the highway divided on 843, he headed north, away from the airport to which she'd suspected he might be heading. She remained about four hundred feet behind, just beyond the focal distance of his rearview mirror, in the lane to the right of him, maintaining his speed.

Cass went about six miles, then branched west on 83. He was zipping along now, well over seventy, and Tim called to say he was falling behind. He respected his age and couldn't drive much over sixty. After an hour, he was at least fifteen miles behind and worried that he wasn't going to do her much good.

"Keep me company," she told him.

"He's headed to Skageon, I figure," Tim answered. You could find nice country in any direction from the Tri-Cities, but Skageon to the north was by far the most popular destination. Unlike the prairie to the west and south, the land in Skageon was rolling, with panoramic vistas over the many lakes. Tim said he seemed to rec-ollect a feature story talking about Paul's family retreat up there. Evon thought she remembered the same thing, once he mentioned it. Maybe Cass had taken over that, too.

The Hyundai exited on 141, a two-lane road.

"He's going to the Berryton Locks, I bet," Tim said. These days, most people traveled to Skageon by following the winding course of the Kindle through the Tri-Cities and then heading upstate on the other major highway across town, 831. But from here, you could still reach the eastern shore of the Kindle by a ferry that departed from Berryton, where the Wabash and the Kindle met in a small falls that had been forded by locks erected in the 1930s as a WPA project.

The ferry, a massive white thing, was already docked when Evon arrived there in half an hour. Even on Friday afternoon in late May there was not much of a crowd. That would start changing in a week or two, once the Tri-Cities schools were out. On summer weekends, the cars in line to board could stretch back a mile and the ferry often filled, meaning at least an hour's wait until the next departure. But now, with about ten minutes to spare before the 4:35 embarkation, there was still plenty of room. Six cars were between the Hyundai and her when she paid her fee. She followed Cass down the gang-way into the iron innards of the ferry, which always reminded her of being in the belly of Jonah's whale. A flagger kept the cars straight within the bright yellow lines. When the lane beside Cass filled, she saw him get out of the Hyundai. The profile was still Paul's. He took the stairs up to the cafeteria, where he, like most folks, was going to wait out the thirty-minute ride. Cell phones didn't work inside the iron hull, and even in the cafeteria everyone tended to lose reception for a few minutes out in the middle of the water.

Once Cass was out of sight, Evon stretched her legs. She asked the flagger how long before the ferry departed.

"Three minutes."

At the rail, she got enough reception to call Tim. There was no way he was going to make it. He'd been on 141 for only a few minutes.

"I'll wait for the next ferry," Tim said. The plan to start had been to give Cass no choice: Tell us the truth about Dita's death, or we have to call the police right now and tell them about the identity switch. They'd planned to let Tim deliver that message, and that still seemed the better course.

"He's just going to take me as Hal in another body," she said. "It's a lot more likely that he'd trust you enough to make a deal." They knew for certain that Cass wasn't going anywhere for half an hour. The Hyundai was parked in by now.

A moment later, she could feel the ferry lurch as it unmoored. It would take another ten minutes, while the locks brought the vessel up about thirty feet to the level of the Kindle, before they started across the river.

She hung over the rail to feel the sun. It was a great early spring day, upper sixties, with high clouds plump as doves. When the little breeze kicked up periodically, it carried some of the chill of the water. She took a second in the ladies' room, then returned to her car and thumbed through her e-mail the rest of the ride.

When the other shore came into sight, heavily wooded between the little shacks that served as marinas and restaurants, drivers began to filter back down to their vehicles, starting their engines once the vessel banged to rest. The iron mouth of the ferry slowly opened, admitting daylight into the dungeon darkness.

The cars on both sides of her slid forward, but there was no motion in her lane. After another minute, horns were blaring, and the PA blasted an announcement asking for the driver of the red Hyundai with New York plates to move his vehicle before it was towed. Evon knew Cass wasn't going to appear. Eventually, an orange-vested flagger got into the coupe, in which the keys had apparently been left, and drove the car off the ferry.

She had no cell reception until she was onshore.

"He burned us," she told Tim.

31.

He Speaks

Tim was on 141, about five minutes from the ferry launch at Berryton Locks, when he saw Sofia's gold Lexus coming toward him. It was the mid-size model, close to ten years old, which was what clicked first, even before he recognized the vanity plate, RECNSTRCT. He saw two figures in the car as it surged past, Sofia in a headscarf and dark glasses, and someone in back. Tim pulled onto the shoulder and waited for a break in the traffic before crossing the road and taking off behind her. Something had to be up. He tried Evon's cell, but she was out of coverage on the ferry.

On the two-lane road, he could keep pace. The land began to roll here and every time he hit a rise he could see the Lexus several hundred yards ahead of him. Outside Decca, a hay wagon pulled by a pickup swung on in front him, doing no more than twenty-five. At his age, it froze his heart solid when he pulled into the oncoming lane to pass, but he needed to get closer. He fell in with two cars between Sofia and him.

When Evon called, he didn't even let her talk.

"I think I got him," Tim told her. "Never saw a surveillance the damn Feebies didn't muck up." He just wanted to make her laugh, and she did. The Feds, in fact, were usually better at the cloak-and-dagger. Talking it over now, she and Tim decided Evon should get on the highway on the other side and meet him at the Indian Falls Bridge about fifty miles north, the next point to cross the Kindle.

Near Bailey, the two vehicles that filled the gap between Sofia and Tim exited, and a few miles on, the speed limit lowered to thirty, as the road passed through Harrington Ridge. Tim now recognized the second figure in the back of the car. It was the dog.

"They could have had a second car up there at the ferry," Evon said, when he told her he still didn't see Cass.

"But Sofia's headed away from home," Tim said. "And she ran out on a reception room full of patients. Odds are she's running somewhere we wanna go."

Here, the footprint of the glacier had left undulant farmland, a picture from the *Saturday Evening Post*, with red barns and white farmhouses rearing up against the broken black soil, some stubbled by soybean sprouts. Occasionally the long vistas were interrupted by stretches of the old-growth forest of hickory and oak. The Indians had burned down much of it centuries ago so they could drive their prey into the open and see enemies across a distance. The white settlers had leveled more woods to farm.

As he expected, when 141 intersected with the highway, Sofia got back on 83. She took off north on the interstate, driving faster than Tim was willing to go, doing at least seventy-five. Before she disappeared, Tim thought he could make out another head beside her in the passenger seat. If it was Cass, he must have been reclined before, sleeping or hiding.

"If they don't take the bridge at Indian Falls, we're probably going to lose them," Tim told Evon over the phone.

There was nothing to do about that. Tim put his audiobook back on. The narrator, with a plummy, Anglicized voice, recited several versions of the story of the Gemini, the identical twins Castor and Pollux, born to Leda after she was raped by the swan. Driving along, Tim found his mind drifting from the book to the imponderable details of Dita's case. When things suddenly clicked, he nearly swerved off the road.

"I'm an idiot," he told Evon, when he reached her. "It's right in front of our faces." He reminded her about Father Nik telling Georgia that he'd seen Cass on TV, or Dickerman saying Paul's prints matched those of the man who'd entered Hillcrest. Eloise, the attendant at St. Basil's, said that when Lidia's son visited her, sometimes she called him Cass and sometimes Paul. "This little masquerade we've been watching. What says it hasn't been going on for twenty-five years?"

Tim had driven past the entrance to the roadside rest area, which was slightly elevated from the highway, when he caught sight of the gold Lexus parked there. He braked and pulled to the shoulder. Looking back, he saw Sofia rushing toward the one-story brick square that housed the restrooms. A plume of air shimmered behind each exhaust pipe, meaning her need was too urgent even to bother cutting the engine.

The ramp exiting the rest area was ahead of him. Tim inched his way along the gravel shoulder. The egress was posted on both sides with the red circle of the DO NOT ENTER signs. Tim waited for two campers to depart, then swung a hard right and drove in. A guy in an SUV with his family had seen the stunt and waited, but he hung his head out the window as Tim passed. "If you're too old to read, you shouldn't drive."

Tim nodded humbly and continued. In the meantime, he finally saw Cass, who alighted from the passenger's side, circling to the driver's door. He'd abandoned the disguise—the prosthetic was gone, and he'd recombed his hair and changed glasses. Sofia was on her way back now, and with one foot in the car, Cass called out to her, probably to say he was ready to drive. But the Lab took the opportunity to squeeze past him and flew out in a blur, charging over to the dog walk, where she tried to frisk around with the other hounds, one of whom reared up on its leash and began barking ferociously. Both Cass and Sofia gave chase.

While they were gone, Tim pulled in beside the Lexus. Its motor remained running. Tim went around to the open door, killed the engine and grabbed the car key. He threw it under the mat in the trunk of his rental car, a blue Chevy Impala, then called Evon for just a second. "I got them," he told her and hung up, because he could see the two strolling back, with the dog now leashed. Sofia caught sight of Tim first and stopped dead about ten yards away.

"Tim, please," she said.

"How about the three of us sit down at one of those tables over there and have a conversation? Won't take long."

"We don't owe anyone any explanations," Cass said. He was a pace ahead of Sofia. "Least of all Hal."

"Well, I'm not sure about that. My best guess is that you pled guilty to a crime you didn't commit."

Cass took that in, then motioned to Sofia to proceed.

"I don't think you're going very far," Tim said. "I have your key."

Cass charged past and peered through the Lexus's driver's side window. When he turned back, his expression was hateful.

Tim said, "You don't really want to beat up an old man with all these people around."

"I was thinking more about calling the police."

"Cass, that would be the wrong move. I'd have to give them the whole story, at least what I know. They'd take your fingerprints, and then they'd go over to Paul's law office, and his senatorial office, and you'd end up arrested for fraud, and false personation of a public official, impersonating a lawyer—God knows what else. Why don't we talk first?"

Sofia reached for Cass's hand, and Tim could see him slump in resignation. The three proceeded to a picnic table near the low brick building that housed the bathrooms and vending machines. The tabletop was a smooth speckled plastic meant to inhibit graffiti, but that still hadn't hindered the gangs from engraving their signs, probably with cordless Dremel tools. There was also a huge white splash of hardened bird poop, beside which several kids had used permanent markers to draw hearts containing their initials. Youth.

The dog continued to bounce around at the end of her lead, and was soon wound up in the steel legs that bowed under the table. Tim played with her a second. In his house, Maria and he had always owned dogs, mutts, but they'd been some of the best friends of his life. Part of his daughters' sales pitch for moving to Seattle was that with so many people to help him, Tim would be able to get another pup. Living here, he'd hesitated, unsure how his leg would do with three long walks a day in every kind of weather.

"She's a good one," said Tim. "How old?"

"Eighteen months," said Sofia. "She hasn't read those books that say she's supposed to have stopped acting like a puppy."

"Whatta you call her?"

"Cerberus. Paul named her."

"Cause she's such a ferocious watchdog," said Cass, and shook his head at the folly.

"That was the dog that kept people from escaping from Hades, right? With three heads?"

"I'm waiting for her to grow the first one," Cass answered. "But she's definitely got the part down about keeping us in hell."

"She'll settle down," Tim said. "Just like kids. They all grow up, just at their own rates."

None of them said any more then, so that the great humming roar of the highway surrounded them—the engines' throaty growl and the tires singing on the pavement and the spumes of rushing air spilling off the vehicles speeding along. The dog had actually taken a seat at Tim's feet as he scratched her ears.

"Cass, how about you tell me what happened the night Dita died?"

"Why are you so sure I didn't kill her?"

"Well, she was hit on the left side of the face, for one thing, which means the assailant was probably right-handed. You're a lefty."

"That didn't bother you twenty-five years ago."

"Not sure I knew that twenty-five years ago. Which is pretty odd in itself. Like you or Sandy were trying to avoid pointing a finger at somebody else." Tim reviewed the mounting evidence against Lidia.

"What about my fingerprints? And semen?"

"Dita's girlfriends all said you were skivvying up there every night to make out with her."

Sofia pushed Cass's arm. "Just tell him."

Cass closed his eyes. "I don't believe this. And if I tell you, who do you tell?"

Tim offered the deal Evon and he had already agreed upon. Hal was entitled to know the details of his sister's death. The rest—phony noses and switching places—was an interesting sidelight, but not essential for Kronon. That stuff could stay right here.

"Assuming one thing," Tim said.

"Which is?" Cass asked.

"That nobody else got murdered."

Cass started to say something in protest, then shushed himself and scanned the rest area. He was in his blue suit pants and a white shirt with the sleeves rolled halfway up his arms. His striped Easton rep tie, which he wore every day, was probably in his jacket, which was on the back seat of Sofia's car.

"I can only tell you for sure what I know."

Tim said that would make a good start. Cass pressed his face into his palms to give himself the heart to begin.

"The night Dita died," he said, "Paul and I left Zeus's picnic together and went to the Overlook and sat on the hood of my car and drank a few beers. We actually talked mostly about our love lives. There was a lot of ribbing until I told him I was going to ask Dita to marry me, which, to put it mildly, was not well received. Around 10, since we weren't talking to each other any more, we headed back to our parents'. Our dad was in a state. My mom had told us that Teri would take her home, but she hadn't turned up and Nouna Teri hadn't seen her since six. I checked our answering machine, thinking maybe she'd called our number for some reason. Instead, I had this hysterical message from Dita, who said my mother had been there belting her around."

"That was the call from her phone to yours?"

"Right." Cass nodded, a weighty motion involving his whole upper body. Lie number one, Tim thought. Cass told the investigators that Dita's only message was a request for him to call, which he'd immediately erased. "Paul hopped in my dad's car to look for my mom and I sped over to Dita's. I climbed up to her room and let myself in through the French window. I didn't even notice the broken pane until I was inside, when I saw the blood. It was all over the place, on the wall and the window. Dita was on the bed and there was a ton of blood there, too, soaking the pillow and smeared on the headboard. And she was dead. I checked her pulse. She was already cool to the touch."

"And you realized your mother had killed her?"

In reply, Cass grimaced and seesawed his shoulders. He took a second to give each shirt cuff another roll.

"I definitely didn't like the way it looked," he answered.

"Which is why you didn't call 911 or wake up the Kronons."

"Right. Which is why I just jumped down off the balcony—"

"Leaving the footprints—"

"I guess. And I ran back to the car. She had to be on foot. I figured that without a car, she'd walk down to Greenwood Village and call my dad to pick her up, so I went in that direction. About halfway there, I saw her. A hundred people must have driven past her. She was sitting up but somehow she'd gone down on the other side of a culvert. This bloody towel was still around her arm. She'd gotten blood all over her face somehow, and she was pretty much out of it. I had her home in twenty minutes."

"That's the type-B blood we found in your car?"

"It was Mom's, right. My father was insane, of course, but Paul and I knew that taking her to the hospital was as good as turning her in. So we called Sofia."

Tim turned to Sofia, who, up until now, had been listening as she held on to Cass's arm. Now she frowned. Even twenty-five years later, she was probably embarrassed at having had a part in fooling Tim. Nonetheless, she shared her part forthrightly.

"Lidia had severed the radial vein. No one would answer when I asked how she'd done it, but I knew they were afraid of taking her to the ER. Both boys were claiming Mickey's illness had made her phobic about hospitals. In any event, closing the wound wasn't a problem, but the amount of blood she'd lost concerned me. I thought she was on the verge of hypovolemic shock, which could have caused heart failure. Her BP, all things considered, wasn't horrible, but I told them if she developed a high fever, or any one of ten other symptoms, she had to be transfused. I came back the next day to check on her. She wasn't good but she was better."

"And did she admit she killed Dita?" Tim asked.

Cass wound his head about vehemently.

"Never. Absolutely never. She was literally too confused to talk about it for a few days. She admitted that she 'slapped' Dita—Mom's word"—Cass made the quotation marks in the air—"and agreed that Dita might have 'bumped' her head, but she said Dita was still shouting at her when she left. Of course, once we knew Dita died of an epidural hematoma, that made sense. But Lidia absolutely denied that she took hold of Dita's jaw or whammed her skull against the headboard. Nothing like that. No beating."

"And what did you think of that?"

"We believed, Paul and me, that that was what she wanted to think. And you know, the blood loss could have affected her memory."

"Did you think she'd killed Dita?" Tim asked again.

"Our mom had quite a temper. '*Tha sae deero*!'" Cass abruptly sang out. He had a finger raised and his voice lifted into a high-pitched rasp that sounded like the Wicked Witch of the West. He was imitating his mother, threatening a smack on the behind. "Those were terrifying words in our house. She'd hit us with a ping-pong paddle. There was no sitting down for days. She was rough when she was angry. But Dita was fit and strong. I couldn't see our mom overpowering her that way. So to be honest, no, I don't think I've ever made myself believe it.

"Of course, a prosecutor probably wouldn't have much doubt. There were a thousand people to testify how odd it was for Lidia to have shown up at that picnic, let alone end up in Dita's room. Plenty of folks knew my mom was convinced that my father would never talk to me again, if I married Dita. And my mom had given up any hope of convincing me to break it off, so there was a reason for Dita and her to get pretty heated.

"But even assuming a prosecutor believed my mom's version, that she hit Dita once and Dita knocked her head accidentally—the best Lidia would have come out with was a plea to aggravated assault. With a death associated, especially the daughter of a guy who was on the verge of becoming governor, Paul and I both expected that she'd catch serious pen time. Lidia said she'd kill herself before she ever set foot in prison. She never backed away from that. I mean, people do that, don't they?"

"Threaten it? Often. Carry through? A lot less." Tim had seen a few suicides on the way to the slammer, young men all with obvious worries, a couple of them addicts, too, who couldn't face withdrawal.

"But even that wasn't what made it complicated," Cass said.

"Sounds complicated enough," Tim answered.

Cass gave him a small, sick smile, somehow meant to be at Brodie's expense.

"Suppose," said Cass, "Mom came forward and told the truth. Gave you guys the same story she told us, and you took that as gospel. Where did Dita's other injuries come from? I'm the only other person who was in Dita's room before Zeus found her dead. My fingerprints are there, my footprints are in the flower bed. Dita's message said she was calling the police. My brother and my dad would have to admit that I headed over to the Kronons'. The prosecutors would say I got into a struggle with Dita to keep her from turning my mom in. Or because she was supposedly going to drop me."

Tim drew back. "You were afraid we'd charge both of you?"

"Why not? Plead my mom to the assault and give her immunity and force her to testify against me. Or better yet, let two different juries sort it out—immunize both of us and call me to the stand in my mom's trial and her in mine. Pretty, right? Mother against son, and son against mother. They could do it. Each of our stories implicated the other. Maybe the prosecutors would find a medical expert to say that Lidia's slap and my supposed wallops were each contributing causes of Dita's death. Not that they needed to legally. In separate trials, they could pin the whole thing on each of us one at a time."

Tim rolled all of this around. He'd like to say that cooler heads would have prevailed, but Cass had a point. With all the hysteria and the press attention, a lot of prosecutors would have ended up charging both Lidia and Cass.

"My mom, of course, she'd have lied and owned the murder to save me. But Lidia Gianis on page one as a killer? Her plan was to swallow hemlock—you know my mom would have the perfect dramatic touch—but letting her claim the whole crime was like handing her the cup." Cass smiled wanly. Down in the parking lot of the rest area, a couple's voices were raised in a quarrel. They were arguing about paying for a motel. "And we weren't sure she could carry it off anyway."

Tim made a mouth as he thought, arguing it through with himself. They'd never thought about gender-testing the blood in 1982. It wasn't routine, and everything said it was a man's crime anyway. But even back then, people knew about chromosomes. The blood in the room would have corroborated Lidia, if she said she was the murderer. But with Cass's fingerprints on the doorknob, and with fresh shoe-prints outside, any good investigator would have been pretty sure she was covering for her son.

"It was a mess, a horrible mess, no matter what we did," Cass said.

"So you pled?"

"So I pled."

Tim stared straight at Cass. "And Lidia Gianis let her son give up the prime of his life, while she walked away?"

"That's what happened."

"No, it's not," said Tim. He reached down again to play with the dog. She was still young enough to nip at his fingers and hold on. "I been following you more than a week now, Cass, watching you stick on a phony nose every morning and go to work and play your brother. And what finally hit me today is that this costume party didn't just start. You couldn't pretend to be Paul—practice law, be the state senator—unless you'd been doing that for years now. I think the two of you traded off the time inside. That's why you made such a big deal about minimum security. Because there's not one of those facilities you can't just walk away from, especially if your brother's waiting nearby to take your place. All you had to do was go for a walk in the woods and swap out your jumpsuit with him. So you were each Paul sometimes, and sometimes Cass."

"That's quite a theory."

"The prints for the man who entered as a prisoner at Hillcrest—they don't match the prints of the man who was in Dita's room. They're Paul's. I say he went into the joint first, just in case this whole charade didn't work. Can't keep the wrong guy in prison, can you?

"And the beauty of it, of course," Tim said, "is that you could talk your mom into doing this. You and Paul would each be out, at least at times. You'd both have a life, even if it was one you'd be sharing." Tim glanced at Sofia. She wasn't ever playing in the World Series of Poker. From the look of pure terror that had enlarged her eyes and stretched across her face, Tim could tell he'd gotten this right. "Must have been a little complicated at home, when Cass was sleeping in his brother's bed," he said. "I suspect that's how you all ended up in your current predicament."

Sofia looked away quickly and announced she was going to walk the dog.

"That's quite a theory," Cass said again.

"I'm pretty sure it's what happened. Only part I'm wondering about is what you said I'd wonder about—how Dita is dead when you get there. Truth is, though, your mom's version makes some sense to me. It took a pretty strong person to overpower Dita that way. That's one more reason we were sure it was a man. Hard to believe a woman of your mom's age could wham Dita around like that."

"As I said," Cass answered.

"Which means you may have killed Dita, after all."

Cass smiled slyly. "See? Five minutes ago you were telling me I was innocent. But I end up guilty when you weigh everything."

Tim leaned over confidentially, with a quick look askance at Sofia, who was clapping at the dog fifty yards off.

"It's just us," he said quietly. "Did you?"

"It would be really easy for me to say it, wouldn't it? I've already done the time."

He was right about that. On the other hand, there were some guys that could just never get the words out of their mouths. But overall, Cass had every reason to own the crime.

"Think I believe you," Tim said.

"Thanks." He didn't mean it. "But just so you know. That stuff about phony noses and switching in and out of prison—that's crap. I did the time because I was going to do it anyway, and this way we kept my mom out, and alive."

"Well, saying yes to what I just outlined, that would mean admitting to several felonies, for both you and your brother."

"It's BS."

"Whatever. Like I said. I just want to know who killed Dita."

"And I said I'd tell you what I knew."

Tim nodded ponderously. Cass seemed to have been good to that deal.

"Only one more thing bothers me just yet," said Tim. "I can't figure out what's become of your brother."

"He's fine."

"Is he? Then why are you running around pretending to be both of you for weeks now?"

Cass looked down at the table.

"Because you scared the crap out of Beata, and they needed some time together. She's pregnant, to tell you the truth. At forty-five, she won't get a lot more chances. So it seemed like a good idea for them just to get away from the freak show."

"And you agreed to cover for him everywhere?"

Cass smiled tightly. "I owe him a favor or two at the moment."

Tim couldn't suppress a bit of a smile himself.

"Have to say, your personal lives, that's none of my business, but I'd be happy to listen if you ever want to tell *that* story."

Cass was done smiling. He told Tim he had it right to start. That part was none of his business.

"How about we all just visit Paul?" said Tim. "He's alive and well, you know that's the end of it for me. But you can't expect an old homicide dick to walk away from any chance of a murder. Like I told you to start, I need to be sure about that."

Sofia and the dog were back.

"Tim wants to see Paul," Cass said. "He thinks I killed him."

Sofia stilled for a second, and then the air of gravity fled her entirely and she laughed out loud.

Cass stood up. "Just follow us."

"No, I think I've chased you around enough for this lifetime. How about we all get in my car and we go say hello to Paul? Once I see him, I'll give you your key and you guys can get on with whatever make-believe you're carrying out."

"And waste another hour driving back here?" Tim actually found Cass's response heartening, since it took for granted that Paul was alive and not all that far away.

"Cass, just get it done with," said Sofia.

32.

The New Paul

Tim agreed to let Cass drive his rental car, the new Chevy that had the lingering acrid odor of somebody who'd broken the rules by smoking in it. Sofia and the dog were in the rear seat.

"I need to call to let Paul know we're coming," Cass said.

"So he has time to put on his phony nose?"

"He doesn't have a phony nose. You'll see for yourself. It was convenient during the campaign for me to go out and be Paul. I admit that."

"Nope, how I've got this figured, whoever was being Paul was wearing that prosthetic. If Paul's nose really was broken like that, he could never have gotten away with being Cass at Hillcrest."

"Which is why that's all jive." Cass took out his cell. "I can't just show up there. There might be a scene. We're barely speaking as it is. I told you. Beata's up here to avoid stress."

"I think you were headed for Paul all along to talk over how to handle the fact that I was on to the disguise."

Cass rolled his eyes, and claimed that Sofia and he had just leased a cottage for the summer ten miles farther on. He dialed his phone without waiting for Tim to say yes. On the call with his brother, Cass's tone was no better than businesslike, but he'd explained to start that Sofia and he were in the car with Tim. Once Cass finished, Tim phoned Evon, who'd left several messages. He said he'd see her at the bridge in roughly an hour.

"That's all you can say right now?" she asked.

"That's all."

"You're OK?"

"Never better."

Cass and Sofia and he spent the rest of the drive talking about Sofia's sons. Michael and Steve were relieved the campaign was over, and especially that Hal's crazy ads were no longer on TV. Michael, the older boy, would graduate next month. He was headed for Teach for America, with law school likely after that. Steve was at the end of his sophomore year and talking about medical school. Tim wondered what it must have been like for those boys, with their uncle turning up periodically and their father disappearing. It was a burden on children to keep a secret like that, but they frequently handled it better than adults. Tim had seen a couple of instances of that with families living on the lam.

As Tim had expected, they headed over the Indian Falls Bridge. He saw Evon's car in a wayside there, but decided not to push his luck by asking if she could join them.

The land up here was beautiful, pines and poplars amid the rocky outcroppings, and a series of streams that sourced from the Kindle. Every mile or so, as they drove, they passed another placid little lake. People were outside now, restoring their houses for the season. You could feel their joy that it was finally spring, a celebratory emotion that inhabited the entire Midwest at this time of year.

Cass took a left on a country road, and then in half a mile turned up a hill. Paul had built a rich man's retreat. Sitting atop a knob, the large stone house had a shake roof and varnished pine timbers rimming the flagstone porch. The three emerged from Tim's rental car in the circular gravel drive. The dog dashed free, ran a giant circuit in the yard and came back with a tennis ball that she dropped at Cass's feet. He whipped it for her once underhanded, just as Paul strode from the house. He was in a plaid shirt and jeans and he crossed his arms as soon as he caught sight of Tim.

Beata emerged next. She wore an old chambray shirt, but Tim could see that Cass had told him the truth about her. She was starting to show. Paul reached back for her hand.

"Are you satisfied?" Cass asked Tim.

Paul looked like Paul, with that big broken bulge at the nose. It had always seemed strange with a wife who was a plastic surgeon that he'd never gotten it fixed, but then again Sofia hadn't had herself cut on either. But of course, Paul's nose wasn't broken at all. It was his disguise.

"You mind if I take a close look at you?" Tim asked him.

"Why?" asked Paul, clearly irritated.

"He's got another theory," said Cass, "that you and I traded places in prison for the last twenty-five years and pretended to be each other, by using a nasal prosthetic."

Paul considered that with a hooded expression, but descended the three steps from the porch. He even removed his heavy black glasses for the sake of the inspection.

"Make it quick," he told Tim.

Tim approached, fumbling in his own pockets for his reading glasses. He got close enough for a smooch, then came around the other side. It looked real, no doubt of that, but so did the prosthetic. He held still then, gripped by an idea, almost as if it was a dare to himself. He acted as if he were turning away, then revolved back and grabbed the bridge of Paul's nose and pulled like hell. Paul actually wailed in pain and swatted at Tim, and then Tim felt a heavy blow from the side and the harsh impact when he hit the ground. Beata was on top of him.

Cass arrived to pull her off, but stood by without offering a hand as Tim slowly climbed back to his feet. He could feel a hot pain on the side of his face that had struck the gravel. In the meantime, Sofia had taken both of Paul's cheeks in her hands, turning his head from side to side to examine him.

"It's time for you to go," Cass said. "Just give me my car key. Paul can drive me back to the rest area."

Beata was now at Paul's side along with Sofia, who was tossing her head back and forth looking at Tim.

"Mr. Brodie," she said, "I think you're getting demented. You could have broken his nose. You may have."

"I'm sorry," said Tim. "I thought I had this all figured out. I'm sorry." He had felt a hard ridge of bone and cartilage. Paul's nose was real.

"The key," Cass repeated.

Tim dusted off his coat and his pants leg. His shoulder was hurting, too. And the bad leg didn't feel any better either, having largely given way under Beata's weight.

He opened the trunk of the Chevy and reached under the mat for the key. When he came up with it, he noticed some kind of pinkish residue on the outside of his right thumb. He circled it against his index finger. Pollen was his first thought, but the substance was oily. Then he realized. It was makeup. It hadn't been on Paul's nose, rather under his eye where blood collected and bruises showed after an injury at or above the ocular orbit.

"The key," Cass demanded.

Tim tossed it. He threw it on Cass's left side and as Tim expected he reached across his body to catch it.

"Nice catch, Paul," Tim told him.

"I'm Cass."

"No, that's Cass," Tim said, pointing at the man who'd returned to the porch. "The guy who's been hiding out up here, while his nose healed after Sofia operated on it to put that bulge on it permanently. That was so you guys could make the switch once and for all. But you're Paul. I bet you were great at playing Cass in the joint. But you're not used to doing it out here. That dog, she's eighteen months old, and she's glued to you. Not the man you say trained her. And by the way, I watched the way you threw that ball for her underhanded. I bet you and Cass learned to eat and sign your name with the other hand—same crappy illegible signature from both of you—but throwing a ball overhand from the wrong side, that's hard to master. Here. Prove me wrong. Throw me those keys back overhand."

The man he'd been calling Cass up until now just stared at him. They were Zeus's eyes, too, dead black.

"Should I ask you to stand back to back with your brother?" Tim said. "Wanna bet that Paul is the one who's just a tad taller now? Cass is going to be Paul from now on. And you're going to be Cass. But living with your wife. Which is nice to know," said Tim. "And Beata, she's been Cass's girlfriend for years, whenever he was out of the joint pretending to be Paul. I understand her wanting to be up here with him, especially given her condition, but I don't think she's feeling too fragile," said Tim and rubbed his shoulder. "She's just been avoiding me. Which is her right. I hope you all live happily ever after. I truly do. I'm not sure I understand what the hell you're doing. But it's not really my business."

Sofia stepped down from the porch. She took her car key from her husband, then approached Tim and put a hand up to his cheek.

"That's going to bruise, I'm afraid. I'll get some ice. Anything else hurt?"

"No worse than usual," he told her. He wasn't really sure about his leg.

Sofia headed into the house and murmured something as she went so that the other three followed her in. The dog crashed out of the woods at that point and stood at the door with the ball in her mouth. Her tail wagged, and now and then she looked back expectantly at Tim.

"Don't ask me, Cerberus," he told her. "I don't understand anything around here."

In a few minutes, Sofia returned alone. She carried a plastic bag of ice cubes, a tub of water and a spray bottle. She washed the wound and had him close his eyes while she spritzed him with an antibacterial. Then she handed over the ice.

"Ten on, ten off," she said. Tim got into his rental.

Sofia knelt down to peer in. "Just between us?"

"Of course."

"You're right."

"I know that. Your husband's a pretty good guy. Cass and Lidia were both in a jam. But that's a hell of a thing for a brother to do, volunteer for prison, even if it's only part-time."

Sofia looked down to the gravel drive for an instant, as if the truth might be located there.

"You learn a lot about love married to identical twins. It's not for everyone. Especially if you want to feel like you're number one. They grow up in a world of individuals, and we all tell them to think and behave like us. But they can't. At least not these two. Their fundamental experience is different. It's probably the ultimate bond. The whole switch thing was Paul's idea. He was certain Lidia would do herself in. But more than that, he just couldn't tolerate the idea of his brother bearing that kind of trouble without him sharing it."

"You involved, too?"

"Little by little. I suppose I was in on it as soon as I sutured Lidia. Certainly when I started falling for Paul. I came up with the idea for the nasal prosthetic. We needed a facial characteristic so prominent that it would obscure the other minute differences between them, especially the ones that would develop as they aged. And you know the saying. 'Plain as the nose on your face.' It's the best way to differentiate two people's appearance. Hilda, my anaplastologist, she must have figured it out by now, but she's never said a word. The whole thing was manageable because they wore the prosthetic only when they were on the outside, being Paul."

"And they just glided in and out of the facility for twenty-five years?"

"There's a back road at Hillcrest. Whoever was out would drive up. The other one would go for a walk through the woods. Exactly as you said."

He shrugged. All those minimum-security places were the same, outside some small town where they needed the jobs.

"Occasionally there'd be a problem," Sofia said. "Somebody on the road. In twenty-five years, there was only one inmate who got suspicious. They did their visits in the attorney room for a while—Paul was always listed as Cass's lawyer—and swapped clothes there, until a CO came in and found them both without shoes. He nearly wrote Cass up, but Paul told a story that Cass was hungry to try on his new loafers.

"They changed places every month usually. But occasionally it would be for a day, if one of our boys had an important game or a teacher's conference. There were some weird times." She rolled her large eyes. "Lots of stories."

"I bet. And no trouble practicing law?"

"Paul didn't know any more than Cass about practicing criminal law when he started in the PA's office. You don't really learn how to be a prosecutor in law school. It's on-the-job training. And both of them picked up a lot from Sandy Stern during Cass's case. A few years later, when Paul went into private practice, he got into a big case in Illinois and needed to be admitted to the bar there. Cass stayed in the joint for six weeks and studied, and he was the one who took the bar exam and passed it.

"So practice was never the problem. It was the details of life. They wrote down as much as they could for one another in those letters they sent every night, but I must have apologized a million times over the years for Paul's poor memory. The hardest part was the kids. The prosthetic had to come off at night, and with it or without it, each boy could tell their father from their uncle by the time they were three. It was a big chance telling each of them the truth, when we finally did. We had this pact among the three adults that there would be no recriminations if one of the kids blew it. But they didn't. Kids don't like to be different, it's the kind of thing they keep to themselves naturally. At this point, they're grateful. They feel like they have two fathers. A lot of children of identicals will tell you that."

"And what's going on now?" Tim asked. "What's the point of changing identities?"

"Paul's had his fill of politics, Cass hasn't. Paul is going to be happier opening that charter school. It'll be for ex-cons and kids out of juvenile confinement, young men fourteen to twenty-six. The curriculum will go from high school through junior college, with a big emphasis on job training and internships. The notion is that the cons will teach the kids to stay straight. It's a neat idea. And it's the right job for 'Cass.'" She made the quotation marks in the air. "A con teaching cons? Paul's already talked to Willie Dixon about it and the county will fund it. And Cass wants to stay in office. So it makes sense. Doesn't it?"

"Not for me to say. But I hope you all live in peace. You're entitled." Tim thought about what Sofia had said. It was a lot to take in. "How was it having your kids while they were swapping places?"

"Paul was always home when they came." She looked Tim in the eye. "And when they were conceived. I can tell the brothers apart."

Tim laughed out loud.

"You settled for half a husband?"

"Lots of spouses spend time apart. Think of families in the service. Besides, I was twenty-four and crazy in love. And I thought any man who loved his brother that much would love me the same way."

"Were you right?"

She smiled a little, philosophical, as he'd expect of any grown-up.

"I think so. I think our marriage really is another reason Paul's willing to leave public life. So we have a space to build a more normal relationship. Until February, I hadn't lived with my husband longer than two months straight in twenty-five years."

"Working out, I hope."

"It's been great, thank God. I won't pretend we weren't both worried. But you know, Mr. Brodie, Tim—as hard as it's been at times, I always thought about the way you and Mrs. Brodie were while Kate was dying. And afterwards. You two really were my model. God knows, it wasn't my parents."

She'd surprised him. "Did it truly look that good?"

"Yes. Really good. Really solid."

"And do you think Maria was happy?"

"I'm positive she was, Mr. Brodie. Positive. Don't let her death take that away from you. I remember one day when I was in high school, I was over at your place, and I passed through the kitchen, and at just that moment Mrs. Brodie, Maria, lit up like somebody had turned on the power, just beamed. And I couldn't understand and then I realized she was looking out the window at you coming up the walk. I wasn't more than fourteen or fifteen, but I thought, That's what *I* want. *That*."

Tim, as often happened these days, found himself near tears.

"You couldn't have told me anything, Sofia, that means more to me."

She smiled. "I'm glad." When she straightened up, she looked into the car for another second.

"I told them that you were a person of your word. That you won't tell anyone about this part. The last switch?"

He nodded then and she leaned in to kiss his cheek. As always, she told him to say hi to Demetra.

Evon was still parked at the foot of the bridge. She jumped out of the car as soon as she saw him coming.

"Who hit you?"

"My own damn fault," he said. He told her about grabbing Paul's nose and getting attacked by Beata.

"Paul's nose is real?"

He nodded and didn't say anything else.

"That kind of screws what you were saying on the phone, right?" Evon asked.

"Maybe. But whatever they were doing, or are doing, I guess it's not our business. That's the deal we said we'd make, right?"

"Right," Evon said. "I don't know why I should care."

It was late now. The sun was starting to set into the river in an astonishing display of color. They leaned on the hood of Evon's Beemer, the sight soon lost on them while Tim told her what he'd heard about the night Dita was killed.

"So," he said at the end, "either Lidia lost it more than she admitted or recalled and is the killer. Or Cass is lying and he killed Dita. Or someone else took a turn whomping on young Ms. Kronon."

"And what's your bet?"

"Cass didn't do it. I'm convinced of that. And there's no skin under Dita's fingernails. She'd have fought off Lidia, especially after

Lidia slapped her. But she didn't raise a hand to whoever killed her. Which means, probably, that it was someone she never ever expected it from."

"Like someone in her family?"

"That's tonight's guess," said Tim. "Hermione, she was a wafer, she never had the strength. So that leaves the two men."

Evon stared at him. "Hal?" she asked.

V.

33.

Zeus—September 5, 1982

*B*etween the row of Corinthian columns that surround the drip-
ping porte cochere at the front of his grand house, Zeus raises
his palms to signal to his fleeing guests that he accepts the judgment of the gods: The picnic is over. Sheltered by umbrellas and
newspapers and, in a few cases, the plastic cloths filched from the
tables, his fellow parishioners rush down the hill toward the lower
meadow where their cars are now sinking into the mud. His suit,
swan-white at the start of the day, has been grayed by rain, but he
keeps his place, waving, throwing kisses, shouting to the boys from
the caterer to assist the old yiyas, many of whom stop to touch Zeus
and bless him as they depart. Diane Trianis, built to the same stately
proportions as her mother, comes close again to kiss his cheek. She
remains lovely, even with her hair reduced to a fringe of wet scraps.
"Call the campaign office Tuesday," he tells her again. She has just
divorced, needs work. He slept with her mother twenty years ago,
and the fleet thought of what may be ahead with Diane sends a jolt
to the part he has been known to refer to as his thunderbolt. So
much happening, so many people—real people he has known for
years—in his thrall. The picinic is always a wonderful day. Hermione

has him by the elbow and he turns at last to the darkness of the house and the gloom he dwells with whenever he steps out of the circle of light that shines on him in public.

His wife, miraculously if predictably, has remained almost completely dry. Hermione is always in precise control of her appearance, so much so that years ago she had her eyebrows plucked out, preferring to draw them in perfectly in pencil each day. She remains sleek and elegant in the expensive garments she has had tailored, even if she looks like a ruler once her clothing has been shed. But she is reliable. Her smile has been fixed faultlessly for six hours now. Without doubt, she is exhausted, but Hermione is too rigid to complain. Yet no one in a marriage ever fully forgets its worst moments, which in Hermione's case involve alcohol and a torrent of shrill anger that she finds difficult to dam once it bursts forth. In those times, usually when he himself is drunk and has in Hermione's presence chatted too amiably, canted too close, hungered too openly for a young woman, she calls him a callous monster, whose ego is a well that can never be filled. He accepts these outbursts, even her judgment, in silence, knowing he has brought it on himself. The truth, of course, is that he is not a good person. He is entranced by his power and impressed by the way it has grown up in him like the trunk of a strong tree. But the immensity of the appetites Hermione deplores often shocks even him. She is right. He will never be happy.

Hermione inevitably restores order to their marriage. Ordinarily it is the next day when she comes to him and says simply, 'I am grateful to you, Zeus. I am grateful for my life.' This is enough, and far more than most men receive within the walls of their homes. He knows that. Thanks to his late father-in-law, Hermione understands their relationship the way a man would, as a deal well made on both sides.

Zeus has stopped in the living room, amid the brocades and the treasures. Phyllos brings him a glass of whiskey. Pete Geronoimos, who has been upstairs in Zeus's office using the phone, comes down the stairs whistling.

"I've got a plane to take us to Winfield at 6 a.m. The Farmers thing is in line." The UF, United Farmers, is going to endorse Zeus. He will talk about his family in Kronos, at the foot of Mount Olympus, who kept sheep and goats and horses, a few of which they had not stolen from someone else. His father had actually come to the US because a posse of local men had spent a full day tracking him like a wolf. But Zeus will limn Nikos as a gentle shepherd.

Pete is a food importer, but he has loved politics since they were boys together. By all rights, he should be the candidate, but Pete stands five foot three and is built to the same proportions as a kitchen stove, and has been busted three times Zeus knows about, propositioning undercover cops who told him they were sixteen. Last year Zeus finally acceded to Pete's repeated requests to run. Pete undertakes most tactical decisions, attends to all operational details. Zeus's job is to make them love him, a task he relishes, talking about his modest start in life, the war, business, the glory of America, selling his whole story, which he knows they yearn to believe. The voters are still angry with the Democrats and that weak cluck Jimmy Carter in his cardigan, telling Americans to turn down their thermostats and perk up from their funk. People want strength. Eighty percent of the people who will cast a ballot in November have no idea what the governor actually does besides live in a mansion and attend parades. Zeus is strong. The idea of standing on the balcony of the governor's mansion after his inauguration and waving to a throng of thousands is as exciting to Zeus as sex.

When Hal and Mina come into the living room to say good night, Pete heads home to his dog and a few hours' sleep. Zeus's daughter-in-law-to-be embraces him and praises every aspect of today's event—the food, the music, the warmth of the people from

St. D's. Hal, who is learning to follow her example, repeats every word as if he had thought of it himself. Hal is a good boy, far younger than his age, but dear to Zeus, due especially to his eagerness to please his father. Hermione is in despair because the couple cannot be married at St. D's. The rules are absolute, Father Nik says, he does not make them. Were Mina a Catholic, a Presbyterian, anyone who accepts Christ and the Trinity, she could receive the sacrament. Zeus could not care less. He is a Greek of ancient sensibility, who believes more in the gods on Olympus than some mystical three-headed ghost. He takes Mina with him when he gives speeches at synagogues.

As Hal and Mina head off, Dita, his treasure, flashes by. Zeus calls her. She answers him, as always, with impatience.

"What?"

He considers her as she stands there, an extraordinary beauty with her sharp features and penetrating eyes. There is no love in his life like the ravening desperate love he feels for his beautiful daughter, his only true child. It precedes everything else. He is dirt and muscle and bone; but first he loves Dita. This love holds power over him, so much so that at a terrible moment it was beyond his control. Which is why she despises him in a way that will never ease. She needs him, too, as children always do, and is twisted on the rack by that antagonism, between her hatred and her need. But neither of them will ever fully escape that darkness in the past, a cataclysm that resides in the same place in Zeus as the chaos of war. It was a sad drunken time in his life, right after his mother died. He rarely lets his memory turn there, and neither Dita nor her mother nor he ever speaks a word. But the lock on her door is always a reminder.

"Thank you for being so gracious to our guests," he says.

"You're welcome. I hate this fucking day," she tells him. "Those people bore me to death. Greek this, Greek that. They don't seem to know they're living in a cage."

He ignores her. That is all that he can do. She will be twenty-four in a few days and remains under her father's roof with the implicit proviso that she will be free from any criticism, including much she unquestionably deserves.

"Your boyfriend is Greek, if I'm not mistaken."

"Cass? I'm just about done with him. His family hates me. What in the hell did you do to them, Dad?"

"Nothing. It was a misunderstanding. Lidia unfortunately married below herself. Mickey is really nothing but a Greek hillbilly. He has more pride than ability. He felt humiliated by my kindness to his family and I only meant well."

Zeus spoke to Lidia today, the first words in many years. Teri believes Lidia attended the picnic because she is beginning to accept that Cass will marry Dita, as he well may, despite tonight's hard words from Zeus's mercurial daughter. Lidia is stout now and gray. Yet the woman he so desperately longed for remains visible to him. For years, especially when he entered the service, he retained the hope that he would return in glory and marry Lidia, whatever her father had to say. When Zeus learned that she had wed herself to a creature as simple as Mickey, it was like a stabbing. Zeus has always recognized that he married Hermione in part because the only woman he ever envisioned as his partner was gone. He wants so many females in other ways. Even now, he can saunter across some broad avenue, stricken by longing for half the women who come into sight. Any manifestation of beauty is enough to stimulate his ardor—good legs, a full bosom, a pleasant face. But he had truly yearned to marry only Lidia, who then chose her father over him. In reprisal, in time, Zeus fucked her. It was the way the gods always served him. He saw that the instant that Terisia asked him to give her best friend a job.

'She is desperate,' Teri had said.

So I will fuck her, Zeus thought. Desperation had cost Lidia the power to say no. But even so, she remains one of the few losses in his life. He never sees her, even now, without wondering whether he might have despaired less in himself if she had been his wife, if her strength would have made him less brutal.

Dita has departed without saying good night. Zeus climbs the stairs, pained by his life. Hermione is asleep. He steps into his pajamas and lies beside her. Hermione lets her arm come forward and rest sweetly on his flank. He touches her hand, grateful for its familiarity, and drifts deeply into the grip of his own troubled dreams until he is roused by a clamor down the hall. The rain has cooled the night and Hermione has opened the French door. From there, he hears what is surely glass breaking and soon after, Dita's scream. There is often noise from Dita's room, late at night. It is her revenge. But there is no pleasure in these sounds. As he struggles into his robe, he is certain he hears the front door slam.

He tries the knob on Dita's door and is surprised to find it unlocked. He knocks and enters, asking if she is all right, but his heart clenches when he sees the blood. It is slathered on the French door and looks like a splatter painting on the wall.

"My Lord! What is this?"

Dita is on her bed, her robe parted to expose one long well-shaped leg. She is rubbing the side of her face, and greets her father with a baleful expression.

"What?" he asks again.

"You were right about them being hillbillies."

"My God. What are you saying?"

"Cass's mother was here."

"Lidia?"

"And beat the hell out of me to get me to stop seeing her son."

"Here. In my house? She beat my daughter?"

"She told me a pretty good story." Dita at that point seems to recognize the flimsiness of her attire and grabs a quilt at the foot of her bed. "I mean really, Dad. Is there anybody around here you haven't fucked?"

In him, something gives way, some sluiceway of raw emotion that is always contained for Dita's sake. There is a clear implication in her words—'anybody'—and he has always known that if she speaks, she will destroy him. Not because he wouldn't lie. Zeus has long accepted that lying well is an inevitable attribute of power. But it would mean she has abandoned him forever. The thought of that fills him with both fury and terrible dread.

"Your filthy mouth," he says. The closest thing to changing the past is to leave it unspoken.

"Oh, that filthy mouth used to suit you fine," she answers.

He slaps his hand across her lips and slams her head back to stop her. For a time all he knows of himself is rage and strength. But he feels in that brief instant as he drives her skull back several times that she is offering no resistance because she knows this is what she deserves.

When he lets go finally, he takes a step back. His heartbeat is all the way into his shoulders and he is breathing like a horse under a heavy plow. She is winding her head, touching her brow, but finally focuses on him with scorching hatred. The worst has happened, he knows. He has lost her for all time.

"Fuck you," she says. "Fuck you forever." And then she does what Dita never will—gives way to tears. She wails, his child, as she did when she was young.

He steps forward to comfort her, his arms open.

"Get out," she screams.

He has taken one step to the door when he sees the smear of blood on the headboard, and worse, a crimson bubble rising from her crown. She realizes he is staring.

"What?"

"You're cut," he says. He lifts a hand in warning. "Don't touch it.

Don't infect it. I'll get a towel." He goes to the powder room across the hall. He is trying to explain what has happened in his own mind. But there is only one explanation, which he has always known. He is a bad man.*

When he returns to Dita's bedside, her look has changed. Her beautiful eyes no longer seem to move together. She is slumped to one side and from the desperate way her arm swipes out at the sight of him, he somehow knows she has lost the ability to speak.

He runs down to wake Hermione.

"Something has happened to Dita," he tells her. Later, he knows, he will think of other things to say, a way to contain this in better words and entomb it in the past. He is Zeus and always finds a path. But not now. By the time they return to Dita, his daughter, his precious child, his treasure, is dead.

34.

Good-Bye—May 31, 2008

About 6:30 Saturday morning, Evon was awakened by a flat-handed thumping on her apartment's front door. She needed sleep, and nearly ignored the racket, but the sound was authoritative and urgent, and she finally jolted awake at the thought of fire. By the time she had her robe on, she realized who it had to be. Cleverly, Heather had stepped to the side, so she was out of sight of the fish-eye in the door. For the sake of her neighbors, Evon had no choice but to open up, albeit with the chain secured.

"Please," Heather said, as she stepped forward, "please." She pressed her face to the breach between the jamb and the door. On her breath, Evon could smell the stale reek of alcohol. As so often, Heather had affected her look of reckless dishabille. A slinky sleeveless top of iridescent fabric, which she'd donned for her night in the bars, hung off one shoulder, raising the inevitable question of whether it had been shed in pleasure a few hours earlier. From one finger a pair of glittery six-inch heels rocked, along with a ring of keys, on which Evon could see the garage fob. The doorman was on notice and would have barred Heather, but she'd sneaked in through the building's subterranean parking garage. The code for the electric door was still programmed into her car, and she'd used the fob to get upstairs from there.

"No," Evon said. "That's my line. 'Please.' Please, let go. Please. For both our sakes. You're making both of us totally miserable. You know I have a protection order. Please don't do this to yourself or to me." She spoke with a kinder tone than she'd managed in several weeks, but she still closed the door. Heather slammed it once with the flat of her hand, then hammered several times with what sounded from the sharp impact to be the heel of one of her shoes. She stopped after a minute.

Evon went through the useless exercise of lying down in her bed, but she remained wide awake and heard her phone buzz. There was a text. "Look downstairs," it read.

She thought of replying, "No," then decided that no response was better. But after lying still another second, she recognized an omen in the message and went to the living room window and peered down to the distant street. From this height, the avenue always reminded her of a scale model, with inch-high people and cars like crawling scarabs. She didn't spy anything at first. At this hour, traffic was sporadic and on the sidewalk there were only a couple of pedestrians, both out walking their dogs, joined by early-morning runners who flashed by.

Then she saw what she'd been intended to notice. Her BMW had been nosed into the street from the garage driveway. Heather still had that key, too, apparently. But even at that, Evon was confused. Was she supposed to beg to save her Beemer?

In a second the car moved, inching forward at first. Then it shot straight across the breadth of the street in a blur and rammed into the old-fashioned iron lamppost on the other side of Grant Avenue. Heather had floored it. The front end of Evon's sedan crunched like a soda can underfoot, and the lamppost leered to the side. The orange electric cables below it, which had been abruptly jacked out of the ground, appeared to be all that was keeping the streetlight from toppling. If Heather hadn't put on her seat belt, which she frequently refused to do, she might be seriously injured.

Barefoot and still in her robe, Evon descended in the elevator, completely uncertain about what she was hoping to find. There was smoke coming from the front end of the Beemer, but that was because the engine was still running, grating against some part of it-self. When Evon pulled open the driver's door, Heather was pinned in the seat. The airbag had deployed and the seat belt, which she'd fastened after all, had also retracted to hold her in place. Heather had clearly terrified herself and was crying with abandon. But her soft blue eyes were wide open and she turned them on Evon, even though she seemed slightly dazed.

"Just tell me you never loved me. Just tell me that and I'll leave you alone. But you can't," said Heather. "You can't say that."

"I can't," Evon said. Then she crouched down so Heather and she were more or less eye to eye. She actually held her hand, a disconcerting act after not touching for months this woman whose every caress once had so thrilled her. But she folded her fingers tenderly over Heather's. She had blamed Heather since January for being all kinds of crazy and hiding that from her, but something else was suddenly clear to Evon. "I can't say that. But I shouldn't have. I shouldn't have fallen for you. And that was my fault. Not yours. I couldn't accept you as you are, so I wanted to pretend you were someone else. And even worse, I wanted to believe I was somebody I'm not. It was so exciting. But I can't be that person. I can't. So you have to forgive me, baby. I wish I had known myself better."

There were sirens already. One of the dog-walkers, apparently, had called 911. A police cruiser arrived only seconds after the big square ambulance, both vehicles with lights flashing and their sirens sounding discordantly at two different pitches. The combined wailing was sharp and disturbing, like something used to keep prisoners awake during interrogations. Evon's neighbors were going to be pissed.

In instants, the paramedics had Heather out of the car and strapped to a stretcher, while the officer remained behind to question Evon. As the EMTs lifted Heather inside the rear of the ambulance, she cried out Evon's name, then the doors closed and the ambulance screamed off toward County Hospital, the nearest facility.

Evon responded to the officer tersely, but told him the truth. She shared as much of the story as the cop asked for. Yes, it was her car. No, she hadn't given Heather permission to drive, but yes, she hadn't bothered to retrieve the key, or the garage fob, so she wouldn't file a complaint for auto theft, or break and enter. Her reluctance was not an obstacle for the cop. He had already had a whiff of Heather, and they'd be required to take blood from her at the hospital in order to treat her. Heather would be charged with DWI, reckless driving and malicious damage to county property. Then there was the protection order, which the cop learned about after recovering Heather's purse from the car and calling in the information from her driver's license to central command.

"She's also walked about a thousand bucks in parking tickets," the cop told Evon. He was a tall black guy, calm by nature. He was going to bring Heather's purse over to the ER while he waited for her to be checked out. If she was discharged soon, he'd take her in cuffs straight to County Jail.

"I'd bet you've seen the last of her. Violating a protection order means she can't just sign a recognizance bond. She'll have to wait in a cell for a bail hearing. In the tank, she's going to be meeting some different kind of chicks. The judge will tell her straight out they'll jerk her back in there if she comes anywhere near you. That'll be part of her sentence, too."

Wearing a used jumpsuit was probably going to be the worst part for Heather. Yet whatever the deterrent, Evon knew the cop's prediction was almost certainly correct.

She thanked the officer for his efforts, then went upstairs. She waited until nine to call Mel Tooley at home. Mel groaned sympathetically as she told him the story. He said he'd send an associate over to the jail. It was early enough that, assuming Heather wasn't held too long in the ER, they'd probably be able to get her a bail hearing by late afternoon. Those hearings, these days, were conducted by TV, with the judge in a courtroom upstairs in the jail, and the prisoners below parading before a camera.

"And her with no makeup," said Evon.

Mel chuckled, but Evon, as it turned out, couldn't laugh at her own joke.

35.

Truth—June 1, 2008

Nella and Francine had a cabin on Lake Fowler and Evon spent Saturday and Sunday with them. Nella, another former jock, had been trying to convince Evon to take up golf. She'd thought initially that the game was too sedentary, but she was starting to warm to the challenges, and they ended up playing both days.

Driving back into town Sunday night, Evon decided to pay a call on Aunt Teri. It was past 9, but Evon had been waiting to see the old lady. The doorman downstairs put Evon on the phone and Teri invited her up. The old woman in a brocaded caftan was at the door with her cane, her face averted so she could hear the sound of Evon's approach. Teri's face was a glistening pond of cold cream, and she'd put up her hair for the night. The tiny pink plastic curlers were wrapped tight, exposing the elderly woman's pale scalp, except on the back of her head where she'd covered the mess with a sheer net. Without her sunglasses, Teri's eyes proved to be surrounded by pouches of brown flesh that looked like used tea bags.

Teri touched her head. "Well, I suppose if you came to get laid, this jinxed it."

Despite herself, Evon laughed. "Sorry, Teri. Timing is every-thing."

She didn't mind the banter with the old lady, but the truth was that Evon had always been slow to get to the point of sex with anyone. The bar scene never held much charm.

Teri used her cane to orient herself and clumped along to her golden living room. German had apparently roused himself when he heard Teri moving about and was standing there in his paisley silk robe, still looking tidy with his fuzz of cropped gray hair. Teri told him he could go.

"Watches those ridiculous reality shows," she told Evon once he left. "People eating goats' eyeballs and seeing who can stand the most paper cuts. So fucking stupid. What about a drink?"

Evon seldom indulged, except at parties, more or less out of def-erence to her father who'd never taken it up, but she thought the old woman might be more relaxed if she had company. Evon said she'd have whatever her hostess was drinking. Teri made her way with her stick to the tea cart holding a troop of brown bottles, and then handed a cut-glass crystal tumbler to Evon, while she settled herself on her overstuffed sofa.

"OK, shoot," said Teri. "*Ti yenaete?*" Hal often used that phrase, which apparently meant 'What's up?'

Evon realized she had not planned what to say, but she told Teri that Tim had finally cornered Cass Gianis.

"He says he didn't kill Dita. And I have a feeling you have a good idea who did."

"Ah." Teri took a healthy sip.

"The first thing—I guess the most important thing—is I need to be sure that it wasn't Hal."

"Hal? Oh no no no." Teri found the idea amusing. "My nephew might be better off if he had a little more killer in him. The best I know is that he was still out necking with Mina when Dita was murdered. He walked in to find that crazy scene. He's the one who called the police, if I'm remembering. Tim didn't recall that?"

Tim probably never knew. By the time he took over the case a week later, the family members had all been cleared because their blood didn't match what had been spilled in Dita's room.

"Well, Tim's pretty sure it wasn't Lidia." She repeated to Teri what Cass had told him.

"Same as Lidia told me."

"Right." Evon took a second. "That's one reason I'm here. I figured from what you said last time that you probably talked to Lidia about Dita's murder."

"Not immediately," Teri said. "But she finally put it all on the table with me maybe three months after Dita was killed. Lidia was just in a state. You know, we spoke every morning in those days. And every day it was the same thing. She couldn't finish her sentences. She burst into tears over nothing. Finally, I said, '*Afto einae anoeto!*' 'This is craziness!' 'You have to tell me what's going on.' We met at St. D's and sat in the pews in the sanctuary and talked for hours. Oh, and she *cried*. Cried and cried. And so did I, of course. Dita was my only niece and I saw more than a little bit of myself in her."

In the church, Teri said, Lidia had told her about Zeus and the twins, and Lidia's plan to ask Dita to stop seeing Cass. "I understood why she couldn't tell her sons. But why not come to me? If anyone could talk sense to Dita, I was the best one to try. But I guess Lidia was embarrassed that she'd kept the secret from me for so long. Maybe she was afraid I wouldn't believe her after all that time. Anyway, Dita had smart-mouthed her way into getting slapped. Probably would have done my niece some good if that happened more often, but not that hard. Apparently, Lidia caught her with a full swing. She shocked herself."

Evon asked if Teri believed that Lidia had hit Dita only once. She did, Teri said, but not for the reasons that convinced anyone else.

"Lidia wouldn't have done that to me," said Teri. "Hal and Dita, they were all I had. She wouldn't have taken either one from me, no matter how angry she got. But when I asked Lidia who else could have beat up Dita, I thought she was more evasive."

"She believed Cass had killed her?"

"Well, if Dita was OK when Lidia ran out of the house and dead when Cass left, it seemed fairly obvious to me. And it must have worried her, too. When I heard a few months later that Cass was pleading guilty, I wasn't surprised. He was always the more excitable of the two boys. My heart broke for Lidia, of course."

"Tim doesn't believe Cass did it either. Not any more." Evon picked up her drink but only so she could look down into it. "I guess that means your brother killed his daughter."

Teri didn't answer, but even without much sight, she was reluctant to face Evon. The old woman was silent some time, which made for an unusual moment.

"Do you think we have obligations to the dead?" she asked Evon.

"I visit my parents' graves when I go home. Is that what you mean?" That was almost a lie, since she prayed a lot longer over her father.

"Not really. Here," she said, and raised her tumbler but only to gesture with it. "Truth told, I never knew exactly what to make of my brother. Of course, I loved him like crazy. You had to. He was the biggest thing on earth, so grand, and he carried it off. He was a good brother, loyal, always looked out for me, and a good father to Hal, who looked up to Zeus so much. Zeus had his points. But he was too much like our father, who I may have told you was just a big stinking turd." Teri wound her head around in lingering contempt and disbelief, then paused again to reflect.

"I sometimes think," Teri said, "we're all sort of like twins—who we want to believe we are, and the person others see. They look alike, but you know, most folks probably make out someone in the mirror a little more appealing than how it might strike somebody else. But my brother, that was an odd thing with him. He knew the worst about himself. Didn't face it often, and forgot it as fast as he could. But it was always there stuffed down inside him somewhere, like a loaded musket. And he was dead set on never letting anybody else find out. So do I ignore that?"

Evon told her the truth. That was Teri's decision.

"Sure it is," said Teri. "You bet your ass. But here's the problem. As you might have noticed, dear, I'm *old*. And what I know—it could matter if this blame parade starts up again somehow. So I'll trust you. But this is a truth that would hurt a lot of people."

"Hal?"

"Especially. So you need to keep this to yourself, unless there really is no choice."

"What if I tell Tim?"

"I'll leave that to you. But Tim's definitely another of the folks who would be hurt."

Evon was too startled to respond. Teri looked up to the ceiling, where there was a gilded molding she could probably no longer see, then said abruptly, "All right. Let's get this done." She adjusted her position on the sofa and took another solid mouthful from her drink.

"You probably know, from the time of Dita's death, my brother wanted to rebury her on Mount Olympus."

"So she could be among the other gods and goddesses?"

"Whatever. He certainly thought that was where he belonged when his time came. Zeus, he really sometimes seemed to believe in the Greek gods. At least when it suited him. What he liked was that so many of them behaved so badly, so often. Nothing like Jesus. Zeus, if he got drunk enough, would tell you Jesus was a wimp. Zeus, the god Zeus? He truly was my brother's role model. All-powerful and full of vices.

"At any rate, on the fifth anniversary of Dita's death, Hermione and he thought they could bear the trip. Hal and Mina had three small children at home, but I went. Most of Olympus is a national park, but my people, they build churches everywhere, and Zeus had found a little chapel there with a graveyard. The old priest came out to say some prayers. It was a beautiful ceremony. A few of Hermione's Vasilikos relatives had come up to Thessaly from different parts. And Dita's casket was returned to the earth. In my bedroom, I've got some thyme I picked out of the rocks there to remember her.

"Afterwards, we went back to the villa Zeus had rented. Hermione's relatives and some locals came to pay their respects, but they weren't there long. Pretty soon it was Zeus and Hermione and me. My brother was in an absolutely black mood. 'I am a bad man,' he said as he sat there on that sofa. That was not the first time I'd heard that from him, by the way, but I doubt he'd ever made those kinds of remarks to that silly little clothes rack he'd married. But now he looks up and says, 'I killed our daughter.' Just like that. Like, 'It snowed.'"

Teri, now that she'd decided to share this, was engaged by the storytelling. She had scootched herself forward on the sofa and was waving her whiskey around now and then as she spoke. Zeus's description of the killing was brief. Lidia's visit had caused Dita to make some awful comment about her father, which Zeus never specified, but which he admitted led him to strike his daughter in rage.

"Afterwards, of course, he was mortified he'd be discovered. So he weaseled around so that the police put your friend, Tim, in charge, figuring Tim was bound to be more unsuspecting of Zeus. And afterwards, he gave Tim a healthy retainer every year, just to be sure he kept seeing Zeus in a kindly light."

"God," Evon said. She now understood Teri's warning that the truth could wound Tim. She finally took a nip of her drink. To her it would forever taste like gasoline. She said to Teri, "I know Zeus didn't realize Cass was his son, but did he care at all that a twenty-five-year-old was doing his time?"

"Oh, he said something silly at one point, that no expert could say for sure that it wasn't Lidia's slap that caused Dita's death. As if that justified sticking Cass in the pokey. But, no, like I said, Zeus was a lot like our father. He just convinced himself that bad stuff he'd done hadn't happened. But reburying Dita had waked it all in him and he said he had decided to turn himself in as soon as we got back.

"It was a minute before either Hermione or me could react, but then she started carrying on. I'd never seen her act like that, throwing things and screaming. She spit on Zeus, smacked him. He just sat there. Not that she wasn't entitled. He'd killed their daughter. But once she was done calling him a monster for that, she said that what he was going to do would only make things worse—abandoning her in old age, bringing shame on their family, and shattering Hal. And why? In order to spare Lidia, who Hermione always somehow felt he loved more than her.

"I just left her to the screaming, and tried to sleep. As far as I could tell, they were up all night.

"The next morning, Zeus seemed to have settled her down enough that she'd agreed to take a walk with him back to the grave-yard. So off they went, and no more than an hour later, I hear all this shouting and hear sirens up the mountain. The servants in the villa were in a tizzy and dragged me out with them. And there was Hermione telling the police about these strange men who had followed Zeus and her. She said she was walking alone, fifty paces in front of him, when she heard Zeus scream. Next she sees is these men tearing off and Zeus way down below, broken on the rocks like a child's toy."

"Did you believe that? That strangers had tossed him down the mountain?"

"*Ohee*," Teri said, moving her head from side to side. She actually laughed at the idea. Zeus's enemies would not kill a father in mourning, according to Teri. But Hermione was a Vasilikos and the Greek police couldn't wash their hands of the matter fast enough.

"Hermione never cracked. Once we came back, I saw next to nothing of her, except on family occasions. She became another one of these Greek widows, keeping company with almost no one but her son and grandchildren, and dressed in black. Designer stuff, of course. But black." Teri cackled.

"And Cass stayed in prison."

"Yes. That was sad. Of course, I returned from Greece determined to honor my brother's wishes and go to the prosecutor in Greenwood County. I hired a lawyer, a fellow named Mason. Ever heard of him?"

"George?" He was a judge now, but still one of Evon's closer friends. "You couldn't have done better."

"Well, he listened to all this and said, 'Is your sister-in-law going to back you?' 'Fuck no,' I said. I knew better than that. Admit she had a motive to push her husband off the mountain? Blacken his name and devastate her son? And reward Lidia, who she despised? I'm no lawyer, but I knew that wasn't going to happen. Your friend George just shook his head. 'A prosecutor is going to look at this and laugh. You come forward only after your brother dies, when you can conveniently lay the whole thing at his feet with no consequence to him. His wife, who was in the room, denies he ever said anything like that. And who do you hope to free as a result? Only the son of your best friend. We can do it, Teri, but I'll tell you right now there isn't a soul in that courthouse who is going to believe you. Frankly, I think I might deserve a bonus if you don't end up charged with perjury.' If it was just about me, I might have carried on anyway. But to tear Hal apart with no point? Cass wasn't getting out. Your friend Mason convinced me of that."

"And you never told Lidia."

"How could I? She'd have demanded that I go to the prosecutor. What else would a mother do? A lot of people thought Hermione was dull, but she was a survivor. She knew I was cornered."

The old lady emptied her tumbler. She was done.

"A secret," she said to Evon again, as punctuation.

Evon went to set her glass down on the tea cart, but Teri reached for it when she realized where Evon was headed. She made a remark about wasting good whiskey and took a long draught.

"Forgive me for not showing you out," she said. "I'll probably just fall asleep here."

Evon offered to help her to bed but the old lady was content with her bad habits.

"How is your life, dear?" she asked, as Evon picked up her purse. "What happened to Loopy Loo?"

She described yesterday's events to Teri. "She probably got out of jail last night. I never checked to find out."

"And how do you feel?"

"Like I got trapped in a washing machine on spin cycle."

Teri liked the description and had a long laugh.

"It'll probably take you a while to recover, but don't give up hope."

"That's what Tim tells me. Anyway, I can't escape my own nature. It's what I want, deep inside."

"Course it is. You ought to try to be happy for your own sake, but if that doesn't convince you, then try because there were so many of us who never even got the chance."

That thought, a new one, pierced Evon straight through the heart.

"Come give your old Aunt Teri a hug."

She did. The old woman still smelled like she was wearing an entire cosmetics counter. Teri looked up, unseeing, and touched Evon's cheek. She told Evon again she was a good girl.

Evon stopped at Tim's house on Monday morning on her way to work. He was up and welcomed her, ushering her back to the sun-room. She was worried about what to tell him, but by now he'd figured it all out on his own.

"You don't need to beat around the bush. It was Zeus, wasn't it? Kept me on his side all these years, didn't he? I've been a fool before. But never for money."

"Tim—"

"It's OK," he said. "I should have looked that gift horse in the mouth a long time ago. I knew Zeus's colors. But he got the drop on me with the grieving-father stuff. A fella like Zeus, they always know the soft spots. Damn him to hell anyway."

"I knew you were going to take it hard."

"Of course I am. Let an innocent man go off to prison? Now how's that for a capstone on my career? Oh, jeepers," he said, and looked bereft as he stared at the floor. "I certainly have worked my last for ZP."

"You don't need to do that."

"Yeah, I do. Time anyway. I'll go out to Seattle and see how much I like it. Lot of hills and young people. I'm still not sure it's the right place for a gimpy old man. I guess I'll find one of those graduated dying places, where you get a little help to start and eventually leave in a box."

"I think they call them assisted living."

"Whatever."

She told him she had to get in to the office, but promised to return to have lunch. Once he saw her to the door, Tim sat in the sun-room and put Kai and J.J. on and listened to them play. All the time Tim tooted on the trombone as a kid, he believed he was going to be that good, and there was no more chance of that than of his becoming a 747. And he thought he was a good cop and a decent man, but he was willing to buy all of Zeus's palaver because it bought him a little more comfort in life. None of the investigators, so far as Tim recalled, had even thought to cast a look in Zeus's direction, because of the blood. But Tim was the guy experienced enough to have seen through it.

The truth was often so damn painful. People couldn't stand to live with it. And him thinking he was in the truth business. No one really was. You took as much as you could and called it quits.

But there was music and sunshine. And maybe when he got himself around other people every day, he might even find some cute old gal. Evon had said the same thing a lot of folks did. In those places a guy who could still drive was more popular than a billionaire. Maria would forgive him. What Sofia had told him had helped. Sitting here on his plaid couch, he again felt his love for Maria, which would last as long as he did.

He put his hands over his face to give the rising shame and indignation about Zeus another second to drain. It would come and go for days. But he slapped his thighs.

Life, thought Tim, almost age eighty-two, goes on.

When Evon got to the ZP Building, Hal was locked in the giant conference room with a battalion of bankers and lawyers, a few of whom would emerge now and then and scurry to a side office for conferences or phone calls to superiors. The meeting had been expected to last two hours and was now in hour four. On the business side of ZP's offices, there was a portentous silence. A lot of people seemed to be holding their breath.

Finally, after lunch, Hal's assistant, Sharize, told Evon he was free. The bankers and lawyers were filing out, men and women in blue suits who looked like teams of pallbearers in training, one face grimmer than the next.

She entered the vast conference room, which was normally partitioned into three, but Hal was on the phone with Mina and he held up a hand. Evon sat in a chair in the hall until he was finished, a good fifteen minutes.

When Sharize brought Evon in, Hal's suit coat was on the back of his chair. He'd removed his tie, and his white shirt was darkened by large spots of sweat. He sat in front of the vast bank of windows over the spangled river, peering abjectly at the wall. Another portrait of Zeus was over there, in the center of the sycamore wainscoting, so perhaps that's where Hal had started, but now he seemed to be indulging his habit of looking at nothing at all. When he finally saw Evon, he withdrew his middle finger, on which he'd been nibbling, from his mouth, and gave her a quick smile, but it was in the nature of a wince.

"It's over," he said.

"What is?"

"ZP."

Evon found she had sat down, still a good thirty feet from her boss.

"How could that be?"

"Housing prices are dropping, even collapsing at YourHouse's end of the market. The bankers have locked arms and want another 150 million dollars in collateral on the YourHouse deal, which has to come out of the equity on the commercial projects. But the other lenders—often the same frigging people—won't give up their senior positions. In fact, retail is down. And, according to the economists, going down further. Which means the shopping centers' values are tanking, too, because rents have to drop. I thought we were pretty conservatively leveraged, but unless there's a giant change, we'll be in bankruptcy by the end of the year and the ZP shareholders, starting with me, will be wiped out. I may even vote for Obama." He smiled wanly then. "Joke," he said.

She repeated herself. How could that be?

"Well, I asked the same thing. But it's just arithmetic. I never imagined all of this stuff would go down at the same time. Nobody did. The bankers will reassess at year-end, but we need to make a public announcement now, which will crater the stock. It's doom."

"How do you feel, Hal?"

He laughed.

"Awful. My dad started with a duffel bag of cash he'd borrowed from my grandfather and worked his whole life, built an empire, and I've lost the whole thing. In a couple of months. I'm glad he didn't live to see it. I truly am. I can't even imagine what he would say."

Evon pondered. "If he was honest, I'm sure he'd tell you he'd made a lot worse mistakes."

"I doubt that." His fingernails were back in his mouth. Evon considered telling Hal that it was Zeus's honesty, not his mistakes, that was subject to doubt, but she couldn't see what good it would do at the moment.

"Do you want to talk about the Gianises?"

He flipped a hand. Who cares?

"Long-short, Cass says he didn't do it. He pled because the way the evidence was going to shake out, there was a good chance both Lidia and he would end up in prison."

"So Lidia did kill my sister?"

She ran him through all the reasons to doubt that. He nodded as if he understood, but Evon realized she had only a small fraction of his attention.

"So who beat her up like that?" Hal asked.

Evon waited, then went with the answer she'd planned.

"We don't know. We just don't know."

"Huh," he said. If Hal ever sat down to do the math, about who was in the house, who was strong enough, there would only be one person left in the equation. But Hal might not work that out in this lifetime. His father probably had to stay up on the mountain for Hal to be who he was.

"You know what my wife said when I told her I just lost a billion dollars?" he said to Evon.

This was going to be a classic. "What?" Evon asked.

"'It will be better for us.' How do you like that? I mean, we'll have enough. No plane. I'll have to get rid of the horse farm. Stuff like that. But I won't have to keep the lamp lit for my father. I can do what I want, instead of trying to maintain his monument. That was her point. She might be right. I feel too crappy now to know."

"Good for Mina," said Evon.

"She's a good one," he said.

She felt sorry for Hal, terrible, the more so as she thought everything over. At end, Hal for all his many faults had been the most honest guy around. He had acted for the most part as a loyal brother and son pursuing the truth. And now in his mid-sixties he was going to have to see if he had the strength to become somebody else.

"You better shine up your résumé," he told her. "Get it out on the street."

She hadn't thought of that yet. She was going to be out of a job herself, assuming Hal was right. Whoever bought up ZP's properties would probably be a bigger operation. They'd come in and clean house. It didn't matter. Since she'd started making big money, she'd always kept two years' living expenses in cash and she'd find another job anyway. Headhunters called all the time. She just needed love. That was really the work she had left.

"I'll give you the greatest reference ever," Hal said. "Which you deserve."

"I appreciate it."

She walked over and gave Hal a hug, which was a first.

"I really don't think your dad would have done any better, Hal. Give yourself a break on that."

"I just didn't see any of this coming," he said. "I should have. It's right in front of my face. Of everyone's really. The same economists who told me that the housing market had bottomed out are now saying there's going to be a plague of foreclosures soon, because people won't be able to sell their houses for what they owe. The banks, everybody holding those mortgage bonds, everybody will be doing the hurt dance. How could we all miss it?"

She puffed up her lips. She could say it again, but it had become a tired phrase. People see what they want to.

"I'm going to take a couple of hours," she said. She had lunch with Tim—she preferred he didn't end up sitting alone for long stretches today. And she wanted to air out her head. Maybe go for a run along the river.

Hal repeated something to her in Greek.

"What does that mean?" she asked.

"My dad used to say it all the time. 'May the gods guide us gently.'"

A Note About Sources

My fascination with twins began before I was three years old, when my sister, Vicki, arrived. The twin whom my mother had carried with Vicki was stillborn. That event loomed over my childhood, and thus what it meant to be and have—and lose—a twin, and the inevitable contrast to other love relationships, has been a preoccupation of mine at some level ever since, and one that I knew would eventually find its way into one of my novels.

I had been working on *Identical* a few months when I realized I had salvaged some of the raw details of the central crime from one of Chicago's most infamous unsolved murders, that of Valerie Percy, which occurred in September 1966, a few miles from my parents' house. The daughter of the wealthy industrialist Charles Percy, then running—successfully, it would turn out—for the United States Senate, Ms. Percy was killed in her father's lakeside mansion in Kenilworth, Illinois, while family members, including her identical twin sister, slept nearby. Although I've clearly scrambled elements, I should say unequivocally that there is no resemblance intended between any member of the Percy family and any of the wholly imagined characters of my novel, including all of the Kronons and Gianises.

A far more self-conscious inspiration for the novel came from what I had always taken as one of the most touching of the Greek myths, the story of the Gemini, Castor and Pollux. The identical twins were said to have been born after their mother, Leda, Queen of Sparta, was raped by Zeus, who had taken the form of a swan to catch her unaware. The myth has many variations, but one of the most common is that the sole difference between the twins was that Pollux was immortal, like his father, while Castor, like his mother, was not. When Castor was fatally wounded, Pollux could not bear the loss and asked Zeus to let him share his immortality with his twin. The brothers therefore alternated time in Hades and on Mount Olympus. For those familiar with the myth, the parallels between it and my story should be plain, as is the fact that I did not allow the old tale to be any more than a fabric on which I did my own embroidery.

I had a lot of wonderful help in writing this book. I am especially indebted to two friends, Dr. Julie Segre, senior investigator at the National Human Genome Research Institute of the National Institutes of Health, and Lori Andrews, a professor at Chicago-Kent College of Law and a renowned scholar in the area of law and genetics, as well as a novelist. Both Julie and Lori took considerable time coaching me on the state of DNA learning circa 2008. A few lines of Dr. Yavem's dialogue have clear roots in a speech Lori gave to the annual meeting of the American Society of Human Genetics in San Francisco, November 7, 2012. I take it for granted that despite both Julie's and Lori's patient teaching, I misunderstood something; the resulting errors are solely my fault.

I also want to thank Camille Rea, MAMS, CCA, a board-certified clinical anaplastologist at the Maxillofacial Prosthetics Clinic at the University of Illinois at Chicago Medical Center. Ms. Rea welcomed me to her lab and was illuminating on details that found their way into the novel. Again, she bears no responsibility for any factual mistakes I've made.

My gratitude also to Emi Battaglia, at Grand Central, my pal Nick Markopoulos and his friend George Chalkias, and Tina Andreatis, who all corrected some of my blunders about Greek language and customs.

Finally, I had several discerning advance readings of the manuscript from friends and relations. They are, alphabetically, Steve Drewry; Adriane Glazier, who also contributed the title; Jim McManus; Dan Pastern; Julian Solotorovsky; Ben Schiffrin; Eve Turow; and my most faithful advance reader, Rachel Turow. My editor, Deb Futter, was everything a good editor can be: patient, incisive and invaluable. Likewise, my wonderful agent, Gail Hochman. Loving thanks to them all.